G000115866

When *the*
Bough Breaks

Books by Denise Grover Swank

Rose Gardner Investigations
Family Jewels
For the Birds
Hell in a Handbasket
Up Shute Creek
Come Rain or Shine
It All Falls Down

Neely Kate Mystery
Trailer Trash
In High Cotton
Dirty Money

Rose Gardner Mysteries
Twenty-Eight and a Half Wishes
Twenty-Nine and a Half Reasons
Thirty and a Half Excuses
Thirty-One and a Half Regrets
Thirty-Two and a Half Complications
Thirty-Three and a Half Shenanigans
Rose and Helena Save Christmas (novella)
Thirty-Four and a Half Predicaments
Thirty-Five and a Half Conspiracies
Thirty-Six and a Half Motives

Magnolia Steele Mystery
Center Stage
Act Two
Call Back
Curtain Call

The Wedding Pact Series
The Substitute
The Player
The Gambler
The Valentine (short story)

Discover Denise's other books at
denisegroverswank.com

When *the* Bough Breaks

Rose Gardner Investigations #6

Denise Grover Swank

Chapter One

F alse alarm," the nurse said with a disapproving look. "*Again.*"

I cringed with embarrassment. This was the second time in a week that I'd come to the hospital in false labor.

The first time I'd called Joe at two in the morning, dragging him out of a deep sleep, and he'd rushed out to the farm and brought me to Fenton County Hospital. The nurses had admitted me, hooked me up to a monitor, and checked to see if my cervix was dilated.

"Nope," the friendly labor and delivery nurse had said. "You're locked up tighter than a drum down there." Then she shot an ornery grin at Joe, who was standing close to my head. "You know, they say sex can get things going."

My face flushed beet red, but Joe took it in stride, grinning as he winked and said, "We'll keep that in mind."

It was easier to let it go rather than to tell her that while we were together, we weren't *together*. Not that it was anyone's business.

My contractions faded to nothing mere minutes after she told me to get dressed, and I apologized profusely to Joe. He'd just pulled me into a hug and told me it was okay, his manner as reassuring as always.

By mutual agreement, Joe had moved into Neely Kate's old room after that, which had been our plan for after the baby was born. Although he'd lived in the farmhouse last fall, he'd moved out months ago, after my first meetings with the criminals in the county. I'd become their mediator, for lack of a better word, and Jed had quite rightly said it would be safer for Joe to (temporarily) move out given his role as chief deputy sheriff. But the meetings had stopped months ago, and the matter was mostly moot. The fact was, I needed Joe. And I wanted him around too.

This morning, four days after the first false alarm, the contractions had started again while I was getting ready for work. Joe, of course, had already left. These contractions were irregular, but stronger than the Braxton Hicks contractions I'd been having for the last month. I'd tried to ignore them at first, not wanting to make a fool of myself again, but part of me had wondered if this was the real thing. I was still two weeks from my due date of May 3, but at my last visit, Dr. Newton had said, "The baby's headfirst but not dropped yet. Nevertheless, I hope you have your bag packed, because you could deliver at any time now."

My bag was packed, perpetually in the car, and I'd arranged for Maeve to dog-sit Muffy while I was in the hospital. So I'd brought her to work with me this morning, just in case.

The contractions had continued all morning, sporadic at first but then ten minutes apart. They'd stopped briefly at lunchtime, making me glad I'd held off telling anyone, but they were back an hour later, this time only five minutes apart. So I'd taken a walk around the block to see if they'd stop. They hadn't, so an hour later I'd called Joe and pulled him out of an important meeting, only to end up hearing those fateful words.

False alarm.

I cried as soon as the not-so-nice nurse walked out of the room, and Joe sat down next to me on the bed.

"I'm so sorry, Joe," I said through my tears. "They were coming all day and then they changed to five minutes apart." I looked up at him. "I'm sorry."

"Hey," he said with a warm smile, his eyes shining with what looked like happiness. "You've never been in labor before. How are you supposed to know what it feels like?"

"But you were meetin' with the sheriff and someone from the state police."

His smile stretched wider. "And that meetin' was borin' as shit. You did me a favor."

I knew his statement was a partial lie. While I'd accept that it might have been boring, I knew it was important. He'd told me so the night before, but he'd insisted that I call him anyway if I went into labor.

"How can you look so happy?" I asked through my tears. I'd been extra weepy lately—which was saying something. "I'm a mess."

"Rose, you're havin' a baby. *Our* baby. How can I not be excited?"

"But I'm not havin' it *now*. I'm just a fat whale, waddling around like a penguin."

He laughed. "You're not a fat whale. You're pregnant. You were a beautiful woman before, but now you're glowing."

If I was glowing, it was only because I was perspiring. I was hot all the time.

He wrapped an arm around my back and gave me a sweet smile. "Let's get you dressed and take you home so you can rest."

"I don't want to go home," I said in a grumpy tone. "I hate bein' alone out there. Yesterday I dropped a wooden spoon, and try as I might I couldn't reach it. I had to have Muffy pick it up and jump up on the sofa so I could get it from her."

"Just imagine how handy she'll be with fetchin' diapers," he said as he helped me slide off the bed. "How about you get dressed and we'll do something together?"

"I'm supposed to see Ashley and Mikey tonight, remember?"

Mike had agreed that I could take them out to dinner, which was nothing short of a miracle. After my sister, Violet, had died last October, my former brother-in-law had kept me from seeing my niece and nephew. But then I'd run into them at Walmart the week before. Ashley, my six-year-old niece, had cycled through shock, excitement, then anger to see that I was so pregnant, given she hadn't known I was expecting. I'd tried my best not to shame Mike in front of them, and when Ashley said he'd been telling them for months that I was too busy to see them, I just shot him a dirty look and suggested I get them for a few hours *this week*.

"I'm totally free," I'd said with a bright smile. "Any day."

With no graceful way out, he'd settled on tonight. When I'd offered to pick them up from daycare, his body had stiffened. "I'd have to add your name to the list of approved people," he said in a short tone. "So just pick them up from my house."

I used to be on the list of approved people, so I had to wonder why he'd gone to such lengths to push me away. What was he really up to? Then again, I'd been wondering that very thing for months.

I was fairly certain he had some criminal ties that circled back to James "Skeeter" Malcolm, the crime lord of Fenton County, Arkansas, though I had yet to figure out any details. I was even more sure Violet *had* known. Other than a few personal items, she hadn't left anything to the kids, instead leaving her one-third share of the nursery to my best friend, Neely Kate, and everything else, including our childhood home, to me. Her attorney had said she'd given him an envelope for me to open after her death, some sort of directive that would help me understand the terms of her will— including her wish to grant me custody of her children (something she couldn't do without just cause)—but his office had been broken into after the funeral. The only thing missing was that envelope.

I'd given the theft a lot of thought over the last few months as I tried to figure out how to handle the Mike situation, and I'd come to the realization that it had been intended as a message.

I'm powerful. Don't mess with me.

And the only person in the county powerful enough to stand up to the Lady in Black, my alter ego in the criminal world, was my ex-lover and the biological father of my baby.

The aforementioned James Malcolm.

But it was hard to get information out of someone who refused to see you. James had made it clear he wanted nothing to do with the baby, so back in February, I'd sent him a letter asking him to meet with me to sign the forms that would relinquish his paternal rights. I'd also hoped to ask him about Mike's illegal activities. He'd very grudgingly agreed to a meeting at our mutual attorney's office, but ultimately, he'd been a no-show. Or rather, he had shown, and then slipped out before Carter sent me back to meet him. He'd left behind the paternity relinquishment papers with a sticky note that said, *I'm not signing.*

So not only was I none the wiser about Mike's criminal involvement, but now I was waiting for Skeeter Malcolm to try using my baby as a pawn.

Because the criminals in the county couldn't find out James was my baby's biological father—they needed to continue thinking he or she was Joe's in all ways, rather than just by choice, and James knew it.

When Joe had first suggested that we raise the baby together, I'd balked, worried I was taking advantage of him, but he'd convinced me that he wanted to be a parent. He aspired to be the kind of father he'd never had, and I knew beyond a shadow of a doubt that he would be. Because Joe Simmons had done a lot of growing up over the last two years, and I had no doubt he would put our baby before everything else. That he'd be there with me through the good *and* the bad. That he would never, ever take off just because things were hard.

James hadn't offered me any of that. And wouldn't.

Most of the people in town thought Joe and I had been together and split up but agreed to raise our baby amicably. We'd come up with the plan for him to build an apartment in the barn—a plan that had been put on hold after I'd agreed to shelter rescue horses—but lately, I'd been thinking of asking him to stay with us more permanently. I wasn't sure how I felt about him romantically. Frankly, my emotions were too all over the place for me to know for certain, but I *did* know that he'd helped make what could have been months of despair into a much more hopeful and joyful time. And I knew that I loved him. I just wasn't sure what that love meant. My love for James had been too blinding for me to see anything else.

But the shine had long since tarnished, even more so since James had refused to sign those papers. I might have understood if he'd come to me and said he wanted to be part of the baby's life. Or if he'd reached out to explain himself. But he'd remained eerily quiet. When I'd attempted to quiz Carter about his client's intentions, he'd confessed he was in the dark. In fact, he had suggested it might be a good idea for me to find another attorney. An impartial one who was *very* good at family law.

I'd hesitated to do that—partially because it seemed like a bad idea to bring the whole thing to court, but also because I couldn't bring myself to believe the man who'd professed to love me would use our child to hurt me. Still, I knew James had changed. Everyone around me said so, even his ex-best friend, Jed. James saw my decision to keep the baby as a betrayal, and he was someone who retaliated for that kind of thing. So I *had* gone to a lawyer in the end, only for her to tell me it would be best to wait James out. If I brought him to court, everyone would learn the truth about the baby's parentage.

But Joe was looking at me now, obviously waiting for an answer, and I hadn't the first idea what he'd said.

"I'm sorry," I said. "What did you say?"

He smiled patiently. "I said how about I don't go back to work, and I'll go with you to Mike's to pick up the kids. I'm as excited to see them as you are."

It was true. He'd loved the kids, and vice versa, but I also suspected he was worried Mike would give me grief, and while Joe was beyond excited at becoming a father, the closer I'd gotten to delivery, the more protective he'd become with regard to my safety.

Understandable given two of his ex-girlfriends had been killed, both while pregnant.

"Okay," I said. "They'll be excited to see you."

"It's nearly five. How about we get you checked out, pick up Muffy from the office, then head over to Mike's a little early?"

"Sounds good." I doubted Mike would give Joe, the Fenton County chief deputy sheriff, trouble for showing up a half hour early.

I grabbed my clothes from a chair, and he hesitated at the door. "I'll wait in the hall."

"No," I said, keeping my back to him. "You're gonna get an eyeful and more when the baby's born. Stay."

He hesitated a moment. "Okay."

I turned my back to him and reached behind me, fumbling to untie the strings of the faded hospital gown, but then Joe walked up behind me and tugged on the top string. The neckline fell to my chest, and I placed my hand on it to hold it.

His fingers lightly brushed the skin of my back as he slowly untied the next string with a tenderness that caught me by surprise. A shiver ran down my back, and my nerves tingled in anticipation. I sucked in a breath, telling myself it was a reflex, nothing more, but there was no denying I felt an unexpected yearning. It was sexual to be sure, but it was more than that. It was a soul-deep ache.

Joe's hand was gone, and he sounded strangled when he said, "I'll go check on that discharge paperwork."

He bolted out the door, leaving me to wonder if he'd run because he was horrified by my reaction or because he dared to hope it meant something.

Our relationship had changed since he'd offered to be the baby's father. We'd spent a lot of time alone together, especially over the last few months as we prepared for the baby's arrival, and I'd noticed subtle signs that his feelings were shifting. A soft smile. The way he tenderly cradled my arm—or wrapped his around my back—when he worried about where I was walking. The way he brought me things—decaffeinated coffee drinks or a bouquet of flowers to brighten my day. Then for Easter, he'd built multiple raised gardening beds so I could plant the vegetable garden I had mentioned in casual conversation. The effort he'd gone to had made me choke up with tears—they were decorative in addition to functional, and he'd even thought to wrap chicken wire around the sides to keep out wild animals. He was still working on the chicken coop he'd designed to look like the farmhouse.

Joe hadn't told me that he'd fallen in love with me again, but I knew. I could read it on his face as easily as if it had been printed across his forehead. While part of me thought I should have nipped it in the bud weeks ago, I wasn't so sure I *wanted* to nip it in the bud. I could see parts of the Joe I'd fallen in love with nearly two years ago—the fun-loving, carefree man—and parts of the man he'd always wanted to be—strong, loyal, and in charge of his own destiny.

That man was sexy and desirable and exactly the type of partner I'd always wanted, because despite my reckless fling with a wild and lawless man, I wanted stability for my children. I wanted a man who would be there when I needed him, not when he felt like showing up.

Joe deserved to be with a woman who truly loved him for everything he was worth. He deserved more than someone who was settling.

Only the more I thought about Joe, the more I wondered if having him permanently in my life would be settling after all.

Chapter Two

When I walked into the hallway, Joe greeted me with an easy smile, as though nothing had happened, but I was having a harder time pretending. How had I forgotten how handsome he was? He was tall, with dark hair and brown eyes, and had the look of a man who wasn't afraid to get his hands dirty. But then I realized I hadn't forgotten—I'd just been too lost in myself over the past six months to notice.

"Why don't we get you a snack? How about some cheesy fries from the Burger Shack?" he asked.

I narrowed my eyes. "You must really be pityin' me if you're willin' to go to the Burger Shack. You hate that place."

"I know you've been cravin' 'em," he said, wrapping an arm around my back and steering me toward the exit. "That and peanut butter toast. Since I can't get you the latter, I'm willin' to make the sacrifice."

"I'm not cravin' cheesy fries anymore. I've moved on to Chuck and Cluck's coleslaw."

He laughed. "Random, but who am I to argue? Chuck and Cluck it is."

We headed to Chuck and Cluck, and Joe ordered my slaw through the drive-thru. I ate it in his car as he drove to the landscaping office. By the time he pulled into the parking space next to my truck, my contractions had completely stopped, making me feel like an even bigger fool. When I confessed what I was feeling, he said, "Just think of the stories we'll have to tell the baby years from now. Every kid loves to hear about when they were born."

"Not me," I said. "My momma never said nothin'." Then I added, "Only I guess she would have been lyin' since she wasn't my birth mother."

He picked up my hand and squeezed. "We'll make sure our baby has plenty of stories. Happy ones."

"Yeah," I said, squeezing back. "We will."

Joe got Muffy out of the office through the back door, and then we climbed into my truck since Joe had installed Ashley and Mikey's car seats in the back the night before.

He insisted on driving, and ordinarily I would have protested, but my stomach was so huge it nearly touched the steering wheel. Besides, I was tired. I decided to save my energy for the kids.

When Joe pulled in next to Mike's truck in the driveway, the state of Mike's house caught me by surprise. He was usually the tidy type, but the yard needed to be cut and the landscaping looked overgrown. All of the blinds and curtains were shut.

An uneasy feeling twisted inside of me.

"Something's off, Joe," I said as I reached for the door handle.

He gave the house a long look, shifting into chief deputy mode. "Maybe you should wait in the truck, Rose."

"I'm not waiting in the truck. I'm going to get my niece and nephew." Mike had finally relented, and I wasn't about to let him change his mind. And if I saw any evidence he wasn't taking care of those kids, I would find a way to help them. Legal or not.

Before Joe could reply, I pushed the door open and slid off the seat. I was about to close the door, but Muffy jumped out and immediately peed in the yard.

Smart girl.

"Rose," Joe protested as he met me at the hood.

"I realize Mike is irritated with me, but he's not gonna hurt me. Especially with you here."

Joe's grim look suggested he wasn't appeased, but he didn't stop me either. Instead, he followed me to the front door. Muffy trotted along next to my feet. She didn't seem overly concerned, just curious. As crazy as it seemed, I trusted her. She was a great judge of character and great at assessing dangerous situations.

I knocked on the front door while Joe stood at the bottom of the steps and glanced around the yard. When no one came to the door after a few seconds, I knocked again.

"They're not home?" Joe asked, turning his attention to me.

"That doesn't make sense. Mike's truck is here." Was he hiding inside, pretending not to hear me knocking? I didn't see how— Ashley would have been running to the door.

"Maybe they took a walk," Joe said, climbing the steps to stand next to me. "It *is* a nice day."

"Maybe," I said, but I wasn't buying it. Something was off.

I knocked on the front door again, more insistent this time. "Mike. It's Rose. I'm here to pick up the kids."

"Maybe they're in the backyard," Joe said when no one answered the door after a few more seconds.

"Maybe…" I said as dread burrowed in my gut.

I walked down the porch steps, shooting a scowl at Joe as he reached up to take my hand and help me down.

"I'm perfectly capable of walkin' down steps, Joe Simmons," I snapped.

"Can you even see your feet?"

That was beside the point.

When I reached the bottom, we were about to walk around to the back when the front door finally opened, and Mike appeared in the barely-there crack.

"The kids are sick," he said. "They can't see you tonight."

I almost called him a liar, but the fact that he didn't look so well himself stopped me. Dark circles underscored his eyes, and his face was pale.

"What's wrong with them?" Joe asked, wrapping an arm around my back and resting his hand on my hip.

"The flu," Mike said, his gaze darting to the street then back to us.

"Are you sick?" I asked. "Do you want me to get you anything?"

"No," he said so quickly it was obvious he was trying to get rid of us. That and his darting glances added to my suspicion that there was more to the situation than he was saying. "We're fine."

I took a step toward the porch. "Maybe I should come in and check on them."

"No," both men said at once.

Joe grabbed my wrist and held me in place. "You can't go in there, Rose. You can't risk gettin' the flu."

He was right, but Mike wasn't being truthful with us. I glanced down at Muffy, but she sat at my feet, looking at Mike. Normally, she'd be trying to run in and see the kids.

What was holding her back?

"Are your parents helping?" I asked.

"No," Mike said, "I don't want them to get sick either."

"You're sure we can't get you anything?" I asked.

"No," Mike said in a broken voice, then shut the door, leaving me a lot more worried than when he'd opened it.

I stared at the house and Joe's hold on my wrist tightened.

"You can't go in there, Rose."

I knew he was right, but I needed someone I trusted to tell me that my niece and nephew were okay. I'd spent months fretting about not being able to see them. This was different. Part of me feared something had happened to them, or that maybe they were sicker than Mike was saying. "I can't, but you can."

"Mike's not gonna let me in, and even if he did, I'm not gonna risk comin' down with the flu and infectin' you and the baby."

I knew he was right, but it still felt wrong.

"How about we see if Jed and Neely Kate have plans for tonight?" Joe said, tugging me toward the truck. "We can invite them over for dinner. It might be our last chance before the baby comes."

"If I ever *have* the baby," I grumbled.

"You'll have the baby," he said in a teasing voice, but he cast a glance back at the house as he led me to the passenger side. His gaze found mine, all teasing gone. "But on the way back to the farmhouse, you're gonna make a call to Mike's parents and ask them a few questions because, just like you, I know something's goin' on and I plan to do a little diggin'."

"Thank you," I said, relieved he was taking this seriously.

He frowned. "Those are Violet's kids, and I promised her I'd make sure they were always protected. Always safe. I won't let her down. We'll make sure they're okay. I promise."

I was counting on it.

He got in the truck, and as we drove away, I placed the call and put the phone on speaker. Mike's mom answered.

"Hi," I said, "this is Rose." When she didn't respond, I added, "Violet's sister."

"I know who you are," she said curtly.

Joe's eyebrows rose.

"I'm just callin' to check on Ashley and Mikey," I said. "I dropped by Mike's to pick them up like we'd arranged, but he said they have the flu."

"Oh dear," she said, her voice softening. "I hadn't heard."

"Mike didn't look well himself, and I'm kind of worried. If you happen to check on them, can you let me know that they're all okay? I'd be more than happy to make some soup or drop off some juice."

"Don't you have more important things to worry about?" she said, her snippy tone returning. "Like havin' your illegitimate child?"

I gasped, and Joe whipped the truck over to the side of the road and snatched the phone from my hand. "Excuse me?"

"Who is this?" she asked.

"It's Joe Simmons. The baby's *father*."

"Like that makes it any better," she snapped. "Gallivanting from one woman to another. Even Violet had her sights set on you for a time." She tsked. "There's a reason Mike keeps those children from you, Rose. You're a terrible influence. Perhaps you should consider *that*." Then she hung up.

Joe and I stared at each other for several seconds before he said, "Rose, she's just one old woman whose opinion doesn't amount to a hill of beans."

But it wasn't just one old woman. Plenty of them felt that way, something I'd discovered firsthand last month. Neely Kate and Maeve had hosted a baby shower for me, and Maeve had invited the Garden Club. They'd shown up, but they'd looked down their noses at my bare ring finger.

The others had been content to emanate quiet disapproval, but Miss Mildred had taken it upon herself to try to force a *literal* shotgun wedding. She'd tricked Joe and Jonah into coming to the shower, then stuck a bridal veil on top of my head and held a gun on the minister, telling him it was his ordained duty to make sure our baby wasn't doomed to hell. Joe had talked her down, telling her he'd be sure to make an honest woman out of me someday, although hopefully not at gunpoint. Jonah convinced her to hand over the gun—which, thankfully, hadn't been loaded—but Officer Ernie, responding to a 911 call about a hostage situation, showed up just in time to witness the exchange. He tackled Jonah to the ground, knocking over the refreshment table, and the diaper-shaped cake flew into the air and landed directly on Ernie's butt. It took a while for the dust to settle, but we finally convinced Ernie that

Jonah was innocent, Mildred's plan wasn't truly criminal, and he had no just cause to arrest Neely Kate for attempted murder for baking the cake that had assaulted him. Needless to say, my shower had been the talk of the town for weeks.

I hadn't let the incident bother me too much then, but now I wondered if the whole out-of-wedlock thing was a bigger issue than I'd realized. "What if it really *is* my character that's influencing Mike to keep me from the kids? Maybe I'm just imaginin' that he has criminal ties."

"I wouldn't jump to that conclusion," he said. "Of course he's gonna spin it like that for his parents."

"Maybe," I said, staring down at my phone.

"Rose."

I looked up at him.

"She's full of shit. You're no more of a bad influence on the kids than the donuts Mike gets for 'em at Dena's cupcake shop."

"Dena makes donuts now?" I asked, trying not to cry.

He grinned. "So I hear. I can't step foot in the place."

My stomach sunk. Dena was his ex-girlfriend, and she whispered malice-laced gossip about me into the ear of every person who walked through the doors of her bake shop. "You're givin' up so much for me, Joe."

"If you think I gave up Dena for you, then you've got another think comin'. I broke it off with Dena because I came to my senses." He gave me an ornery grin. "Besides, I hear the donuts at the Stop-N-Go are ten times better."

"Liar."

He laughed and shifted the truck into drive. "Enough of that nonsense. Let's go pick up some steaks, and I'll grill 'em for dinner. You call Neely Kate."

Just as I was about to place the call, Joe's phone rang. He glanced at the screen and frowned before he answered. "Chief Deputy Simmons."

There was a moment of silence, then Joe shot me a glance and said, "I'll be there as soon as I can."

He hung up and gave me an apologetic look. "I'm sorry, Rose. I have to go into work. I'll drive downtown and pick up my car."

"It's okay."

"It's not, but one of the conditions for me takin' two weeks off after the baby's born is that I have to be called in on all big cases until the baby's born."

"It's a big case?"

He frowned, then said, "They found a body at a neighborhood construction site."

I tried not to flinch. It had been months since there had been any murders in the county, so I took it as a bad sign that this was happening now.

He put a hand on my arm. "Don't be lettin' your imagination run away from you. It could have been a squabble between two coworkers."

"Or it could have something to do with Hardshaw or James."

The Hardshaw Group was a crime syndicate based in Dallas. They were like a cancer, spreading out and metastasizing in small towns and counties all over Texas and Oklahoma, leaving death and destruction everywhere they'd taken over.

Neely Kate had landed on their radar years ago in Oklahoma, when she'd killed (in self-defense) the son of Arthur Manchester, one of the three men who ran the group. We'd taken to calling them the Hardshaw Three: Tony Roberts, Arthur Manchester, and Randall Blakely. All successful businessmen in their own right, but greed had driven them to try their hand at illegal pursuits.

Their interest in Neely Kate had likely been further stirred upon realizing she was an unrecognized Simmons child. And so they'd planted Ronnie Colson in town years ago to spy on Neely Kate. He'd married her even though he didn't love her. Even though he was already married to someone else.

And sometime in the last few years, they'd also sunk their hooks into Skeeter Malcolm. He had been working with them on the sly, without telling any of us, helping to lay a foundation for them to come in and set up shop. All while Joe, Neely Kate, Jed, and I had been trying our hardest to keep them out.

After I'd discovered James's betrayal, Tim Dermot, a criminal with a group of men of his own, had banded the criminals of the county together in an attempt to stop Hardshaw from moving in. Dermot and Jed had asked me to lead them as the Lady in Black, and I'd held several meetings with an eye toward forming a plan for keeping Hardshaw out of the county. Only my mediation hadn't helped much, and we'd never really gotten anywhere.

Then we'd discovered the FBI was investigating Hardshaw, and we'd disbanded the group and let our guard down. We'd lulled ourselves into complacency, and now...now I was scared to death Hardshaw was still a threat and that my baby was in danger.

Joe gave me a sympathetic look. "All the more reason for me to take part in the investigation. Don't be borrowin' trouble until we know more."

But Joe seemed to forget that trouble dogged my footsteps like I was the Pied Piper.

Chapter Three

I hate that I'm leavin' you alone," Joe said, his brow furrowed.

"I'll be fine," I said. "I'm feelin' tired from all the excitement anyway."

"Are you sure?" He cast a glance toward me. "You can still call Neely Kate."

"Nah. Muffy and I will have a nice quiet night at home. But I want you to let me know when you get home. Even if you have to wake me up." When he hesitated, I added, "Please. Otherwise I'll just worry about you."

"Okay," he said, "but I'll likely be home long before you're in bed."

For some reason, that filled me with relief. Heavens knew I'd been nesting lately. I'd cleaned out the linen closet a couple of days before. Maybe needing to have the baby's daddy close was part of it. "Good," I said softly. "I like havin' you around."

He flashed me a grin, and neither one of us said anything more until he pulled my truck into the parking space next to his car. He put the truck in park and turned to me with a worried expression. "What are you gonna do for dinner?"

"I just had that coleslaw," I said. "I'll figure something out. Don't worry about us." I placed my hand on my swollen belly. "We'll be fine."

Joe put his hand next to mine, then leaned down and said quietly, "Take care of Mommy until I get home. And while I'm excited to meet you, little man, I'd appreciate it if you'd hold off for a few hours."

I snorted. He'd insisted the baby was a boy because he'd heard that boy's heart rates ran faster than girls, and since he'd come to almost every doctor's visit, he'd heard it enough times to draw his own conclusion. He was so confident that he'd bet me twenty dollars he was right. I'd abstained from making any kind of counter bet. "I think you're safe there."

He straightened and smiled. "You never know." He opened the door, then looked back at Muffy, who was sitting in Mikey's car seat. "I'm countin' on your guard dog abilities, Muff. Will you watch over your momma?"

She looked right at him and let out a tiny bark.

"You trained her to do that," I said with a laugh.

"I'll never tell," he said, sliding out of the driver's side door. "But it's amazing what she'll do for a piece of a hot dog."

"You spoil her," I complained as I scooted into the driver's position on the bench seat.

"I just show her how much I love her." He grabbed the seat belt and handed it to me. Once I was buckled in, he turned serious. "I worry about you bein' out there all alone."

"I've been alone for months. I'll be fine."

He nodded, but it looked like he wanted to say something—something he'd clearly decided to swallow instead, because he shut the door without another word.

I watched him walk over to his car, then backed out of the parking spot and headed home.

I'd told Joe I was tired, but I was also restless. After putting my purse in the house, I grabbed two apples and let Muffy out through the kitchen door. We walked out to the barn to say hello to the two rescue horses that Margi, the local vet's sister, had moved in. The tan one, a mare named Buttercup, walked over, leaning her head over the fence. I handed her one of the apples and rubbed over her nose. "Did you have a good day, Buttercup? Did Margi come out to see you?"

Margi had coerced me to let her keep horses in my unused barn and pasture, and in exchange, she'd paid to have the barn fitted to house them as well as fix the broken fencing. It had taken her longer to get the money for the repairs than she'd expected, but the barn and pasture had been ready to go by early March. Buttercup had moved in a week later.

The horse had come to the farm impossibly thin and skittish, her body covered in sores. Margi had told me she'd been neglected by her previous owner, but it was nothing some good steady meals and a lot of love wouldn't fix. And since I'd grown up knowing what it felt like to be unloved, Muffy and I had made a habit of coming out at least once a day to talk to her and tell her what a good horse she was.

She'd been scared of me at first, but I'd won her over with sugar cubes and apples. Now she seemed eager to visit with me whenever she saw me walking across the yard. I'm sure the treats helped. Margi said the mare would soon be well enough to saddle, and after I recovered from delivering the baby, she'd teach me to ride.

Joe didn't approve of any of it. He didn't trust Margi and didn't think I should have granted her free access to my farm, something I'd struggled with too at first, but he'd told me his opinion in a reasonable tone, and it hadn't been an order or unreasonable demand. A far cry from how he would have handled it nearly two years ago when we'd first been together.

The other horse, a gelding, stayed back, eyeing me with caution. He'd only been on the farm a couple of weeks, but he was taking longer to come around than Buttercup had.

I held the other apple out to him. "You want a treat, Ninja?"

He eyed the fruit but didn't come closer, not that I was surprised. He only came to get the apple when I left it on a fence post. Over the last few days he'd allowed me to run my hand over his neck while he ate, which I considered progress.

Tonight he came to get the apple right away and eyed me as though waiting for me to pet him. I stroked his neck as he crunched the fruit, and murmured to him softly like Margi had taught me. He let me touch him for nearly ten seconds before he skittered away.

Buttercup edged over and let me know she wanted more attention, so I loved on her for another few minutes, then told her goodnight. Madison, a horse-obsessed teenager who helped Margi, would be out later to bring them into the barn and get them settled in for the night.

I went inside and dropped a slice of bread into the toaster, but I was still feeling restless. I wasn't sure what to do about Ashley and Mikey, although when I really thought about it, there wasn't anything to *be* done. Mike looked terrible, which only confirmed that they likely *were* sick. The family illness would also explain the state of the house. I needed to accept his explanation and hope he'd be willing to reschedule. Even if I had to badger him into it.

While I waited on the toaster, I opened the cabinet to get out the peanut butter, then started pulling out cans and boxes of macaroni and cheese, and before I knew it, all the cabinets were completely empty and the counter and kitchen table were covered in food, dishes, glasses, and a whole host of other things.

I was deep in thought, trying to decide how I wanted to rearrange everything, when I heard a knock at the door.

"Rose, I'm here with dinner," Neely Kate called out.

I walked over to the doorway, bracing my lower back with my hand. "Joe asked you to come."

"He did," she admitted as she walked through the living room toward me. She was wearing jeans and a pink shirt that gave her complexion a soft glow. Her long blonde hair was hanging loose in waves. "But to be fair, I'd planned on comin' over to see you anyway. I figured I'd bring you something for dinner since Joe said you'd likely be eating peanut butter toast again."

"Well, he's wrong," I said in mock indignation. "I put the bread in the toaster about a half hour ago, then completely forgot about it."

"What have you been doin'?" she asked. "You been out with the horses again?" She made it to the edge of the kitchen and stopped in her tracks. For a moment I saw it from her eyes—it looked like a tag sale on someone's front lawn. "What in the heck happened in here?"

"I'm nestin'," I said, making a face, as though that said it all.

"Nestin' or takin' out your frustrations on your poor cupboards?"

I shrugged. "I've always thought the nestin' thing was just somethin' people said, but lately I've felt this overwhelmin' urge to organize everything in this house."

"Well, let me feed you, and then I'll help you put it all back together." Since the kitchen table was covered, and it was such a nice late April evening, we took the food out to the front porch.

I eased down into a chair, which took some doing these days, and Neely Kate handed me a Styrofoam container, her bright shiny engagement ring nearly blinding me. Jed had proposed to her only a few weeks ago, and she'd been on cloud nine ever since.

"I swear, that thing keeps gettin' shinier and shinier," I said with a laugh.

She sat in her own chair and held her hand out in front of her, her eyes lighting up with pure joy. "I know, right?" Shaking her head, she said, "I still can't believe he picked this out all by himself."

"He knows you, Neely Kate. He loves you." I wasn't about to tell her that he'd asked for my input.

"I know," she said softly. "I'm *so* lucky."

Not for the first time, it occurred to me that we both had what the other wanted—Neely Kate desperately wanted a baby, and I wished I were in a loving, committed relationship.

"Have you guys picked a date yet?"

"No," she said, opening her Styrofoam. "But it will likely be soon." She shot me a grin. "After you have the baby, of course. I want you to be the maid of honor."

Tears stung my eyes. "Of course. I'd be honored."

"Good," she said with a nod. "It's settled. Now eat your dinner."

Using my belly as a tabletop, I opened the container and moaned in happiness. "Merrilee's meatloaf and mashed potatoes."

"I figured this would be better than peanut butter toast."

I was too busy eating to respond, which was probably all the response that was needed.

"I wasn't lyin' when I said I'd planned to drop in anyway," she continued. "I wanted to see Ashley and Mikey. I miss them too."

"Obviously Joe told you about the kids."

"He did—and the fact you went to the hospital in false labor again."

"The man can't keep a secret to save his soul," I grumbled, but I knew that wasn't true. He'd kept plenty for me.

"He's worried about you. The false labor. The kids. It's a lot in one day."

"I'm fine," I pushed out with a sigh.

"You're worried, and that's okay. But how about we check up on the kids another way?"

"Investigating on our own? We haven't investigated anything in months. Not since Kermit was arrested for his drunk and disorderly." I cringed, because Kermit's arrest was a sore subject.

To my surprise, Neely Kate didn't rehash the circumstances of our PI mentor's incarceration. She lifted one shoulder in a delicate shrug. "Just because Kermit got locked up in the slammer doesn't mean we can't do a little investigation of our own."

"Technically, it does," I countered. "Now that we've started our PI training, we're only supposed to investigate under a licensed PI."

She smirked. "You're not gonna let that stop us, are you?"

Lifting my eyebrows, I gave her a pointed look. "When did we ever follow the rules?"

"True," she said with the hint of a grin, although it quickly morphed into a look of irritation. "And it wasn't just a drunk and disorderly. That man took a ten-foot rocket to the town square, strapped himself to it with a bungee cord, and attempted to light the fuse because he thought it would shoot him high enough into the air so he could take photos and prove that the Earth is flat. If he hadn't fallen off and given himself a concussion on the sidewalk, he'd be six feet under."

I pursed my lips. "His head didn't land on the concrete. It landed on his sister's DSLR camera. Probably didn't help that she beat him with it once she realized it was broken." I'd seen the whole thing from my office window, while Neely Kate had been working at the nursey.

"I still can't believe I missed that."

I shrugged. "I sent you video."

"You should have gotten closer!" she protested. She obviously still hadn't forgiven me for not capturing more details.

"He was sittin' on a live rocket, Neely Kate! The thing was gettin' ready to go off!" And it would've—with Kermit or without him—if Carter Hale hadn't come out of his office, tossed the contents of his soft drink can on the fuse, then handed Kermit a business card and told him to call him for representation after he was arrested.

She rolled her eyes. "Excuses."

"So, about the investigation," I said, hoping to change the subject, and not just because we'd discussed the Kermit situation at least ten times. I really liked the idea of being proactive instead of just sitting around and doing nothing. "Do you have anything in mind?"

"I do," she said, sitting up, her eyes shining with excitement. "Let's run by the daycare tomorrow and ask Portia when the kids got sick and when Mike thinks they'll be back."

My spirits lifted. "That's actually a good idea."

There was a chance the daycare director wouldn't tell us because of Mike's ban, but she'd been friendly to me during Violet's illness. I suspected she'd understand my need to make sure they were okay.

Neely Kate beamed. "I have a few of them from time to time."

We discussed her plans for the wedding as we finished eating. She and Jed had decided to have it at their house, and they wanted to get married soon after my baby was born. She wanted cut flowers, and I promised I'd help her make the bouquets and boutonnieres. We chatted for a while about what she wanted them to look like, and she showed me a dress she'd found online for herself. At first glance, the dress surprised me. I'd figured she'd go for something simple since she was having the wedding in her backyard, but once I saw it, there was no doubt the dress had been made for her. It was a ball gown with sparkles and tulle, and an off-the-shoulder cut that reminded me of Cinderella. She saw Jed as her Prince Charming, and this was her chance to be a princess for a day. The whole affair was to be completely different than her wedding to Ronnie, which had been an elaborate three-ring circus.

"It's beautiful, Neely Kate," I said with a soft smile. "You'll be the most beautiful bride ever."

"Do you think Jed will like it?" I was surprised to hear the worry in her voice.

I turned in my seat to face her. "You could walk down the aisle wearing a housedress from Walmart, and Jed would absolutely love it simply because you were wearin' it." I grabbed her hand. "Neely Kate, that man loves you with every breath of his being. You deserve a good man like Jed Carlisle, and he's as lucky to have you as you are to have him."

She must have heard the wistfulness in my voice, because she gave me a sad smile. She started to say something, then stopped herself. "I thank the good Lord for him every day. Every. Single. Day."

When we finished eating, we went back inside to start putting the kitchen back together. Before long, we had over half of it put away, but Neely Kate had turned strangely silent, all the wind going out of her sails, and I could tell she had something on her mind that she wasn't sharing.

Finally, I held up the can in my hand and turned to her. "If you don't tell me what's botherin' you, I'm not responsible for what I do with this can of green beans."

"What are you talkin' about?" she asked, but she refused to look at me.

"I know you, Neely Kate Rivers. I know when something's eatin' at you, so just spit it out already."

She made a face. "I don't want to steal your thunder with the baby."

I set the can on the counter. "What in Sam Hill are you talkin' about?"

Her mouth twisted and tears filled her eyes.

I walked over and grabbed both of her arms. "Neely Kate, honey, I can't think of a single thing that would steal my thunder over this baby." My brow shot up. "Do you mean your weddin'? I couldn't be more excited for you. Why can't we have two happy things happenin' at the same time?" I gave her a soft smile. "We need to embrace all the happiness life gives us. If you're happy, I'm happy."

"It's not just the weddin', Rose. There's something else."

Fear seized my heart. "Are you okay? Are you sick? Is it Jed?" Then I gasped in horror. "Has Kate contacted you?" Her half-sister Kate was a sociopath who'd killed multiple people and attempted to kill several others—including me. She'd also kidnapped Neely Kate last summer and brought her on an excursion—Kate's word—that had illuminated Kate's entanglement with the Hardshaw Group. She intended to ruin them too, or so she said, but we hadn't heard from her since. The more time that passed without contact, the more I hoped she was gone for good. But I also knew that was too good to be true.

"No, Jed and I are both fine. And not a peep from Kate." She pushed out a breath, then tugged me toward the door to the living room. "Let's go sit down. You need to get off your feet anyway."

She grabbed her purse, which struck me as a little odd—was she planning on leaving?—and we sat down on the sofa.

"What's goin' on?" I asked.

She took a deep breath, then said, "You know how much I want a baby, but Jed and I realize it's unlikely I'll ever carry one. So back in February Jed contacted an adoption agency. We've had a home study done and filled out tons of paperwork, but we were told it could take years. But then out of nowhere…we found out that we're getting a baby."

I gasped. I couldn't believe she'd gotten so far in the process and hadn't told me. It stung a little, truth be told, but this wasn't about me, and I was sure it had to do with her continuing disappointment over her infertility. The fewer people she told, the less people who'd know if she suffered another disappointment.

"There's a teenager in south Fenton County who picked us, Rose. *Us.*"

I pushed any hurt over her secret to the side, and let my excitement take over. "Well, of course she did! When?"

"She's due in a month."

My eyes flew wide. "*Oh, my word.* You were worried I'd be upset? How could I be upset?" Excitement raced through my veins. "Neely Kate! We'll get to raise our babies together!"

"You're sure you're not upset?" she said, her eyes full of worry. "After the way I freaked out when you told me you were pregnant, you're allowed to be upset."

I stared at her in disbelief. "Why would I be upset! I'm so excited for you my heart could burst!"

I wrapped my arms around her and hugged her as close as my stomach would allow.

She pulled free and reached into her purse. "I have a photo." With a sheepish look, she handed me a picture of an ultrasound. "We're havin' a girl."

I took the photo and touched the image. "She's beautiful."

Neely Kate laughed. "You can't see much, but Jed says we'd think she was beautiful if she came out with three eyes and a pair of horns."

"Yeah," I said, smiling softly. "We definitely would."

"You're sure you're not mad?"

"Never! I'm so excited for you! *And* for me." I grabbed her hands. "Neely Kate! This is so perfect I'm about to cry!"

"No cryin'," she said, even though her eyes were glassy. "Or I'll start bawlin'."

"This is all so sudden," I said, shaking my head a little in disbelief. Soon we'd both have babies. We'd be going through this together. "You won't have much time to talk about names."

A playful look filled her eyes. "We already know."

"How can you already know?" I asked. "You only started this process a couple of months ago." Joe and I still hadn't picked a name and we'd had months.

"We just knew," she said. "Especially for a girl. We're naming her Daisy Mae Carlisle." Her smile widened. "Isn't it pretty?"

"It's beautiful." It had been Jed's baby sister's name, and I knew he was still haunted by the pain of losing her when they were kids.

"Jed wants us to get married before the baby is born. We'll get her the day after she's born, which means we only have four weeks or less to tie the knot." She laughed. "It's a shotgun weddin'." She winked. "We'd better not invite Miss Mildred or she might take that a little too literally."

I laughed. "And we know *that* from firsthand experience." I put my hand to my forehead, still in shock. "Oh, my word! There's so much to do! We have to get your nursery ready and host a shower, not to mention plan your wedding…"

"And have your baby," she said.

"Don't you worry about that. You have your weddin' whenever you want," I said. "We can have it this weekend, because I'll still be pregnant at the end of May. The way I'm feeling, I'll be pregnant next May."

She laughed. "You're not even due for another two weeks. I think we're safe to wait. You *have* to be at the wedding, so we'll see when you have…Are you ever gonna name that baby?"

"We still haven't decided on names yet," I admitted.

"I can't believe you haven't opened that envelope."

"We decided we want to be surprised." When I'd had my ultrasound back in December, the doctor had written down the baby's sex and put it in an envelope, and so far we hadn't opened it. Joe had deferred the decision to me. In the beginning, he had deferred *a lot* of things to me. At the time, I had fully intended to open it before the baby's birth, when the time felt right, but I'd waited, and waited some more, and it had begun to feel like a big deal. At this point, we'd gone so long without knowing, we both figured we might as well go the whole way. "Besides, you know we made the nursery neutral so it works for either gender." I shook my head. "Enough about my baby! I want to hear more about yours."

"The mother just turned eighteen and realizes she can't take care of a baby. She's really smart, Rose, like valedictorian smart. She has a scholarship to LSU, and she knows she can't have the life she wants if she keeps her."

"So she's not only book smart but has common sense too," I said.

Her smile widened.

"The agency matched you?"

"No," she said. "It's a private adoption. Jed found out from her older brother that she was thinkin' about giving up her baby. We met with her, and she even came to our house to see where the baby would live. At the beginning of the week, she called and said she had picked us. I'm scared she'll change her mind, but our attorney says she's 99% sure she won't."

"We have so much to do!" I said.

Her face glowed with happiness. "I can't believe I'm getting everything I ever wanted."

"Oh, Neely Kate, you deserve every bit of it and then some." The baby kicked, and I grabbed her hand and placed it on my belly. "See? My baby's excited to meet his or her new cousin." My eyes widened. "Have you told Joe? Because I'm gonna have a terrible time keepin' this a secret."

"I think Jed accidentally spilled the beans this mornin', so you go ahead and tell him."

I pursed my lips. "He never said a word to me."

Laughing, she said, "I think Jed threatened to skin him alive if he told you before I did."

I looked at the ultrasound photos again, and then we got up and finished putting my kitchen back together. She yawned as I put the last plate away, so I sent her home, telling her I'd meet her at the nursery in the morning and we could go to the kids' daycare together.

I got ready for bed and plopped on the sofa. I was exhausted, but it was hard to get comfortable. I couldn't stay in any position for long, and every time I lay still for any length of time, the baby started his or her acrobatics. Plus, I was too excited to sleep. While I'd suspected Neely Kate and Jed would adopt, I hadn't expected it to be this fast. Some things were just meant to be.

I was dozing when the front door opened. The Netflix show I'd been watching had turned off, and the room was only lit by one lamp. Joe walked in and frowned when he saw me stirring.

"You didn't need to wait up."

"I didn't," I said, putting both hands behind me and shifting my weight to sit up. "I thought I'd lie down in front of the TV for a while, but I fell asleep." I groaned. "And your son or daughter has decided it's Gymboree time."

A grin lit up his face. "He's movin' now?"

"Yep."

He sat down next to me and placed his hand on my belly. I grabbed it and placed it where the baby had been kicking. "Wow. He's really got a kick."

"I think that's an elbow," I said. "Sharp and pointy."

He looked up at me with eyes full of concern. "I'm sorry you're uncomfortable."

I smiled at him. "I'm not complainin'." Because other than the last week or two, I'd loved every minute of being pregnant. "How did it go at the crime scene?"

He sat back, leaving his hand on my stomach. "Too soon to know anything for certain, but he was an electrician subcontracting for several building contractors in the area."

I shifted to get a better look at him. My ex-brother-in-law was a contractor, and sick or not, there was no denying he'd acted strange this afternoon. "Did he do work for Mike?"

"I don't know. We're still tryin' to get ahold of his records." He gave me a pointed look. "I'm not supposed to be tellin' you any of this."

"I won't tell anyone, Joe."

"Not even Neely Kate, Rose."

That one was harder, but I wouldn't break his trust. "I won't. I promise, but I heard you learned some other juicy news from Jed this morning."

Guilt washed over his face. "Rose, Jed threatened bodily harm if I told you."

"I know, and it's okay. No offense, but I'm glad I heard it directly from Neely Kate."

He laughed, leaning back on the cushion and shifting to face me. "I figured."

We sank into the sofa and turned toward each other, a habit we'd formed over the last few months. Even before he moved in, he'd taken to spending all day Sunday at the house, as well as a few weeknights. We'd formed a kind of day-to-day intimacy I'd never shared with anyone other than Neely Kate. As I stared at his smiling face, I realized we'd formed a deep trust.

I trusted Joe with my secrets, my baby, my life…so what was stopping me from trusting him with my heart? He was no longer beholden to his father's whims, and while I told myself that was because his father was dead, I knew the man before me would stand up for the people he loved, no matter what the cost.

Part of me ached to reach out and touch his face, sink my fingers into his thick, dark hair. To close the distance between us and kiss him. But Joe had been hurt too many times, and I didn't want to be the next person to do it. I had to be certain, or I might ruin everything.

Still, I edged a bit closer to him, because being next to him felt like being home.

Joe was the type of man to build a life with, and while I was sure I was falling in love with him too, something held me back. I needed to find my way past it, and soon.

I smiled at him, surprised at the pure joy radiating through me. I was worried about my niece and nephew, to be sure, but it felt like I was getting the one thing I'd always wanted—a big, loving family, because if I'd learned anything over the past years, it was that family had nothing to do with blood. "I can't believe Neely Kate and Jed are adoptin' a baby girl."

"I have to admit that I was caught by surprise," he said, "but I think it's a good thing. Especially since it's been so hard for Neely Kate to watch you through your pregnancy. This way we can raise the babies together. Now give me details, because Jed didn't mean to tell me anything, and he shut up tighter than a clam once he realized what he'd done."

"Her birth mother's due to give birth in another month."

His eyes flew wide. "That fast?"

"Apparently they started the adoption process a couple of months ago and didn't tell us."

"And it happened already?"

"Yeah." I told him what Neely Kate had said.

"And they know they're havin' a girl?" he asked.

"They're namin' her Daisy Mae."

He leaned back into the cushions again. "I think it's just now hittin' me that I'm gonna be an uncle."

And he really would be since Neely Kate was his sister.

"Yeah," I said with a soft smile. "Uncle Joe."

He grinned again. "Uncle Joe and Aunt Rose."

"And they've decided to get married in a few weeks. Jed wants them to be married when the baby comes."

He nodded slightly, staring off with a faraway look.

"What are you thinkin' about?" I asked.

He gave me a tight smile. "Don't you worry about that." He stood and offered me his hand. "Let's get you upstairs and to bed. It feels like the baby's gone to sleep, so maybe you can get some sleep too."

I took his hand and let him pull me to my feet. When I stood, he wrapped an arm around my back and held me close.

"Do you wish we knew the baby's gender?"

"Sometimes," I admitted. "But I like that it's a surprise. A good one. We need more of those, don't you think?"

He leaned over and kissed my forehead. "Yeah. I do."

Flutters filled my stomach.

One more surprise to add to a pile of others. Now I needed to sort out what it meant. Or maybe I knew, but I was just struggling to accept it. So what was holding me back?

The real question was who.

Chapter
Four

The next morning, I walked into the nursery, and Maeve and Anna oohed and aahed over my huge belly. The baby was moving, so I let them both feel his or her kicks.

A customer pulled into the lot, and Anna reluctantly left to see to them. I suspected she was getting baby fever, but Bruce Wayne had told me only a few weeks ago he wasn't ready to become a father. Not even close.

Maeve looked at my belly with a longing that broke my heart. Her only daughter had been pregnant when she was murdered a couple of years before, and her son, Mason, wasn't even dating anyone. She lived vicariously through me, not that I minded. I was only glad she still wanted to be part of my life given Mason and I had a past.

"Would you mind watchin' Muffy?" I asked her. "Neely Kate and I are gonna run over to the daycare."

Maeve's eyes widened. "I thought you planned on keeping the baby with you at the landscaping office."

That was the plan, but now I wondered if Neely Kate had a childcare plan for after she got her baby. I couldn't imagine her putting Daisy in daycare. Jed had enough money that she didn't need to work, but she claimed she liked her job, especially the time she spent at the nursery now that she was part owner.

I didn't want to worry Maeve over Ashley and Mikey, and apparently neither did Neely Kate, because she gave the older woman a warm smile as she said, "It's always good to keep your options open. Right, Rose?"

"That's right. Anyhow, we better get goin'."

Muffy tried to follow me out the door, but Maeve picked her up to keep her from bolting after us.

When we got outside, Neely Kate asked, "Do you want to take my car or your truck?"

"If I get in your car, I'll need a tow truck to pull me out," I said.

She laughed. "Okay, but I'm drivin'. I'm not sure you can even reach the steering wheel."

"Fine by me." I handed her the keys and we both got in.

Neither of us spoke until she pulled out of the parking lot. Then I finally asked, "Do you know if you're gonna keep workin' after the baby?"

"I'm not sure," she said slowly. "I know you're plannin' on workin' your landscapin' schedule around your baby, but I'm not so sure that would work so well at the nursery."

"If that's what you want to do, we could try it," I said. "We can fit a travel crib in the back room." I'd already gotten one for the landscaping office. I just hadn't brought it in yet. "We can fix it up so it's not so dark and a bit cheerier. And it might actually be easier with Anna and Maeve there, dotin' on her." I cast a glance at her. "When are you plannin' on tellin' everyone?"

"Not until we get her. I don't want to jinx it," she said, gripping the steering wheel tighter. "Our attorney says the birth mother seems adamant about her future plans and LSU, but we can't count our chickens, you know?"

"Yeah," I said. "I understand." I'd heard of too many adoptions that had fallen through to question her logic.

She pulled into the daycare parking lot, and as she shut off the engine, she turned and looked me in the eye. "Maybe we should go about this another way."

"How so?"

"What if Mike told her that she can't share anything with you?"

"Then this will be a wasted trip," I said. "Unless we see Mikey playin' outside in the playground."

"Exactly," she said. "So we'll go in pretendin' you're lookin' for daycare for baby bruiser there, and we'll throw out some *won't it be awesome that your baby will be goin' to the same daycare as his cousins.*"

"So you think the baby's a boy too?" I teased.

"Joe's reasoning has convinced me, not to mention I've felt him kick. After dealin' with my cousins, I'm convinced that's a future bear wrangler in there."

"What?" I shook my head. "Never mind. It's a great plan. We'll go with it."

I opened the truck door, and Neely Kate laughed as I slid out.

"That's right, make fun of the twenty-eight-month-pregnant woman."

She was still laughing as she met me on the sidewalk. "Elephants aren't even pregnant that long. Two weeks will pass before you know it. And I'm not laughin' at you. I'm laughin' *with* you."

"Only I'm not laughin'," I said, trying to suppress my grin. "I've missed you." I'd had too much solitude lately. Having Joe around was a relief, and I loved being with Neely Kate. It made me feel more like myself. James had been important to me—in some ways he always would be—but he wasn't the only person who mattered. Far from it. The months I'd spent alone at the farm had convinced me of that.

"I've missed you too. Now let's go get some answers."

We walked into the entry and rang the buzzer parents pushed to gain entry to the secure area. A woman showed up at a sliding window open to the lobby. "Can I help—oh, hi, Rose!" she said, obviously recognizing me from when I used to help with Ashley and Mikey. "Oh! You're havin' a baby of your own!"

"I am," I said, placing a hand on my belly.

"I didn't realize you'd gotten married."

An all-too-familiar defensiveness washed through me. "I didn't."

She blinked. "Oh. I never took you for the type…" Her voice trailed off as she realized her faux pas. "Sorry. None of my business."

"*In any case*," Neely Kate said with plenty of attitude. "Rose was gonna keep the baby with her at work after she delivered, but now she's havin' second thoughts."

"I've decided to check out my options," I said, hoping this would work. "I know I was in here all the time with Ashley and Mikey, but is there any way I can take a tour?"

"Sure," she said brightly. "Normally we have people make an appointment, but it's a bit slow this morning, and I'm sure Portia wouldn't mind if I give you a quick tour."

"Thanks," I said. "I'm due any day now, so I really don't want to wait."

"Let me buzz you back."

The buzzer rang out, and Neely Kate opened the door for me, holding it so I could enter.

As soon as I walked through the door, I immediately began to scan the room for Mikey. Ashley was in first grade, so she wouldn't be here until after school, but Mikey would be in the three-year-old class.

The woman met us at the door and held out her hand to Neely Kate. "I'm Amanda, by the way."

Neely Kate offered her a big smile and shook her hand. "Nice to meet you, Amanda. I'm Neely Kate."

"Welcome," she said. "We'll head on back to the infant room."

"But we'll get to see the older kids' rooms, right?" I asked. "Because if my baby goes here, I don't want to have to change daycares once they reach preschool age."

"Of course," Amanda said, guiding us into the huge communal room at the heart of the daycare. "I'll bring you through the entire facility."

She led us to the infant room, which held six babies ranging in age from three months to nearly a year. "When they reach their first birthday, they move to the toddler room."

As she said so, she moved down to a sunny room with five babies crawling and walking around while a worker blew bubbles.

"The teachers have been trained in the newest ways to interact with the babies and encourage their curiosity."

Glancing around the room, I had to admit it wasn't the dark, dreary prison I'd expected. The babies all looked happy.

"When they turn two, they move out to the big kid room." She led us across the communal room to a classroom against the back wall.

"We have two teachers in a room with eight to twelve kids," Amanda said. "The younger the age, the more teachers."

The two-year-olds were singing a song with sign language. After we watched them for a moment, Amanda took us to the three-year-old room. They sat in a circle on the floor with their teachers, looking at giant flash cards displaying letters.

I glanced around and turned to Neely Kate. "I don't see Mikey."

"Actually," Amanda said, "I'm glad you mentioned that. Mikey and Ashley haven't been here most of the week."

"So they really *are* sick," I said.

Amanda's eyes widened "They're sick? We weren't sure what happened. Mike never called in and he hasn't responded to our voicemails."

"Has Ashley been going to her elementary school?" Neely Kate asked.

"No," Amanda said. "Her teacher called here to see if we knew what was going on."

A sick feeling filled my stomach. "When was their last day here?"

"Last Friday," Amanda said.

The day after I'd seen Mike with the kids. Had he pulled them in some elaborate scheme to keep them from me? That seemed crazy.

"So they've been gone three days?" Neely Kate asked.

"That's right," Amanda said. "We're starting to get worried." She lowered her voice. "I shouldn't have mentioned it to you—confidentiality rules and all—and I'll admit to using your question about Mikey to my advantage. But if you tell anyone, I could get in big trouble. Mike made it very clear he doesn't want us sharing anything with you."

"Don't worry, Amanda," I said. "We won't tell a soul."

She gave me a tight smile. "Thank you." Then she seemed to shrug it off and asked perkily, "So do you want me to add your baby to the waiting list?"

"There's a waiting list?" Neely Kate asked.

"Oh, yes," she said. "We're one of the best daycares in the area. Most people put their baby on the waiting list the moment they find out they're pregnant. Shoot," she said with a laugh, "sometimes we know before their friends and family."

"Um…" I said absently, trying to figure out my next course of action. "Sure. How long's the waiting list?"

"Eight months."

Neely Kate shot me a look of surprise, but I shrugged. Who knew if I'd change my mind about daycare, and it wasn't a bad idea to leave the option open.

We thanked Amanda and accepted a handout about pricing—making me reconsider being added to the wait list. I might have to take out a mortgage on the farm.

We were just about to walk out when Amanda asked, "What's your baby's name? So I can put them on the waiting list."

"The baby doesn't have one yet. We don't know if we're having a boy or a girl."

Amanda didn't hide her surprise. "Wow. I've heard that some people don't know, but I've never seen it in the wild."

I laughed. "That's me. The free-range pregnant lady."

Neely Kate shot me a worried look, then grabbed my arm and dragged me out the door. "I think all those pregnancy hormones have finally addled your brain."

Part of me wondered if she was right.

After we got into the truck, I asked, "So what do we do now?"

Neely Kate rested both of her hands on the steering wheel. "I say we go to Mike's and demand some answers."

"He's never gonna tell us anything," I said. "And if they have the flu, we can't risk gettin' it either."

"We'll go over anyway. At least it's a place to start."

Not to mention, at the moment, it was the only thing we had to go on.

Chapter
Five

Neely Kate pulled up in front of Mike's house, and the first thing I noticed was his truck was gone.

"Maybe he went to work," Neely Kate said. "Do you think he took the kids to his parents' house?"

"If they're sick, I don't see how he could. His dad has respiratory problems. He wouldn't want to risk him coming down with it."

"Maybe he's checkin' on some job sites," she said, "and he's lettin' them stay inside the truck."

That was a possibility. "Last I heard, Mike was building some houses in that new neighborhood south of town. Maybe we should head over there and see if we can find his truck."

"Good idea," she said, shifting the truck back into drive. "Let's head over there now."

I gave her a sheepish smile. "Thanks for takin' this seriously."

"Of course. Those are Violet's kids, and I promised her I'd watch out for them too. We all did."

"I should have fought harder," I said, "but my family law attorney is worried that he might make my Lady in Black activity public."

"You have a family law attorney?" she asked in surprise. "Are you thinkin' about suing Mike for visitation rights?"

My shoulders tensed. I hadn't told her about my encounter with James in February, and part of me was scared to tell her now. Partly because it would make it feel more real, but also because I suspected her feelings would be hurt. Then again, she'd kept the news about baby Daisy from me too—maybe this protectiveness was part of being a parent.

"Neely Kate, there's something I need to tell you," I said, deciding to come clean. "In February, I asked James to sign papers legally giving up his rights as a father. I had Carter draw them up, which he eagerly did. He didn't charge me a cent, because he thought it was the best way to get his client out of a difficult situation. James wanted to just sign them, but I insisted on meeting in person at Carter's office. I wanted to see his face when he signed them, to be certain he'd leave us alone, and truth be told, I'd also hoped to corner him and ask him about Mike."

"I take it he didn't tell you anything."

"No. I never saw him. He showed up for the appointment, but he left out the back door before I got there." I paused. "He didn't sign the papers, Neely Kate. He refused to give up his rights."

She shot a quick glance at me, terror in her eyes. "Does he want to be a daddy to your baby?"

"Honestly? I doubt it. I suspect he refused so he'd have something to use against me."

"Oh, Rose."

I pushed out a breath. "After that, it seemed wise to retain a family law attorney. But my new lawyer doesn't want to do anything yet. She thinks we should wait until he makes a move, otherwise the baby's paternity will become public knowledge. I know she's right, but it feels like I'm sitting on a ticking time bomb that could go off any minute."

"How's Joe takin' it?"

"I haven't told him."

"Rose!"

"I don't want to worry him."

"So you're takin' the worry all on yourself?" she asked in disbelief. When I didn't answer, she said, "Rose, seems to me that bein' a parent is worryin' about your baby for the rest of your life. You're lettin' Joe be the baby's daddy, but you're not lettin' him do his job."

I hadn't thought about it that way, but I realized she was right. Joe wasn't going to abandon me or the baby if things got tough— wasn't that why I wanted him to be the father? Tears stung my eyes. "How'd you get so smart?"

She preened for a few seconds, her attention flicking from me to the road, but her expression turned serious again all too soon. "Seriously though, I'm worried the message he'll take from this is that you don't think he's capable of bein' a daddy."

"That's not it at all!"

"*I* know that," she said, "but he's already worried he's on shaky ground."

"Which is why I don't want to worry him unnecessarily about James."

"He's a strong man, Rose. He can handle this, and it's gonna hurt his feelings that you've been carryin' this all alone."

Tears filled my eyes. "This is all my fault."

"What are you talkin' about?" she asked.

"If I hadn't been stupid enough to think I could handle having a fling with James…if I'd been more careful…if I hadn't slept with the crime lord of the county, I wouldn't be in this situation. I wouldn't be puttin' Joe through this."

"And you wouldn't be havin' this sweet baby, Rose."

"I know," I said with a sigh. "I wouldn't wish the baby away for the world, but it's all so confusing."

"Look," she said, "we all make mistakes. Me included. I blamed myself for my infertility, even though I got all those STIs through no fault of my own."

"*I* knew full well what I was gettin' into," I said. "I just chose to believe I could have a different outcome."

"Granny always says live and learn," she said. "And that there's no sense hangin' on to the past." She paused. "It doesn't really matter how we got here, Rose. All that matters is what we do with the here and now."

"I'll tell Joe tonight."

She gave me a sad smile.

We reached the neighborhood and Neely Kate turned in. The addition was new enough that it didn't have any inhabitants yet. There were over a dozen houses in various states of construction scattered down the street.

One of those houses was cordoned off with crime scene tape, and I could feel in my bones that my worst fears had been confirmed. The murder really did have something to do with Mike.

"What in the world…?" Neely Kate exclaimed as she pulled over between two beat-up pickup trucks.

"That must be where they found the dead body yesterday," I said with a shaky breath.

"What?" she screeched.

Joe had told me not to tell Neely Kate anything, but there was no hiding crime scene tape. What else was public knowledge? I pulled out my phone and did a quick internet search.

"You knew there was a dead body and didn't tell me?" she asked, sounding affronted.

I continued searching on my phone. "That's where Joe went last night, but he didn't say much about it." I found an article and opened it. "This says a body was found at a new home construction in the Wild Vista neighborhood and that neither the name of the victim nor the cause of death has been released yet. The murder is under investigation."

"There haven't been any murders in Fenton County in months…" she mused. Then she gasped. "Do you think this is tied to Mike?"

I pinched my lips tight.

"You *do* know something." When I didn't respond, she exclaimed, "Rose!"

"I only know that he was an electrician and Joe's lookin' to see if there's a connection. It could be a coincidence."

She stared at me in disbelief. "Do you seriously believe that?"

"No, but this is an official investigation. I didn't tell you earlier because Joe trusted me enough to tell me a few things and asked me not to talk about it. I don't want to screw that up."

Her lips twisted as she gave it some thought. "Okay."

My mouth dropped open. "You're gonna let this go?"

She lifted her shoulder into a half shrug, then said in a flippant tone, "If you can't tell me, you can't tell me."

I didn't believe that for a minute. But if she was thinking of poking around, she wasn't alone. I couldn't walk away from this, not if Ashley and Mikey were really missing. "Let's look for Mike's truck, then start askin' around."

"About Mike or the dead guy?" she asked.

I grinned. "If we find out more about the dead guy because of our questions, then Joe can hardly object to you knowing. I wouldn't have told you anything."

"Good plan."

"And I really don't know much anyway."

"Okay."

Either her own impending motherhood had mellowed my best friend, or she was up to something. I supposed it didn't matter since I was up to something too.

She drove to the end of the street—and the construction. We passed the house Mike's crew was currently working on, with no sign of Mike or his truck, and I wanted to burst into tears. I needed to see those babies with my own eyes to know that they were safe.

As Neely Kate started to turn, she asked, "Did you see Mike's truck?"

"No," I sa   "   [saw a sign for his construction company in front of one of t   uses. Let's go inside and ask around about Mike and the kids."

"Do you have a plan?" she asked.

"Do we ever?"

She laughed as she pulled over to an available parking spot on the road in front of the house. "Sometimes we start with a plan, but it usually goes sideways."

"Then let's just trust our guts," I said.

She glanced at my stomach and flashed me a cheesy grin.

I rolled my eyes and groaned. "Come on."

As soon as my feet touched the ground, I realized I had a problem—the yard was a dirt pile with massive ruts and there wasn't a driveway. While the exterior of the house was up, and plywood had been attached to the outside walls, there weren't any windows in the multiple holes cut into the exterior of the house, let alone stairs to the front door.

How the heck was I going to manage *that*?

"Maybe I should go in and ask the questions," Neely Kate said.

I started to argue with her, but then my common sense kicked in. "Yeah. I'll wait out here."

As Neely Kate picked her way through the minefield of ruts toward the house, I walked into the middle of the road and started to scan the neighborhood. Mike's house was two houses and one empty lot down from the house with crime scene tape.

Neely Kate walked through the gaping two-car garage into the house, then called out to the guys working inside, "Hey!"

I put a hand on my belly, trying to figure out where to start first and how to go about it. I'd learned from Mike that the world of contractors in Henryetta was pretty small—everyone knew everyone else, which meant there was a good chance the murdered electrician and Mike had known each other, especially given he'd been murdered in a neighborhood where Mike was working. The real question was if the electrician had ties to Skeeter Malcolm. I'd have to be more careful finding the answer to that question.

A shiny black pickup turned into the neighborhood, driving toward me. I moved to the side of the road as I continued to consider the situation.

The truck pulled over to the side of the road about twenty feet ahead of me, and when the driver's door opened, a large man wearing jeans and a button-down shirt with the sleeves rolled up to the elbows got out and started ambling toward me.

"Well, hello, little lady," he said with a big grin in an accent that sounded like it came from Texas, not Arkansas or Louisiana. "Are you looking for a house for your expanding family?"

It was a legitimate question, and even though he made me cringe, I could work with this. "I'm considering it. I live out in the country, and with the baby comin', I thought it might be nice to be closer to town."

He pursed his lips and nodded, as though taking my statement to heart and intending to personally solve my dilemma. "When kids have an accident, they can go from happy and healthy to dying in seconds flat." He snapped his fingers to punctuate his statement. "It would be better to live closer to the Fenton County Hospital, which is only ten minutes away from here."

I jumped, both because the snap had caught me by surprise and a sudden fear had mushroomed inside of me that I was putting my baby in danger by living out on the farm.

"You got any other kids?" he asked, propping his elbow on a rounded belly that wasn't quite as large as mine and resting his chin on his fisted hand.

"No," I said. "But I'd like to be prepared if I have more. I'd really rather not move again."

His gaze drifted to my naked left ring finger. "So it's just you and the baby, then?"

I bristled, but I told myself he wasn't judging, he was appraising my financial situation. "And my fiancé."

His eyes lit up. "And what does your fiancé do?"

I definitely didn't want to scare him off, so I went with what I hoped was an innocuous answer. "He's in security."

He nodded his approval. "Then he knows the importance of a safe neighborhood."

I made a face and moved closer, lowering my voice. "But *is* it safe?"

I nodded to the house with the crime scene tape.

He let out a huge sigh as though he'd just finished pushing a five-hundred-pound boulder uphill. "That is an unfortunate circumstance that has nothin' to do with common criminals and everything to do with greed."

"Oh?" I asked. "How so?"

A smile spread across his face, but it looked forced. "Now, don't you worry about that, little lady. You let the menfolk take care of it."

My own smile wavered. "I'm about to be a mother—it's my job to worry, Mr....?"

"Just call me Tex," he said, reaching out to shake. When I offered my hand, he squeezed tight and pumped several times. "Everyone does."

"I take it you're a builder, Tex?"

"That's right." He gestured to the house next to Mike's. "That's one of my houses right there."

It looked slightly further along than Mike's. I decided to drop a line in the water and see if I could get a bite. "I was interested in the house next to it."

"Mike Beauregard's house?" He pinched his mouth together and shook his head disapprovingly. "*That* would be a big mistake."

"Oh? Why?"

He leaned in closer. "I know for a fact he cuts corners."

"You don't say."

"Yep."

When he didn't elaborate, I pressed. "How so?"

He studied Mike's house for a second, then as though shaking himself out of a stupor, he said, "Now, don't you worry about that." His grin lit up his eyes, but he didn't look quite as jovial as before. "You stick with one of my houses and you'll do just fine. Are you lookin' for a three- or four-bedroom?"

It took everything in me not to give him a tongue-lashing, but Neely Kate emerged from Mike's house just then, walking toward me, dodging the ruts in the torn-up yard.

I lifted my hand in greeting. "Hey, I was talkin' to Tex here about buyin' a house. He says to stay away from the builder of the house you just left."

She put a hand on her chest as her mouth dropped open in shock. "What? Why?"

Tex gave her a smug look. "He cuts corners."

Neely Kate gave him a deadpan look as she reached us. "The corners all looked square to me." Turning to me, she added, "Should we bring a protractor and measure them?"

It took everything in me not to burst out laughing.

Tex looked like he was fighting hard not to roll his eyes. "Not those kinds of corners, little lady. He's sloppy and tries to get by with shoddy work."

"Don't they have inspections to protect buyers against things like that?" she asked.

"He doesn't cut the kind of corners that would show up on inspections."

"Then what kind of corners is he cuttin'?" I asked.

"Cheaper plywood. Furnishings pulled from other job sites. Using unlicensed subcontractors but having a licensed one sign off on the work…"

"Why doesn't anyone turn him in?" Neely Kate asked.

He shrugged. "Not all of it is illegal."

Which insinuated that some of it was.

Neely Kate pointed to the cordoned-off house. "The men I just talked to said a man was killed down there."

Irritation flickered in Tex's eyes. "Like I told your friend, the victim was someone who'd gotten greedy. It's not cause for alarm over movin' into the neighborhood."

"How'd he get greedy?" Neely Kate asked.

He shook his head. "Don't you worry about that, little lady. It's none of your concern."

It was as though he were a doll with a pull string, and every other sentence was *don't you worry, little lady*. I was in no mood to deal with nonsense, but I suspected we might be able to get a little more out of him. I put my hands on my hips. "It's my concern if a man was killed two houses down from the house you're tryin' to sell me."

"It might be haunted," Neely Kate said with a nod. "We'll need to conduct a séance, but first we need to know how he died."

"I don't know how he died," Tex said. "And you don't need to conduct the séance. It's not haunted."

"You don't know that," Neely Kate said, pouring on the drawl. "He died last night. His spirit hasn't had time to get settled yet." She tilted her head to the side and made a face. "All the more reason to hold a séance ASAP to stop him from gettin' a foothold."

"It didn't happen at one of my houses," Tex said. "Besides, it's a full two houses away from mine. You don't need to worry."

"Of course I need to worry," Neely Kate said. "It's my civic duty to make sure that house is safe for the family that moves in. We very well might need to hire the ghost hunter we saw on that PI reality show." She scrunched up her face. "What was her name?" She pointed at the contractor. "Piper Lancaster. If you like, I can find out how much she charges and get her over here."

"I'm not payin' for a ghost hunter," Tex said, becoming indignant.

"That's what I'm tryin' to prevent," Neely Kate said. "Which is why we should march over there right now to make sure that spirit doesn't get a foothold. But we need to know his name first."

Tex rubbed his forehead, looking frustrated. "Mark Erickson."

"And you don't know how he was killed?" Neely Kate asked.

"I heard he was shot."

Neely Kate scrunched up her face. "I can work with that. Come on, Beth Ann."

A smile twitched on my lips. She hadn't used my alias for months. "You know how much I hate evil spirits," I said. "So we'll definitely need to get rid of it before I even *consider* movin' into this neighborhood."

"You're gonna hold a séance right *now*?" Tex asked in disbelief.

"Well, yeah!" Neely Kate said. "The sooner the better!" She grabbed my wrist and started to drag me down toward the house.

"We can't go in there, Neely Kate," I protested in a whisper. "The crime scene tape's still up."

"But is it *really*?" Neely Kate asked. "Look, some of it's down on the side."

True enough, it was lower on the east side, but it was plain as day that it was still cordoned off. "Neely Kate... Joe's gonna have a conniption."

"He'll be fine."

"I'm not havin' my baby in a prison cell!" I hissed.

"You won't. Joe won't let that happen. Don't worry so much."

"What do you hope to find in there, anyway?" I asked. "Don't you think Joe and the sheriff's deputies would already have found anything of importance?"

"I don't know. Maybe, but I also know Mike's up to something, and it's more than cuttin' corners on his houses."

I pulled her to a halt in front of the crime scene tape strung alongside the street. "Why? What did those guys say?"

"They said that Mike didn't pay them last week, and that he hasn't shown up this week, except for a couple of times and he was lookin' like crap."

"Like he was sick?"

Her eyes narrowed. "He's hidin'."

"Hidin'? Hidin' from who?"

"They think he owes money to someone. They don't know who, but they think he's scared."

My stomach somersaulted. "Neely Kate, what about Mikey and Ashley?"

"They haven't seen them and didn't know anything about them being sick."

The blood drained from my head.

"Rose," she said insistently, "we'll go to his house and look for them after we finish here, but while you and Joe saw Mike last night, *they* haven't seen him for two days."

"I don't have a good feeling about this."

"Yeah, neither do I. It can't be a coincidence that Mike went into hiding around the same time an electrician was shot near one of his build sites."

I tried to swallow my fear. "Agreed."

We studied the house, and even though Neely Kate tried to convince me the crime scene tape had drooped enough to qualify the scene as open for business, I refused to cross that line. For one thing, the yard wasn't much better than the one at Mike's construction site, and two, I wasn't in the mood to tug at the skirts of the law. I was too tired and cranky, and I was craving a biscuit sandwich.

"You can go inside, but I'm stayin' out here," I finally said. "You can take lots of photos and show me. And if you do happen to get arrested, I'll try my best to scrounge up the money to bail you out, but I have no idea how much those two false labor visits are gonna cost me since I'm not sure they're covered by insurance, so no promises."

"You used to be more fun," Neely Kate said with a frown.

"Yeah," I said, grumbling. "You wouldn't be sayin' that if you'd known me two years ago."

She laughed. "Come on. Let's get you that biscuit I heard you mumblin' about under your breath."

"It wasn't under my breath. I *wanted* you to hear it."

We headed back to the truck, and Tex, who was standing in the doorway to his spec house, gave us a wave. I waved back, but my attentions shifted to the house with the crime scene tape as we drove past. I had every intention of finding out what had happened to Mark Erickson. We'd just have to go about it another way.

Chapter Six

On the way to Mike's, I called Joe and put him on speaker to fill him in on what we'd found out at the daycare and the neighborhood under construction. He listened and asked a few questions, then finally got to what I knew he'd been dying to ask since I'd told him where we'd gone.

"Did you two go in that house?" he asked in a firm tone.

"Which one?" Neely Kate asked with a huge grin that would have given her away if Joe had been there to see it.

"You know which one," Joe snapped. "*Did you?*"

"No," I said, not in the mood to hear them squabble. "We stood at the curb and looked from there. I wasn't about to disturb a crime scene."

He was quiet for a moment, then said, "Because you figured you'd get the information another way. From me."

"I wasn't *countin'* on it," I said. "We have other resources."

He released a low groan. "You're both gonna be the death of me."

"I sure hope not," I said. "I kind of need you to stick around."

"I'm not goin' anywhere, darlin'." He took a breath, then said, "What are you two doin' now?"

"We're headed to Mike's house to see what's goin' on with the kids."

"I'll send a deputy over," Joe said.

My breath caught in my throat. By bringing in his men, Joe was taking this to the next level, which was a good thing. Something might actually get done, but it also meant this wasn't as simple as Mike trying to keep me from seeing the kids. They were in danger. "But Mike's house is in Henryetta city limits."

"You let me worry about that," he said. "In fact, if Mike's in trouble with some criminal, I'm not sure I want either one of you anywhere near his house."

Neely Kate started to protest, but I held up my hand. "We'll head over, but we'll wait on the street until the deputy gets there."

I was sure he was going to shut me down, so he surprised me when he said, "All right. Just stay in the car, okay?"

"We'll stay *by* it," Neely Kate said, then hung up the call and gave me a sideways glance. "You know *I* didn't promise, right?"

I crossed my arms over my chest, my forearms resting on my belly. "I'm *fully* aware of that."

Neely Kate offered to pick up a breakfast sandwich from Merilee's, but I told her I'd had second thoughts. I was too worried to eat it. All I wanted was to make sure my niece and nephew were safe.

When we pulled up in front of their house, the driveway was ominously empty.

"He's still not home."

"Maybe his truck is in the garage," Neely Kate said.

I shook my head. "It wouldn't fit. But if he's not here, where is he? And more importantly, where are the kids?"

A sheriff's car was heading toward us, and the deputy parked behind us. We both got out, and I was relieved to see Deputy Randy Miller get out of his cruiser and walk toward us. Randy was my friend, and I knew he'd take this seriously.

"Hey, Rose," he said, sounding subdued. "You look like you're ready to deliver any day."

"So they tell me," I said with a sigh, "but I'm not convinced."

"She's got two more weeks until her due date," Neely Kate said, "but she's over it."

He gave me a sympathetic look. "My cousin went through the same thing. She was three weeks late, and then she was in labor for three days. They finally had to cut the kid out. But don't you worry. You'll be holding that baby soon enough."

I gaped at him in horror. Three weeks late and three days of labor? Three weeks late would mean I had five more weeks to go. Over a month.

Oblivious to my internal crisis, he turned his attention toward the house. "I hear something fishy's goin' on with your niece and nephew."

I shook myself out of my self-pity. There were more important things to deal with. "They haven't been to school or daycare in days, and Mike hasn't called in to tell either place what's wrong. He told Joe and me that they're sick with the flu, but his parents didn't know anything about them bein' ill, and now Mike and the kids aren't even home."

"Maybe they're at the doctor."

"Maybe," I conceded. "I can probably find out if they are."

He narrowed his eyes. "The doctor's office isn't supposed to release any information to me without a warrant…so how about I walk up to the front door and around the house, and you call whoever your source is and find out without my involvement."

I pulled my phone out of my purse. As he headed to the front door, I called my doctor's office. The receptionist answered, and I said, "Hey, Loretta, this is Rose Gardner."

"Is everything okay? We heard about your false labor yesterday."

I suppressed a groan. "I swear I'm not goin' to the hospital again until I feel the baby fallin' out." I paused and softened my tone. "But that's not why I'm callin'. I'm worried about my niece and nephew—Ashley and Mikey Beauregard. They've been out of school with the flu, and I'm checkin' to see if I can swing by and pick up their prescription for Tamiflu."

Neely Kate shot me a surprised look, which quickly morphed into a grin. She liked it when I did things on the sly.

"I don't see a prescription up front for them, although that's something we can call into the pharmacy. Did you check there?"

"I did, but they don't have it," I said, resisting the sudden urge to feel my nose to see if it was growing.

"Let me place you on hold and check."

"Thanks, Loretta."

I put the phone on mute in case Loretta picked up, and said to Neely Kate, "It's workin' so far. She's checkin' for a prescription, which means she's lookin' to see if he brought them in."

Randy stood waiting on the front porch after knocking several times. He walked down the steps and started around the corner of the house toward the back.

"Rose?" Loretta said.

I turned the mute button off. "Yeah?"

"Do you know where their daddy took them? I'm not seein' any record of them bein' here."

"Are you sure?" I asked, my stomach twisting with worry.

"Yep. I triple-checked."

"Okay. Thanks, Loretta. Maybe he took them to the urgent care." I hung up and held the phone to my chest. "Neely Kate, Mike never took them to the doctor."

"Well, you already suspected they weren't sick, so why are you so freaked out?"

"Because if they aren't sick, then where are they?"

Neely Kate's gaze drifted past me, and I turned to see Joe getting out of his car and walking toward me.

He took one look at my face and closed the distance between us, pulling me into his arms.

I buried my face into his chest. "They never went to the doctor, Joe. I just checked."

He held me close. "We'll find them." Dropping his hold on me, he pulled out his phone and placed a call. "Mrs. Beauregard? This is Chief Deputy Joe Simmons."

Mike's mother knew Joe, which meant he'd included his title to make sure she understood the authority behind the call.

"I need to ask you about the whereabouts of Ashley and Mikey." He was silent for a long pause. "I need to know the last time you saw them, not when Mike said he had them, when *you* saw them with your own eyes." His brow lifted. "Five days ago. And when did you last talk to Mike?" A pause. "Yesterday after I spoke with you...and did he give you any indication of what might be going on or why the kids hadn't been to school?"

Randy appeared at the corner of the house, and Joe motioned for him to join us.

"I'm gonna need to take statements from you and Mr. Beauregard... Yes, it's necessary because this is turnin' out to be a serious matter, but first I'm gonna need one of you to come over and let us into Mike's house." He frowned. "Yes, Mrs. Beauregard, this is necessary too. Your grandchildren have been out of school and your son hasn't notified the school. We're just here to make sure everyone's okay." A look of disgust washed over his face while he listened. "You can be upset with me all you want, but I'm about to call child protective services *and* break a window to get into Mike's house, so I suggest that you or your husband come over here with a key so you'll have one less thing to worry about."

I could hear her angry voice, although I couldn't make out the words.

"Oh," Joe added, looking completely unflustered by her tirade. "If Mike happens to contact you, you go ahead and tell him that the Fenton County Sheriff's Department is looking for him and his children. He knows my number." He hung up and lowered his hand to his side.

"She didn't know anything," he told me.

"What if she's lyin'?" Neely Kate asked.

"Unfortunately, I don't think she is," Joe said, then turned to Randy, who had just walked over to us. "Deputy Miller, I'm gonna call in another deputy, and once he shows up, I want you both to take the lead in goin' through the house. I'll follow behind."

"Why are you doin' *that?*" Neely Kate asked.

"To help negate any claims of bias should we find something," Joe said. "Ideally, since I have personal ties to the case, I wouldn't go in at all. But this is a small town and county, which means I can't avoid everyone I know." His jaw twitched. "Plus, I promised Vi."

I put my hand on his chest and looked up into his face. "You're keepin' your promise, Joe."

Like he always did.

He glanced down at me, and his worried expression stirred up my own anxiety, making me feel like a shaken beehive.

Taking a deep breath, he took a step back and started making calls and issuing orders. The second deputy showed up, and they were about to break into the house when Mike's parents finally showed up a half hour after Joe had called. They'd brought a familiar-looking younger woman with them, and it took me a second to realize who she was.

"They brought an attorney," I said, almost under my breath.

"What?" Neely Kate asked, craning her neck to check the woman out. "How do you know?"

I could understand why she'd asked. The woman was dressed in a pair of jeans and a bohemian shirt, but she didn't look all that different from when I'd first met her at the Henryetta Police

Department nearly two years ago. "It's Deanna Crawfield. Violet called her for me when I was taken in for questioning about Momma's murder."

Joe was standing closer to the house with Randy and the other deputy, who had arrived about ten minutes earlier. Deanna approached them with a determined look in her eyes. "Do you have a search warrant, Deputy Simmons?"

"If I had a search warrant, would I be asking Mr. and Mrs. Beauregard for a key?" Joe asked in a good-natured tone, but I could see he was holding back his anger.

"There's absolutely no reason for you to go into the Beauregards' home," Deanna said. "If Mike's parents aren't worried, then why are you?"

"If your clients aren't worried, then why did they bring *you*?" Joe asked. "Seems to me they're plenty worried—we're all just worried about different things. I'm worried about the safety and welfare of two young children. Your clients are worried about their son. Seems to me they'd be worried about both and welcome the sheriff's department's concern. If the Beauregards can confirm the whereabouts of their grandchildren, we'll happily walk away. Otherwise, we *are* going in that house."

"This isn't a sheriff matter," Deanna said. "We're still in Henryetta city limits, which means it's under the jurisdiction of the Henryetta Police Department."

"While I understand why you'd make that assumption," Joe said, "this is actually part of an ongoing investigation the sheriff's department took over from the Henryetta police last fall."

"The break-in at Violet's attorney's office?" Mike's mother asked in shock. "What on earth does that have to do with this?"

"Mrs. Beauregard," Deanna warned.

Mike's mother turned to her in outrage. "They came around askin' him all kinds of questions, insinuating he knew something about it. Why on earth would he have anything to do with a burglary? She left him absolutely nothing! Not even her life insurance policy to take care of the kids! He was countin' on that money!"

"Mrs. Beauregard!" Deanna said, increasing the sternness in her voice.

But Mike's mother wasn't backing down. She shifted to face me. "This is your fault! You turned her against him!"

"Now hold on there," Joe said in a slow, good-natured tone. "No one said anything about Mike breaking into Mr. Gilliam's office. We only want to know who did. Seems to me all y'all would want to know too."

"She left Mike and her kids with nothin'!" Mike's mother said through her tears. "Absolutely nothin'!"

I stifled a gasp. I understood why Mike's parents saw it that way, but what did Mike think? Did he truly believe I'd stolen his children's inheritance, or had he figured out Violet knew what he was up to?

Joe gave her a sympathetic look and lowered his voice. "And while I know that must have hurt you all deeply, the simple fact is that your grandchildren haven't been seen in days, and now your son can't be located. We only want to make sure they're all okay."

Deanna frowned and turned back to Mike's parents. They formed a huddle and whispered for nearly a minute. When Deanna finally stepped away from the Beauregards and approached Joe, she had a key in her hand.

"By allowing you into their son's home, they are not confirming that their son has done anything wrong."

"Funny," Joe said as he took the key, "I never once insinuated that I thought Mike Beauregard had done anything wrong. For all we know, the family's unconscious in the home. What makes your clients jump to that conclusion?"

No one said anything for several uncomfortable moments before Joe spun around and handed the key to Randy. "Deputies, after you."

Just as they started walking up to the front door, sirens wailed in the distance. Joe looked up in surprise, although his expression quickly turned to a scowl when he saw the two Henryetta Police Department cars approaching us. The car in front was flying down the street, much too fast to be safe in a neighborhood, while the second car followed at a much safer speed.

The first car skidded to stop, but the officer must have underestimated how much distance he needed to stop, because it plowed into the rooster mailbox of the house across the street, sending mail and painted aluminum feathers everywhere.

Joe had run over and pushed Neely Kate and me against the side of my truck, shielding us with his body, which was a good thing since a flying yellow feather whizzed through the air where we'd been standing and lodged into a tree trunk.

Seconds later, we heard creaking metal, and Joe stepped away to walk around the front of my truck into the street.

Mike's parents and their attorney had resumed their huddle on Mike's driveway and now stared at the scene in shock.

The patrol car's driver's side was smashed in, and Officer Ernie was pushing on his door with all his might, trying to get it open.

The second patrol car came safely to a halt on the other side of the street, and Officer Sprout got out, his mouth dropping open as he took in the state of Officer Ernie's patrol car.

Officer Sprout traipsed over, making a horrified face. "The chief ain't gonna like this, Ernie."

"Well, there ain't nothin' I can do about that now, is there?" Ernie shouted, jerking on the door. "Help get me out of here!"

I sidled over to Joe, staring in disbelief. The metal rooster's face had gone through the windshield, its body jutting out in the air, but a sudden breeze sent it bobbing like one of those pecking rooster toys.

Officer Sprout braced himself and tried pulling on the door handle. "It's stuck."

"I know it's stuck!" Officer Ernie shouted. "That's why I asked you to help me get out!"

The homeowner of the rooster's house, an older woman in a housedress and curlers in her hair, burst out the front door, panic on her face as she threw her hands in the air. "You can't pin it on me!"

"What's she talking about?" Neely Kate asked, standing on the other side of Joe.

"I have absolutely no idea," he said, "and at the moment, I've got my hands full enough that I'm not sure I *want* to know."

"Pull harder!" Ernie shouted.

"I am!" Officer Sprout protested, tugging with all his might. He put a foot on the door for more leverage and pulled again.

"Um…" Neely Kate said, trying not to laugh. "Should someone tell him that he's actually keeping the door closed with his foot?"

"Or that Ernie only has to scoot over to the passenger side and open that undamaged door?" I said.

"Don't either of you dare," Joe said, shaking his head. "Hopefully, that'll keep them busy while we go through the house."

Officer Sprout released a loud grunt and then fell several feet back, landing in a large puddle I was pretty sure was the homeowner's attempt at a water garden.

As Officer Ernie released a loud string of curses, Joe spun around. "That's my cue to get started."

"Don't you go in that house, Chief Deputy Simmons!" Ernie shouted, turning to face us.

Joe turned back and cupped his hand to his ear. "What did you say? Good luck with the search? Thanks!"

He headed toward the house while Ernie started kicking his door with both feet. "Call the fire department!" he shouted at Officer Sprout. "We need the Jaws of Life!"

A confused expression settled on Officer Sprout's face. "I thought that was just for dyin' people trapped in cars."

"And if I don't get out of here, *I'll die*, Sprout!"

Officer Sprout's eyes narrowed as he tried to see Ernie's reasoning, but then his face lit up and he nodded. "Yeah. I guess that's true."

He wandered over to his car, presumably to make the call.

I turned from the circus in front of me to watch Randy and the other deputy walk up to the front door with Joe behind them. Wearing a pair of gloves, Randy unlocked the door and pushed it open.

"Fenton County Sheriff's Department," he called out. "We're here for a welfare check." He waited for several long moments, then the two deputies and Joe walked into the dark house.

Neely Kate and I stayed on one side of the driveway, while Mike's parents and Deanna waited on the other. I expected his mother to give me dirty looks, but some of her persistence seemed to have faded and now she looked genuinely worried.

Deanna's phone rang and she stepped away to take the call.

Officer Sprout emerged from his car and returned to his task of trying to open Ernie's door.

"Gee," Neely Kate said in a mock congenial tone. "I wonder who called the police department?"

"Mike's house is in Henryetta city limits," his mother said, lifting her chin. "We needed someone to take charge."

"And how's that workin' out for ya?" Neely Kate said, her brows lifted.

I tapped her arm and frowned. "I'd like to think we all want the same thing—to find Ashley and Mikey, safe and unharmed."

"And Mike!" Mrs. Beauregard snapped. "He's missing too."

"And Mike," I said, because I was hoping the kids were with him, and because he *had* been my friend for years before turning on me. While his betrayal hurt, I couldn't help remembering the way things used to be.

More sirens sounded down the street, and a Henryetta fire truck came speeding toward us. It slid to a halt in the middle of the street, and a couple of firefighters hopped out and made their way over to Ernie's patrol car, where Officer Sprout was still struggling to get him out.

"You called us for this?" one of the firemen said in disgust, his hands propped on his hips. "All you need to do is file a report and call a tow truck."

"But he's stuck in there!" Officer Sprout protested, pulling on the door handle to prove his point.

"I'm about to starve to death!" Ernie said, sounding panicked. "And I'm running out of air!"

The other firefighter, a woman with a long blonde French braid and a no-nonsense swagger, walked to the passenger door and lifted the handle, popping the door open. "How about you get out over here?"

Officer Sprout's mouth dropped open and his eyes lit up with puppy love. "You're amazin'."

I could see why he was entranced. She was pretty *and* competent.

She gave him an *are you serious?* look. "Nothin' common sense couldn't fix."

Her comment passed right over his head and took off for the heavens. "You saved his life."

"And you just cost me a half hour in paperwork," she grumbled as she headed back to the fire truck.

Ernie scrambled over his console and out the door, falling to his knees and holding his hands up to the sky. "Thank you, Lord, for savin' me! I swear I'll be a better person now!"

Ernie and the fire department were a great distraction, but Joe and the other deputies had been in the house for several minutes, and my anxiety had nearly reached the breaking point. Joe stepped out of the house then, talking on his phone. He looked up at me, and I could tell something was wrong.

Obviously Neely Kate could too, because she put an arm around me.

Officer Ernie caught sight of Joe and made a beeline for him. "Get out of my house!"

Joe's brow shot up to his hairline, and he didn't look like he was in any mood to get into a territorial war with Henryetta's finest. "Your house? Did you pay the property taxes on this place, Officer?"

Officer Ernie stopped short. "Well, no…"

"You're lookin' a little pale," Neely Kate said, taking a step forward. "Are you sure you're okay after your near-death experience, Officer Ernie?"

The officer's anger faded. "You're right. I haven't had anything to eat in nearly forty-five minutes. I bet my blood sugar has plummeted."

"I have a protein bar in my purse," Neely Kate said, wrapping an arm around his shoulders and steering him toward my truck. She shuddered a little as she touched him, but she steeled her back.

"I don't like protein bars," he whined, leaning into her, which caused her to shudder again.

Neely Kate was really taking one for the team.

"I have some grapes too. Or a turkey sandwich." She cast Joe a dark look and mouthed, *you owe me big time* as they headed for the truck.

Joe gave her a grim nod.

"What did you find?" Mike's mother called out.

Joe hung up the phone and strode toward her, casting a glance at Deanna, who was standing next to the car, engaged in a heated phone call.

"Mrs. Beauregard," Joe said, "I need to know if Mike has been on edge this week…acting out of the ordinary…"

"He's been on edge," she said, clenching her shaking hands in front of her. "I know he's got a lot of spec houses right now and he's overextended himself. We offered to give him money, but he said he had a house closing soon."

I was relieved to see she was being more cooperative.

"Do you know if he's borrowed money from anyone?" Joe asked.

She shook her head and glanced at Deanna, who had her back to us. "He has multiple loans. I think he may have taken out a second mortgage on the house, but there wasn't much equity, so it mustn't have brought much in." She lifted her fingertips to her lips. "What did you find?"

"I'm not at liberty to say, but your grandchildren are now officially listed as missing persons."

I gasped, and Joe shot me a worried looked.

Panic had me in its grip, but I knew he'd have a hard time focusing on doing his job if he was worried about me, so I gave him a reassuring smile. *I'm okay.*

He still looked concerned, but he returned his attention to Mike's mother, who had started to cry.

"I knew we should have come over last night," Mike's father said. "I knew something was up when he wouldn't let us talk to the kids."

Mike's mother's wail had caught Deanna's attention, and she quickly ended her call and hurried over. "Please do not talk to my clients unless I'm present." She glanced from Joe to Mike's mother and back. "What did you find in there?"

"Nothing I can tell you about right now, but we have reason to believe the children are missing."

"What about Mike?" his father asked.

"We're not sure," Joe said, "which makes it imperative that you tell me if he contacts you."

Mike's father nodded.

Joe shifted his attention to me, leading me several feet away and out of earshot. "I'm gonna need you two to leave."

"What did you find, Joe?" I asked in a whisper.

His gaze held mine. "I need you to trust me, Rose. Can you do that?"

"You don't think they're dead, do you?" I asked, my knees weak.

"No, darlin', I swear to you I don't. There's no blood or anything to lead me to believe they're hurt. But I found a note that leads me to believe they've been taken, and that's all I can tell you, okay? I shouldn't have even told you that much."

I opened my mouth to protest, but a sense of tranquility washed through me. I was terrified for Ashley and Mikey, but if I could pick anyone to look for them, it was Joe. "Yeah."

His eyes widened in surprise. "Really?"

I wound my arms around his neck and his arms wrapped around my back, holding me as close as my stomach would allow.

"I'll find 'em, Rose," he said, his voice thick with emotion. "I swear it."

"I know," I said, clinging to him. "If anyone can, it's you." I pulled back and kissed him on the cheek. "I'm gonna head to the office."

He kept an arm around me and placed a hand on my belly. "How are you doin' with all of this? How's the baby?"

"We're both fine. Now go look for our niece and nephew," I said, my voice breaking. "And be careful, Joe." Because something big was going on in this town, and I had a feeling Joe was about to walk into the middle of it.

Chapter Seven

W e're not really headin' back to the office now, are we?" Neely Kate asked, incredulous. She stood next to the truck, still in front of Mike's house.

Officer Ernie had eaten her grapes, the turkey sandwich, a tin of breath mints, and a can of kidney beans she'd had in her purse for some ungodly reason. He'd convinced the firefighter to open it for him. Then, after all of his bluster about going in the house, he'd gotten into Officer Sprout's patrol car, saying he needed a rest after his near-death experience, and the two of them had driven away.

I'd told Neely Kate that Joe had asked us to leave so he could investigate without worrying about us, and while she *had* agreed to leave, we still hadn't reached an agreement on where to go next.

"Okay, if not the office," I said, "then the nursery."

"Rose!"

I put my hand on my stomach. "Come on, Neely Kate. I can't be chasin' bad guys right now." When she didn't look appeased, I leaned closer and lowered my voice. "You know we can't go in there, and Joe's not allowed to tell us anything."

That and I had a couple of other sources I planned to contact, but the first person had asked me not to tell anyone that he'd contacted me months ago, and the second…

I still wasn't convinced I should contact him. If Neely Kate knew that I was considering it, she'd lock me up in the landscaping office.

No, it would be better not to tell her just yet. I'd rather ask for forgiveness after the fact.

"You can't be serious," she protested.

"Come on," I said, opening the passenger door to the truck. "Let's go."

Grumbling, she walked around the truck and got inside. "I can't believe you're letting this go," she said once she was settled behind the wheel.

"I'm not lettin' it go," I said. "I'm lettin' Joe take care of it."

"Since when did we walk away from a mystery? And why would we walk away from one involving Ashley and Mikey?"

"Because I have to think about my baby, Neely Kate," I said, feeling the press of guilt. Was I making a mistake by keeping this from her?

Maybe so, but I'd do anything to help my niece and nephew.

"Yeah," she said with a groan. "You're right. I'm sorry. I guess I miss investigatin' cases."

"I do too," I admitted. "Maybe when our babies are older." I needed to think about something other than Ashley and Mikey and where they might be now. I sure couldn't think about them being dead. "I know you found a wedding dress on the internet, but you should try some on in person. We could go shopping."

Her mouth dropped open. "You want to go shoppin' for weddin' dresses *now*?"

Tears flooded my eyes, and the dam broke loose on my tears. "No."

"Oh, honey."

I tried to stifle my sobs. "Where are they, Neely Kate? Who could have taken them?"

"I don't know, but instead of going back to town, how about we go see Jed?"

That was a good idea. Jed used to be James's righthand man, which meant he had a lot of contacts in the criminal world, and most of the people he knew actually respected him. Besides, he was good in a crisis. Lord only knew he'd gotten me out of plenty of scrapes. I had trusted the man with my life more times than I could count. I took a deep breath, trying to calm down. "Okay."

She nodded. "Okay."

I started talking about nonsense, anything to keep my mind from wandering to all the worst-case scenarios running through my head.

When Neely Kate pulled into the parking lot of Jed's garage, all three bay doors were open and filled with cars. Jed walked out of one of the doors as we crossed the parking lot toward him.

"What are you two doing here?" he asked, wiping his hands on a shop rag.

I took a ragged breath, dangerously close to crying. But something on my face must have made him realize something bad had happened. Panic filled his eyes and he snuck a quick glance to Neely Kate.

"Ashley and Mikey are missin'," she said, her voice breaking.

Jed rushed over and wrapped an arm around my back and led me inside.

I pushed his arm away. "I'm fine."

If I let him or anyone else baby me, I'd fall apart. And I couldn't afford to fall apart. My niece and nephew needed me to be strong.

"Let's go inside," Jed said. He and Neely Kate flanked me as though prepared to catch me if I fell to pieces.

"What's goin' on?" Witt asked as we walked through the garage. Then he added in disbelief, "How big are you gonna *get*, Rose?"

I shot him a glare that should have killed him in his tracks.

"Okay," he said. "Point taken. But what's goin' on?"

"Let's go to the lounge," Jed said, opening the door in the back that led to the offices.

Once we were in the employee lounge, Neely Kate said, "Ashley and Mikey are missing."

"When you say missin'…" Witt said, moving his hand in a *go on* gesture.

I started pacing while they watched me. "They haven't been in school or daycare most of the week. No one's seen them since last Friday. When Joe and I went to pick them up last night, Mike refused to let us see them, telling us they had the flu, but he never called them in sick or took them to the doctor. And now he's missin', and his parents say he owed a lot of money to the bank, and an electrician was killed a few houses down from one of Mike's…"

My voice broke and Neely Kate reached out to me, but I pushed her hand away.

"Rose," Jed said in an irritatingly reasonable tone. "Maybe you should sit down."

"Maybe *you* should sit down," I snapped, then shook my head and ran my hand over my hair. "I'm sorry. That was uncalled for."

"It's okay," he said.

"Joe found evidence that they were taken, but he didn't say a word about Mike," I said, still pacing, knowing I couldn't tell them about the note and hoping I hadn't already told them too much. I wanted Joe to trust me—no, I *needed* Joe to trust me, and I hoped I hadn't just broken his confidence. "Someone kidnapped them. But who? We know that James had some kind of control over Mike. Was it him? Did James take my niece and nephew?" My voice rose and I knew I sounded hysterical, but I'd kept my fears bottled up on the drive, and now that I was giving voice to them I couldn't figure out how to stop.

"Rose, honey," Neely Kate said. "Let's just take a moment to catch our breath."

"I still think you should sit down," Witt said. "You look as pale as a sheet hangin' on Granny's clothesline."

A Braxton Hicks contraction grabbed hold of me, and I stopped pacing and rested my hand on my belly as I waited for it to subside.

"What's goin' on, Rose?" Neely Kate asked in a panicked voice.

"False labor," I said, trying not to tense and make it worse.

"Maybe we should get you to the hospital," Witt said.

"I'm not goin' to the hospital!" I protested, my voice rising. "I'm not goin' just to have them send me home again. Heaven only knows how much I owe them, and I haven't even had the baby yet. And besides, Joe's busy lookin' for Ashley and Mikey, *so I can't be havin' this baby right now!*"

Witt stared at me with unadulterated fear.

"Okay," Neely Kate said slowly. "You're not havin' the baby now."

"I have two more weeks," I said, "and anything before then is just stupid Braxton Hicks, so don't anybody be suggestin' I go to any hospitals."

I knew I was raving like a crazy woman, but I was thirty-eight weeks pregnant, I'd spent the last four weeks dealing with Braxton Hicks, and my niece and nephew were missing. I was due a little crazy.

The contraction began to ease. "What are we gonna do to find them?" I demanded, staring Jed in the eye.

A lesser man would have cringed or at least paused, but Jed didn't hesitate when he said, "First I need to catch up. Maybe you can explain it all a little slower this time."

So I did. I started with seeing Mike at Walmart with Ashley and Mikey and arranging to see the kids. This time I told them about the weird vibe I'd gotten at Mike's house last night—how he'd looked like crap and the house had been closed up. Neely Kate finished by telling them about our visit to the daycare and everything that had happened this morning.

"So Mike's mother said he's in a lot of debt?" Jed asked.

"Yeah," I said. "She said he's got several loans and maybe took out a second mortgage on his house. His parents offered him money, but he told them that he was about to close on a house."

"Where does the murdered subcontractor fit in?" Witt asked.

"We don't know that his murder is for sure tied to Mike," I said, "but it seems like a huge coincidence."

"Maybe," Jed said, deep in thought. "I need to see his books."

"Don't you think Joe's gonna take those?" I asked.

"Yeah," Jed said. "But depending on what they found at the house, they may concentrate on that evidence first. Does he have an office for his construction business, or does he work out of the house?"

"Both, I think. He worked at home a lot when he had the kids full time, but he used to go to his office when Violet lived with him while she was sick."

"Can you get into his office?"

I gasped. "You want us to get Mike's books?"

"I don't want to take them," Jed said. "Just get a copy. I know it's a lot to ask, but it might tell us something."

"Do you think we should just let Joe handle it?" I asked.

He paused. "I have no doubt that Joe will do everything with the power available to him, but he has limitations." His eyes narrowed. "I don't."

"What do you think happened to them?" I asked.

"I don't know," he said, "but we've known for months that Mike likely has criminal ties. It's time to find out what those might be. Maybe someone kidnapped the kids for blackmail."

The thought made me sick to my stomach, but at least it was better than the alternative. Still, I needed to stop dwelling on what had happened and start doing something about it. Which meant I needed to get those records for Jed. But how? I'd meant what I'd said to Neely Kate—I wasn't about to start stepping over crime scene tape or breaking into buildings.

Then it came to me. "Mike's mother might help us."

Neely Kate's brow shot up. "Joe had to threaten her to get her to come over and unlock the house. What makes you think she'll help get into his office?"

"Because once she realized the kids really were in danger, she started sharing *everything*. If she thinks we have a way to get to them faster, I think she'll help."

Jed nodded. "Then call her. Joe's gonna get the books sooner or later, and we need to beat him to it."

I felt like a traitor, but my loyalty to Violet's children trumped my loyalty to Joe. I only hoped he'd understand.

I pulled out my phone and called Mike's mother's cell phone. She answered right away.

"Rose," she said, sounding like she'd just finished a crying spell. "I owe you a huge apology. If I'd only listened to you and Joe last night, we might have stopped this."

"I don't think it would have mattered, Barb," I said, my voice breaking. "Based on the fact he wouldn't let us see them and acted so strangely about it, I suspect they were already gone."

She started to cry. "Why wouldn't he call the police? He would *never* hurt those children, Rose. He loves them. They're his everything."

"I know," I said. "I've never once doubted that he loves them." I took a breath. "But there's a reason I'm calling. I need to ask you to help me get access to something. I think it will help me find Ashley and Mikey faster than Joe can."

"You think you can find them?" The hopefulness in her voice made my heart skip a beat.

"I have a couple of friends who will be helpin' me, and they're known for gettin' results. But I need to see Mike's books for the construction company."

"His books?"

"They might be able to help us figure out who took the kids."

"You really think someone took them?" she whispered.

"Yeah."

Mike's mother was quiet for so long I was sure she was going to tell me no, but then she said, "They're on the computer at his office, but the staff won't let you in. Especially if they recognize you. He's told them you're not allowed to see the kids, and I know they won't let you have access to his computer."

While I knew he didn't want me seeing the kids, it still hurt to hear her say it. "Then what do you suggest we do?"

"I'll let you in through the back door."

Going in through the back sounded a better idea in general. The fewer people who knew we were in there the better.

"When do you want to meet me?" she asked.

"As soon as possible. We can be there in fifteen minutes." Even if Jed was right, and Joe started off by looking into a different angle, it wouldn't be long before they made it to Mike's books. We needed to get the information as soon as possible.

She hesitated. "We?"

"Me and Neely Kate. I can't do this without her." Neely Kate had bookkeeping experience. She'd be able to figure out what we needed more quickly than I could. Then, of course, there was the whole I-was-a-waddling-penguin thing…

"Okay…" She didn't sound happy about it, though, and before I could confirm she was still on board with the plan, she hung up.

I turned to Jed. "She's going to help me in through the back door."

"And she's good with Neely Kate coming too?"

"She didn't say no." I turned back to Neely Kate. "We need to leave if we're gonna meet her in time."

"Joe's not gonna like this," she said, holding my gaze. "Do you want to piss him off this close to havin' the baby?"

The look she gave me reminded me that I had yet to share another piece of information liable to upset him. The whole incident with James. But this was different—this was about doing everything within our power, legal and not so much, to help my niece and nephew. That, I had to believe, Joe would understand.

"I'd rather keep this from him," I said. "At least for now."

"If the files are on his computer, copy them to a flash drive," Jed said. "If they're in a ledger, get photocopies. But you need to hurry because Joe's not gonna hold off on his office for too long. You'll need a flash drive."

"I have one in my bag," Neely Kate said, patting her purse.

"Jeez, woman," Witt said. "Is there *anything* you don't have in there?"

She propped a hand on her hip. "Try me."

"An ice cube tray."

She pulled out a small silicone tray with bird indentations. "Stork ice cubes, left over from Rose's shower."

"Okay," Witt said, cocking his head. "How about cookies?"

Rolling her eyes, she said, "Amateur." She pulled out a zippered bag containing three chocolate chip cookies, then shrugged as she shot me a glance. "I couldn't let Ernie eat *all* my food."

"Can we play this game later?" I asked. "We're on a deadline."

"Take my car," Jed said, handing Neely Kate the keys. "It'll be less noticeable."

"If we're looking for stealth, then I'm not sure I'm cut out for this mission." I waved a hand over my belly. "I'm noticeable."

Jed frowned as he looked me up and down. "You have a point."

"We're sneakin' in through the back," Neely Kate said, heading for the door. "No one's gonna see you."

She was right. Mike's office was in a strip mall on the south side of town. We could likely go unseen if we parked behind the building, especially since we were bringing Jed's nondescript car.

We were silent on the drive over, and I was relieved there weren't any sheriff cars out front of the office when we pulled into the parking lot. Thankfully, Mike's mother's car was parked directly in front of the door. Neely Kate drove around the building, which wasn't in the least bit busy, and I texted Barb to let her know we were there. The back door opened about a minute later, and she stuck her head out and motioned for us to enter.

"I sent the receptionist to lunch," Barb said as she led us down a short hallway to Mike's office, "and the designer has an appointment at a job site. You have about a half hour before anyone else comes back."

I walked into the office, taking in the details of the generic space, the walls plastered with photos of houses Mike had built, a couple of civic award plaques, and photos of the kids and Violet.

"That should be plenty of time," Neely Kate said as she moved behind the cheap desk in the center of the room and pulled out the desk chair. "Do you know the login and password?"

Mike's mother frowned. "I do for the computer, but not for the bookkeeping program."

"Hopefully the fields will autofill," Neely Kate said, then looked up at Barb, waiting for the computer login information.

Her face turned pink. "It's *Violet Mae*, no space, and the password is their anniversary."

Neely Kate glanced at me with tears in her eyes.

I leaned over the desk and typed in the date, and the computer sprang to life.

The loss of my sister caught my breath, and I placed my hand on my chest to help ease the sharp pain in my heart. Needing a moment, I walked into the front room and tried to catch my breath and fight back tears. I knew I needed to get it together—for all I knew, the receptionist was a workaholic who'd take a five-minute lunch—but I needed to regain my focus. I had to think about finding Vi's kids, not crying for the millionth time over the loss of my sister.

"It hurt him, you know," Barb said quietly behind me, having apparently followed me out of the room.

"What hurt him?" I asked, staring out the windows at the parking lot. I couldn't bring myself to look at her.

"When Violet chose you over him. When he couldn't be there with her at the end."

I swallowed the lump in my throat. "Is that why he kept the kids from me? To punish me?"

"That. And other things."

I turned to look at her. "What other things?"

She pressed her lips together and shook her head.

"Does it have anything to do with why the kids are missing?"

"Mike's missing too," she said, almost in a whine. "Are you looking for him as well?"

"I'm sure Joe is."

"But you're not?" she countered.

I turned to face her. "He's not my priority, Barb. If I find him along the way, then so be it."

Bitterness filled her eyes. "I never should have let you in here. I never should have agreed to help you."

"You did it to potentially save your grandchildren, who were put in this situation through no fault of their own. Mike, on the other hand…"

"You're one to talk," she snapped. "You were cavorting with criminals."

For a moment, I thought she'd found out about my personal relationship with James Malcolm, but then I realized she was talking about our cooperation to bring down J.R. Simmons, Joe and Neely Kate's father. "I was working with law enforcement," I said. "I wore a wire to get him arrested. I was held at gunpoint."

She remained silent.

"You know what's funny?" I asked in a humorless tone. "Mike kept me away from the kids supposedly because he worried my association with the criminal element put them in danger, but I suspect it was his own involvement that put them in harm's way." Then I spun around and started to head back to the office.

"Are you really not going to get married before you have that baby?" she asked in disgust. "Are you gonna make that poor baby a bastard?"

I stopped in my tracks and turned back to face her. "Do not mistake my concern for your grandchildren with tolerance for your hateful opinions." I walked into the office. "Neely Kate, are you almost done?"

She looked up at me with worry in her eyes. "Yeah. I'm almost finished copying the files onto a flash drive."

I nodded as I scanned the photos of Violet and the kids.

"You okay?"

"Just peachy."

She cast a glance past me into the front room and frowned. "What did she say?"

"Nothing important. Finish that up so we can get out of here."

"Almost done. Got the login and password too, so we can sign in from another computer, but I suspect it might be risky to log back in." She made a few more keystrokes, then beamed. "Done."

As she started to stand, Barb called out. "There's a sheriff car pulling up out front."

Relief filled Neely Kate's eyes. "Just in time."

We both poked our heads out of the office to look through the front window. Sure enough, a sheriff car was pulling into a parking space in front of the office.

"Get out of here," Mike's mother said, sounding agitated. "I'll keep them busy while you go out the back."

A deputy was getting out of his car, and Barb pushed open the front door and went out to greet him. She pointed down the street, and Neely Kate and I slipped out of the office and down the hall to the exit. Once we were outside, we pushed the back door closed, hoping he hadn't noticed the sunlight filling the office, there and then gone.

We hurried into the car—well, Neely Kate hurried, and I waddled.

"Can we get out of here without him seeing us come around the building?" I asked.

"Yeah." She turned on the engine and headed down the narrow lane to the end of the building. "Ideally we'd pull in behind the strip mall next door and keep going, but a delivery truck's blocking the lane, so we'll have to drive in front of the building. He probably won't see us or put it together."

Probably...but if he was still in front of the office, he could see us pull out. "Wait here for a minute. Mike's mother might be stalling him, thinking we need more time."

"Good idea."

She veered around the building and pulled to a halt, letting the engine idle.

"Did you see anything fishy in his books?" I asked.

"No, but I wasn't really lookin'. I was just tryin' to download it all as quickly as possible. If I'd dillydallied even a little, we might have gotten caught."

I nodded distractedly, and Neely Kate placed a hand on my arm. "We're gonna find 'em, Rose."

"Yeah. We've probably waited long enough for the deputy to go inside. Let's get that flash drive back to Jed."

The more I thought about what could be on it, the more anxious I became. It had to be helpful. Because I didn't trust my other plans to lead anywhere.

Chapter Eight

While Neely Kate called Jed to let him know we were on the way back, I got a text from Bruce Wayne.

There's an issue with the azalea bushes at Sonder Tech and the manager wants me to come check it out. I can't get away, is there any chance you can do it?

Bruce Wayne was working on a multiday install that had been set back a couple of days due to weather. Still, the fact that he'd asked meant he likely didn't know the kids were missing. I considered telling him no, but I knew it would take some digging to find anything of significance in the books, and I would be worthless in that endeavor. Besides, I still needed to contact my two sources, and I suspected the one I planned to talk to first would require some advance notice.

I glanced at Neely Kate. "Bruce Wayne needs me to check on an old install, so once we get back to the garage, I'm gonna take the truck over there."

She stared at me as though I'd announced I was going to invite my old neighbor, Miss Mildred, to move in with me. "You're kiddin' me."

"No," I said defensively. "It's not like I can do anything while you're searchin' the books, and I'll just drive everyone crazy, pacing and looking over your shoulder. The best thing I can do for everyone concerned is to get out of your hair."

She narrowed her eyes. "You're up to something."

In a way, I was, but not at the moment. "I'm going to check some azalea bushes, Neely Kate. It's nothing to get a bee in your bonnet about."

She paled a little at my statement, but then she nodded. "Yeah, you're right. Better to keep busy."

"You'll call me as soon as you find something, right?"

"Of course," she said.

I pulled into the parking lot, and she put the car in park.

"You're sure you're gonna be okay on your own?" she asked.

"Perfectly fine," I said, already getting out of the passenger side. "I need to do something or I'll lose my mind."

"Call me if you need me."

She'd gotten out too, and I gave her a warm smile over the hood of the car. "I will. And the same goes for you."

"Jed's probably not gonna approve of this plan, you know," she said.

I grinned. "Which is one of multiple reasons I'm not going in there first."

She laughed. "Coward."

"I prefer to think of myself as cunning."

She gave me a boost into the driver's side of the truck before heading into the garage, and sure enough, Jed was coming out of the garage as I was about to pull out of the parking lot. He gave me a strange look, so I waved and then turned the corner to head back into town.

I hadn't been to Sonder Tech since I'd gone through the punch list to ensure everything had gone according to plan after the install last November. They had come to Henryetta from Dallas, and I'd been suspicious of them, especially since they'd specifically requested RBW Landscaping. Of course, I'd been suspicious of everything associated with Dallas last summer and fall, with plenty of reason. I'd wondered if their sudden appearance in a town no one with half a brain would willingly move to was another of the Hardshaw Group's attempts to infiltrate the county. But Sonder Tech seemed to be on the up and up, and Jed had found nothing to explicitly link them to organized crime, let alone to Hardshaw. When I'd made my pitch to them last October, one of the managers, Stewart, had told me they were bringing most of their employees with them but planned to hire three or four Fenton County residents. They must have done better than expected, though, because they'd hired about fifteen local employees since last November. From what Jed had discovered, most employees seemed to love working for them.

I pulled into the parking lot, choosing an empty space in the back even though there was an empty visitor spot by the door. There were large windows overlooking the parking lot, and I had no desire to put on a show as I got out.

Grabbing my phone and a notepad, I started to take notes and photos. Some of the flowers we'd planted a few weeks ago—an addition to the landscaping plan—weren't looking as healthy as I'd like, so I made a note to check the soil as well as the sprinkler system. By the time I reached the building, I could see that the azaleas were dying—no, they were basically *dead*—which made no sense. Bruce Wayne's crew had come out to plant the flowers. They definitely would have noticed if there was a problem. Which meant this had happened recently. I could only think of one reason a hardy plant would fail so quickly.

"Rose…wow!"

I turned to see Stewart.

"Hi," I said, resting my hand on my belly. "Good to see you."

"I see there have been some changes since I last saw you."

I laughed. "A few." I pointed to the bushes. "When did you first notice there was a problem?"

"It happened really fast. They were blooming last Friday, but they looked a little anemic come Monday morning. Now, as you can see, most of the leaves and flowers have fallen off."

He was right. The blooms had completely shed, and the few leaves that clung to the bushes were yellow and brown.

"Do you know what happened to them?" he asked.

"It looks like they've been poisoned."

"Poisoned? Why would someone poison our bushes?" he asked.

"It could be environmental." I glanced around. The bushes were in a raised bed and had good drainage. "But I don't think so. I think someone must have put something on them."

"Someone purposely poisoned our bushes?" he asked in disbelief.

"I don't know. I'm merely guessing. Have you upset anyone? Any unhappy customers?"

"Most of our customers are out of state, but aside from that, no."

"Any disgruntled employees?"

"No," he said, at a loss. "We've never even fired anyone. Everyone seems happy."

I frowned. "I could be wrong, but I'd like to test the soil before we replace the dead plants. We need to make sure it's healthy for them. We'll have to send the sample to Little Rock, though, so it will take a few days to get the results."

"Okay," he said, with a frown. "Now I'm worried that we've got someone pissed at us."

I gave him a sympathetic smile. "A number of things could have happened, and most of the possibilities aren't malicious." I took a deep breath. "Sorry, I really shouldn't have mentioned that your business might have an enemy. I'm a little distracted today, and my mind just seems to automatically wander to criminal activity."

"That murder south of town seems to have everyone upset," he said. "But you've definitely given me something to think about."

I cocked my head. "Your employees are upset about the murder?"

"No one's thrilled about it, obviously," he said. "Especially since there hadn't been a local murder since last year, but Calista seems especially shaken up."

"Calista?"

"One of our account specialists." He grimaced. "That's what we call our salespeople. It sounds fancier."

"Did she know him?"

"Not that I knew of, but I'll be honest…I didn't ask."

I nodded, my mind already whirling from what he'd told me. "Thanks, Stewart. I'm going to grab some soil sample kits from my truck so I can make the collection."

His gaze lowered to my stomach. "No offense, Rose, but can you get down and back up by yourself?"

I hated to admit it, but he had a point. Still, I wasn't going to saddle Bruce Wayne with this. It made me wish that I'd brought Neely Kate, but then I remembered she was doing something much more important, which brought back the reality that Ashley and Mikey were missing.

"Uh…" I said, giving myself a moment to recover from the wave of fear. "I hate to ask this, Stewart… I can get down to get the sample, but I'm going to need help getting back up."

"I really hate to ask you to do it at all," he said, looking worried.

"No, really," I said. "I get down all the time to take care of my dog, but I usually have a piece of furniture to grab."

"I don't mind helping," he said, "but it feels wrong to have you do it at all."

After I assured him again that I didn't mind collecting the samples, I got the kits out from under the passenger seat, grabbed my bottle of hand sanitizer, and headed back to the dead azaleas. It didn't take me long to gather soil from the bases of two of the bushes, and when I was finished, Stewart offered me a hand to help me up. An offer he likely regretted given I nearly pulled him over on top of me and covered his hand in dirt.

"I'm so sorry." Then I cringed. "I hate to ask any more from you, but can I use your restroom?"

He released me and looked at his dirty palm. "Of course. You'll want to wash your hands."

It was more that I had to pee, but I'd use that excuse. Stewart opened one of the double glass front doors, and I headed toward the restrooms.

I went into a stall, tucking the sample bags under my arm as I sat on the toilet. As I was finishing up, the door opened and I heard a woman's hushed voice urgently say, "I told you not to call me at work."

I sat still even though my legs had already started going to sleep from sitting on the toilet for less than a minute.

"I don't care!" she said insistently. "The same thing's gonna happen to us if you don't keep your mouth shut." She released a little whimper. "Mark."

My breath caught. Was this Calista?

After several seconds of silence, she said, "I'll meet you after work, but don't call me again. Text."

I heard retreating footsteps. Then the door opened and closed.

Calista knew something about Mark Erickson's murder.

And I was going to find out what.

Chapter
Nine

I hurried out of the stall and washed my hands, frustrated that Calista had a head start on me. It would have been helpful to know what she looked like.

When I left the bathroom, I took my time walking to the front exit, scanning the desks in the main part of the office. There were six of them, four men and two women. One of the women was older and deep in conversation with the man at the desk next to her. I ruled her out as soon as I heard their conversation. The other woman was younger and kept her gaze on her computer screen.

I headed toward her desk, deciding I'd ask her if she could loan me a pen to add something to the sample tubes. Although it wasn't the best excuse, she'd almost certainly say something in return—I'd hear her voice, which would tell me if she was the woman I'd overheard.

"Excuse me," I said as I approached, but she jumped as though I'd snuck up on her. "I'm sorry. I didn't mean to scare you."

She placed her hand on her chest and gave me a confused look. "Are you here to see Stewart?"

My hunch was right. This had to be Calista.

"I already talked to him," I said, "but I was wondering if you have a pen I can borrow so I can add something to my soil sample tubes."

Her gaze dropped to the bags under my arm. "Soil sample?"

"I'm trying to figure out why the bushes are dyin'."

She gave me a look that suggested she thought I was annoying, then handed me a pen.

I took it and pulled out one of the tubes, trying to figure what I could possibly write that wouldn't mess up the test given I'd already filled out the label, but it soon became obvious it wouldn't matter—she'd already turned back to her computer. I pretended to write something on it, wondering if I should try to question her. She was absorbed in whatever was on her screen, so I decided not to risk it, instead placing the pen on her desk. "Thanks."

She gave me a quick wave that suggested she wouldn't give me another thought.

But my niece's and nephew's lives were at stake, so I wasn't willing to accept this as a wash. On a whim, I reached out and put my hand on her shoulder, forcing a vision as I focused on the question: *What does Calista know about Mark Erickson?*

The office space faded to a dark room, and I could barely see. But I could feel, and what I felt caught me by surprise, to put it mildly. I was naked, sitting on top of a man, only I wasn't just sitting on top of him. I was…

"You have to be more careful than Mark," I moaned in Calista's voice, every nerve in my body taut with expectation as I lifted myself up and then lowered down slowly, throwing my head back as a small wave of pleasure coursed through me.

"I ain't as stupid as him," the man grunted, his hands digging into my hips and pulling me down even more.

I moaned louder. He was close to pushing me over the edge.

"The cops are sniffing around. They're gettin' too close," I said, but it took effort to focus on the words.

He thrust deeper, sending me into an earth-shattering orgasm.

The office came back into view, and instead of blurting out what I'd seen, I cried out as the last wave of her orgasm shivered through me.

The entire office was staring at me in shock, although a couple of the men wore dazed expressions. The room was so silent I could hear a car driving down the street in front of the building. And I suspected it was one of those quiet, fuel-efficient models.

Oh, sweet baby Jesus. What had I done?

Calista looked up at me in horror and shoved my hand away as if I were diseased. With wide eyes, she forced through gritted teeth, "If you don't get out of here right now, I'm going to call the police."

I took a step back, wondering if I should try to explain myself or turn around and bolt out of the room.

But it didn't take me long to figure out the obvious—there was no explaining this—and the running away plan won out.

When I got to the truck, it took me three attempts to start the engine. I pulled out of the parking lot and drove away with no destination in mind. I just knew I had to get the heck off the property.

As soon as I was certain I was out of sight, I pulled over into the parking lot of an abandoned Sonic restaurant and called Neely Kate.

"Hey, Rose," she said when she answered. "We haven't found anything yet."

"That's not why I'm calling." I rested my face in my free hand. "I need to know if it's possible to die of embarrassment, because if so, I need you to promise to raise my baby."

"What are you talkin' about?" she asked, her voice sounding high-pitched. "What happened?"

"I forced a vision!" I shouted. "That's what happened!"

"Slow down," she said in a calm voice. "You forced a vision and something embarrassing happened?"

"I saw her havin' sex, Neely Kate! I was havin' sex!"

"Was it good?" she asked, "because last time I checked, you haven't had any in months."

She had a point, but now didn't seem like a good time to admit it. "She was havin' an orgasm, Neely Kate! Instead of blurtin' out what I saw, I…I…"

"Are you sayin' you had a *When Harry Met Sally* restaurant scene sort of vision? Oh, my stars and garters. Where were you?"

I cringed. "At Sonder Tech. In their sales room."

"Why were you forcin' a vision? I thought you were just checkin' on some plants."

"Because the manager told me one of the employees, a woman named Calista, was taking Mark's death hard. Then when I went in to use the bathroom, I overheard a woman's phone call. Right away, I knew it had to be this Calista because she mentioned the name Mark and then told the person on the other line they shouldn't have called. She said they'd discuss everything in person after work. I decided to force a vision to see if she knew anything about Mark Erickson."

"And all you got was her havin' sex?"

"She was talkin' to whoever she was havin' sex with. She told him he had to be more careful than Mark. That the cops were sniffin' around. He said he wasn't as stupid as him."

"And you didn't blurt any of that out?"

"Nope. Just the moan. And then Calista threatened to call the police."

She made a strangled sound.

"Are you *laughin'*?"

"Of course not, honey," she choked out, clearly trying to hide her giggles.

"This isn't funny, Neely Kate! It was unprofessional! I'll never be able to show my face there again."

She burst out into laughter. "I know. I'm sorry. But I doubt she'll call the police. Sounds like she wants to avoid them."

Thank goodness she was probably right.

"We need to have someone follow her after she gets off work," I said. "I'd do it, but I suspect she'd run me off the road, then beat me with a baseball bat for being a pervert. I was holding on to her shoulder when I…moaned."

Neely Kate burst out laughing again. "Jed'll take care of it. What's she look like?"

"Strawberry blonde, freckles on her cheeks. I don't know what kind of car she drives. I don't even know her last name."

"I'll tell Jed. We both know he can work with what you've got. I'll let you know when we find something."

"*If* you find something," I said.

"We will," she said assertively. "We will."

I hung up and took a deep breath. I hoped she was right. If not, I'd mortified myself for nothing.

Still parked in the restaurant lot, I finished filling out the paperwork, then sealed everything up in a mailer. It needed to go to the post office, but I picked up my phone again. It was time to move on to my first source.

Taking a deep breath, I scrolled through my contacts and sent Mason a text. I'd met with him back in November to tell him about the break-in at Violet's attorney's office and ask if he knew anything about Mike's presumed criminal activities. He hadn't heard anything, but he'd cautioned me to proceed carefully. The kids had lost their mother—did I really want to take their father from them too? I'd agreed with him at the time, but now I wondered if I should have pushed it. Could I have prevented this from happening?

Guilt ate at my stomach as I texted him.

There's been a new development. Any chance you can meet with me today?

I stared at the phone for several seconds, hoping he'd respond right away, but the three telltale dots failed to appear, so I started the truck and proceeded to the post office. After I dropped the envelope in the mail, I headed out to Bruce Wayne's job site. He and his crew were working on a gazebo in the client's backyard, and it was over halfway finished.

He saw my truck pull up to the house and headed over to greet me.

"I checked out the azaleas," I said, meeting him a few feet from the curb. "I think they've been poisoned."

"Poisoned?"

I pulled out my phone and showed him the photos. "Stewart said they were perfectly fine last Friday, then they were dying by the time everyone returned to work on Monday. And now they're pretty much dead."

He frowned as he scrolled through the photos. "Does he know what happened to them?"

"No, and when I asked him if they'd dealt with any disgruntled employees or customers lately, he assured me they hadn't."

"Something happened to these bushes," he said, still scowling. "They almost look burnt."

"You think someone poured some type of acid or bleach onto the soil?"

"Maybe…?"

"I took a couple of soil samples and sent them off to Little Rock. We'll need to replace the plants, but no sense doin' that till we know something about the state of the soil."

"Good thinkin'," he said, "but if I'd thought you'd need to take samples, I never would have asked you to go."

"It's my job, Bruce Wayne."

"Still…" he said, giving me a worried look.

I knew I was about to make him a whole lot more worried, but there was no avoiding it. I swallowed the lump in my throat and said, "Ashley and Mikey are missing."

His head jutted back. "*What?* Why didn't you lead with that?"

"I don't know," I said, my eyes burning. "I don't like thinkin' about it, I guess."

"Rose…"

I told him everything I knew, from Mike's ruse about the flu to Joe's search of the house, leaving out only what Neely Kate and I had done.

"Is Joe issuin' an Amber Alert?" he asked.

I stared at him in surprise. "I hadn't thought about that."

"I haven't seen an alert come through my phone, but from my understanding, the case has to meet certain criteria. Maybe it's too soon."

"Maybe…" Or maybe Joe was trying to keep it quiet for some reason. I'd call him after I left. "As far as I know, Joe doesn't have any leads."

Bruce Wayne started to say something, then stopped and pulled me into a hug. I couldn't get over the fact that this was the same man I'd met in a private courthouse room toward the end of his murder trial. He'd been nervous, jumpy, and scared of his own shadow, and no wonder—anyone would likely feel that way if they were being tried for a murder they hadn't committed. Months later, I'd offered him a job, little knowing he'd become not just my business partner, but the man I could count on to run our business when I was running around solving mysteries, taking care of my dying sister, and soon to have a baby. My boyfriends had come and gone, but Bruce Wayne had been my rock, the one man in my life whom I could count on without fail for the past year and a half. And now he was offering his support again, and that was what broke the wall I'd erected around my fears. It came tumbling down, and I found myself sobbing into his chest.

His arms tightened around me and he stood stock-still as I cried my heart out into his shirt. When I finally finished, he loosened his hold on me and I stepped back, wiping my face with the back of my hand.

"Thank you," he said, his voice rough.

I glanced up at him in surprise. "What are you thanking *me* for? I've gone and ruined your shirt."

"Ever since we first met, you've done nothing but give and give to me." His Adam's apple bobbed as he swallowed. "And I've never been able to give much back to you."

"What are you talkin' about?" I asked. "You end up carryin' most of the load half the time when I'm off dealin' with some kind of drama. Shoot, I'm about to take a few weeks off to have the baby."

"You're takin' off longer than a few weeks," he said firmly. "You need to stay home and heal and bond with that baby."

"I'm havin' this baby at the worst possible time," I protested. "This is our landscaping business's busiest time of the year."

"Rose," he said emphatically. "We need to focus on what's really important. Your baby. Neely Kate and I can carry the landscaping load."

Except Neely Kate was getting a baby of her own, which meant she wasn't going to be able to fill in for me. She'd be taking her own time off, and based on what she'd said, she might not return at all. But I couldn't tell him any of that. It was Neely Kate's news to share.

We'd figure it out. Ultimately, he was right—I had bigger fish to fry.

I reached up and kissed him on the cheek. "You're a good friend, Bruce Wayne Decker, and I'm lucky to have you."

"Joe will find those two kids," Bruce Wayne said. "He loves 'em nearly as much as you do."

I nodded, but somehow I expected the legal route wouldn't see them home. "Something feels off to me about all of this," I said. "If Mike was involved in something illegal, wouldn't some of the other criminals in the county know about it? From my experience with them, they seem to be chatty about their buddies."

"Maybe he's not workin' with local criminals."

I stared at Bruce Wayne in shock. "Hardshaw."

He shrugged. "It's something to consider."

Did that mean the subcontractor who'd been murdered was also working for Hardshaw? Or had he heard something he shouldn't have? All the more reason to talk to Mason.

"You gonna suggest it to Joe?" he asked.

"Yeah. As soon as I leave." I pointed to the truck. "I'm gonna go pick up lunch, then head to the office. Can I get you anything?"

"Nope," he said, glancing back at the gazebo. "I brought my lunch today. Besides, we've got a few hours of work left in us."

I left him and picked up Muffy from the nursery, telling Maeve that Neely Kate had taken the afternoon off. I thought she might ask questions, but she took it in stride.

Muffy hopped in the truck with me, smothering me with kisses from across the bench seat. I partially rolled down the window, and she stuck her head out of the opening. She got excited when we pulled into the Burger Shack parking lot, recognizing the building after the many times I'd taken her with me through the drive-thru to feed my bacon cheeseburger craving. After I placed my order for a bacon cheeseburger, fries, and a mini hamburger for Muffy, I tried calling Joe. When he didn't answer, I left him a message asking him to call me when he got a chance. I'd just gotten my food when a text from Mason popped up on my phone.

Can you meet me at your farm in a half hour?

I answered right away. **Yes**

I headed straight out to the farm, feeding Muffy pieces of the hamburger. I only ate a few bites of my own food before I was full. There wasn't much room left for it to go.

Mason's car was parked in front of the house when I pulled up, and he was sitting on the front porch in a dress shirt and tie, eating a sandwich. For a moment, it felt like time had gone and rewound itself, and Mason and I still lived at the farmhouse together. But so much had changed since then—everything, really—and the thought crumbled into dust.

He stood as I got out of the truck, and Muffy jumped down after me, her tail wagging when she saw Mason moving to meet me at the top of the porch. He bent down to pick her up. The bag that was slung over his shoulder slid forward, but he adjusted it as he stood, his eyes glued to my stomach.

"Yeah, I know," I said. "I'm huge."

He grimaced, then smiled, rubbing Muffy behind the ear. "Sorry. I didn't mean to stare. It's just that I haven't seen you since before Christmas."

I couldn't help wondering if he was thinking about the pregnancy scare we'd had when we were together. We'd had so many plans back then. Before I became the Lady in Black.

"That's okay," I said, lumbering up the steps. "I'm due in two weeks, so I'm supposed to be this big. Let's go inside." I unlocked the front door and headed to the back of the house to turn off the alarm. Mason set Muffy down and followed me inside.

"Want to sit at the table or in the living room?" I asked.

"Whichever is more comfortable for you."

"Want a cup of tea?" I asked, grabbing the kettle and filling it with water.

"Sure. When I spoke to Mom earlier, she said Muffy was with her."

"Neely Kate and I had to run a few errands, and it didn't seem wise to bring her. I picked her up before heading out here to meet you."

He tilted his head. "And did those errands have anything to do with your text?"

"As a matter of fact they did." I gestured to the table. "We can sit while the water boils."

He sat in a chair and set his bag on the floor next to him, while I took a seat at the head of the table. "Ashley and Mikey are missing."

Mason sat up so quickly it looked like someone had held a lit match to his butt. "What? When?"

"Joe made it official this morning," I said, surprisingly matter-of-fact. "But we both knew something was wrong last night." I told him everything, except, of course, the bit about Neely Kate and I making off with copied information from Mike's office. "I was wondering if you ever found out anything about Mike being involved in any illegal activity?"

His gaze dipped to my stomach for a brief second, then lifted to mine. "I did find something, but I never reached out because it's all part of an investigation and nothing has been confirmed. But first I'd like to ask you some questions about Mike."

He hadn't guaranteed that he'd tell me anything, but if he was going after Mike, I was willing to help. "Sure."

He pulled a legal pad and pen out of his messenger bag. "When Mike went to Houston to see Violet, did he ever mention making any stops in Dallas?"

My breath caught. Was Mike involved with Hardshaw?

"No. But he'd stopped talking to me by the time Violet left for Houston. After everything came out about me being involved with taking down J.R."

He shifted uncomfortably. That was when he'd abandoned me too.

Glancing down at the table, he nodded, tapping his pen on the blank page. "So he never told you that he'd gotten a contract for a Dallas-based company opening an office here in Henryetta?"

"Do you mean Sonder Tech?" I asked. Did this mean they were tied to Hardshaw after all?

His brow lifted slightly. "So he *did* mention it?"

"No," I said, rubbing my forehead. "I did a big landscaping job for them. I'm not sure how they got my name, but they contacted us for a bid after they moved to town."

He nodded slightly, but I noticed he wasn't writing anything down.

"But you knew that already," I said, fear prickling my nerves. "You're questioning me about my *own* involvement."

"No," he said carefully. "I know you're not involved with Hardshaw. In fact, as I've mentioned before, I'm certain that you're trying to stop them." He paused. "But don't you think it's strange your brother-in-law got a contracting job with a company that has links to Hardshaw, and then they asked you to make a pitch for the landscaping? Don't contractors recommend subcontractors like landscapers?"

At first, I thought he was insinuating I'd worked with Mike, and then it hit me what he *was* insinuating. "Mike was workin' for them."

Doing what? Watching me?

James had confirmed that he himself was working with Hardshaw, and I knew his arrangement with them had begun before our falling-out. Last August, James had backed away from me, saying it wasn't safe for him to see or talk to me. Had they slipped in Mike to keep an eye on me, or rather on the Lady in Black, in his place? But if so, they'd chosen poorly—Mike refused to have anything to do with me anymore.

"I didn't say that," Mason said, but he made a face that suggested I was onto something. "You're a smart woman, and we both know you're good at finding out things law enforcement often can't. So if you were to put things together, well, that wouldn't be outside of what you usually do in these situations."

I stared at him for a long moment. "You want my help."

"Let's just say we could potentially help each other." He drew in a breath and shifted in his seat. "I can't share what I know with local law enforcement. I'm not happy about it, but it's not my call. It's coming from the state."

"But if I figure things out, I can share my suspicions with Joe."

He gave me a tight smile. "We're just two friends having a chat. If you deduce things that I'm investigating, I can't help it or even stop you." Then he added, "But I can't confirm it either."

I glanced out the window. Mike was involved with Hardshaw? I wasn't sure why it hadn't occurred to me before Bruce Wayne had mentioned it, but it made perfect sense. It explained why the county criminals didn't know anything about him, and why a certain someone might have stolen those papers from Violet's lawyer's office.

What was currently messing with my head was that I'd ruled out any Hardshaw involvement with Sonder Tech. My instincts were usually spot on, but this mistake made me question everything.

The kettle flicked off, and I started to stand to make the tea, but Mason got to his feet more quickly than I could. "I'll make it. Is everything still in the same place?" His voice sounded a little strained.

"Uh… no. I felt a nesting urge, so Neely Kate and I moved everything around last night. The cups are on the right of the sink and the tea bags are above them."

He headed to the cabinet and pulled out two cups. "We know for a fact that Mike bribed a building inspector," he said, dropping a tea bag into both mugs. "He admitted that to me last year after J.R. Simmons threatened you. But it's a big jump to go from bribing inspectors to working with a crime syndicate from Dallas."

I shook my head. "I'm just as baffled as you are. How did he even get hooked up with them?"

"*That* is a very good question," Mason said, turning back to face me. "He bribed the inspector because he was struggling to provide for his family. What would he need money for now? Did he help pay for Violet's medical bills?"

"She was covered by the insurance we got through the nursery, but the bone marrow transplant wasn't completely paid for by her insurance, and when I asked the attorney about it, he said there weren't any leftover medical bills from Houston. Only what she owed for her hospice care."

"How did the Texas bills get covered?" he asked.

"I didn't ask," I admitted, feeling foolish. "In hindsight, I should have."

"You were grief-stricken," Mason said, scooping sugar into my tea, preparing it just how I liked it, and bringing both cups over. "And you shouldn't have to think about it. You trusted Violet's attorney to take care of the details."

"Which was likely a huge mistake. Especially after the break-in."

"Even the best attorney in the world could have had a theft, Rose," he said softly.

"But he didn't notice until days later."

"Perhaps he should have checked the safe, but I read Joe's report. There was nothing to suggest the safe had been breached. And I suspect a couple of days wouldn't have made a difference anyway. Whatever Violet had left for me to read in that safe was gone, and whoever took it made sure not to leave any evidence behind." Then he added, "Which eliminates Mike. He doesn't have that kind of expertise."

"But maybe the person he works for does."

"True," he conceded. "We just need to figure out who broke into the office. Someone with Hardshaw?"

I was pretty sure I knew who broke into that safe, and it was past time to confront him.

I was going to ambush James Malcolm.

Chapter
Ten

I'd already made up my mind to talk to James, but obviously, I couldn't tell Mason. I couldn't even tell Joe. Although I hated the thought of keeping something else from him, I knew this was something I had to keep to myself and do on my own.

Even if I had no idea how to go about it.

But there was something else I still hadn't figured out. "Mike's in construction. What could he possibly have done for Hardshaw other than remodel Sonder Tech's building?"

"If anyone finds out that the information I'm about to tell you came from me, I could not only get fired but perhaps be prosecuted, Rose. You have to be careful how you use it."

I reached over and covered his hand with mine. "I will. I swear."

He looked into my eyes, and I didn't see the hope and regret I'd seen there in our last few encounters. I saw resignation and something else—a kind of professional acknowledgement, for lack of a better word. Like maybe he thought we could work together to bring Hardshaw down.

He pulled his hand away and made like he was about to start writing on his legal pad.

"The connection between Sonder Tech and Hardshaw is a loose one," Mason said. "The owner is friends with Anthony Roberts, one of the alleged Hardshaw leaders."

"The Hardshaw Three."

His brow rose slightly. "Excuse me?"

"That's what we call them. The Hardshaw Three." Three ruthless men who'd think nothing of ramrodding everyone and everything until the world looked the way they wanted it to. My friend Carly's father, Randall Blakely, was proof enough of that. She'd had to change her name and go on the run, because if she didn't stay hidden, he would find a way to kill her.

"Look, I'm the first one to be lookin' for ties," I said, taking a sip of my tea, "but the fact that they're friendly doesn't necessarily mean he's caught up in their trouble." I was proof enough of that.

"Fair enough," he admitted, "and obviously we haven't established any clear-cut ties. So far, Sonder Tech has behaved beyond reproach."

"Well, they've had trouble brought to their doorstep," I said. "Someone poisoned their azalea bushes."

He sat up. "You're sure it was malicious?"

"I've sent soil samples off to be tested, but I can guarantee someone did it on purpose." I told him about Stewart's reaction to my suggestion—seemingly genuine shock—and then about overhearing Calista in the bathroom.

"I also forced a vision of her," I admitted, my face flushing.

"What did you see?"

"She was talking to a man. She told him the police were sniffing around, and he needed to be more careful than Mark."

"Mark Erickson? The murdered electrician?"

"She didn't say his last name, but Stewart said she was upset over his death."

"Has Joe talked to her?"

"I haven't even told him yet. I called and left a message that I had some helpful information, but he hasn't had a chance to call me back."

"That all sounds mighty suspicious," Mason said, then raised his hand with a look of alarm. "Calista, not you."

I pushed out a breath of relief. Last summer, Mason had threatened me with legal action if I was caught acting as Lady, and the worry that he'd turn on me was still in the back of my mind.

I shook my head. "I still don't know how you came to the conclusion that Mike's workin' for Hardshaw just because his construction firm did the Sonder Tech remodel. Besides, he's been acting strangely for longer than six months. Violet asked to move in with me in August. She must have gotten proof of whatever he was doin' at around that time." I narrowed my eyes. "But let's say he *is* working with them. What do you think they're havin' him do? I know he wasn't watching Neely Kate or me because he avoided us every chance he got."

"Maybe he was keeping an eye on something else," Mason said.

James? But as soon as the thought occurred to me, I doubted it. James had promised me that Mike wouldn't give Violet any trouble over moving in with me—and he hadn't. He also hadn't given her any grief about taking the kids whenever she wanted them.

I shook my head. "I have no idea who or what that could be, and honestly, my head hurts just thinkin' about it."

Worry filled his eyes. "Then I should leave and let you get some rest. We're just speculating at this point, and I need to get back to the office anyway."

Both of us stood.

"Thanks for agreeing to meet with me, Mason."

He nodded, and his gaze dipped to my stomach again. He started to say something—then cut himself off by clearing his throat. For a moment, I thought he'd leave without saying his piece, but he met my eyes and said, "I wish things had been different."

A lump formed in my throat. "I used to wish that too. I hope you find what you're lookin' for, Mason, because in the end it wasn't me."

He nodded, his eyes glassy. "I wish you the best, Rose."

"And you too."

"I'll let myself out." He turned and walked through the living room. Seconds later, I heard the latch of the front door.

I sat back down as tears flooded my eyes. I wasn't entirely sure why I was crying. Mason and I would never have worked in the end, and I didn't regret that we weren't together now. But a part of me did feel the loss of the simple life I'd envisioned with him. The possibility of normalcy.

My life was anything but normal now.

But I didn't have time to dwell on the life I would never have with Mason. The life I knew I didn't want any longer. I needed to find James and make him tell me everything he knew, which was easier said than done. I couldn't just waltz into the pool hall, and I no longer had James's cell phone number. The only other way I knew to get ahold of him was through Carter Hale, but I doubted Carter would want to get involved. Plus, James would likely refuse to see me.

Which meant I had to go to his house.

Today was Thursday. James used to go to his house on Thursday nights. Had he stuck to his routine?

I was about to find out.

The baby gave me a hard kick, as if reminding me I wasn't alone in this, and I pressed my hand against the side of my stomach. Fear washed over me. How would James react when he saw me? Would he try to hurt us? Last summer, I would have said never. But I no longer knew what to expect or believe. It was best, I figured, to expect nothing good.

My phone rang, and I felt a stab of guilt when I saw Joe's name on the screen, quickly followed by relief. I wasn't sure what I'd tell him about James, but I was thankful to hear his voice. It was a measure of how much I'd come to rely on him over the last few months.

"Hey," I said. "Have you found anything?"

"No, darlin'," he said, his voice full of sympathy. "Not yet."

I nodded even though he couldn't see me. "Like I said in my message, I discovered a few things." Then I told him about Sonder Tech—the bushes and my vision of Calista, although I kept the racy parts to myself. (Which I didn't feel guilty about in the least.)

"You didn't get a last name for Calista?" he asked.

"No. But I told Neely Kate, and she planned to tell Jed."

He hesitated, then said, "I think Jed should hold off on doin' anything."

"Why?" I asked. "The Erickson case has something to do with the kids, doesn't it? Do you have a lead from that note?" Then I quickly added, "And before you ask, no, I didn't tell them about the note, even if I have no idea what it said."

"We're holdin' it for evidence," he said carefully.

"Which means you aren't gonna tell me anything else," I said with a sigh.

"Rose...just know that I'm doin' everything I can," he said emphatically.

"I know," I said, suddenly exhausted. "And you have no idea how relieved I am to know you're the one in charge of finding them. I take it you haven't found Mike either?"

"No, but we're lookin' for him too."

"Bruce Wayne brought up a good point. Why haven't you issued an Amber Alert? In fact," I added, "why haven't you publicized it at all?"

Silence hung over the line for a second. Then he said, "We're not ready to make this public yet."

"Why not?"

"This is one of those times I need you to trust me," he said quietly. "Can you do that? I know in the past I've given you reason to doubt—"

"No, Joe," I said. "Stop. I trust you. That's all water under the bridge. All of it. We're both different people now, aren't we? We're not the same people who met and fell in love two years ago."

"Yeah," he said quietly, sounding sad. "We're not."

"We've both grown, and I'm pretty proud of the people we've become. You're the man you always wanted to be," I said, wishing we were having this conversation in person instead of over the phone, yet I felt like it needed to be said. "And me…I'm no longer that naïve young woman you met on your front porch, afraid of my own shadow."

"You weren't that fearful when I met you, Rose," he said tenderly. "You were brave from the moment I saw you behind your mother's house, lookin' at the cut electric line. But I agree, we're both different. We grew apart."

"Maybe not so far apart," I said with tears in my eyes. "We're about to raise a baby together. I think that means we found our way back to each other."

He didn't say anything for so long that I thought he'd hung up. Finally, he said, "What are you sayin', Rose?"

"Let's talk tonight," I said. I needed to go see James before I made any kind of commitment to Joe.

"I'm probably gonna be workin' late," he said. "In fact, I'd feel better if you stayed with Neely Kate and Jed."

"Don't worry about me," I said, trying to push away my guilt. He would hate it if he knew what I was planning. "Just focus on finding the kids. And the talk can keep. We've got plenty of time." We had our whole lives.

"Are you feeling okay?" he asked. "Any more Braxton Hicks?"

"Just one this morning. I'm fine. Muffy and I are at home, and I'm feeling kind of tired, so I think I'm going to stick around the farm for the rest of the afternoon."

"You're at home?" he asked in surprise.

"Yeah, I met with Mason to find out if he had any more information about Mike. Mason thinks he has ties to Hardshaw."

"What? Why?"

"He wouldn't give me many specifics, and he told me to be careful who I shared the information with because it could get him in a heap of trouble. I know you and Mason have had your issues in the past, but I'm beggin' you, Joe, *please* don't tell anyone where this came from."

"Rose," he said so gently I could almost feel his arms around me. "I'll be careful. I would never jeopardize his career, let alone whatever type of arrangement you two have. His—and your—secret is safe with me."

I pushed out a breath of relief. "Thank you, Joe." It wasn't lost on me that he never would have handled this so calmly a year ago. "Mason also thinks Sonder Tech has ties to Hardshaw. They've discovered that the Sonder Tech owner is friendly with Tony Roberts."

"Shit." His voice sounded tight. "They requested that you and Bruce Wayne make a bid for the landscapin' job. *You were out there today.*"

"Joe," I said. "I'm okay. The baby's okay. Nothin' happened."

"You can't go back there, Rose. It's not safe."

"I didn't know before I went there this morning," I said. "But I do now." I hoped he noticed I hadn't promised not to go. My instincts had always told me they were on the up and up, but then again, I'd almost always dealt with Stewart, and he'd always struck me as honest. What if he was oblivious to the company's ties to Hardshaw? *That* was something worth looking into. If he knew that his boss was shady, he might be willing to give us information.

If I was even allowed back on the premises after my little display.

I heard voices in the background, and someone calling Joe's name.

"I've gotta go," he said, "but we'll talk more tonight, okay? And reconsider spendin' the evenin' with Jed and Neely Kate. If you want to sleep in your own bed, I can even swing by to pick you up on the way home."

"I'll consider it," I said, my guilt rushing back like an avalanche. "Now go find Violet's kids."

I hung up, trying to think of what else I could do to aid the investigation. James wouldn't be at his house for hours, so the rest of the day loomed before me. I would be terrible at any kind of surveillance, since rule number one was blend in so you go unnoticed. But at least I could make phone calls.

First I pulled up Violet's attorney's number and placed the call. When his receptionist answered, I asked to speak to Mr. Gilliam, surprised when she put me right through.

"Rose. Pleased to hear from you," he said, sounding anything but, which was fair considering our previous encounters.

"Thanks, Mr. Gilliam. I have a few more questions about Violet's affairs."

"We haven't heard any new developments regarding the break-in," he said, "but then again, you'd be in a better position to know than I would."

I grimaced. "Joe doesn't have any new information, but I'm calling about something else."

"Okay," he said, but I could hear the hesitation in his voice. "I'll answer if I can."

"It's regarding Violet's medical bills. You said the estate only had to handle the hospice bills. Do you know anything about the medical expenses from her bone marrow transplant?"

"No," he said. "She never mentioned it."

"MD Anderson hasn't reached out to you for payment?"

"I doubt they would. They would be sending the bills to the address on file."

Which would have been Momma's house since Violet had been living there before she'd left for Texas. I'd been collecting the mail for over a year and had yet to see a bill. "Do you think they could have gone to Mike?"

"Perhaps," the attorney said. "Her divorce attorney might know. Let me give her a call and get back to you." He was so eager to get me off the phone he hung up before I could answer. The last thing I expected was to hear back from him soon, but he called back about ten minutes later.

"I've solved the mystery of the medical bills," he said, sounding like he'd just won a gold medal. "Violet's divorce attorney said that Mike was responsible for any copays or expenses not covered by her insurance through the nursery for two years after the divorce. Which explains why you haven't seen any bills. In fact, you aren't even responsible for the hospice bills. We can send them to him if you like."

I was so shocked it took me a few seconds to respond. "No. I've already paid them and I don't want to saddle him with those too." I shook my head, sick to my stomach. "Mr. Gilliam, do you have any idea how much he had to pay?"

"Not a clue, but it's nothing for you to worry about. It's Mike's problem."

But I suspected it was a *huge* problem—the kind that might have driven him to crime. Had Violet known? "And if I wanted to find out?"

"We might be able to find out by calling the billing department. I can do that if you like. I'll just tell them I'm the attorney handling Violet's estate."

"Yeah, that would be great."

"If I can get a copy of any bills, I'll email them to you." Then he added, "but I assure you, Rose, that you are *not* responsible for those bills. The divorce decree makes it very clear that Mike is the responsible party."

"Thanks. I'll keep that in mind."

I wasn't sure what else to do. I considered calling Neely Kate to see if they'd found anything yet, but it would be pointless. She'd let me know if they'd discovered anything important. Instead, I sent her a text telling her that Joe thought Jed should let the sheriff's department handle Calista.

She sent back: Jed got your message.

Which meant he wasn't going to take Joe's advice. I was relieved to hear it, although it made me feel guilty all the same.

I headed up to the baby's nursery to see if anything needed to be washed or organized, and Muffy trailed behind me. Truth be told, I'd already done all the chores that needed doing, but part of me needed to see the baby's room, to feel the assurance that he or she would soon be coming home.

I hoped we found the kids before the baby was born. Of course, we couldn't find them soon enough to suit me, but selfishly, I didn't want the baby to be born while we were still so upset and worried. Despite Mike's resistance, my daydreams about the baby had always included my niece and nephew.

I couldn't even let myself think about where they were, who they were with, or what was happening to them. I had to stop midflight up the stairs as a wave of dizziness hit me, and Muffy began whining at my feet.

"I'm okay, girl. Just so, so worried."

After my head cleared, I climbed the rest of the stairs, then walked to the end of the hall and turned right into the baby's nursery.

The walls were sage green, decorated with white birch trees, which Neely Kate and I had painted a month before. The crib and dresser had arrived shortly afterward, and Joe and I had spent a weekend assembling the furniture and putting everything in its place.

It was hard to believe that our baby would be sleeping in the crib within a few weeks.

I sat in the rocking chair—the chair that had been in my own nursery, which I'd only gotten to use for a few weeks before the death of my birth mother. Joe had painted it white, and Neely Kate and I had added a seat and back cushion, and sometimes I liked to sit in the chair and imagine holding my baby.

I started to drift off to sleep, but then my phone buzzed with an incoming email. When I saw it was from Mr. Gilliam, I opened it.

Rose, attached is a statement that shows the balance on Violet's account, including what was paid and what is still owed. Keep in mind, it reflects Violet's full stay at MD Anderson, including her chemo and radiation treatments. Let me know if I can do anything else to help.
Regards,
Gary Gilliam

My stomach in knots, I opened the attached file and zoomed in, and nearly vomited when I saw the total.

Mike owed four hundred and seventy-three *thousand* dollars. And fifteen cents.

While I'd known the insurance through the nursery wasn't great, and that they'd been reluctant to cover the bone marrow transplant, I had no idea the balance was this bad. How on earth could he pay off such a debt? But the simple truth was he couldn't. He'd be forced to declare bankruptcy and lose everything.

No wonder Mike had been so bitter about Vi's choice to move in with me. No wonder he hated me for getting—aside from Neely Kate's inheritance of a third of the nursery—every last one of her assets.

Mike was in deep, deep debt. Had Hardshaw offered him money to help him out of it?

What on earth had they asked him to do?

I called Joe, but he didn't answer, so I left him a message saying that Mr. Gilliam had sent me information about the small fortune Mike owed for Vi's medical bills. I followed up by forwarding him the email.

Suddenly, everything felt like too much.

Muffy and I went into my room and both of us settled in for a nap, Muffy jumping up beside me on the bed, her small body curling against mine. A few hours later, I woke up stiff and groggy, but I forced myself to get out of bed. I had several texts. One from Neely Kate saying they'd found some cash deposits, but they weren't sure who they were from. I texted her back, letting her know about Mike's debt, and then forwarded the email from the lawyer to both her and Mason, chastising myself for not having sent the information to them sooner. The more people who were looking for Ashley and Mikey, the better. The other text was from Joe, thanking me for the email, saying it was more helpful than I knew.

It was after six, time to go. I knew I should eat something, but I was too nervous, so I grabbed a container of leftover pasta and told Muffy she had to stay behind. While James and Muffy had gotten along, he'd never fallen in love with her like Joe and Mason had. While I wanted to believe he wouldn't hurt her to get to me, I couldn't be completely sure. Everyone said James had changed since I'd last seen him.

With that in mind, I got my handgun from my dresser drawer and checked the clip. I had no idea what to expect when I saw James, but I wasn't leaving until I got answers.

I was on autopilot as I drove to James's house south of town, but I repeatedly checked my rearview mirror to make sure I wasn't being followed. No one appeared to be tailing me, though.

Of course, I hadn't been with James in months. No one was following me anymore, and everyone in the county was well aware I was living with a deputy sheriff. Nevertheless, with Mike and my niece and nephew missing, it made sense to be more vigilant than usual.

I still had his garage door opener in my glove compartment. When I pulled up in front of his house, I put the truck in park and scooted over to dig it out. I held my breath as I pressed the button, hoping he hadn't changed the frequency. The door opened, and equal parts relief and dread washed through me when I saw the garage was empty. James wasn't here yet. If he still came at all. For all I knew, he hadn't been out here in weeks or months, but I was committed to seeing this through.

Once I pulled inside, I closed the garage door, then found a step stool and used it to unplug the door opener from the outlet. I wanted the element of surprise, which would be blown if he saw my truck before he saw me. He'd likely be on edge when he walked through the front door, but it was a chance I was willing to take. Especially since I had my gun.

I went inside and found the kitchen and living room spotless. Another wave of worry washed through me—had I come here for nothing?—but then I opened the fridge and checked the contents. There was a half-empty carton of eggs with an expiration date a week away, a slightly empty half gallon of unexpired milk, and a partially consumed package of deli turkey. But it was the loaf of bread that brought tears to my eyes. It wasn't the fact that it was fresh; it was where I found it. Last summer, I'd told James that it was better to keep bread in his pantry than his fridge. He was still following my advice.

I wasn't sure why that stupid bread made me emotional, but I walked into the living room and broke into sobs. James Malcolm was domesticated enough to put his bread in the pantry, but he couldn't handle the thought of me having a baby, *his* baby.

I knew they were two entirely separate things, yet my heart broke all over again. But even in my grief, I told myself I'd always known there would be no happily ever after with James…so why couldn't I let the man go?

My belly began to shake, and I couldn't help smiling when I realized the baby had the hiccups. Wiping my tears with the back of my hand, I said, "Oh, sweet baby. I didn't mean to upset you. I promise that when you are born, there will only be happy tears."

I wasn't sure what to do while I waited. I considered going upstairs to see James's room, but I couldn't bring myself to do it. Too many memories, yet there were memories downstairs too. We'd had nearly two months of pretend domestic bliss, and our make-believe life together had made me lower my guard and consider the impossible. It had made his sudden departure from my life hurt that much more.

It was getting dark outside, but James always left a living room lamp on. I sat on the sofa and turned on the TV, reasoning that he'd designed the house so he could see any visitors' cars as they approached. When I saw James's car, I'd turn off the TV and wait for him to walk in. Then I'd confront him.

If he showed.

And perhaps my plan would have worked if I weren't nine months pregnant and exhausted all the time, because one minute I was watching Food Network, and the next I was staring into James Malcolm's face.

Chapter Eleven

At first, I thought this was another dream. I'd had many of them last fall—dreams where he came to me as James and not Skeeter Malcolm. Where his face was soft and love and adoration filled his eyes, not the scorn and hate that had replaced it.

I smiled, happy that I was seeing him the way I wanted to remember him, but then his expression shifted to wariness and I realized this wasn't a dream.

I had fallen asleep, and James had found me sprawled out on his sofa.

I jerked to sit upright, but my center of gravity was off, and I flopped like an upended turtle.

Dammit. This was not the first impression I'd intended to make.

He was sitting on the coffee table, and he slowly reached out a hand as though any sudden movement might make me lash out and bite him.

I batted it away, pissed at him. Pissed at me. Pissed that Mike had put my niece and nephew in harm's way. Pissed that James had known what was going on and hadn't warned me.

And that was what wiped away the last bit of my happiness at seeing him. He'd known that Mike was working for Hardshaw—he must have—and he'd never once warned me. I nearly laughed at my idiocy. *James* had been working for Hardshaw. If he hadn't told me what he was up to, what made me think he'd reveal Mike's secrets?

This man does not have your best interest in mind.

James stood and backed up to the fireplace, and I realized the TV was off. He'd walked in, turned off the TV, and sat beside me, watching me sleep. He could have hurt me. He could have hurt the baby.

Why had I been so careless?

I finally got to a sitting position, then rocked up to my feet.

"What are you doin' here, Rose?" he asked softly, without anger or accusation, but I realized he didn't look surprised. I supposed he wasn't. He knew everything that happened in Fenton County.

Which meant he also knew Ashley and Mikey were missing. Somehow deep down I'd known…I'd just failed to let myself acknowledge it.

He not only knew my niece and nephew were missing, he likely knew how and maybe even where to find them. And yet he'd done *nothing*.

A protective fury rose up in me, making me see red, but I couldn't lose my cool. I had to play his game, because I'd come to realize everything was a game with him. He was only honest or forthright if and when it served his purposes.

Stupid me. I'd thought I was different. Turned out, I was just like every other person in his life, including his supposed best friend, Jed—disposable. Just another plaything to amuse him until he grew bored and decided to move on.

Why had I expected anything else? He'd told me his limitations in the beginning. He'd been honest about that, at least.

But I was here for answers, which meant I couldn't just ask for them outright like any mature adult would do. I'd have to beat around the bush to gain what would likely only be nuggets of information.

I was exhausted of it already.

I needed a game plan, and since he didn't seem to be in a hurry, I took a moment to think this through. Skeeter Malcolm didn't like people getting the best of him, yet I didn't feel like kowtowing to him. I never had before, and I wasn't about to start now.

"Do you know where my niece and nephew are?"

He leaned his shoulder into the smooth river rock and asked in a lazy tone, "Are you askin' me if I have them?"

I lifted my chin, trying to control my temper. "You read into my words what you will. I merely asked if you knew where they were."

"No."

His answer filled me with equal parts relief and anxiety. If he'd known, I might have found a way to convince him to give them to me.

"Do you know where Mike is?"

He released a soft laugh. "No. Trust me, I wish I did."

"You have answers and I need them."

His mouth stretched into a smile, but now I was facing Skeeter, not James. This was his crime boss persona, hammered into place over long, hard years. "Do you now? What are you willing to pay for them?"

"Not a damn thing," I said with plenty of attitude. "How about you be a decent human being and just tell me for the sake of doing the right thing?"

"Come now, Rose," he said with a slow drawl that let me know this had become a game. "We both know I'm not capable of either of those things."

A small part of me was ready to blast him, but I knew he believed what he said. He always had, although I'd started to make him believe differently when we were together. It seemed he'd snapped all the way back.

Who was right? James? Me? A combination of both?

"What do you want?" I asked, deciding to be blunt. It was a terrible negotiation tactic, but I wasn't in the mood for this dance.

He laughed as he pushed off the fireplace and sauntered into the kitchen—and then out into the garage.

I hesitated for a moment before following him to the doorway.

James grabbed the step stool and moved it to the center of the garage.

"Should you be climbing up on things in your condition?" he asked in a curious tone lacking the previous animosity.

"No," I conceded. Then because I'd decided to throw games out the window, I added, "But I needed the element of surprise and it seemed the best course."

"Force me through the front door," he said approvingly as he reached up, his arm long enough to easily plug it back in. "Good plan."

"If I hadn't fallen asleep."

"And that is what likely saved your life," he said, his breath a bit shaky as he climbed down the short ladder. "I walked in, gun drawn, ready to shoot to kill."

"So you knew someone tampered with the opener?" I asked, trying not to think about what could have happened.

Putting the step stool back in place, he said, "Whenever anything goes wrong, I *always* presume someone has worked things to their advantage."

"That's no way to live, James," I said softly, in disbelief that I was standing here, talking to him in a civil tone.

He finally turned to look at me, his face void of any expression. "It's too late to turn back time, Lady."

Lady. He was talking about his criminal doings, not our relationship. Because we had no relationship. He'd thrown that away last year.

I backed up, keeping my gaze on him as he headed back into the kitchen.

His smile was genuine as he said, "Good girl. You remembered what I said about never turning your back on an adversary."

"Are we adversaries, James?" I asked, the small of my back hitting the edge of the counter in front of the sink.

He closed the distance between us. "You made sure of that last October."

I would have expected some heat behind those words, but the only heat I sensed was of a sexual nature.

My breath caught. I was as huge as a barn. Surely I was imagining things.

"When I decided to keep the baby?"

His eyes hardened. "When Lady took a stance against me by turning half the county against me with those meetin's."

"You're working with Hardshaw. We had to figure out how to take a stand," I countered, remembering why I was here, and it wasn't for a trip down memory lane. While I still wanted to ask him why, I doubted he'd tell me. And the time for explanations had passed. "Did you bring Hardshaw to Fenton County?"

"Hardshaw was comin' here with or without me," he said, taking two steps back before turning to walk to the fridge. He opened the door and pulled out a beer.

"I thought you weren't supposed to turn your back to your enemy," I said harshly.

He kept his back to me as he twisted off the cap.

"Are you my enemy, Rose?" he asked softly. Then he took a long pull from the bottle. I would have thought he was handling our discussion as though we were two friends who'd had a spat over a borrowed muffin tin, but the fact that he downed nearly half the bottle made it clear I'd caught him off guard.

I didn't answer, deciding to wait to see if he'd offer any information.

Lowering the bottle, he turned to face me. "So this is what it takes for you to show up at my doorstep. More damn kids."

My anger rose again, but I stuffed it back down. For one, *he* didn't sound angry, more like a child who had been caught doing something naughty and responded by pointing out that his brother had done something worse. And two, I wasn't going to waste my time on petty arguing. I was here for information to help me find my niece and nephew.

"You have control over Mike," I said, presenting what I knew in a logical tone. "Or at least you did. I'm guessing things might have changed based on what you said about wishing you knew where he was now."

A grin tilted the corners of his mouth up, lighting his eyes too, as he pulled out a barstool and took a seat.

"You told me not to worry, that I'd still be able to see the kids after Violet died. That didn't happen."

He lifted his bottle to his lips and took a sip. "Your decisions made that agreement null and void."

"Is that what we had?" I asked, unable to keep the anger out of my voice. "An agreement?"

"Wasn't it?" he asked casually. "Friends with benefits? It was your suggestion, if I remember correctly. You're the one who changed the terms."

He sounded perfectly reasonable, but the slight tremor of his hand clutching the bottle gave him away. My presence had shaken him, and it wasn't just because he'd believed he had an intruder.

"When did you pair up with Hardshaw?"

He studied me for a long moment. "That is irrelevant to the reason you're here."

"Is it?" I asked, taking a step toward the island. "Did you get Mike hooked up with them?"

He paused, then took a drink, and as he lowered the bottle, he said, "Figured that part out, did you?"

"Yeah," I said. "Although admittedly, it took me longer than it should have." Resting my hands on the island counter, I held his gaze. "Violet put it together somehow. She had evidence he was up to somethin', and she gave it to her attorney to be released to me after her death. The day after she died, there was a break-in at her attorney's office, only her attorney didn't realize that his safe had been opened until a few days later, when I went in for the reading of her will."

His brow lifted. "Is that so?"

"I know you broke in and stole it, James."

His brow shifted even higher. "That's a bold accusation, Rose."

"And it was a bold and skillful break-in. Totally within your wheelhouse."

He finished off his beer, only to get up and grab another from the fridge. He lifted his bottle to me and said, "I'd offer you one, but under the circumstances…"

His voice trailed off as his gaze dipped to my stomach—then it quickly lifted, as though staring at the evidence of my betrayal was too much to bear, because the other option was that he'd had a change of heart about the baby, and my nerves were too fried to entertain *that* possibility.

He twisted off the cap and took another long drink.

"What did you steal from Violet's attorney's office?" I asked in a hard tone.

"Steal's an ugly word, Rose."

"What did you *take* from Violet's attorney's office, James?"

"*I* didn't take anything from Gary Gilliam's office," he said good-naturedly, then took another long drink.

131

"Don't play games with me, James Malcolm," I said, getting pissed. He'd used the attorney's name to toy with me. When he didn't answer, I let loose. "You think I betrayed you, but you betrayed me long before I found out I was carryin' our baby." My voice broke. "*Our* baby."

He shook his head with a sharp jerk. "That baby sure as hell isn't mine."

"Then why didn't you sign the papers giving up paternal rights?"

"Because you wanted me to." I expected there to be vindictiveness in his voice, but I saw an unexpected flicker of emotion in his eyes.

Fear washed through me. Did he want to be part of the baby's life? If so, that was a good thing, right? But I thought about his life—his garage door hadn't opened, and his response had been to walk into his house presuming someone was waiting to ambush him. How in the hell could he help raise a baby in that kind of environment?

But even if he'd changed his mind, there was no way in hell I'd cut Joe out of his or her life. Family was more than DNA. It was love and commitment, and Joe had shown us that in spades.

"What do you want, James?"

His mouth parted in surprise, but then he recovered, his eyes turning hard. "It's too late for what I want."

"To get rid of this baby? That was never gonna happen. But you clearly want something else, otherwise you would have signed those papers and been done with me. So I'm gonna ask you again: What. Do. You. *Want?*"

He started to say something, but he raised the bottle to his mouth instead, downing the rest of the beer before wordlessly returning to the refrigerator—this time bypassing the fridge and reaching above it to grab a bottle of whiskey.

I was about to tell him that getting drunk wasn't the answer, but I was too hung up on wondering *why* he was getting drunk. It wasn't lost on me that he hadn't kicked me out. Would the alcohol loosen his tongue enough that he would finally tell me how he really felt?

He slid past me to grab a juice glass out of the cabinet, the whiskey bottle in the other hand. Setting the glass on the counter, he filled it halfway and took a generous gulp.

Good. Let him get drunk. Forget his feelings. There were more important things than our *feelings* to deal with here. I needed every scrap of information I could pry out of this man to find Ashley and Mikey. Everything else was wasted breath.

"What did Mike do for Hardshaw?" I asked.

"What makes you think I know?" he asked in a snotty tone.

"For one thing, you're not stupid, James Malcolm. You were able to control him last September, which means you had some authority over him. And that leads me to believe you know exactly what he was doin' for them. What was it?"

"I could tell you, but then I'd have to kill you." He snorted, then took a drink.

I rolled my eyes. "Look, if you want to roll around in bed with Hardshaw, then you accept the consequences, but whatever Mike's been doin' has gotten my niece and nephew kidnapped, so if you have any feelings left for me at all, then I'm *begging* you to help me."

His gaze lifted to mine. "What makes you think I give a single shit about you?"

That stung, but the fact that he was getting shit-faced to have this conversation wasn't helping his defense.

"Fine," I said, "you don't care about me. You made that clear last fall, but you once told me you cared about kids, and the fact remains that two kids are missing, the children of a man who works for Hardshaw, which means you probably have some clue who took them or where they might be."

He shot me a glare. "I'm not tellin' you shit, Rose. Not without something in return."

"What could you possibly want from me?" His look hardened, and I said, "If you're askin' me to choose between you and the baby, don't waste your miserable breath."

He started to say something, then took a generous gulp of his whiskey. "That ship has sailed, sweetheart. I'm not interested in some bitch who tried to trap me into a relationship with a baby."

I flinched. His go-to defense mechanism was to lash out, but I wasn't going to put up with his disrespect. "If that's how you choose to remember it, by all means, live in your land of delusion. In the meantime, tell me how you wish to profit off two *missing children*, James."

"Glad you see it my way," he said, his words sounding a bit slurred.

"*What do you want, James?*"

He turned to face me. "I know your new boyfriend is investigatin' Mark Erickson's murder. I want to know what he's discovered."

My eyes narrowed. "Why do you care about the murderer of an electrician?"

His eyes were unfocused. "I like to keep tabs on everything that happens in this county."

"Seems to me you'd know more than Joe, what with your criminal connections."

He snorted and finished off his glass. "Seems to me your own criminal connections would come into play for you too, *Lady*," he sneered.

"And you have to know that I haven't met with the criminals of the county in months."

"It's too bad that you haven't," he said, pouring more whiskey into his glass. "Especially your buddy Carmichael."

I blinked. "What does Denny Carmichael have to do with this?"

He lifted his glass in salute, his hand waving. "Maybe you should ask him."

Then he turned and walked into the living room, carting the glass and whiskey bottle with him. He plopped onto the leather sofa and flipped on the TV, grimacing when an episode of *Cupcake Wars* came on. He quickly changed the channel to a dirt bike race.

Shooting me a dark look, he asked, "What the hell are you still doin' here? I gave you some information, for free no less. If you want more, you're gonna have to bring me something about Mark Erickson."

I counted to three, trying to get my temper under control. Then I turned around and left.

Chapter Twelve

When I got home, Joe's sheriff's car was parked outside the house and he was sitting on the porch drinking a beer of his own, petting Muffy, who sat on his lap.

He stayed seated while I got out, but when I started up the steps, he rose to greet me. "Decided not to stay with Neely Kate and Jed?"

"I wasn't at Neely Kate and Jed's."

He didn't say anything, but I could tell he'd known that. He'd probably called or texted one of them.

"I didn't lie to you, Joe," I pleaded.

He placed a gentle kiss on my forehead. "I know."

Wrapping my arms around his neck, I pressed myself against him as close as I could get. "Will you hold me?"

His arms were around me in an instant, giving me comfort and strength. I felt like I'd cheated on him, which was crazy. We weren't together, yet we were. He was living with me now, giving me financial support for the baby. We ate together, spent time together. He'd taken me to the hospital for two false labors, and he'd never once acted frustrated or angry.

While I suspected James still loved me, he had no idea how to love me, let alone a child. Joe was different...he'd changed since the end of our relationship. It was like our paths had diverged as we grew in different directions, but they were coming back together. Joe, I knew, would never accuse me of trying to trap him in anything.

"I'm sorry about Ashley and Mikey," Joe said. "We haven't really made much progress."

"I know you're doin' your best, Joe. I never once doubted it."

"Let's get you inside," he said, wrapping an arm around my back and leading me into the house.

"Joe, there's something I need to tell you."

His body stiffened slightly. Then he said, "Should I be worried?"

"Let's sit down on the sofa and I'll explain."

He hesitated. "Okay."

We sat on the sofa together, but instead of taking our usual positions, we sat next to each other. My shoulders were stiff as I prepared for his reaction, and his posture—back stiff and his hands on his knees—told me he was preparing himself for the bombshell I was about to drop on him.

"I saw James Malcolm tonight."

His face paled. "Was that your doin' or his?"

"Mine. I knew James had some kind of control over Mike, so I figured he might know something. I asked him to tell me what Mike was involved in."

"Were you in danger?"

"No. He wasn't excited to see me, but he wasn't hostile." That seemed like a partial lie. While James hadn't been excited, he'd been more cordial than I'd expected.

He drew in a breath. "Did he tell you anything?"

"Not really. Only that I should check with Denny Carmichael."

"Denny Carmichael?" Joe said in confusion. "What does he have to do with Hardshaw?"

"I don't know," I said. "Carmichael was willing to take a stand against them last fall, so I doubt he's involved with them, but your guess is as good as mine." I paused, then added, "There's something else I need to tell you."

He hesitated and worry filled his eyes. "Okay…"

"James said he'd tell me more if I gave him information about Mark Erickson."

"The dead electrician?" He looked lost in thought. "So Malcolm is involved somehow?"

"Not necessarily," I said a little too quickly. "Sometimes he just likes to gather information. I have no idea why he's interested other than pure curiosity."

"Malcolm doesn't seem like the gossipin' type."

"There are all sorts of gossipin'," I said. "At times, I've found the criminals of this county to be worse than fishmongers' wives."

Surprise filled his eyes before he glanced down at my stomach. "So what do you plan to do?"

"I'm not tellin' him anything, Joe. That's why I told you. So there aren't any secrets. So you know you can trust me."

His face softened, but he still held back. "I've known I can trust you for months. But thanks for tellin' me."

Tears filled my eyes. "I don't want there to be any secrets, Joe. I don't want you to think you can't trust me. I don't want you to leave me and the baby because of this."

He took both of my hands. "I'm not goin' anywhere, Rose. I'm here."

I'm here. He wasn't just here for the baby. He was here for me too.

I'd realized something over the last few months of soul-searching on the farm, helped along by several counseling sessions with Jonah Pruitt, my friend and minister: I had a fear of abandonment. My father had abandoned me to my mother's anger. Joe and Mason had both abandoned me when they'd broken up with me. Violet had abandoned me in death, and James...his abandonment had been ugly. But I was finally climbing out of the pit of my despair, excited to meet my baby despite the fear of James's retaliation, and only a few days before, I'd made a breakthrough with Jonah about another fear I hadn't yet verbalized.

"If you're gonna change your mind, I need you to do it now, Joe," I whispered. "It will break my heart if you do, but I'd rather you do it now instead of after the baby's born."

He slowly shook his head. "I'm not changing my mind, Rose. I'm in this. I'm here."

I knew he was, which made the next part even harder. "There's something else you should know."

Fear filled his eyes again, but it was quickly replaced by resolve. "Okay."

"I'm scared James might try to lay claim to the baby." Then I told him about the can of worms I'd opened in February.

He listened in silence. I waited for him to get angry, but instead, he asked, "Why didn't you tell me sooner, Rose?"

"I didn't want to worry you," I said in a shaky voice.

"So you took the worry on yourself and left me out of it."

"I was tryin' to protect you, Joe."

"Don't you know that worryin' is part of bein' a parent?" Raw emotion flashed through his eyes...pain, fear. "By keepin' the worry to yourself, you took part of my job as the baby's father."

Which was exactly what Neely Kate had told me. Somewhere along the line she'd gotten to know her brother well.

"I didn't mean to hurt you, Joe. I was trying to keep from hurtin' you."

"Do you want Malcolm to be a father to this baby?" He swallowed. "Do you want me to step aside?"

I shook my head vigorously. "No. He hasn't expressed any interest in the baby, and instead of telling me what he wanted when he refused to sign, he left me to stew and worry. Even Carter has no idea what he wants." My voice broke. "I'm scared he's gonna use this baby to hurt me for choosing it over him."

"Did he say anything tonight?"

"No. I asked him why he wouldn't sign the papers, but he ignored the question."

Joe was quiet for several long seconds. "What do you want to do?"

"Jonah convinced me that pretendin' it wasn't a possibility wasn't doin' me a speck of good. It's only makin' me more anxious. A couple of months ago, he suggested I hire an attorney and prepare to protect myself, the baby, and you." Joe's eyes widened in surprise. "The attorney said it would be best to wait him out. If I sue for full rights, he might push back, and it would likely become public that James is the biological father."

"So we wait," he said, but the uneasiness in his eyes broke my heart.

"It might get hard, Joe. It could get ugly, and if it becomes public, it could ruin your career."

"I don't care about my job, Rose. I care about the baby."

"Are you sure?" I whispered again, close to breaking down. "This is so much more than you bargained for, so if you change your mind, I understand."

He cupped the side of my face. "I'm not changin' my mind, Rose. If I'm honest, I'm scared to death that you're gonna change yours. Especially after you saw him."

I slowly shook my head. "He made his choice. I'm holdin' him to it, not that he's changin' his mind."

He studied my face for a moment, and determination filled his eyes. "I decided months ago that this baby is mine. I don't care whose DNA makes up half of his genes. I'm his father, and I'll do *everything* in my God-given power to protect him, even if it means protectin' him from the man who helped create him."

I smiled through my tears. "You're so convinced this baby's a boy. What if he looks like James?"

A fierce look filled his eyes. "I'll still love him, Rose. I look like my own father, but I hope to God I'm nothin' like him."

I covered his hand with mine. "You're not, Joe. You're a good man."

"The last thing I want you to worry about is that I'll treat this baby unfairly because of his parentage."

I wrapped my arms around his neck, burying my face in his chest, thankful once again that I'd accepted his offer. "I don't. If I'd had one speck of doubt, you wouldn't be here now."

We sat like that for a moment—my head nestled against him, his arm around my back, and his other hand resting on my huge belly between us.

The baby moved and he pulled back. "He kicked me. That was a strong one."

I laughed, and he put his hand on my stomach as the baby moved again.

"He's gonna be a football player," Joe said.

"Not a chance," I said. "I'm not riskin' my baby gettin' a concussion. If you want to go to the high school football games, he can be in the band."

"A band geek?"

I shot him a glare. "You got a problem with that?"

Joe grinned down at me. "None at all. No football, but if he's gonna be in the band, can he at least play the sax?"

I laughed. "We'll let him decide. We have to promise not to pressure him into doing anything he doesn't want to do."

He turned serious. "We'll support him no matter what choices he makes."

Suddenly, I could see our lives together so clearly—Joe, me, and our baby. I saw Joe and I sitting together, watching him grow. Joe and I holding hands. His arm wrapped around my back.

I saw us *together*. As a couple.

And I liked it. I liked the life I saw with Joe. I liked the thought of the three of us having a loving, happy home. And the thought of having more babies with Joe.

But I couldn't bring it up now. There was too much going on. And I didn't want to propose this after seeing James for fear Joe would get the wrong message. I needed him to know he wasn't some sort of panic rebound.

Chapter Thirteen

I didn't sleep well. Between my anxiety and my heartburn, I tossed and turned until I finally got up around midnight and went downstairs for a glass of water. Muffy came down with me, and I turned off the security alarm to let her out the back door.

The water didn't help, so I slipped on a pair of boots I kept by the back door, pulled a sweater from the coat tree over my nightgown, and followed her outside. She sniffed around the back of the house for a few seconds, but then her back stiffened and she raced around the corner of the house toward the front yard.

I followed her, worried about what she'd found and whether it would hurt her. Joe had found evidence of a raccoon getting into the trash the week before, and I knew Muffy wouldn't back down if she came face-to-face with one.

But it wasn't a raccoon she was running after—it was a car. A station wagon was parked on the side of the driveway under the shadows of the trees by the county road, its lights off and its nose pointed toward the house.

And Muffy was tearing toward it.

Despite the dim light, I recognized the station wagon. I'd seen this car, and the woman who drove it, twice before. The first time was back in December. Vera had come into the nursery holding a little boy, but she'd reacted strangely to my offer to help. Then, out of nowhere, she'd revealed that she knew my pseudonym: the Lady in Black. I probably would have been able to get more information from her, but a vision had stolen over me of Vera hiding in a closet with a little girl, scared to death of the man calling out to her.

When I'd blurted out my vision—*He's gonna kill you*—she'd freaked out and run off. I'd attempted to follow and had fallen instead, breaking my clavicle and scaring everyone to death. The next time had happened a couple of months later—I'd noticed her sitting in the driver's seat of the station wagon outside the nursery. But she'd torn out of the parking lot before I could approach her or get her license plate number.

And now she was parked in my driveway at midnight.

"Muffy!" I shouted as my little dog ran for the car. "Come back!"

The headlights turned on and the engine started.

Muffy continued running for the car.

"*Muffy!*"

The light in Joe's bedroom flicked on.

The car shot forward, kicking up gravel as it headed for Muffy. Then the car swerved sharply, perhaps because the driver saw Muffy, or perhaps because she was simply desperate to escape, but it was too late.

As the station wagon skidded sideways, its back tires spinning out, Muffy disappeared underneath it.

"*Muffy!*" My foot slipped on the wet grass and my arms flailed as I tried to keep from falling. Once I had my balance, I raced after her again.

The front door burst open and Joe ran out, in pajama bottoms and a T-shirt, chasing after me on bare feet as the car sped toward the county road and spun left, barely slowing down, its tires squealing on the pavement.

"*Muffy!*" I screamed, trying to see her in the darkness.

Joe gained on me and wrapped his arms around my chest from behind, pulling me to a halt, but I fought against him, trying to break free.

"Rose," he said, his voice breaking. "Stop. What happened?"

"That car..." I hiccupped through a sob. "It ran over...Muffy."

"Stay here!" He released his hold on me and took off running toward the road, calling her name. I followed, slower this time, partially out of fear I'd fall and partially because I was terrified of what I'd find.

Joe dropped to the ground, murmuring softly, and I heard Muffy whimper.

"Rose, get my car keys and my shoes," Joe said, his voice strained. "And a towel."

I started to ask him how bad she looked, but I was too scared to hear the answer.

I took off for the house. I ran inside and grabbed Joe's shoes by the front door, plus a clean towel from the laundry basket in the kitchen. I snatched my keys from the bowl by the door, then locked up the house and drove my truck to Joe, who was still kneeling in the gravel.

I pulled to a stop, and I got out of the truck, hurrying over with the towel. "How bad is she?"

"I'm not sure," he said, laying the towel on the ground. "But I already called the vet. He's gonna meet us at his office."

He scooped her up and lifted her onto the towel. She released a loud whimper, which made me start to cry again.

I couldn't lose her. Muffy had been with me since my new life had begun. Since Momma had died. She'd been with me when my heart had been broken, and she'd been with me through my greatest joys. She was as much a part of me as my hand, and I couldn't imagine my life without her. A sob wracked my body.

Joe looked up at me as he wrapped the towel around her. "Rose. You okay to drive or do you want me to?"

I hesitated. "I can drive."

"Okay, good," he said, scooping her up and holding her tight to his chest, "because I plan to hold her, and I wasn't sure whether you'd be able to."

I knew he was talking about my stomach, which was a fair concern. I opened the passenger door, and Joe climbed in. I shut the door and got into the truck, then finally shot a glance at Muffy. Her head stuck out of the towel and I could see blood on her fur.

Dread flooded me, and it must have shown in my eyes, because Joe spoke to me in a low, calming voice. "Rose," he said, "it's gonna be okay."

I nodded, because I couldn't let myself fall apart. Muffy needed me to get her to the vet's.

I started driving, gripping the steering wheel with both hands.

"What happened?" Joe asked. "What was Muffy doin' outside?"

"I couldn't sleep," I said, trying to settle down. "I had bad heartburn, so I went downstairs to get some water. It didn't help, so I figured I'd take Muffy out back, but she must have sensed the car, because all of a sudden she took off running for the front of the house."

"Why didn't you come inside as soon as you saw the car?" he asked in a panic. "Your niece and nephew are missin', Rose. What if whoever took them is tryin' to kidnap you next?"

"I wasn't thinkin' about that," I admitted with a sniff. "I was only thinkin' of Muffy. She ran right for the car. I kept calling her back, but she wouldn't listen."

He pushed out a breath, and I wasn't sure if it was in relief or frustration. "She's gonna be okay. She's a tough little dog."

I glanced over at her, worried that she lay so still, releasing a tiny whimper every few seconds. "You said Levi's going to meet us there?"

"Yes," Joe said. "Sounded like he was still awake."

While I saw Levi's sister at least once a week given our arrangement with the horses, I hadn't seen Levi since last year. We'd gone on a few dates at the beginning of the summer, but it had never gotten serious—nowhere approaching it—so it hadn't been too awkward to end things. I'd chosen James, although Levi hadn't known that. I'd told him I wasn't ready to move on after the end of my relationship with Mason. He might think I was a bit of a hypocrite given Joe had moved in with me a few months later, and I'd discovered I was pregnant a few months after that, but I wasn't worried about facing him. He was a professional, and he loved Muffy.

In fact, what struck me most about my short trip down memory lane was that my relationship with James, which had shaped my life in so many ways, had been so short.

"Did you recognize the car?" Joe asked as he turned slightly, causing Muffy to whimper again. "Do you know who it was?"

"I think it was that woman who showed up at the nursery." I'd been concerned enough to tell Joe about her both times I'd seen her before. "Or at least it was her station wagon. The car was parked under the trees, and I couldn't see inside."

"She was watchin' the house?" he asked.

"I guess."

Flashing lights from a sheriff cruiser approached from the other side of the road. Joe's phone rang and he answered it with, "Simmons." He was silent for a moment, listening, and then said, "We're on our way to the vet now. Rose is with me. I want you to do a thorough search of the property and be on the lookout for the same late model station wagon I had you looking for a few months ago. Let me know what you find out." He paused, then said, "Thanks, Benson," before he hung up.

"You already called it in?" I asked.

"Someone was on your property and hurt our dog," he said in a growl while tenderly holding Muffy. "Of course I already called it in."

Our dog.

Warmth filtered into my heart, but guilt was fast behind it. I couldn't help but think I'd brought this on us by traipsing around in a black hat and heels.

"I'm sorry," I said to both Muffy and Joe. "This is all my fault. That woman came to see the Lady in Black. She was here because I couldn't leave well enough alone."

"Rose, it's not your fault," Joe said emphatically. "In fact, given the timing, I suspect it has something to do with Mike."

"But she knew I was the Lady in Black."

"It doesn't mean anything."

I was too upset to reason this through right now. "How's Muffy?" I asked, my voice breaking.

"She's hanging in there," he said. "Her breathing is steady and she's lookin' at me."

I glanced over and saw the top of her head in the glow of the dashboard lights, her bloody face pointed toward his.

I sped up, driving over the speed limit, figuring that this was truly an emergency and I had the chief deputy sheriff with me. When I pulled into the parking lot of the veterinary clinic, the lights were on and Levi's truck was parked in front. Joe jumped out and raced for the door, Muffy in his arms, and Levi opened it before he reached it. They were already in an exam room by the time I got inside.

Muffy was lying on the table, the towel unwrapped. Blood soaked her mangled back leg and covered her head. Her entire body was shaking. She saw me walk in and began to whine.

I nearly lost it again, but I told myself I had to be strong for her. I could fall apart later.

"How bad is it?" I asked, walking closer but afraid to touch her. The last thing I wanted to do was hurt her any worse.

"That's what we're trying to figure out," Levi said in a calm voice as he pulled the stethoscope from around his neck.

She whimpered as he pressed it to her chest, keeping her gaze on me, but I was still too scared to touch her.

"Did you see what happened?" Levi asked as he moved the stethoscope to her side.

"Uh…" I said, pressing a hand to my chest. "She ran toward a car parked in the driveway. I told her to stop, but she just kept running. She seemed intent on chasing it down. Then the driver pulled forward and started to make a U-turn, and she was going so fast she couldn't stop—Muffy went right under the car." I took a breath to keep from breaking down. "Joe heard me yellin' and came runnin' out and took over after that."

"Did you see her get run over by a wheel?"

"No."

Levi nodded as he studied Muffy. She yelped as he lightly pressed on her belly.

"I'd like to get some x-rays," he said. "Margi's on her way in to help, but Muffy's back leg is clearly broken, and I suspect that she has some internal injuries. Her abdomen is distended and painful to the touch."

"Oh no," I cried out.

Levi gave me a soft smile. "The x-rays will tell me if she has any other broken bones and what we might be looking at. We'll go from there, okay?"

I nodded. "Yeah. Of course."

Levi smiled down at Muffy. "I'm gonna pick you up, girl. This might hurt, but I'll be as gentle as possible."

He rewrapped her in the bloody towel, then slid his arms under her body and picked her up. She let out a yelp, then whined as Levi cooed and murmured what a good dog she was, carrying her through the door to the back.

As soon as he walked out, Joe asked, "You okay?"

"Yeah," I said, trying not to be hurt that he'd stayed on the other side of the room. I wanted so badly for him to pull me into a hug. I needed to feel his arms around me. But while he moved closer, he didn't reach out.

Still, his voice was tender as he said, "She's gonna be okay, darlin'."

"I never should have let her outside," I said, starting to cry. "But I was up, and she wanted out and no one's bothered us at the farm lately…"

"This is not your fault," he said in a firm tone.

"I tried to get her to come back."

"She must have sensed danger. She was tryin' to protect you."

I still wanted his comfort, and part of me wanted to make the first move, but he was wrestling with the demons I'd brought to his front door. If he wanted space, I had to give it to him.

Levi cleared his throat from the doorway.

"What's the word, Romano?" Joe asked stiffly, and I could hear the fear in his voice.

He gave Joe a grim look, which he then shifted to me. "In addition to the break in her leg, she has internal bleeding and some broken bones in her pelvis. I need to do surgery."

I nodded, tears flooding my eyes again. "Of course."

His stance softened. "I'll do everything I can for her, Rose. I swear it."

"I know." I trusted him with my dog's life. Literally.

"Why don't you and Joe head home and I'll call you when we finish. I have no idea how long the surgery will take, and she won't be able to go home for a few days." A wary look washed over his face before he said, "I hate to bring this up, but I need to know if you have a financial limit for her care. We're looking at over a thousand dollars for certain, likely more. I can call you once I have a better idea."

"No limit," Joe said, his voice tight. "Whatever it takes."

Levi gave Joe a warm smile. "I'll do everything I can, and I'll call you with updates."

"Rose doesn't have her phone right now," Joe said. "Call mine."

Levi nodded and jotted Joe's number on a paper towel. Before I knew it, he was heading toward the back. Which when I realized we wouldn't be seeing Muffy again tonight.

"I don't get to tell her goodbye?" I asked Joe, wishing I'd rubbed her head or at least touched her so she knew that I loved her.

"There's no need to tell her goodbye when we're going to see her tomorrow morning."

I had to believe him because I couldn't handle losing someone else I loved.

Chapter
Fourteen

Joe wanted to get back to the farm and meet with his men, but he was worried about bringing me with him, so he'd convinced me to stay at Jed and Neely Kate's house. Under normal circumstances, I would have protested that I wasn't a fragile flower in need of protection, but frankly, I was out of fight. Between Ashley and Mikey's disappearance, my encounter with James, the distance with Joe, and then Muffy...all I wanted to do was sleep.

Joe called Jed as we headed north to fill him in on what had happened and to let him know he was dropping me off. We pulled into their driveway a few minutes later, and warm light shone through multiple windows of their two-story white home. Neely Kate must have been watching for us because the front door burst open as we pulled up in front and she ran out to greet us.

"I've got her, Joe," she said, opening my door. He hesitated for a moment, but then he nodded and went in to talk to Jed, several feet from the car and out of earshot.

As soon as I got out of the truck, Neely Kate gave me that hug I'd been wanting, wrapping her arms tightly around me and squeezing. I wanted to cry all over again, but I'd just about cried myself out.

"How's Muffy?" she asked in my ear, her voice breaking.

I shook my head as she pulled away. "I don't know. Levi's operating on her. He's going to call Joe as soon as he knows something."

She nodded, looking grim, as she led me through the front door. "Jed said it was the station wagon from the nursery."

"Yeah, but I couldn't see inside, so I'm not sure if it was Vera or someone else."

"Do you think it has anything to do with Ashley and Mikey?" she asked, stopping in the entryway.

I shook my head. "I have no idea, but Joe seems to think there's a connection because of the timing, if nothing else." I glanced out the front door to make sure Joe was still outside with Jed. "I take it you didn't find anything else in Mike's books?"

"Not much more than I already told you. It looks like he was gettin' cash payments and usin' them to pay off his debts, but he was pretty sloppy about recordin' them." She shrugged. "Still, there was nothin' to tie him to Hardshaw or anyone else."

"That's something, I guess. What about Calista? Because I know there's no way Jed backed off."

"Witt went to follow her, but she must have left early. He stayed until all the cars were gone and never caught sight of anyone who fit her description."

I nodded.

She started to tug me toward the kitchen. "Can I get you something to eat or drink? I made an angel food cake."

I shook my head. "I just want to go to bed."

Giving me a worried look, she said, "I got the guest bed ready. In fact, I got it ready earlier, when Joe said you might be staying with us."

I grimaced as I headed for the stairs. "Yeah, I've got plenty to tell you tomorrow." I was halfway up the stairs when I stopped and turned back to face her at the bottom. "I don't have my phone. Can you tell Joe to call you or Jed to let me know when he hears about Muffy? If I'm asleep, wake me up."

"Yeah," she said. "Of course."

Since I'd stayed in the guest room before, I knew where I was going. I entered the cheery room with its red and white toile comforter and the stuffed red chair in front of a window draped with white sheer curtains that matched the white plantation shutters. My feet sank into the soft red and white rug when I kicked off my boots. Then I slipped out of my sweater and tossed it onto a chair. Since I was still wearing my nightgown, I pulled back the crisp white sheets and climbed under the covers. I was heartbroken but too tired and shell-shocked to cry. Instead, I closed my eyes and drifted off to sleep, wondering how God had seen fit to give me a baby when I'd proven I couldn't even take care of a dog.

I wasn't sure how long I'd slept, because the next thing I knew, Neely Kate was softly calling my name. "Rose. Joe's on the line. He has news about Muffy."

I tried to sit up, but it was too much of a struggle, so I just took the phone, staring up at the ceiling. The baby rolled to his or her side and kicked softly as though they were trying to reach out and comfort me. I placed my hand on my belly, feeling an even deeper connection to the soul inside me. "Is she okay?"

Joe hesitated before tentatively saying, "She's out of surgery."

"But is she okay?"

"Levi said he was going to stay at the clinic to watch her."

"But she's gonna be okay, right?" I pleaded.

"She has a couple of broken bones, her right back leg and her pelvis, and there were internal injuries. He cleaned up what he could."

"Joe," I said, my voice breaking. "You're scarin' me. Did Levi say she was going to be okay?"

"He said it's gonna be touch and go for a bit."

"Did he give you any odds?"

He hesitated again. "No. I asked, but he wouldn't say."

I sucked in a breath.

"We're done at the farm," he said quietly. "We didn't find anything to help us figure out who did this, but we're still lookin' for the station wagon."

"Thank you."

"I know you've got Neely Kate and Jed…" He paused. "I can come over and be with you if you want. Or I can leave you be. You tell me what you want, Rose."

I'd spent months alone. Months of suffering with anxiety over James's reaction to my pregnancy, over his refusal to sign the papers. Months of lonely solitude.

I didn't regret the time alone. It had given me a chance to figure out the mess of thoughts in my head, but I'd realized that I didn't need to do everything alone. It was okay to ask for help from the people in my life. Wanting comfort from Joe didn't make me weak. It made me human. The real question was whether it was fair to him. Right or wrong, I was too selfish to care at the moment.

"I want you to come over," I whispered.

His voice softened. "I'll be right there."

I hung up and handed the phone back to Neely Kate, then wrestled myself into a sitting position, propping two pillows behind me. "Muffy has a broken leg and pelvis and internal injuries. Levi's not sure if she's gonna make it, and he's staying at the clinic to watch her."

Tears filled her eyes. "Oh, no."

"She's a tough little dog," I said resolutely. "If anyone can pull through this, she can."

She nodded. "Definitely." She gave me a long look. "Joe's comin' over?"

"Yeah. I hope that's okay."

"Of course it's okay." Then she said carefully, "The question is, do you want me to make up a bed on the sofa for him?"

"No. I'd like him to sleep with me, if he's willin'." I quickly added, "But we're not havin' sex."

She chuckled. "I didn't think you would be."

"The labor and delivery nurse suggested it the other day. She told Joe it might kick-start labor." I gave her a wry grin. "So apparently it's *possible*."

She grinned. "Huh."

"Even so," I said, "we're not havin' sex. We haven't even kissed."

She was silent for a moment. "But you've been tempted." When my eyes widened, she said, "We've spent a lot of time with you two... Rose, Joe's in love with you."

"I know." It was true. Even if I'd refused to acknowledge it until just a few days ago.

"The question is whether you're in love with him. I know you love him, but are you *in love*? Because you have to be sure before you act on it."

Glancing down at the bed, I said, "I have feelings for Joe, but I can't sort out what it means. Or whether it's just because I want a family. He deserves better than someone who doesn't know her own mind." I lifted my gaze. "I saw James tonight. Or I guess last night."

Her eyes bugged out. "*What?*"

"I'm sick of playing games. I wanted to ask him about Mike and the papers stolen from the lawyer's office. It was time."

"Where did you meet him?" she asked in disbelief. "How?"

"I went to his house. I waited for him to show up."

Confusion filled her eyes—she knew as well as I did that he didn't stay in his house every night. Then she sighed. "Thursday." She obviously remembered our schedule. "Did he threaten you?"

"No," I said, getting pissed again, "but he didn't tell me much either. He did confirm that Mike works for Hardshaw, and he suggested Denny Carmichael has a role in this mess."

"Denny Carmichael?" she asked in disbelief.

"I know. He may have said that just to throw me off, but I'm sure James knows something about the kidnapping."

"And he didn't tell you anything solid to help you find them." It wasn't a question.

My heart felt heavy. "No."

"Did he say anything about the baby?"

"No, not really. And he refused to address the paternity papers."

"Are you gonna tell Joe?"

"I already did."

Her eyes flew wide. The fact that she'd expected me to keep it a secret only underlined how badly I'd handled everything up until now.

"No more secrets. He needed to know. I told him about the papers too."

"How did he handle it?"

"He said he's the baby's father and worryin' about our baby is part of his job. He said I was cheatin' him out of fatherhood."

She gave me a sad smile. "He's turned into a really great guy."

"Then why do you look so distraught?"

"Because I'm worried you're gonna hurt him."

It wasn't a good sign that I was worried about that too. "I'm not goin' back to James, Neely Kate. He doesn't want me anyway. But Joe deserves someone who loves him with everything she's worth. I'm not sure I'm there yet."

"There's all sorts of loves, Rose," she said quietly, stroking my hair. "There's hot and fiery. There's calm and steady. And then there's dysfunctional."

I sighed again. "You're talkin' about James with that last one."

"I think you're still hung up on him." When I started to respond, she held up a hand. "I'm not judgin' you. What you had with him was epic, but I think you need to ask yourself if it's real."

"*Was* real," I said. "Past tense."

"Okay," she conceded, even though she didn't look totally convinced. "*Was* real."

"The last time we were together, I told him that very thing. That we were just pretendin' to have a relationship. He tried to tell me I was wrong, but I know better. We were sneakin' around the whole time, actin' like we were doin' something wrong."

"It's more complicated than that, and you know it."

"Maybe so," I said, my back stiffening. "But I'm havin' a baby, Neely Kate. That changes *everything*. The thing is, James was very clear about what he wanted—and didn't want—from the beginning. I can't fault him for that," I said. "I got caught up in… *us*. But other than our trip to Shreveport, our entire relationship was confined to his house."

"Jed and I weren't public at first," she said, "and what we have is real."

"But even then you talked about the future," I said, grabbing her arm. "You actually made *plans*. James and I never planned ahead further than the next time we were going to be together." When she still didn't look convinced, my anger flared. "You never approved of my relationship with James. Why are you pushin' me on this now?"

"Because I think you need to ask yourself who you're tryin' to convince," she said, tears filling her eyes, "me or you."

"*Neely Kate.*"

"I love you," she said emphatically. "You're the sister of my heart, and I will stand by you no matter *what* you do, but I love Joe too. He's taken his brother role seriously and then some. I'm worried he's gonna get hurt in all of this. The kind of hurt that doesn't go away."

She was voicing my own fears.

She must have sensed that I was close to the breaking point, because she leaned forward and hugged me tight. "Maybe now's not the time to sort everything out. Joe's not goin' anywhere, and it sounds like James isn't swoopin' in to lay claim to you or the baby. You've got time to figure it out."

"Yeah," I said, realizing she had a point. I didn't need to have all the answers yet. But I couldn't help but feel angry with myself that it wasn't more clear-cut. James may not have kicked me out of his house, but he hadn't exactly tried to smooth things over. He didn't want me or the baby, and even if he did, would I still want him?

The answer should have been an adamant *no*, but instead it was a big question mark.

"I've got time," I said, maybe more for myself than for her.

So why did it feel like I didn't?

"Can I get you anything?" she asked. "Water? A snack? A crystal ball?"

I released a tiny laugh. "No."

She stood and started to walk out, then stopped in the doorway. "Everything's gonna be okay."

"There's an awful lot of bad stuff goin' on for you to make a proclamation like that."

"I know," she said with a soft smile. "But one way or the other, it's still gonna be okay."

It was the one way or the other part that had me worried.

Joe walked in as she was leaving, my overnight bag slung over his shoulder. He gave me a hesitant look in the doorway. "I grabbed a few things for you, but I'm not sure I grabbed the *right* things."

I started to scoot off the bed. "Thank you. I'm sure it will be fine."

"What do you need?" he asked, still standing in the doorway. "I'll get it for you."

"Unless you've figured out how to pee for me, I think I need to do this myself."

He grinned, but it was still guarded. "You're on your own with that one."

"That's what I figured." I headed to the bathroom, then washed up and went back to the guest room.

Joe had kicked off his shoes and was sitting at the end of the bed with a stack of linens on his lap. When I gave him a questioning look, he said, "I didn't want to bother Neely Kate or Jed, so I grabbed a blanket and a pillow to sleep on the sofa. I was waiting for you to come back so I could say goodnight."

"Will you sleep with me tonight?" I asked, hating myself for being weak, and just when I'd realized that I still had to get my head on straight. "I don't want to be alone."

"Of course." He sat back on the bed and waited for me to climb in next to him, but he was still stiff and guarded.

Why had I asked him to do this? What kind of monster was I? But I decided it was the mother of his baby asking—*she* was the one who needed comfort.

"My heartburn came back, so I need to sit up," I said as I sat on the edge of the bed.

"Not a problem," he said, reaching out an arm and tugging me next to him.

I lay my head on his chest as he held me close. Sinking into him, I took in the familiar scent of his shampoo, which filled me with comfort and strength.

I wasn't the person I had been last summer. Just like I wasn't the person I'd been two years ago before Momma had died. My life had been a roller coaster, and each drop and rise had changed me.

Joe shifted, pulling me closer, and I burrowed into him as his presence filled me with a peace and comfort I'd never known with James.

Maybe that was my answer after all.

Chapter
Fifteen

I woke up before Joe, needing to pee. The sun was beginning to rise, so I grabbed the bag Joe had packed and took it to the restroom. I peed and got dressed, smiling to myself when I saw that he'd packed a pair of regular underwear instead of my maternity panties. At least he'd chosen a maternity dress I could fit into. There wasn't any makeup, but I didn't wear much these days.

When I finished, I took my bag downstairs and pulled out my phone. After I got a glass of water, I went out to the screened-in porch off the kitchen and sat at the small round table.

Birdsong filled the air as I pulled up Levi's number and sent him a text.

Just checking on, Muffy. Thank you for taking such good care of her.

To my surprise, my phone rang seconds later, and Levi's name came up on the screen.

"I hope I didn't disturb you," I said as I answered.

"I was already awake," he said, sounding tired. "And don't be feeling guilty. I have another animal that spent the night and needed some attention. Muffy's hanging in there. I repaired her broken pelvis and leg as well as her internal injuries. She's holding her own right now. I'd like to keep her for a few days and make sure she's stabilized before I send her home."

"Of course. Can I come see her?"

"Sure," he said. "Feel free to come whenever you like. I'll be here."

"Thanks, Levi. You have no idea how much I appreciate everything you've done."

"Just doin' my job, Rose. Muffy's a special dog, so I confess that I have a personal interest in her recovery."

I hung up and walked around to the front of the house. Joe's sheriff's car was parked on the curb, and I wasn't surprised to see him descending the porch steps, rubbing his hand over his tousled hair. The hem of his shirt lifted, giving me a glimpse of his stomach, and a jolt of electricity shot through me. I'd touched that chest, caressed it, but I hadn't felt like this for a long, long time.

His gaze caught mine. "You look startled. Sorry to catch you off guard."

I was definitely caught off guard, just not in the way he thought.

"Just a little jumpy," I said. "I couldn't sleep, so I texted Levi, who promptly called and said Muffy is holding her own. We can go see her as soon as we like."

He stood at the bottom of the stairs and glanced over his shoulder, then turned back to me. "How about I take a quick shower and then we head over now?"

"Thanks, Joe."

"Hey, I'm eager to see her too."

Ten minutes later, we were both ready to go. Neely Kate and Jed still hadn't come out of their room, so I left a note telling them what was going on and promised to check in later.

The car ride was silent for a few minutes, until I spoke. "Despite James saying his interest in Mark Erickson was pure curiosity, I'm guessing Mark's murder had something to do with Mike and the kids' disappearance. Did you find out anything about Calista?"

Something flickered on his face, but I wasn't sure if it was my mention of James or what I'd said. Still, he kept his eyes on the road. "I can't discuss an active investigation, Rose. You know that."

Lips pursed together, I gave it some thought, then asked, "If you knew it *didn't* have anything to do with Mike, would you tell me?"

"Let me handle the investigation." He didn't sound angry, but he definitely didn't sound happy. When he turned to me, his eyes were dark. "The Lady in Black needs to sit this one out. Especially given what Malcolm said about Denny Carmichael."

I shook my head. "I know there are things you aren't telling me."

"It doesn't matter. You're in no condition to deal with this right now."

That made me bristle. "And if I wasn't in this *condition*, would you let me deal with it?"

"You know I've never been one hundred percent behind your...activities. It's one step removed from vigilantism." He shot me another dark look. "And that's bein' generous."

Now didn't seem like the time to point out the good I'd done as the Lady in Black, especially since I agreed that he had a point—I had no business running around the county in my black hat this close to going into labor...not that I'd used the hat in over a year. Every criminal in the county knew I was the Lady in Black. The disguise was no longer necessary.

"I'm not gonna run around as Lady," I said. "I'm just askin' questions."

"And I understand why you're askin', so long as you don't get teed off that I can't answer."

Neither of us said anything for the rest of the drive, and my thoughts turned to Denny Carmichael. I hadn't seen or heard from him in months. Last fall he'd told me that I owed him a favor for saving my life, but he'd yet to collect. The last thing I wanted was for Denny to come anywhere near my baby. While James had always been adamant that he would never harm children to do his bidding, I was fairly certain Denny Carmichael wouldn't say the same.

Joe pulled up in front of the veterinary clinic and we both got out. As we walked toward the door, he stopped and turned to face me with a pained expression.

"I don't like fightin' with you."

I looked up at him in surprise. "Were we fightin'?"

"No, not outright, but we're definitely at odds."

"So we have different perspectives on the situation. That's happened before. We're still in this together."

He started to say something, then stopped, but determination flashed through his eyes, and he started again. Eyes on mine, he asked, "And what exactly are we in together?"

My breath caught. If he'd picked up on my changing feelings, he had to be confused. I'd suggested we talk last night, and then I'd run off and met with James. "I'm still sortin' that out, Joe."

He nodded with a grave expression. "Fair enough."

He turned and left me to follow.

Joe knocked on the locked front door, and Levi appeared shortly afterward with dark circles under his eyes.

"She's still pretty groggy," he said as he led us into the back. "Her temperature is a little low, so I have her under a warming blanket, and I've got her on some powerful pain meds to make her more comfortable."

We walked into a room with multiple metal cages, and I spotted Muffy in the middle, lying on a fuzzy blanket. An IV bag hung on the door and a plastic tube led from it into her leg, which was wrapped with adhesive tape. Levi carefully opened the door, murmuring, "Your momma's here to see you, Muffy."

Her head stirred slightly, but her eyes were unfocused as I crept closer. She was wrapped in the blanket he'd mentioned, and I could only see her head and her front legs.

"Hey, girl." I glanced up at Levi. "Where can I touch her that won't hurt?"

"Her head's a little bruised, so maybe one of her front feet or legs."

I took her paw in my hand, rubbing my thumb over the pad of her foot. "You scared me to death," I said, my voice breaking. "You can't go running after cars, girl. You have to come back when I call you." Then I realized I was chastising her, which was the last thing I wanted to do. She needed to know—*I* needed her to know—how much I loved her. "I can't live without you, Muff. You have to promise that you won't do anything like that again. Please, please don't do anything like that again."

Usually she would have responded in some way, but she just lay still, her chest rising and falling.

"Joe's here," I said as a tear rolled down my cheek. "He wants to see you too."

I stepped back to let Joe get closer. He squatted down next to her and whispered something I couldn't make out. He stayed with her for a few more seconds, softly stroking her leg, before moving to the side and making room for me too.

We stood there like that for a while, side by side, both of us telling her what a good girl she was and how much we wanted her to come home. After a couple of minutes, I could see she was tired and struggling to keep her eyes open, so I told her how much I loved her and that I'd be back later.

"You can come back," Levi said carefully, "but maybe later this afternoon. I'm not sure if you noticed, but she was fighting off sleep to keep watch on you." He gave me a sad smile. "She still thinks she needs to protect you."

A fresh round of tears filled my eyes. "So she can't rest if I'm here."

"It's only a guess," he admitted sheepishly. "But I suspect she'll fall into a deep sleep as soon as you leave."

"And she needs her sleep to recover," I said.

He nodded.

Pushing out a breath, I said, "I'll do whatever I need to do to help her."

Joe and I left, still in silence but for a different reason this time.

"She almost died," he said once we were in the car.

"I know," I whispered.

He gripped the steering wheel but didn't turn on the engine. "I'm scared, Rose."

His admission caught me by surprise. "What are you scared of?"

"That I won't be a good father. That I'll screw this up like my own father did. I couldn't protect Muffy...what makes me think I can protect a helpless baby?"

"Hey," I said, turning to face him. I almost took his hand but stopped myself, Neely Kate's words still fresh on my mind. "I'm scared too. In fact, if anyone's to blame for Muffy's accident, it's me. I let her out to pee. I didn't put her on a leash."

"We never put her on a leash on the farm," he protested.

"Then I should have trained her to obey better," I said. "I called her multiple times to come back and she didn't. This is my fault, not yours."

"We're both wrong," he said, a look of resolve washing over his face as he turned on the car. "The only person at fault was whoever was driving that station wagon, and I'm gonna find 'em."

Chapter Sixteen

Neither of us spoke during the drive back to the farm, but it wasn't our usual comfortable silence of two people who knew each other well. It was filled with a strained tension that put me on edge.

When he dropped me off so I could get my truck, he told me that he'd be sure to check his phone in case I needed him before he came home.

I got out, then leaned into the open door. "Joe," I said insistently, "you're gonna be a great daddy. An amazing daddy. Please don't doubt that."

He gave me a tight smile. "Thanks. Now get to work safe. I don't want to worry about you out here."

The only reason he'd agreed to leave me alone was because I had a landscaping appointment coming up. I needed my truck.

I shut the door and he drove away, leaving me with the overwhelming sense of loss. Muffy's accident was hitting me hard, so I walked around the back of the house, left my bag on the back steps, and made my way to the barn. The horses nuzzled my hands for apples—which I didn't have—and seemed to look past me, looking for Muffy.

As I rubbed their faces and necks, I pondered what James had told me about Denny Carmichael. If he'd truly played some role in either Mark's murder or the kids' disappearance, Lady would have more luck getting information than Joe would. Still, while I could see the sense in not actively pursuing this myself, it didn't mean I couldn't get the advice of a friend.

I fished my cell phone out of my pocket and pulled up Dermot's number.

"Long time no talk," he said when he answered. "Not that I'm complainin'."

"I've missed you too," I teased.

"I take it you've got something on your mind."

"Feelin' up to a chat?" I asked.

He was silent for several seconds, then said, "You still makin' coffee even though you're due to have a baby at any time?"

"Sure am," I said. "I allow myself one cup a day and I haven't had one yet. Plus, I have some leftover cinnamon rolls."

"I'll be at your place in fifteen minutes."

Smiling to myself, I headed back to the house and washed my hands before getting the coffee going. I kept looking at my feet, expecting to see Muffy around me. My chest hurt, the fact that she was critically ill hitting me all over again. She'd make it. Muffy was a fighter. Just like me.

I had to believe that about both of us.

I was warming two of the cinnamon rolls when Dermot showed up at my back door. He knocked once as he peered through the window, then walked in.

"Word has it your niece and nephew are missin'," he said, heading straight to the coffee pot and picking up the mug I'd left out for him.

"Yeah," I said as I stood in front of the microwave. "I was wonderin' if you had any insight into that."

"Seems like we should ease our way into this conversation," he said with a grim smile. "You mentioned cinnamon rolls?"

I couldn't help but smile back.

Tim Dermot and I had known each other for less than a year. But I'd grown to trust him more than any other criminal in the county, even more than I'd trusted James when we'd been together, so that was saying something. He'd helped me bolster my neutral position in the crime world, and I'd accidently helped him take over his own organization. As I pulled the cinnamon rolls out of the microwave, I realized I should have called Dermot days ago.

I set his plate in front of him and sat down opposite him with mine. I'd already set down my coffee. "Did you ever hear anything about my brother-in-law, Mike, havin' something to do with Hardshaw?"

Dermot, whose concentration had been fixed on the gooey baked good in front of him, looked up with raised brows. "Hardshaw? What makes you presume there's a connection between them?"

"Why *didn't* we presume it earlier?" I asked. "Seems like we were all bein' shortsighted with that one."

A grim look covered his face.

"I saw Skeeter Malcolm last night and he confirmed it."

He shifted his gaze back to his cinnamon roll as he sawed off a piece. "I wondered how long that would take."

"Are we talking about Mike bein' with Hardshaw or me seeing James?"

"Malcolm. I wondered how long it would be before he tried to win you back."

"What's that supposed to mean?" I demanded, dropping the fork I'd just raised. "I really don't need this from you, Dermot."

He met my eyes again, his unreadable gaze holding mine. "I saw the way that man looked at you. Acted around you. I never thought he'd let you go so easily."

"Well, I went to him, not the other way around, make no mistake about *that*. And I only did it because of the kids. I wanted to find out what he knew about them, Mike, and the break-in at Violet's attorney's office."

"You're just now askin' him about that?" He finished off the cinnamon roll and glanced over at mine. "You gonna eat that?"

I shoved it over to him. "Consider it a bribe. I'm *not* discussin' my personal life with you."

He chuckled. "And who said we were?" His fork sliced through the cinnamon roll. "Look, Rose. Whether you like it or not, you dipped your toe into this world with that man holdin' your hand. He thinks he created you, and he's not gonna let you go as easy as it's seemed so far. He's just bidin' his time, waitin' to use you again."

Just like Denny Carmichael, and now I might have to approach him again too.

"Well, James didn't seem like he was fixin' to use me for anything anytime soon," I grumbled. "He wouldn't tell me crap. Except…" I took a breath and pushed it out. "He suggested that Mike might be tied to Denny Carmichael."

That caught Dermot by surprise. "Carmichael? He's flat-out against Hardshaw movin' in. So if Mike's workin' for Hardshaw, I can't imagine what he'd be doin' for Carmichael. Unless he was sellin' information to him."

My stomach roiled. Carmichael was not a man to get mixed up with.

"I need to talk to Denny," I said.

Dermot held up his hand. "Now hold on a minute. There's no call to be hasty."

"My six-year-old niece and three-year-old nephew are missin', Dermot. Hasty sounds pretty good to me right about now."

"There's a whole lot of other avenues we can go down first," Dermot said. "Like pursuing what happened to the electrician who was killed two nights ago. He worked for Mike on multiple projects. They definitely knew each other."

I nodded. I wasn't surprised. I also wasn't surprised Joe hadn't told me.

"From the outside, your brother-in-law looks squeaky clean, which is likely one of the reasons Hardshaw picked him, if he's really workin' for them. He's less likely to draw attention from the authorities."

"I heard"—I couldn't tell him it was from Mason—"that he did some work for Sonder Tech, a company out of Dallas. They sought out my landscaping company to do work for them soon afterward, which seems like a strange coincidence. Do you know anything about that?"

He rubbed his chin in thought. "Any connection between Sonder Tech and Hardshaw is a loose one."

"The owner is friends with Tony Roberts, one of the Hardshaw Three."

I told him about visiting Sonder Tech the day before, and Stewart's reaction to my suggestion that the bushes had been poisoned—seemingly genuine shock—and then about the incident with Calista (leaving out the mortifying parts). "Jed sent Witt to follow her and see who she was going to meet, but by the time he got there, Calista was already gone."

"Has Jed done any more diggin'?"

"Last I heard, he's concentrating on goin' through Mike's books."

His brow shot up. "You got ahold of Mike's books?"

"We had a little help. Neely Kate says they haven't found anything useful yet, but it looks like he was gettin' cash payments and usin' them to pay off bills. He wasn't very careful."

"Probably figured no one would look." He rested his hand on the table. "What do you want me to do?"

"That's not why I asked you here, Dermot. I was hoping for information from the criminal underworld, and you've already been helpful."

"Two innocent kids are missin' due to the idiocy of their father," Dermot said, his voice hard. "If I can do something, I will."

A lump formed in my throat, the contrast between James's reaction and Dermot's as profound as night and day. But something else occurred to me, and I wasn't sure what to make of it.

Dermot was everything Fenton County needed—level-headed, firm but empathetic, direct. James had not been any of those things lately. Was Dermot hoping to usurp his position in the underworld? Was he using me to do it?

Was that such a bad thing after all?

I took a drink of my now-cold coffee, then said, "I want to keep Jed, Neely Kate, and Witt out of any kind of investigation. Joe's watchin' this too closely. You'll need to be careful."

"I'm always careful."

I knew that from plenty of firsthand experience. "We need to find out more about Mark Erickson. Calista's connected to Sonder Tech *and* Mark, so we need to find out what she knows." I held his gaze. "But we can't take goin' to see Carmichael off the table."

His lips pursed, but he nodded. "Agreed."

"And if I go to see him, I'll need backup."

His face softened. "There's no need for you to go. I'll handle it if it comes to that."

"They're my niece and nephew." My chest tightened. "Maybe we're goin' about this wrong. Maybe we need to go to him first."

"A day's not bound to make much of a difference," he said.

"Tell that to those scared-to-death kids," I said, my voice breaking.

"Okay," he said, "you've got a point. But I'm not sure you're in any condition to be facin' Denny Carmichael."

He had a point too—Denny Carmichael wasn't likely to forget he thought I owed him a favor. I didn't want to let him use my niece and nephew as pawns, and yet...

"I may not have a choice, Dermot."

His lips twisted into a grim smile. "That's what I'm afraid of." Leaning forward, his gaze lowered to my stomach. "How far along are you? Thirty-seven? Thirty-eight weeks?"

"Thirty-eight."

"The baby's head down and engaged?"

I would have found his questions invasive, but he was a nurse practitioner and he'd done surgery on a boy's leg on this very table. "Down but not engaged. No dilation or effacement but plenty of Braxton Hicks contractions that have sent me to the ER twice. I felt like a fool."

His gaze softened. "My wife had plenty of those with her second pregnancy. We went three times for false labor before she made me start checking for dilation myself."

My mouth parted in shock. "You have a wife and kids?"

His eyes shuttered, leaving him emotionless. "Not anymore."

I had a million questions but knew better than to ask a single one. "Why the questions about my pregnancy?"

He released a quick puff of air. "In case I end up takin' you to see that maniac. I need to know what I'm dealin' with."

"I'm not goin' into labor on Denny Carmichael's property, Dermot." God forbid. I'd hold my legs together first.

"Like I said, I want to know what I'm dealin' with."

I couldn't blame him.

He started to get up, but I reached forward and put my hand over his. "There's one more thing."

Settling back onto his seat, he said in a careful tone, "Okay."

"Someone was on the property last night. I think they were watchin' the house. But I let Muffy out to pee at around midnight, and she took off runnin' after them." I took a deep breath, tamping down my emotion, and said, "They ran her over."

Dermot sat up straighter. "Is she okay?"

"I'm hoping she will be. The vet operated on her, and he's keepin' her for a few days to make sure she recovers."

"Damn," he said, rubbing his hand over his mouth. "Do you know who did it?"

"Maybe." I told him about Vera's strange visits and her old station wagon. "I couldn't see who was drivin', so I'm not sure if it was her."

His eyes darkened. "Every criminal knows better than to mess with you."

"I'm not sure the person who did this meant to mess with me. If it was Vera, she might have been here tryin' to work up the gumption to ask me for help."

"And ran over your dog in the process."

"We don't have enough information to know, Dermot. First, we need to find out who owns that station wagon. Joe did some searches back in February and came up with nothin'."

He nodded. "I'll do some diggin'."

"Thanks."

He started to get up again, then stopped, leaning forward. "I'm about to step on dangerous ground, Rose, but take it for what you will."

"Okay," I said slowly, already preparing myself for some kind of lecture.

"I'm not sure where you stand with Skeeter, but I will tell you one thing—if you're considering goin' back to him, you need to not only think twice, but four or five times. Rumor has it that his operation is involved with some South American drug cartels. Those people don't mess around."

Something in me seized up. What had James gotten himself into? But I shook the feeling off—he'd made his own bed. It had nothing to do with me anymore. It was even more confirmation that I needed to keep my baby as far from him as possible. I wanted no part of that life, and there was no way my baby could be part of it either.

"Is he dealin' with 'em through Hardshaw?"

"Probably," he said, "but it doesn't matter. You need to stay away from that shit. Move on. Marry the deputy sheriff. Have a good life." His voice cracked on the last words and a tight smile stretched the skin around his eyes. "Trust me on that, okay?"

"Thanks for your input, Tim," I said, wondering again what had happened to his family.

He got up and left without another word, and I realized Tim Dermot was just one more mystery to add to the pile.

Chapter
Seventeen

After Dermot left, I took a shower and got dressed in fresh clothes. Before I left for the day, I made sure my gun was in my purse and turned on the alarm.

Neely Kate called when I was in the truck, and I put her on speaker.

"How's Muffy?" she asked.

"Hangin' in there. She was fightin' to stay awake, so Levi said we should go and come back this afternoon."

"But she's gonna be okay, isn't she?"

"I hope so."

We were both silent for a moment. Then I said, "I talked to Dermot this morning."

"Oh, that was a good idea."

"He's gonna look into Mark Erickson, the murdered electrician." I hesitated, then said, "I'm going to go back out to the neighborhood where he was killed. I want to ask around and see if anyone knew if Erickson and Mike were involved in something on the side."

"I thought you were lettin' Joe handle it."

"He can work on things on his end, and we can do the same on ours." But it occurred to me that despite our escapade yesterday,

Neely Kate might be having second thoughts about investigating an active murder case on the sly. She and Jed were in the process of adopting a baby. She wouldn't want to jeopardize that, and I certainly didn't either.

"But on the other hand," I said, "it's probably a bad idea." I still intended to go, but this would give her a way out.

"Oh, no you don't," she said. "Don't you try to pull that on me. If you're bringin' it up, then you're plannin' on goin' over there—but not without me, you're not. I'm on my way to the nursery. Pick me up on your way there." Then she hung up.

That answered that.

Twenty minutes later, I pulled into the nursery parking lot, and Neely Kate walked out of the building and hopped into the passenger seat.

She gave me a frown. "I told Maeve about Muffy and she's pretty upset."

I felt terrible. I should have called and told her. She probably loved Muffy just as much as I did. "Is she mad at me for not lettin' her know?"

"Of course not. She's just worried." She turned to look at me. "Did Joe tell you anything more about his investigation?"

"No…" My voice broke. "He's pullin' away from me, Neely Kate."

She gasped. "What on earth makes you say that? He drove over to my house in the middle of the night so he could sleep by your side. That doesn't sound like pullin' away to me."

"Sure, he held me, because I'm the mother of his baby, but he wasn't there, you know? We've been so close for months now. He's living with me and I love havin' him there. I miss him when he works at night. But after I told him I went to see James, he pulled back."

"He's scared, Rose," she said quietly. "He's lost two babies, and you're weeks away from givin' him one, and then you suddenly go see James. He's probably scared you're goin' to snatch it all away from him."

I sucked in a breath. "I did it to find the kids, Neely Kate. If I wanted to see James, then I would have gone to see him months ago."

"Maybe Joe thinks you just needed an excuse to justify it."

I tried to swallow my hurt feelings, but I was sure I wasn't doing a good job. "Joe thinks that or *you* do?"

She was silent for several seconds before she turned to face me. "Tell me you don't still love James Malcolm."

Oh, how I wished I could. "I don't know if I do or not. I'm so confused."

"How did you feel when you saw him?"

I shrugged. "There was no burning desire to rekindle anything, if that's what you're askin'."

"But there's still something there?"

"I don't know what I feel."

She turned to face me even more directly while I concentrated on the road. "If he showed up at your front door tonight," she said softly, without a speck of judgment in her voice, "tellin' you he'd made a mistake and he wants a life with you and that baby—he's got a big ring, and he wants a wedding and a happily ever after…you have to make a decision on the spot—yes or no. What do you choose?"

I raked my teeth over my bottom lip.

"No thinkin' about it. Yes or no."

"No."

She pushed out a slow breath. "Why'd you say no?"

"Because even before this mess, a life with him would have been dangerous. All the same, some stupid part of me thought love could make it work." I shook my head in disgust, tightening my grip on the steering wheel. "I was so naïve."

"You were in love," she said tenderly. "We have rose-colored glasses on when we're in love. And you saw a different man than the rest of us do." She leaned forward a bit. "I think you made him want to be a better person. You have that effect on people, you know."

"No," I said, feeling an all-too-familiar hopelessness rise up. "I just see the good in people and try to help them see it too. No more, no less. I showed him the good parts of himself and encouraged him to become that man. But in the end, he chose evil, and I don't think I can forgive him for that."

"You said he told you that everything he was doin' was for you."

"I didn't ask him to do any of that, and he *had* to know I'd never approve of him endangerin' himself and other people. And now I found out he's even more entrenched in the criminal world than he was before I ended things with him. Dermot told me that he's involved with South American drug cartels." I shook my head again. "I would never, *ever* willingly step into that. Even if I put aside the danger it would pose for the baby and me, I can't be with a man who would join forces with hardcore killers. And that's not even bringin' up the way he betrayed Jed and me and tried to pay me twenty thousand dollars to abort my baby." My anger was rising by the second. "So no, if he showed up, beggin' me to come back, I'd say no."

"But you still love him?" she asked softly.

I pushed out a breath, wishing my feelings weren't so murky. "I think I'm in love with the fire we had, you know?" I turned to look at her and she nodded. Glancing back at the road, I said, "But that kind of passion never lasts. It peters out. And then you're stuck with mountains of laundry and a sink full of dishes and a man who's pissed because the baby won't stop cryin' and he needs to relax after... what? Making his drug deals with the cartel? So he's pissed that he's in this life he never wanted in the first place, and I'm resentin' him for stickin' me out at his house, probably under armed guard, and offerin' me no help except for a house cleaner a couple of times a week," I said with a huff. "Yeah, I've tried to imagine it. And even if I could get past the fact that he is, indisputably, a criminal, the thing I can't get past is being a prisoner in his world. But even if I could get past all of *that*…" My voice broke. "He hurt me. He's lied to me. He's hidden things from me. He's endangered my life. He refuses to explain why he does what he does or any significant part of his life. He acts like a child when he doesn't get his way and has a vicious temper. Yeah, I see the good in him, but I needed that man to step up last fall. I needed the good side of James Malcolm to say, 'Okay, this isn't what we planned, but we'll make it work.' Instead, his option was to not discuss it with me at all, to *dictate* what I should do, with no regard to my feelings whatsoever."

Suddenly, all the fight bled out of me. "And while I never would have agreed to the abortion, it should have been a discussion. *Everything* should have been a discussion. But he's incapable of sharing 99% of what he's thinking or feeling, and you can't build a relationship on that." Tears sprang to my eyes. "I deserve *better* than that."

She reached over and put a hand on my arm. "Yeah, honey. You do."

I inhaled deeply, then blew the breath out, squaring my shoulders. "I'm havin' a baby, and it's time for me to grow up and make wise, mature decisions, and not one part of pickin' James Malcolm is wise *or* mature."

She gently squeezed my arm, then put her hand in her lap. "But that still doesn't answer the question of whether you love him."

Tears welled in my eyes. "I think some part of me will always love him, just like some part of me will always love Mason, but at some point we have to decide to let go." I gave a slight nod. "And I have to let him go. I have to open my heart to new possibilities,

180

because I don't want to spend my life alone. I want a good man to share my heart and my life. A true partner who's willing to share his heart too. I need a man who will mow the grass and change diapers and call the plumber and pick up the kids from daycare. I need a man who will love and support me and not be there just for the passion but also for the sleepless nights when the baby is sick." Tears flowed down my cheeks. "Joe *is* that man, Neely Kate. He's all of those things and more."

"But Skeeter's still holdin' you back."

I swiped my cheeks with the back of my hand. "I think part of me thought I could get closure by seein' him."

"But you didn't?"

"I did get some," I said. "More of the shine's fallin' off."

"But you're still not ready to commit to Joe."

"No." And nothing made me sadder.

She was quiet for a moment. "Joe will be okay. His pride is hurt, just like yours would be if he was still hung up on Hilary or Dena, but he'll be okay."

I couldn't even imagine how hurt I'd be if the roles were reversed, and the thought that I was causing him so much pain upset me even more.

"Just let him know that you love him, but you're not ready to fully commit. Let him know there's hope, Rose."

I nodded, wiping my cheeks again. "Yeah. I'll do that tonight."

"Good."

I was so desperate to change the subject, and I knew that Neely Kate had her finger on the pulse of Fenton County gossip. "Say," I said, "what do you know about Dermot?"

Her head jutted back. "Dermot? What about him?"

"Well, he asked about my pregnancy this morning. When I told him about my false labor, he mentioned that his wife went into false labor a few times with their second child."

"Dermot's married?" she asked in shock. "He doesn't wear a ring."

"I told him I didn't know he had a family, and he said he doesn't anymore."

"What does that mean?" she asked.

"I have no idea, but now I'm curious."

"I'd never heard of him before you met him through Buck Reynolds, but I'll ask Jed. If anyone will know, it's him."

Of that I was sure. Jed had been James's righthand man for years, which meant he knew all there was to know about the criminals in the county…or at least he used to. Other than helping Lady, Jed had gone clean.

The Wild Vista neighborhood came into view and my stomach twisted into a knot. There was a chance this would tick off Joe, but I had given him valuable information already. If Neely Kate and I could possibly safely get him more, it was worth a try.

"So what's the plan?" Neely Kate asked.

"We need to find out as much about Erickson as we can. Maybe we can find a connection to Calista."

"Yeah," she said. "Good idea."

I drove to the end of the street and turned around, parking in front of Mike's spec house again. Only today, no one was working.

"Now what?" Neely Kate asked.

"We could ask around at the other job sites. Tex over there seemed to know something," I said, gesturing to the man standing in the dirt driveway of the house next to Mike's. "He said the man who died had gotten greedy. We could try to get more information from him. Or we could go over to the other neighborhood Mike's been workin' in. Barb said he was getting ready to sell a couple of houses, and I only see one here."

"I say we try to talk to Tex," Neely Kate said, already reaching for the door handle. "Let me take point on this one, okay?"

"Okay…" I wasn't sure whether to be excited or scared.

I followed her across the torn-up yard, Neely Kate holding my elbow to make sure I didn't fall.

Tex shielded his eyes from the sun and watched us as we made our way to him. "You little ladies are back!"

"I'm really interested in your house," Neely Kate said, "but I had to come over in person to make sure our séance worked."

His smile stretched across his face as he tugged up his jeans. "I'm pleased to tell you that no one's seen hide nor hair of any ghosts! Whatever you did must have done the trick."

"See?" I said. "You should never doubt yourself, Nancy."

Neely Kate made a face. "Umm… I'm not so sure. I'm still feeling some bad energy, Beth Ann."

"There ain't no bad energy in my house," Tex said. "I can give you a tour and you can see for yourself."

Neely Kate extended her arms from her body, pinching her middle fingers and her thumbs together, and began to hum as she slowly turned in a circle, finally coming to a stop and crossing her arms at the wrist as though they were divining rods. They pointed toward Mike's house. "There's bad energy comin' from that house. Bad chi."

"Bad chi," Tex repeated.

Dropping her arms, she turned her attention to Tex, her brow furrowing. "I'm sure it has everything to do with that builder next door cuttin' corners. I'm worried the chi from his house will float over to this one." She pointed to Tex's house beside us.

"Well, now," he said, "that ain't gonna happen, little lady. There's a good ten feet between houses here, see?" He gestured to the narrow space between the houses. "Plenty of space to keep his chi on his side of the property line."

"While chi *does* respect property lines," Neely Kate said with a serious expression, "it latches on to people and falls off 'em like fleas on a hound dog." She lifted her hands. "Now, it's not a problem if it's trapped, as long as I know what I'm dealin' with."

"Well," Tex said with a drawl. "What do you need to know?"

"I need to know how many houses that dead electrician worked on in this neighborhood."

His eyes widened slightly. "Well..."

"It's really important." The bridge of her nose pinched. "What would you say? Five? Six?"

He grimaced. "That sounds about right."

"Which houses did he work on?" she asked. "The *feng shui* makes a difference."

"*Feng shui?*"

She turned to me in horror. "Beth Ann, I don't think he used *feng shui* in his design."

My brow shot up. "Well now, that changes *everything*."

I turned as though I was about to walk back to the truck.

"Well now, hold on there," he said, his hands patting the air. "I never said that. I was just clarifyin' you meant *feng shui* and not...fink shy."

"Oh," Neely Kate said with interest in her eyes. "I've never heard of fink shy, and I like to fancy myself an expert on the existential, isn't that right, Beth Ann?"

I nodded, unsure what Neely Kate was up to, but I was willing to play along. "That's right, Nancy. I keep tellin' you to get business cards." I held up my hands as though I was framing a view. "Nancy Ellis, Expert of the Existential." I gave him a questioning look. "We've never heard of fink shy."

Creases appeared on Tex's forehead and it was apparent he was trying to come up with an answer.

Neely Kate must have decided to go easy on him, because she waved her hand. "Must be one of those west-by-north-south philosophies. *In any case*, if I'm going to shake off that dead electrician's chi, I'm gonna need to know more about him." She dug a pink sparkly notebook out of her purse and held her pink puffball pen at the ready. "How tall was he?"

Tex gave her a look that suggested she'd lost her mind.

"It's important for the Gollum," she said.

"The *what*?"

She waved him off with a look of irritation. "Never you mind about that. But on a side note, how good's the mud around here?"

He shook his head in confusion.

"His height, Tex," Neely Kate said impatiently. "What's his height?"

"I don't know, I guess he was around five-ten."

"Weight?"

"Uh… 180?"

"Hair color?"

"Brown. What's that have do to with his chi?"

"It has *everything* to do with his chi. Was he married?"

"I don't know…"

"Kids?"

"No?"

I still wondered where she was going with this. We could have likely gotten some of this information from Facebook.

"Was he into dark magic?" she asked with a serious expression.

"I don't think so."

"What about gamblin'?"

"I barely knew the guy," Tex said. "I had him work on one of my houses until I caught him fudging on his invoice, so I never hired him again."

"But other builders still used him?" I asked.

"Well, yeah. He had a special deal with some of 'em," he said. "I think it might have been something under the table."

"Like what?" Neely Kate asked. "Drugs? Animal sacrifices?"

"Animal sacrifices?" he asked in confusion.

"Did he work with anyone? A partner or a boss?" I asked. "We could ask them."

"No, he was an independent contractor, but word has it he had some dealin's with a guy south of town."

"What's his name?" Neely Kate asked.

"I don't know."

"Think, Tex," Neely Kate insisted. "We have to get this right."

"Maybe it was Carbunkle?" he said in a questioning tone.

"Carmichael?" I asked, my stomach dropping.

He pointed his finger at me. "That's it."

"Well, okay then," Neely Kate said, closing her notebook and inserting her pen into the spiral binding. "I think we've got enough to get started on that Gollum. Thank you for your time, Mr. Tex. We'll be in touch." Then she grabbed my arm and practically dragged me to the truck.

"What about that tour?" Tex called after us.

"We'll check back once the Gollum is finished," Neely Kate called back over her shoulder.

Once we were inside, I started the truck and pulled away from the curb, while Neely Kate gave Tex a friendly wave goodbye.

"You do know that Tex can easily find out who we are, don't you?" I asked. "RBW Landscaping is clearly written on the side of the truck."

"It won't matter," she said, her fake smile dropping. "We've gotten everything we need from Tex."

She was right. Mark Erickson had been working for Denny Carmichael, which meant everything had gotten ten times more dangerous.

Chapter Eighteen

So now what?" I asked.

"Let me think," Neely Kate said, bending over her phone as she sent Jed an update text.

I considered texting what we'd found to Joe, but for one, I suspected he was already looking into the Denny Carmichael angle, and two, he'd have a conniption if he knew what Neely Kate and I were up to. But we hadn't put ourselves in any danger yet, and as long as we continued to play it safe, we wouldn't.

Jed texted back seconds later saying that he'd take it from here.

"What the Sam Hill does that mean?" Neely Kate asked, pivoting on the seat to face me.

"Probably exactly how it sounds. That he'll handle it from here on out."

"He's cutting us out? You've got to be kiddin' me!"

"You have to admit that things have gone to whole new level now that we know the electrician was working for Carmichael."

She blew a raspberry. "We already knew Mike had some association with Denny. Skeeter told you as much."

I held up a hand. "Look, I'm not sayin' we should stop. I'm just tellin' you what he's likely thinkin'."

"Yeah, you're right," she grumbled.

"We just need to figure out where to go next."

She pressed her lips together while she gave it some thought. "The way I see it, we've got a couple of angles we can work. One, we can try to find out definitively if Sonder Tech is working for Hardshaw. Or we can look into who loaned Mike money."

My brow shot up. "How do you plan to figure out either of those things?"

I already had a feeling I wouldn't like what I was about to hear.

She made a face. "Sonder Tech might prove a bit embarrassing after yesterday."

I shook my head adamantly. "I am *not* goin' back there."

"Rose, you need to have a vision."

"I already did, and look what happened!"

"Well, today you'll be askin' a *different* question. You'll be askin' if they're workin' with Hardshaw."

I had to admit it wasn't a horrible plan, but I had no idea what would happen if I showed my face there again. Would they run me out? Still, if there was a chance it could help us find Ashley and Mikey, I couldn't let embarrassment hold me back.

"Fine," I muttered. "We'll do it your way." A pleased smile crossed Neely Kate's face, but she knew better than to say anything on the drive. Several minutes later, I pulled into the parking lot and turned off the truck, trying to calm my nerves.

"It's gonna be okay, Rose," Neely Kate said. "I'm sure it wasn't as bad as you thought. In fact, I'll bet most of the people there didn't even notice."

"I sure as Pete hope you're right. I'm supposed to be a professional."

"It's gonna be okay," she repeated, then opened her door and got out.

"Wait," I called after her as I got out of the truck and tried to catch up to her, but she was already making a beeline for the front door. "Neely Kate! Hold up!"

We didn't even have a plan, for Pete's sake.

She stopped short when she reached the edge of the building. "The azalea bushes." She stared at the dead bushes. "Those were here—at Sonder Tech?"

For a moment, I was stuck on the fact that I hadn't told her about that yet. I'd told Joe, Bruce Wayne, and Dermot, but somehow I hadn't gotten around to telling Neely Kate. Maybe because I'd been so distracted by the mess with Calista. Then it struck me why Neely Kate had turned pale. She'd buried Pearce Manchester, the son of one of the Hardshaw Three, under azalea bushes.

"Neely Kate. I didn't put it together."

She swallowed and pulled her gaze from the bushes. "This was a warnin' to us."

"Maybe not. Stewart seemed pretty shocked when I suggested they'd been intentionally poisoned. It could be a coincidence."

"You don't seriously believe that, do you?" she asked.

"Look, while I'm not disputin' that the poisonin' was likely intentional, why would Hardshaw poison their own bushes? They're supposedly friendly with Sonder Tech's owner. And the fact that they poisoned azalea bushes doesn't mean a doggone thing. In the south, you can throw three rocks and one of them is bound to hit an azalea bush."

She nodded. "Yeah. You're right."

"I'm not sayin' it *doesn't* mean anything. But the warnin' might not be for us." I drew in a breath and steeled my back. "Come on. We're goin' in."

Wrapping an arm around her, I steered her toward the double glass doors, still unsure of how best to handle this. I'd just ask to speak to Stewart and hopefully avoid the sales department.

The receptionist's eyes widened the moment we walked in. "Oh. *You're* back."

Neely Kate started to giggle and covered her mouth with her hand.

My cheeks felt hot, but I forced a smile. "Is Stewart busy?"

The receptionist cast a quick glance at the sales team room before shifting her focus back to me with a wary look. "He's not here today."

Neely Kate leaned an arm on the counter. "Is he *really* gone or is he just hiding in his office tryin' to avoid Rose?"

Her face flushed. "He's really off for the day."

"Do you know if he'll be back tomorrow?"

"He's home sick, so I'm not sure. You can leave a message if you like."

"That's okay," I said, my face still burning. "I'm here to check on the bushes, and I just wanted to let him know so he didn't think I was lurkin' around."

"Like a Peeping Tom?" she asked me with a lifted brow and judgment written all over her face.

So much for things not being as bad as I had thought.

Neely Kate gave her a patient smile. "I think there was some misunderstanding about what happened yesterday. Rose here"—she gestured to me—"is obviously very pregnant and keeps having false labor. That's what happened yesterday."

If I'd thought my cheeks were hot before, they were on fire now.

The receptionist looked uncomfortable. "Look, my sister just had a baby in January, and I saw her practicing her breathing techniques when I went home for Christmas. What Katie was doing wasn't *anything* like what she did." She nodded her head sideways toward me.

"That's because Rose is tryin' something new," Neely Kate said, then looked back at me with wide eyes. "Right, Rose?"

What was she up to? "Uh…yeah. That's right."

Neely Kate turned her attention back to the receptionist. "Rose found something on the internet that says she's more likely to get through an unmedicated labor if she learns to get in touch with her..." Neely Kate grimaced. "You know, her *flower*."

The receptionist looked dubious. "You're telling me she was practicing her...labor breathing?"

"Not labor breathin'," Neely Kate said, getting more animated with every word. "She's getting in touch with *her body*. Every part of it, so it all works in harmony to help with her delivery."

"That sounds like a crock of bull to me," the receptionist said.

Neely Kate shrugged. "Maybe, maybe not, but they're doin' it in all the big cities."

"Not in Dallas they aren't," the receptionist said. "My sister pays attention to that sort of thing, and she never mentioned anything about havin' fake orgasms."

"Who said it was fake?" Neely Kate asked. Then her eyes flew wide as she realized the implications of what she'd just said.

"Look," I said, pushing Neely Kate to the side a few inches. "I'm sorry for what happened yesterday, and I'd like to apologize to Calista if she's willin'." When she didn't say anything, I added, "I was not havin' a... you know." I cringed, my face flaming again. "I was havin' false labor, and I just sound really weird when it happens."

She didn't look convinced, but she pushed out a sigh. "I'd ask her, even though she made it pretty clear she thinks you're a degenerate and never wants to see you again, but she's not here."

"She called in sick too?" Neely Kate asked.

"Nope. She just didn't show up."

We were all silent for a second before Neely Kate said in a lowered voice, "You mentioned your sister is in Dallas. Is that where you're from?"

"Yeah," she said. "I moved here with Sonder Tech."

That seemed a little strange. Stewart had said they were bringing some of their own employees, but why would a receptionist be one of them?

Neely Kate gasped. "Wow! Sonder Tech must have some amazing benefits to convince you to move all the way to Henryetta. Did anyone else relocate here?"

"Stewart, of course, and Gary and Rebecca. And me and Calista."

"Calista came from Dallas too?" I asked in surprise.

She curled her lip as she looked up at me. "Sure did, but she has a boyfriend, and last I heard, she doesn't swing *that way*."

"Did her boyfriend come with her too?" Neely Kate asked.

"No," she said with a long sigh, then gave me a patronizing look. "Pat's from around here, but she's pretty serious about him, so don't let the short length of their relationship give you hope it's only a fling." Her phone rang and she gave me an apologetic smile. "Now if you'll excuse me, I have work to do."

"Can I use the restroom?" I asked as she reached for the phone.

She waved her other hand in a shooing motion. "Sure. Whatever."

I led Neely Kate into the women's restroom, but given that I'd overheard Calista from a stall on my last visit, I figured I'd better make sure we were alone. I got the balance wrong when I leaned over, though, and almost fell flat on my face on the germy floor.

"What on earth are you doin'?" Neely Kate asked, grabbing my arm and pulling me upright.

"Tryin' to see if anyone's in here."

"Oh, good gravy." She pushed me toward the sinks. "Let me do it." Bending over, she checked underneath all three stalls before joining me. "Empty, but you need to be careful. You've already been labeled as a pervert. Looking under women's bathroom stalls won't help that reputation much," she said, giggling.

"It's not funny," I said, but I struggled to keep a straight face.

"What are we doin' in the bathroom?"

"Stewart called in sick, and Calista plum didn't show up. That's odd."

"Agreed," she said with a nod. "But we could have discussed that in the truck."

"We have the opportunity to gather more information here. We just have to figure out what to look for and how best to find it."

"Yeah," she said, resting her butt against the bathroom counter. "We should focus on Calista's boyfriend, Pat. Based on your vision, he knows something. We need to find out more about him."

"And how do we go about that?"

A bright smile spread across her face, but I already had misgivings. She was giving me her *just go with it* face. "I have a semi-plan."

"Oh mercy. Why do I think I'm not gonna like it?"

Her smile widened. "Well, your reputation is already ruined. Might as well get what we can."

Then she told me what she had in mind.

I adamantly shook my head. "No. I can't do that."

"Oh, come on, Rose. We *need* to check her out."

"So have Jed get her address and we'll snoop on her there."

"She's not there. Marshall watched her house all night and she never turned up."

Marshall being the young man Neely Kate and I had saved from a spot of trouble. He'd been working with Jed and Witt at the garage.

"Maybe she went back to Dallas," I suggested.

"Maybe, but if we find her boyfriend, we can ask him."

She had a point, but still...what she was asking me to do was above and beyond.

"It might help us find the kids, Rose," she pleaded, all teasing gone. "It's a great plan. Sure, it's a little embarrassin'…"

"*A little?*" But she was right. Finding Pat might not get us anywhere, but then again, it might. "Okay. Let's do this before I change my mind."

I took a deep breath, and the baby gave me a strong kick as I exhaled. "Not now, baby. Momma's gotta work."

Neely Kate gave me a questioning look but didn't say anything as she held the door open for me to exit.

Instead of turning left, toward the double doors leading outside, I took a right, heading further down the hall toward the billing department. (Stewart had given me a tour after the remodel.) I'd figured it would be best to talk to someone who hadn't been on the sales floor the previous day. When I reached the open doorway, I knocked on the doorframe and gave a shy smile to the two women there, who were sitting at two cubicles. One looked to be in her fifties, while I guessed the other to be in her twenties.

Neely Kate stood next to the wall, out of their line of sight.

"Hi," I said. "I was wondering if I could ask you a question."

They both glanced down at my stomach before lifting their gazes to my face.

"If you're lookin' for Stewart, he's not here," the middle-aged woman said.

The younger woman snickered. "And if you're lookin' for Calista, she's not here today either."

I knew she wasn't laughing because Stewart and Calista had both taken the day off. Word had clearly gotten around about my mortifying run-in with Calista, and it was hard to mistake me for someone else right now. But her comment gave me an idea of a more natural lead-in to the crazy plan Neely Kate had cooked up.

I frowned. "Do you think they're off…you know. *Together?*"

The younger woman burst out laughing. "Are you asking if they're having an affair? No. Stewart's gay, and Calista has a *boyfriend*."

I leaned into the doorframe. "So her boyfriend…is it serious?"

She laughed again. "It doesn't matter if it's serious. Pat's a hot construction worker, and you're a *woman*, and pregnant to boot."

I tilted my head to the side, dying inside, but I'd keep pressing her until I got every drop of information I could. "So this Pat…he's a construction worker? Like the kind that builds houses or works on highways?"

"The kind that knows how to work with his hands and knows how to use his *tools*, if you know what I mean."

"Rose knows how to use tools," Neely Kate said from her spot next to the wall, still out of sight.

The younger woman leaned to the side, trying to see who had spoken up. She was laughing again when she said, "Rose may know how to use tools, but it's all about having the *right tool* for the job."

"Still," I said, "if they haven't been together that long…"

"She met him back in November when we were movin' in. He was on the construction crew for the remodel of this building."

Neely Kate tried to stifle her gasp.

Pat worked on Mike's construction crew. I'd bet my business that Calista knew something about Mike and the kids.

The middle-aged woman had had enough. "Don't you have somewhere you need to be?"

My mouth stretched into a tight smile. "Thank you for your time."

I started to walk away, but the younger woman called after me, "Do you want to leave a message for Calista?"

I turned back, all pretenses gone, and held her gaze. "Yeah, tell Calista I'm comin' for her."

Chapter Nineteen

Neely Kate kept quiet until we reached the parking lot, but as soon as we were alone, she shot me a worried look. "I don't think that was a good idea."

"Pretendin' to be romantically interested in her?" I asked absently as I tried to figure out what we should do with what we'd learned. "That was your idea from the start, and you're right, my reputation was already trashed. Might as well let them think I'm lookin' for a baby mama."

"Not that," she said, struggling to keep up with me as I marched toward the truck. "Tellin' her you were comin' for her."

I stopped abruptly at the back of the truck, and she stumbled to stay next to me. "Calista didn't strike me as stupid. She'll put together that we're lookin' for her. Now she knows for certain."

Uncertainty wavered in her eyes. "Still…"

"It's already done. Do you think we should look for Pat first or try to talk to Stewart?"

"Rose, you seem on edge." she said, hesitantly. "Maybe we should take a moment or two to let this all sink in."

My ire rose. "Think about *what*, Neely Kate? That Calista was in town for all of a week or two before she hooked up with a guy on Mike's construction crew? Do you honestly think that's an accident?

She probably chose him so she could keep tabs on Mike. She's gotta be in Hardshaw's pocket." I shook my head. "I swear, Hardshaw is like a cancer attachin' itself to *everything*."

"I know," she said. "And I'm frustrated too. But let's take a moment to think this through." A bright smile lit up her face, but it looked forced. "Hey, why don't we call Jed?"

"I'm not about to lose it, Neely Kate," I snapped. "I don't need to be handled."

"I know you don't, but you're hormonal, and you're upset about the kids and Muffy, and you're not runnin' on much sleep..." She gave me a sympathetic look. "Oh, honey, it's all just a *lot*."

"I know." I covered my face with my hand and took a moment to calm down. When I lowered my arm, I said, "I say we try to find Pat. Since no one was workin' at the house next to Tex's today, we should try the other neighborhood."

I could tell she had a mind to protest, but she just pinched her lips and nodded. "Yeah. Okay."

"You don't approve?"

"No. It just feels like this is startin' to get dangerous, you know?"

"That's never stopped you before," I said flippantly.

Hurt filled her eyes. "Are you suggestin' I knowingly put us in unnecessary danger?"

I pushed out a breath of frustration. "No. I'm sorry." I pulled her into a hug. "*I'm sorry.* I'm a total mess right now. Thank you for bein' patient with me."

She hugged me back. "I know it's the hormones talkin'."

"It's still no excuse. And I know you'd never knowingly put us in danger. It's just that we're used to takin' more risks."

"But things have changed." She gave me a wry look, then released a short laugh. "Never thought you'd hear me say *that*, huh?"

"No." But she was right—our lives *were* changing. We were both soon-to-be mothers and our priorities would shift. "Promise me that we won't lose each other once we have our babies. That we'll still be best friends and share our lives."

"We will," she said, lifting a hand to my cheek and staring deep into my eyes. "You're the sister of my heart. You're stuck with me."

I gave her a watery smile. "And you're stuck with me. Sadly for you, even when I'm a witch."

A grin lit up her eyes. "Please…I grew up with Witt and Alan Jackson. I doubt there's anything you can throw at me that would drive me away." She cast a glance at the Sonder Tech building before turning back to me, grinning from ear to ear. "They're thinkin' that you rebound pretty fast after a romantic setback."

I turned slightly to face the building. Several people stood in the front lobby, watching us through the glass doors, and a couple of men had gathered in front of the salesroom window too. The only thing missing from their audience experience was a bucket of popcorn.

"Then we'll give them a show," I said with a grin, and before she realized what I was up to, I leaned over and gave her a quick kiss on the lips. "Now let's go."

She laughed. "You're awful, Rose Gardner. Who knew you had it in you?"

I laughed too. "I think you ain't seen nothin' yet."

I got behind the wheel of the truck and drove us toward Whispering Pines, the other neighborhood I knew Mike had been working in, while Neely Kate pulled out her phone and called Jed. She put him on speaker and filled him in on everything we'd just learned.

"And what are you two up to now?" he asked.

"Heading to one of Mike's other spec houses," I said. "Hoping to find Pat."

"I'm not sure that's a good idea," he said. "What if he had something to do with Mike and the kids' disappearance?"

"All the better," I said.

"No," he said in a firm tone. "You two have gotten some very useful information. Let me and Witt take over from here." He paused. "Have you told Joe yet?"

"I told him about Calista last night, but not about this."

"Can you do me a favor and hold off for about an hour to give us a head start?"

"That's presumin' Joe doesn't already know," Neely Kate said. "He's not sharin' everything with Rose."

I didn't answer, instead mulling it over, uncomfortable with his request. I'd been honest with Joe about everything up until this point. I didn't want to give him cause to distrust me now.

"I'm not askin' you to withhold it from him, Rose," Jed said in an understanding tone. "I'm only askin' you to hold off for a little while."

"Okay," I said, but guilt pressed a weight on my chest. "Besides, he's gonna be upset when he finds out I was at Sonder Tech in the first place. Last night he asked me to promise not to go back." And because I felt the need to explain myself, even though I doubted Jed judged me, I added, "And in case you think I broke my promise, I didn't. I just didn't answer him when he asked."

Jed chuckled. "Amateur. I've learned that particular trick from Neely Kate."

"He's learnin'," I said, suddenly overcome with a sense of melancholy. What if this was the one thing that pushed him over the edge?

When would I ever get over this fear of the men in my life leaving me?

Maybe never, because every single one of them had.

Pushing out a sigh, I glanced at the clock on the dashboard. "It's ten thirty. I'll give you until one and then I'm callin' him."

"Thanks," he said, "but I need to ask again—what are you plannin' on doin' now?"

"I don't know," I said honestly. "We still need to figure that out."

"We thought about goin' to see Stewart," Neely Kate said carefully.

"Absolutely not," Jed growled. "You stay far away from that man. Witt and I will take care of it."

I expected Neely Kate to protest, but she said, "Okay. We won't go see him."

He hesitated. "Let me know what you do end up doin'."

"We will," she said.

"Love you, NK."

"Love you too," she said.

When I heard the click of the disconnecting call, I asked, "So are you lookin' up Stewart's address while I drive?"

"No," Neely Kate said. "Jed's right. It's too dangerous for us."

I heaved a sigh, but I didn't protest. Neely Kate, who'd always wanted to plunge deeper into the mysteries we'd investigated—something she'd been all about before our visit to Sonder Tech—didn't want to take this any further. That told me everything I needed to know.

She narrowed her eyes. "You're not gonna fight me on this?"

"No, you and Jed are both right. I can't put the baby at risk."

"I can't believe you're lettin' it go," she said. "You were all gung-ho about findin' Pat and talkin' to Stewart."

"And so were you. But you're right. We're better off leavin' Pat to Witt and Jed, and Stewart…if he's really with Hardshaw, I have no business goin' to see him." I sighed. "I can't put my baby in harm's way, and you can't do anything to get in the way of you and Jed getting your baby. Which means we need to let Jed and Joe handle this mess from here on out. I liked feeling like I was doin' something to help, but it's become too dangerous."

She gave me a long look. "Really?"

I cast a glance to the dash and groaned when I realized I'd completely blown off an appointment I'd already rescheduled twice. "Yeah, really. In fact, I plum forgot I have a landscapin' appointment in twenty minutes. I can drop you off at the nursery on the way, if you like."

"I'll go with you," she offered. "Maeve and Anna can cover the nursery."

I knew part of the reason she was coming was to babysit me, but I wasn't about to complain. An ominous feeling hung over me, like something bad was about to happen, but I had no idea who was in danger or why, other than the obvious. There were just so many things that could go wrong.

"I think I want to have a vision of you," I said.

"Me?" Neely Kate asked. "Of what? Because I'm not sure I want to know my future."

That caught me by surprise. Usually she was the one asking me to have visions and I was the one resisting. Then again, it was understandable given what had happened to her pregnancy.

"I don't want to have a vision of your baby, Neely Kate. I want to see if we find Ashley and Mikey. Maybe it'll help me figure out what to do next, or what to tell Jed and Joe."

When she didn't answer, I said, "I understand. Trust me, I do. Why do you think I haven't forced many visions over the last few months? I want every detail of my baby to be a surprise, right down to their gender. Now, if I have a vision of you, I might see something you or I don't want to know, but don't you think it's worth it to know we're gonna find them in the end?"

"And what happens if you don't see anything?" Neely Kate asked. "What if you find out they're dead?"

It felt like she'd tossed a bucketful of ice at me. "Neely Kate!"

She gave me a pleading look. "You know I'm prayin' with all my might that they're safe, but they've been missin' for *days*. The longer they're gone…" Her voice broke. "Look, right now we still have hope, and I'm not ready to give that up. I'm all for forcin' a vision that can lead us to them, but I know squat about where they're being kept, so if you have a vision of me, the only thing you're likely to see is the end result of our search."

She was right, and although the possibility was hovering like a specter in the back of my mind, I refused to truly consider it. I couldn't imagine those sweet babies dead.

"But what if I see a happy ending?" I asked. "It will give us the hope to keep *lookin'*."

"We don't need any more hope to keep lookin'. We already have plenty."

I couldn't help but think she was hiding something from me— something she didn't want me to see, but after a few moments of silence, she gave me a tight smile. "Okay, but I'm not sure I want to hear whatever it is that you see."

"How do you propose we manage that?"

She dug into her purse and pulled out a pair of earbuds. "I'll plug these into my phone and turn the music up to drown you out. But do it quick before I change my mind."

I pulled over to the side of the road, casting a glance in her direction as she inserted the earbuds into her ears. She stared straight ahead, her entire body tense.

Part of me regretted suggesting this. There was a chance I'd see something that would hurt her, or something that would destroy me. But I had to take that chance.

I put my hand on her forearm and asked the universe if we'd find Ashley and Mikey. A gray haze filled my vision, which I'd learned to mean the result hadn't been determined yet.

They were still alive. We still had a chance of saving them.

I tried to shift the vision and asked if we'd all be safe when this was over, but it stayed that same murky gray.

There was a chance one or more of us could be killed.

It was always hard to exit a murky vision, so I shifted to something pleasant (or so I hoped). So without thinking it through, I asked to see Neely Kate's wedding.

The vision shifted, and suddenly I was standing behind Neely Kate and Jed's house. The sun was shining and I, as Neely Kate, was staring up into Jed's face.

"I know this isn't the weddin' that you wanted," he said softly, lifting his hand to my cheek. "We didn't want so much sadness hangin' over the start of our marriage, but I'm here for the good and the bad, Neely Kate. I'm here for all of it."

The vision faded, and I found myself looking at Neely Kate's profile as she stared straight ahead, her body ramrod stiff with tension.

"Jed's here for the good and the bad," I said, my heart collapsing in on itself.

What sadness was he talking about?

Did it have something to do with the baby, or was this about Ashley and Mikey?

I dropped my hand from Neely Kate's arm, and she turned to me.

"What did you see?" she blurted out.

I gave her a soft smile, but tears stung my eyes. "Your weddin'."

"So I am still gettin' married?" When I nodded, she asked, "Why are you about to cry?"

Neely Kate had been terrified to know her future. She'd fought and scraped for every bit of happiness she'd found in this life, and now that everything she'd always wanted was within her reach, she was terrified it would get snatched away.

But my visions didn't always come true. Things could change. The sadness could be avoided. I refused to worry her for what could be nothing. There was absolutely nothing she could do to change the outcome, not with such vague information. The best thing I could do for her was let her keep her hope.

I swiped a tear with the back of my hand. "Because it was so beautiful."

As I pulled away from the shoulder, I realized what a slippery slope lying could be. It felt like I was about to dive down a mountain.

Chapter Twenty

I was glad Neely Kate came along for the appointment. The homeowner was a friendly middle-aged woman who took one look at my swollen belly, then shared every gory detail of her two horrific labors while she showed me where she wanted a hydrangea bed.

"And *then*," she said as Neely Kate and I took measurements of the west side of her house, "I just crapped all over the table. Got it in the nurse's hair even."

Neely Kate's eyes bugged out, but I gave a firm shake of my head, trying to drown the client out so I could concentrate on writing down the correct measurements.

By the time we were done, I was traumatized, and Neely Kate looked shell-shocked as we drove away.

"I can't believe…" Neely Kate finally said.

I shuddered. "Don't."

"She was in labor for thirty-six hours, and then she had to have reconstructive surgery six weeks later?"

A tremor of fear ran through me. "Neely Kate."

Gasping, she turned to me. "Oh, my word. I'm so sorry. You must be *freaked out*."

"I don't want to talk about it."

"Fair enough." She turned to face forward with her hands on her knees. I wasn't surprised when a few seconds later, she said, "Can you imagine being in the Piggly Wiggly and havin' your water break in front of the canned food aisle, then someone slippin' in it and buryin' you in a pile of cans of hominy? Hominy of all things. Who eats hominy?"

The problem was that I *could* see that happening to me, which made it all the worse. "Well, I'm still banned from the Piggly Wiggly, so that will not be happenin' to me. And your granny eats hominy. Last I heard, she loves it."

She frowned. "She doesn't count." But she must have come to her senses, because she said, "Oh, Rose. I'm sorry! I'm sure you don't want to rehash what she told us, but I just need to process."

"Go on," I said through gritted teeth. "Get it out of your system. Talking about it will help me too. It's bound to give me nightmares if I just bury it."

We spent the next ten minutes of the twenty-minute drive back to Henryetta repeating what we'd heard while Neely Kate assured me that the woman had been exaggerating, because it seemed physically impossible for you to push out your uterus with your baby still partially inside. I spent the remaining ten minutes silently turning over the vision I'd had of Neely Kate.

Something bad had happened, but it could have been anything. For all I knew, it was something as innocuous as a family member pulling a no-show at the wedding.

But I also couldn't ignore the murky darkness that had answered my previous two questions. There was a possibility we wouldn't find Ashley and Mikey, as hard as that was to accept, and one of us could also end up dead.

I pressed my hand on my belly. All the more reason to leave the investigation to Joe and Jed.

But should I tell anyone what I'd seen? Would it do any good? Or would it be better to keep it to myself? Who was the one person who could shoulder the possibility of heartache with me?

Joe.

I'd been wrong to keep the issue with the paternity papers from him, and I was sure he'd be a comfort and help with this worry. Maybe he could help avert whatever sadness Jed had referred to, although that seemed like a stretch. I'd tell him tonight, but the rest of the afternoon still loomed in front of me. Spending it alone wasn't so appealing.

"Hey," I said as we were about to reach the Henryetta city limits. "Want to get lunch before I drop you off at the nursery?"

"Sure, but I want to go to Merrilee's," she said. "I heard they added a cream cheese French toast to the menu."

"Sounds good to me."

When we reached downtown, I parked in an empty spot a few spaces from the landscaping office. Then we walked across the street to the diner. It was late enough that we got a table right away. We'd just placed our orders and I was about to excuse myself to the restroom when Carter Hale walked in.

Neely Kate's eyes narrowed as her gaze zoomed in on him. "I want to give that man a piece of my mind."

It took me a second to figure out she was likely talking about the paternity papers. While I'd known about them for about two months, she'd only known of their existence since yesterday. "It's not his fault, Neely Kate. Carter wants him to sign them as much as I do."

"He could try harder."

"*Please*," I said with a sigh. "Carter's the one man who still has sway over him, but we both know there's no makin' that man do anything he doesn't want to do. Leave Carter be."

She shot the attorney a scowl. "I will, but only because we're in public."

Carter took Neely Kate's irritation as a welcome sign, which wasn't all that surprising since he spent a good portion of his life dealing with—and reveling in—conflict. He walked straight to our table with a bright smile. "Good afternoon, ladies. Mind if I join you?"

"Yes, we *do* mind," Neely Kate snapped.

"Of course," I said, gesturing to the chair he was standing in front of. One thing was for certain—Carter Hale wasn't a stupid man and he didn't provoke unnecessarily. If he wanted to sit with us, he had a purpose.

Neely Kate shot me a glare, but I ignored her.

"Your pregnancy seems to be progressing," Carter said in a congenial tone, but I heard some tension in his voice as he gestured toward my stomach.

"I'm due in two weeks, and I'd love to deliver with the peace of mind that our future is bright and rosy and *unencumbered*."

"That's what I'd like to speak to you about." He lowered his voice. "My client contacted me a short bit ago."

My heart skipped a beat. "And?"

"He says he's considerin' a change of heart…but there are conditions."

I tempered my reaction when I heard the word *conditions*. "What sort of *conditions*?"

He reached into his pants pocket and pulled out a folded piece of paper. "They're written down here. You think on it and get back to me. Just keep in mind that my client insists that it's an all-or-nothin' deal."

I took the paper, knowing it couldn't contain anything good. "Is there a deadline?"

A grim smile spread across his face. "Read the list."

Then he got up and walked out the door.

"He didn't place or pick up an order," Neely Kate mused. "He only came in here to talk to you. He was watchin' for us."

I didn't argue with her, mostly because I suspected she was right. Dread in my gut, I slowly opened the paper and saw it contained two requests, both written in James's handwriting.

Give up the hunt for the item stolen from Gilliam's office

Spend forty-eight hours with me before the baby is born, no questions asked, no contact with anyone while you're with me

"Well," she demanded. "What does it say?"

I hesitated, then handed it over to her, still trying to sort out what it meant.

She quickly scanned it and looked up, outraged. "You're not giving this serious consideration, are you?"

"I don't know, Neely Kate," I said, my voice rising in panic. *Was I?* There was no way I could give up finding what had been stolen, especially if it contained information that would help Ashley and Mikey. And the second request… there was no way I'd do that one either. Not this close to delivery. Shoot, not at all. After my house call the night before, I was more certain he wouldn't hurt me, but I couldn't imagine why he'd request such a thing. What did he hope to gain? He'd made it very clear he wanted nothing to do with me.

Whatever he was up to, it wasn't for good, that was for certain.

Neely Kate glanced around to see if anyone was watching, and when she was satisfied the patrons around us were more interested in their meals than our conversation, she said, "You have to tell Joe about this."

"Joe will never agree."

"Of course he won't! Only a *crazy* person would." She leaned closer, her gaze holding mine with a blazing intensity as though trying to convince me.

"Of course it's crazy." Only a fool would agree to let James get away with stealing information that might save my niece and nephew. Only a fool would agree to forty-eight hours with him. "But you have to promise me that you won't tell Joe. I need to be the one to do it."

"Rose. Just promise me that you *will*."

"I will." And I would. I just needed to figure out the best time and place.

The waitress brought out our food, and we ate in silence for a minute or so. I'd lost my appetite, but I took several bites of the chicken club and chips. Neely Kate polished off her French toast but gave me a worried look when she saw how much food was still on my plate. "I thought you were hungry."

"I was, but I can't eat much these days. If I eat more than half a plate, I end up with heartburn." I checked the time on my phone, realizing it was after one, several minutes past my deadline to call Joe. "I'm gonna go to the restroom and then take you back to the nursery." I stood. "The fact I've made it almost two hours without peein' is a miracle."

"Okay," she said, pulling out her own phone and starting to tap on the screen. She hadn't told Jed about our chat with Carter, and I was surprised she'd waited this long.

As I did my business, I thought about James's conditions.

Maybe I was a crazy person, because I was considering going to see him again.

I'd take Neely Kate to the nursery and go see Carter in his office. Surely he had some idea of what James was up to, and he'd be able to talk more freely in his office.

Just as I was about to walk out of the bathroom, another false labor pain hit and I stopped, leaning into the bathroom counter as I breathed through it.

Someone knocked on the door, and I called out, "Just a moment."

It was nearly a minute before I walked out, and an older woman who had been waiting in the short hallway shot me a glare... until her gaze lowered to my stomach. "Oh. Sorry for bein' so impatient. I had the *worst* hemorrhoids."

"Thanks," I said, deciding I was going to start keeping a tally of how many women volunteered their personal horror stories about pregnancy and childbirth. When I got back to the table, the bill had already arrived and Neely Kate had placed cash on top of it.

"That took a while," she said, narrowing her eyes in suspicion.

"Just as I was gettin' ready to walk out, a contraction hit, so I rode it out in there. Didn't think people wanted to see the spectacle of me waddling and practicing my new X-rated breathing techniques."

She cracked a wide smile as she stood. "I don't know. I wouldn't mind catchin' a glimpse."

My face flushed, but I shook my head. "Come on."

She followed me out of the restaurant, still grinning.

We headed to the nursery, and Neely Kate told me that Jed was incensed by James's request and was considering paying him a visit at the pool hall.

"No. He can't. He'll only put himself in danger. I'll just ignore it."

"You sure?" she asked with a leery look.

"Yeah. Besides, I want to tell Joe before he finds out from a police report that will inevitably will be filed if James and Jed get into it." Not to mention it was bound to be a bloody mess.

"Yeah, probably a good idea." I was sure I didn't imagine the relief on her face.

When I pulled into the parking lot of the nursery, she turned to me. "I'm still not sure it's a good idea for you to be alone."

"I'm tired and cranky and not up to greetin' people and standin' on my feet at the nursery right now," I said. "I think I'll go lock myself in the office and get some work done, then find out when Joe's plannin' to go home and meet him there. "

"Okay," she said with a frown, obviously not fully on board with my plan. "You call me if you need anything, okay? Maybe we can go see Muffy together after I get off work."

Since I had no idea what would happen this afternoon, I didn't want to commit to anything, but I couldn't just tell her no, so I said, "Let's see how the rest of the day goes."

Thankfully, she didn't look hurt, just understanding, which made me feel all the more guilty for not sharing what I was really planning to do.

As she was getting out, Maeve was coming through the double doors.

Maeve.

I was a terrible friend. I should have called and given her an update.

I opened the truck door. She held up a hand to stop me, but I got out anyway and met her on the sidewalk. I owed her that much.

"Maeve," I said, my voice breaking. "I'm so sorry. I should have called you."

Worry covered her face. "Joe came by and filled me in earlier this morning. Thank goodness you're okay."

I nodded, thankful Joe had thought of it. Just another example of what a great man he had become. "I don't think they were going to hurt me, and I'd like to think that they ran over Muffy on accident."

"Any word on how she's doing? Joe told me it was touch and go."

"Levi hasn't called with any updates," I said as I reached for my phone in my pocket. "But how about I call him and we can hear what he says together?"

Tears filled her eyes and she nodded. "That would be lovely."

I pulled up Levi's cell phone number and he answered right away.

"Hey, Levi. I'm calling for an update on Muffy," I said. "My friend Maeve is listenin' in too." I glanced up and saw my best friend's worried face. I took a step back so we formed a huddle. "And Neely Kate."

"Hi, Maeve and Neely Kate," Levi said in the voice he used when he was comforting patients' owners. Which meant things were still serious.

"How's our girl?" Maeve asked, her face pale.

"Same as this morning when Rose and Joe came to see her. We've had some blood sugar issues, but we're treating her like the princess she is and doing everything we can for her."

"Will it be enough?" Maeve asked.

Levi paused. "I sure hope so."

"Can I come see her?" she asked.

When Levi didn't answer, I said, "Muffy spends a lot of time with Maeve. Maeve's like her grandma. I'm sure Muffy would love to see her."

"Well, okay," Levi said, not sounding happy about it. "But I'm worried that a lot of visitors will stress her."

"I truly think Maeve will soothe her," I said. "Likely more than a visit from me."

Levi sighed. "Rose, I didn't mean to insinuate that you were causing her distress. She needs to see you. She just seemed to be straining to stay awake for you."

"I know you weren't tryin' to hurt me, Levi, and you were right. She was strainin' to stay awake. She thinks she needs to protect me, and for all I know, she thinks she didn't finish the job with that car."

"I'm doing everything in my power to keep her comfortable and help her pull through this."

"But there's a chance she won't pull through?" Maeve asked.

He hesitated. "Let's just say she's not out of the woods yet."

While this news wasn't a surprise, it was still hard to receive confirmation. "Thank you, Levi. I appreciate everything you're doin' and I appreciate your honesty."

"Just doing my job, but I confess I have a soft spot for Muffy."

I hung up and held Maeve's gaze. "I'm so sorry, Maeve."

Surprise filled her eyes. "What on earth are you sorry about?"

"For letting this happen to her."

"Oh, Rose." She pulled me into a tight hug. "This was an accident, plain and simple." She gave me a teary smile. "And we both know that little dog will do anything to protect you. There's no stoppin' her."

I nodded. She was right, but that urge to protect me had nearly gotten her killed…and it still might. Just like it could hurt the other people who cared about me.

Neely Kate gave me a hug. "Maybe you should go home," she said. "All this stress can't be good for you and the baby. Jed could have Marshall come out and stay with you."

A nap sounded good, but I wasn't sure that was in my immediate future. I had no intention of spending forty-eight hours with James Malcolm, but I suspected I'd be seeing him sooner than I'd   like.

Chapter
Twenty-One

I considered calling Carter, but it was pointless. He never discussed anything of importance over the phone, and unless he was in court, he was usually at his office during the day.

I parked close to my office on the square, but once I hopped out of the truck, I headed straight to the other side of the square, toward Carter's office, James's paper in my hand.

The receptionist was at her desk, typing on her computer. She glanced up at me and her face tightened in recognition. "Oh. It's you."

I tried not to roll my eyes. "Is Carter in?"

"He's in his office," she said with a strained smile. "Let me see if he has time to see you."

I expected her to either pick up her phone or walk down the hall, but instead, she leaned to the side and shouted, "Carter, Rose Gardner is here to see you."

"Send her back."

Her face brightened. "He says you can go on back."

"Thanks for lettin' me know," I said as I headed down the hall.

Carter's door was ajar, and before I could knock, he called out, "Come on in."

I pushed the door open and shut it behind me. Then I crossed to his desk and slammed the paper he'd handed me less than an hour before down in front of him. "What the hell is this about?" He started to say something, but I pointed my finger at him and growled. "And cut the bullshit. I'm not in the mood."

A smile spread across his face. "You make a beautiful pregnant woman, Rose."

"What did I say about bullshit?"

He held his hands out from his sides. "I only speak the truth. Maybe Skeeter thought so too after you showed up at his house last night."

"He told you about my visit?"

"Yep."

I sat in one of the leather chairs in front of his desk. "Why does he want forty-eight hours with me?"

"I couldn't say."

"What did I say about bullshit?"

"I'm dead serious, Rose," he protested good-naturedly. "He dropped by, unannounced, told me that you'd come to see him last night and he'd reconsidered signing the paternity papers. He tossed the list on my desk, a lot like you just did, and told me he'd only sign if you agreed to both conditions."

"So let's say I agree to the forty-eight hours…how would I get in touch with him?"

His brows rose. "You're actually considerin' it?"

"I want him to sign those papers," I said. "I'm explorin' my options."

He sat up in his leather chair with a shocked look on his face. "Well, I'd have to contact him."

"No," I said in a no-nonsense tone. "From here on out, I contact him. We'll handle our business without any go-betweens."

He frowned. "That's not a good idea, Rose. Phones can be tapped and traced."

"Please," I groaned. "I'm not the same woman I was a year and a half ago, when he first dragged me into this world. I'm a helluva lot smarter."

He made a face. "One could argue against that given your current state."

My anger boiled. "And one could argue it's not very smart to insult a *very* pregnant woman who has pepper spray, a Taser, and a gun in her purse. But since I'm feelin' agreeable, how about I let you pick which one I use on you?"

"Rose…" he drawled, lifting his hands from the desk in surrender, even though he was clearly not concerned. "I didn't mean anything by it."

"Too bad for you that I *did*. Now give me the number to his burner, because I know he's got one and more to spare, and you won't need to worry about anything being traced because I've got a burner too." When he didn't move, I shouted, "*Now.*"

Startled, he jumped in his seat, then reached for a sticky note. "Has anyone ever told you that you're a mean pregnant woman?"

"My niece and nephew have been kidnapped. My dog was run over by a car and is in critical condition, and my asshole ex has information that might help me find those kids but instead wants to play games. That would be enough to piss anyone off, pregnant or not."

"Fair enough," he said, writing down a number on the blue paper square, "but he wasn't in a good mood when he dropped by, so don't expect him to share anything with you."

I stood and snatched the Post-it from him. "I never expect *anything* when it comes to Skeeter Malcolm."

I marched out and headed across the street toward my office. I was exhausted, likely from my lack of sleep the night before and the fact I was carrying a tiny person in my body, so I headed to the coffee shop to get a latte to hopefully perk me up as I came up with a plan.

There was no way I was going to spend forty-eight hours with James, but I'd agree to that stipulation before I'd give up looking for whatever James had stolen from the safe. With any luck, I wouldn't have to make any concessions. I couldn't think of a single reason he'd want to spend that much time with me unless he was trying to rekindle our romance. That was never going to happen, but if he still cared about me, maybe he could be convinced to help me find the kids. In hindsight, I should have pressed him harder the previous night, but seeing him had thrown me more than I'd thought it would.

Once I got my coffee, I was headed out the door when something caught my eye to the right.

To my surprise, the now-familiar station wagon was parked several spots down, closer to the opposite end of the street.

What should I do? Run after it? Let it go? I could call Joe, but I doubted he'd be able to get someone here in time to detain the driver. I could at least see if Vera was sitting in it.

But as I took a few steps in that direction, the car suddenly jerked in reverse and then pulled forward, tires squealing as it sped away too fast for me to see who was driving.

"Some people need to be more careful," a familiar voice said, and I turned in surprise to see Stewart on the sidewalk several feet away from me.

I took an involuntary step backward, sloshing coffee on my hand. "Stewart, what are you doin' here?"

"I was just at your office, but it was locked up. I was looking for you."

"Uh…" I pulled out my phone and checked the screen. "Did I miss a call from you?"

He didn't seem sick, but he had a wild look in his eyes. "No. I decided to come see you at your office."

Meeting with Stewart in my office seemed like a terrible idea, especially given his crazed look. For all I knew he was in this thing up to his neck.

"Actually, I was just on my way to an appointment." I half-heartedly pointed to my truck.

"This will just take a moment," he said. "It's important."

I gestured to the coffee shop behind me. "How about we go inside and chat here?"

He glanced toward the office. "I was hoping to talk to you alone."

I gave him a hard look. "I'm gonna be frank with you, Stewart. It's the coffee shop or nothin'."

He stared at me with a blank look. "Okay. The coffee shop it is."

I spun around and headed inside the nearly empty dining space, leaving Stewart to follow. I chose a table for two in the back corner a good six feet from the other occupied table and took a seat. He sat across from me, suddenly looking nervous.

"Those bushes," he said, his voice shaking. "Are you sure they were poisoned?"

"I haven't gotten the soil sample results back yet, but I'd be surprised if they weren't."

"I think it was intended as a warning to me."

"A warning?"

He took a breath and glanced out the windows. "A man stopped by the office last week. He asked me some strange questions about my contractor and something called Hardshaw. I told him I had no idea what he was talking about—I still don't—but he threatened to send a warning if I didn't cooperate." He swallowed. "I think the bushes were a warning."

I couldn't believe what I was hearing, but I figured I could get more information out of him if I played dumb. "I'm confused. Why are you tellin' me this, Stewart?"

"I don't know," he said, running a shaky hand over his head. "I guess because he mentioned your name too."

I tried to hide the jolt of fear that shot through me. "You mean in addition to the contractor?"

"Yeah. I told him I barely knew Mike. I saw his contractors more than I saw him."

"Mike Beauregard?" I asked.

"Yeah." His eyes widened. "Is he mixed up in something?" His eyes got even wider, like they were on the verge of popping out. "Are *you*?"

I leaned closer and lowered my voice. "Do you know who came to see you, Stewart?"

He shook his head. "He didn't say, but he gave me this number. He said I should call him when I came to my senses."

He pulled a paper out of the pocket in his button-down shirt and handed it to me.

I studied the ten-digit number written in blue ink on the torn-off piece of paper. "Have you called it?"

"No! I didn't have anything to tell him. I'm not even sure what he expects me to tell him if I call."

"Can you describe him?" I asked.

"Uh…" He rubbed his chin. "Tall. Muscular. Menacing."

"Hair color?"

"Kind of dirty blond."

Oh, my word. Had Denny Carmichael gone to see Stewart? He checked all the boxes.

"Stewart," I said. "Do you know anything about the company you work for?"

His back stiffened. "Sonder Tech? Of course. I've worked for them for five years."

"Did you know they have possible ties to a Dallas crime syndicate?"

His eyes flew wide. "What? No!" Then confusion washed over his face. "How do you know that? And why did that man ask about you?"

"Stewart," I said softly. "I don't know why that man brought up my name, but I do know Mike's children are missin'."

Panic washed over his face. *"They've been kidnapped?"*

"I don't know," I admitted, pulling my phone out of my purse. "But I'm going to call the chief deputy sheriff and ask him to come take your statement."

"What?" Stewart cried out. "No. No sheriff."

"Stewart. You could help the sheriff's department find those two kids."

"If I talk to the sheriff, that man will kill me." He shot out of his seat. "No. I can't do it."

And then he bolted out the door.

Chapter Twenty-Two

I considered running after him for about a second, but I'd never catch up to him, and even if I did, I didn't think I'd be able to change his mind.

Stewart Adams was running for his life.

The barista cast a questioning glance at me, and I forced a smile. "He realized he was late for an appointment."

She tsked. "That man ran out like he had some bad egg salad."

I grabbed my latte and headed out, lingering in front of the coffee shop so I could call Joe.

"Rose, now's not a good time," he said when he picked up his phone, the words coming out in a rush.

"I think Denny Carmichael poisoned the bushes at Sonder Tech."

He hesitated. "What? What makes you say that?"

"Because Stewart Adams just told me so."

There was a pause, and when he spoke his voice was tight. "You promised me you'd stay away from Sonder Tech."

That was a discussion for another time. "Stewart came to me, Joe. He came to the landscaping office, only he found me in front of the coffee shop."

"And he told you Carmichael paid him a visit?"

"He didn't know his name, but the description he gave me sounds like Carmichael, and the guy gave Stewart a number to call."

"Is he at your office now?"

"No, I asked him to talk to you, and he ran off, saying the guy would kill him if he found out he was talking to the cops."

"I'll send a deputy out to search for him."

"There's more, Joe. Stewart said the guy who went to see him was askin' questions about Hardshaw, but Stewart claims he'd never heard of them."

"Chief Deputy, we need you," I heard someone say in the background.

"You said he took off?" Joe asked. "You're safe? Are you with Neely Kate?"

"I'm safe, and Neely Kate's at the nursery."

"I don't want you bein' alone, Rose," he said. Someone else called his name, and his voice was muffled when he called out, "I'm comin'."

"I'll head over to the nursery, okay?" I said. "Don't worry about me. It sounds like you have your hands full."

He lowered his voice until it was little more than a whisper. "We found a big lead. I can't tell you anything more."

"Oh," I said, my stomach in knots. It was on the edge of my tongue to say *that's great*, but something about his tone told me something was wrong. Was this even about Ashley and Mikey? I wanted to ask, but I knew better than to poke him, especially since he wasn't alone. "Go take care of whatever it is you're workin' on, and don't worry about me. I'll go to the nursery."

"I'll call you later," he said. "I suspect I'll be workin' late." Before he hung up, I could hear him calling out orders to his deputies.

I hadn't had a chance to tell him that the mystery man (probably Denny) had inquired about Mike *and* me, or about seeing the station wagon, or Calista's boyfriend Pat, or mentioned anything at all about James's conditions for signing the paternity papers. If he had a big lead, he might not need the other information I had.

Unsure what to do next and not ready to go to the nursery yet, I headed to the office to think things through. I needed to call James, but I also wanted to share what I'd learned with Dermot, and Neely Kate and Jed.

I booted up my computer. It always took a while, so I flipped open my work bag and started going through it, organizing and restocking pencils and business cards as I let my mind sort through its current overload of information. Who should I contact first, James or Dermot? Because once I went to Neely Kate, I doubted she'd leave me alone for long enough to pee.

A contraction grabbed hold of me, but it was milder than my usual Braxton Hicks, and I continued organizing through it, realizing I was nesting again. Since there was no point in fighting the inevitable, especially when it was so useful, I sat down to work on my desk drawer—which was when someone rapped on the front door. The teenage boy who stood behind the glass was tall and lanky, and it was obvious he was still in his socially awkward stage.

"We're closed," I called out to him, realizing I hadn't put the closed sign in the window. The baby hiccupped in my stomach, and I placed my hand over my belly out of a protective instinct.

"I've been told to give you a message," he said, his voice muffled by the glass. He held up a pale yellow envelope, the kind used for greeting cards.

A message? Or had my mail been delivered to the wrong place? The likelihood that it was the former suggested I shouldn't let him in. He seemed harmless enough with his neatly trimmed hair and bright, eager face, but looks could definitely be deceiving.

I walked closer to the door and pointed to the mail slot embedded in it. "Just slip it in through the slot."

Then I held my hand underneath to take it.

He slid the envelope in through the rectangular flap, passing it to me.

"Thanks," I said, looking over the smudged, dirty envelope. It hadn't been addressed to anyone.

My gaze jerked up, but he was already walking away.

Crappy doodles.

I quickly unlocked the door and rushed through the opening, holding the door open with one hand. "Excuse me!"

The kid turned to face me with a questioning look.

"This envelope." I held it up. "Where did you get it?"

He walked closer. "A woman down the street asked me to give it to you. I asked her why she didn't want to give it to you herself, but she said it would be more of a fun surprise this way."

Propping the door open with my back, I broke the seal, pulling out a birthday card that had a popular children's character on the front and read *Happy Second Birthday*. When I opened it, there was the standard cheesy greeting card rhyme. It had been signed, but the signature was scratched out and someone had written on the other side:

I can tell you where those kids are, but you have to come alone. Meet me at Shute Creek Park at four.

My heart raced as I lifted my gaze to the teenager. "Where is she? Is the woman still nearby?"

"I don't know," he said, looking nervous, like he'd just realized this was no joke. "She seemed like she was in a hurry. She got in her station wagon and drove off."

My head felt faint. "A station wagon? Was it an older model with wood paneling?"

Relief washed over his face. "You know her, then? Thank God. I was starting to worry something shady was goin' on."

I wasn't sure what to tell him. Something shady *was* going on.

"Uh…are you okay, ma'am?"

Neely Kate would have punched him if he'd called her ma'am. "Yeah."

"I'll be goin', then," he said, taking a couple of steps backward.

"Wait," I called out. I couldn't just let him go, not without asking more questions, but I was facing a choice: call in the authorities or deal with this myself.

Except it didn't feel like much of a choice. Vera, or whoever had given the boy the card, was clearly afraid of something or someone. The cops would scare her off, especially given how pissed Joe was about Muffy. While I was beyond angry myself, I couldn't ignore this note.

Hopefully, Joe was about to find the kids and it wouldn't matter. But I couldn't ignore the little voice in my head that said *what if*. What if Vera knew something they didn't? And what if I was the only person she'd tell?

"What's your name?" I asked.

Wariness crept into his features. "Preston."

"Hi, Preston, I'm Rose." I forced a smile and held up the card. "This is part of an elaborate practical joke between me and my friend."

Relief filled his eyes. "Oh. Good."

"Do you have a moment so I can ask you some questions? You could help me with my next move."

"Should you really be playin' games when you look like an alien is about to explode from your body?"

My smile faltered. "I'm not *that* big."

His eyes widened and he nodded. "Oh, you're that big all right."

I considered giving him a lesson in manners, but my need for answers overrode my ego. "*In any case*, like I said, anything you can tell me will help. Would you like to come in so we can talk?" Then for some bizarre reason, I added, "I have some leftover Girl Scout cookies."

He gave me a leery look, like he was Hansel and I was the witch in the woods trying to lure him in. Which was a funny thought. I'd been leery of him at the start of this, and now the tables had turned.

"Or we could go down to the coffee shop," I suggested, my smile a little too bright. "If you'd feel more comfortable there. I'd be happy to buy you a coffee for your trouble."

My coffee shop suggestion seemed to put him at ease. "No, your office is fine."

I held the door open for him, taking a quick glance up and down the street to see if the station wagon was lurking anywhere, but it was nowhere in sight.

"Why don't you take a seat in front of my desk?" I asked, gesturing toward the two chairs. I considered locking us in, but I'd already freaked out this kid enough. I didn't want to send him running.

"Okay." He looked nervous as he took a seat, and I couldn't really blame him. Walking behind my desk, I pulled a box of Thin Mints from my drawer and put it on the desk in front of him. "Would you like a bottle of water?"

"No…" he said hesitantly. "This is good. What do you want to know?"

I picked up a notepad and pen as I sat behind my desk. "Can you tell me what she was wearin'?"

"Yeah, she had on a housedress like my granny wears and a pair of boots. Like this army kind, but they looked really worn. And muddy."

I nodded, taking notes. "What color was her hair?"

"I thought you knew her," he said suspiciously.

"I do, but sometimes she likes to dress up," I said. "You know, get in character."

His eyes widened. "Oh, like cosplay."

I blinked. "What?"

He seemed to be becoming more relaxed and reached for the cookie box. "You know, cosplay. When people dress up as their favorite characters."

Huh. "Yeah, just like that. So what color was her hair?"

"A dingy brown and kind of stringy." He winced. "Sorry. That sounds mean."

"Oh, don't you worry," I said. "She was wearin' a disguise."

"Whew!" he said, sinking back into his chair. "I'd hate for anyone to look that beat-down in real life."

That gave me pause. "She looked beat-down? How so?"

"You know," he said excitedly. "Dark circles. Pale skin. She even had bruises on her wrist that she tried to cover up with this chunky sweater she was wearing."

It was Vera. I was sure of it. The last time I'd seen her, she'd been pale, even for fall, and had the look of a woman who was used to being squashed under the boot of a man. Or his fist.

"Was she alone?" I asked.

"I didn't see anyone with her," Preston said. Then his face brightened. "But I saw a kid in a car seat in the back."

"Oh!" I said in fake glee. Vera had been carrying a little boy on her hip. "That's good! Anything else?"

"Um…" He rested his chin on his hand. "Her eyes were a kind of gray, and she had a bit of bruising around one of them." Turning to me, he said, "Whoever did her makeup was really good."

"That Trixie's something else," I said. "Did you happen to see her license plate?"

"Her license plate? Why are you askin' that?"

"Because sometimes she switches out her license plate as a clue." He started to protest, and I held up my hand. "I know. But you saw her makeup. She takes things a little too far."

"I think it was a Louisiana plate," he said with a frown. "Yeah, it was."

228

Louisiana? No wonder Joe hadn't gotten very far in his search. "Do you remember any of the numbers?"

"Nuh-uh."

"That's okay," I said, pulling out two business cards from my desk drawer and handing them to him. "I'd appreciate it if you'd give me a call if you remember anything else, and would you mind leavin' your name and number with me in case I think of another question? You can write the information down on the back of the other card."

"I guess," he said, taking a pen out of the coffee cup that held an array of pens, pencils, and markers. "You sure do take your pranks seriously."

"You have no idea."

He wrote his name—Preston Calhoun—on the card along with his number. "I've gotta get goin'," he said, lifting to his feet. "I was supposed to meet my friends at the coffee shop. I would have let you buy me that coffee you offered, but I wouldn't hear the end of it. My friends would be ribbing me about the hot pregnant lady tryin' to pick me up."

I wasn't sure which part of that statement to react to—the fact he'd called me hot or that his friends would think I was trying to pick him up. The smoldering look he was giving me suggested he was having second thoughts about turning me down.

I stood and walked him to the door.

He paused at the opening. "Would it be okay if I got a raincheck for that coffee when my friends aren't around?"

My mouth dropped open. "Uh…"

His glance dipped to my left hand and back up to my face. "I noticed you weren't wearing a ring."

I lifted a brow and grinned. "I think I'm a little old for you…and encumbered."

He shrugged. "I figured it was worth a shot."

Watching him walk away, I released a wry laugh. "I guess it's nice to know I have options."

The baby gave me a sharp kick, and I rubbed the spot. "I was joking, baby. You've already got the best daddy in the world."

And he or she did, so why was James Malcolm on my mind?

Because he'd all but guaranteed it by offering me impossible conditions in return for his cooperation.

I decided to call James first. I wasn't sure he'd answer, but it was a good place to start.

Taking a deep breath, I got out the burner phone I kept in a zippered compartment in my purse and entered the number Carter had given me. To my surprise, James answered on the second ring.

"Lady, I've been expectin' your call."

I frowned. How had he known it was me? But then I realized Carter had put on a bit too much of a production handing me that number. This had been their plan all along.

"I'm sick of the games, James Malcolm," I snapped. "Why do you want forty-eight hours?"

"Why not?" he said with a short laugh.

"Do you know how difficult it would be for me to get away for that long with everything else going on and my baby due in two weeks?" When he remained silent, I realized he *had* thought about it. He knew I'd likely have to lie to get away from Joe and Jed and Neely Kate, and that they would never accept whatever excuse I offered, not to mention Neely Kate had seen the list and would know exactly what I was up to.

He was purposely trying to hurt me. To rip at my relationships with the people who had stuck with me when he'd turned his back.

Tears stung my eyes. The man I'd known was truly gone. There would be no playing on his emotions or his supposed affection for me. This was part of his punishment for my betrayal.

"And if I refuse?"

"Well, I guess it's pretty simple. I won't be signing those papers."

"So you can hold them over my head?" I asked, my voice cold. "While I raise my baby, waiting for you to initiate some vindictive scheme?"

"Vindictive scheme," he scoffed, sounding ten times colder than he had the night before. "It's business, Lady, pure and simple."

"I'll buy the stolen evidence as a business matter," I said. "But the forty-eight hours... that one seems personal."

"Guess you'll find out."

"I'm not spendin' forty-eight hours with you, James. I'll be happy to meet with you somewhere to discuss whatever you like, but not two days."

"I made the conditions clear," he said in a hard tone. "All or nothing." And he hung up.

I stared at the phone, so ticked I almost threw it across the room.

I got up and paced around the office, trying to expel some angry energy before I called Dermot, but another contraction took hold, and I had to breathe through it, long slow breaths. When it passed, the baby got another round of hiccups.

I rubbed my belly. "I'll protect you, sweet baby. No matter what it takes."

The question was whether it would mean spending forty-eight hours with James.

Chapter
Twenty-Three

I sent Dermot a text. **We need to talk.**

It was no surprise when he called less than a minute later.

I didn't waste time on pleasantries. "I have more information."

I started with the Sonder Tech angle. I told him about Calista's boyfriend, the fact that Calista had been a no-show at work today, and my talk with Stewart in the coffee shop.

"I'd bet money it was Denny Carmichael who confronted him," I said. "It sounded like him, although I was surprised he paid a personal visit off his property."

"It's a rare occurrence," Dermot said. "He usually brings people to him. Gives him more power. But it sounds like it was the first time he'd met the Sonder Tech manager. Did the guy seem on the up and up when he told you his story?"

"Yeah. He was terrified. When I suggested he tell his story to a sheriff deputy, he freaked out. He said the man who'd confronted him would kill him."

"He has good reason to fear for his life," Dermot said flatly. "Two bodies were found in a ditch off Highway 83 outside of town about an hour ago."

I gasped. "That must be what Joe was workin' on earlier. He wouldn't tell me what was goin' on, but he seemed pretty preoccupied when I called to tell him about Stewart."

"Rose, the bodies are of a man and a woman, both young, likely in their twenties."

I sat down in my office chair, feeling like I was gonna throw up. "Calista and Pat."

"That's my best guess."

"I just saw her yesterday," I said in a small voice. "I had that vision of her."

"I hear they were tortured."

I knew better than to question how he knew these things. James used to have someone on the inside at the sheriff's department to feed him information (arranged by Jed). It made sense that Dermot would have the same arrangement.

"Someone wanted information from them," I said flatly.

"And I suspect we both know who did it."

"Denny Carmichael."

Panic raced through my blood. "Oh God. Oh God. They worked for Hardshaw and Mike's missing." I started to cry. "Denny must have killed him too."

"We don't know that," Dermot said in a firm voice. "For all we know, Carmichael tortured them to get to Beauregard."

I nodded, tears streaming down my face. But what if Denny Carmichael had kidnapped the kids to get Mike to talk? What if they were in the clutches of that evil man?

"Rose," Dermot said, "there's a whole lot we don't know. Speculatin' might help us figure out what to do next, but it won't do much good beyond that. Hell, we don't even know if that's Calista and Pat out there on the side of the road."

"Except we do," I said softly.

"If I were a betting man, I'd say there's a ninety percent chance it's them. But that doesn't mean the same thing happened to your ex-brother-in-law and the kids." He paused. "We're gonna find 'em, Rose. Which leads me to another piece of information."

"Okay."

"The construction workers I spoke with said that Mark Erickson was livin' with a woman. They didn't know her name, but we tracked down Mark's brother in Baton Rouge, and he told us he thought it was Riviera Pullman."

"That's an unusual name," I said. "That should make her easier to track down."

"It might be more difficult than you'd think. The construction guys figured Mark for a prepper livin' out in the hills."

"Like the Collard boys?" I'd had a couple of private run-ins with the family, both of them contentious.

"Yeah."

"Would they know where Erickson and his girlfriend live?"

He took a second before he responded. "You want to go ask the Collard boys?"

"Well, not their *daddy*," I said with plenty of attitude as I stuck out my elbow to brace my right hip with my hand to help ease my lower backache. "But I do have someone I can ask. I just need to figure out how to contact him."

"Hopefully, it won't come to that," he said.

"Got any other ideas on how to track down his girlfriend? The guys didn't know where she works?" I asked just as another Braxton Hicks contraction hit. I started a breathing exercise to try to control it.

"They didn't know anything. They said he never spoke about her…" His voice trailed off. Then he asked, "You okay?"

I realized I'd been holding the phone too close to my mouth, so he had heard my breaths.

"I'm fine," I said, trying not to tense up and make the contraction hurt worse.

"Are you sure you're okay?"

"Yeah," I forced out, losing the war on tensing and now my stomach was a tight ball squeezing the breath out of me.

"You sound like you're workin' out at the gym."

"Well, I'm not," I snapped again. Looked like Dermot was meeting the evil me that popped out when I had intense contractions. Lord only knew what I'd be like in actual labor. Maybe having Joe with me in the delivery room was a bad idea after all.

After a few seconds, the contraction began to ease enough for me to speak. "Which leads me to part two of my own three-part information session," I said grimly. "I received a message from Vera, the woman with the station wagon. It was hand-delivered to my office a short while ago."

"She came to see you?"

"No." I told him about noticing the station wagon parked on the square before I saw Stewart, and then how the teenage boy had shown up at my office with the message. "There was no name on the envelope, and inside was a birthday card for a two-year-old. I'm guessing it was for her son because she had a little boy with her in December. She'd scratched out the name signed underneath the birthday message."

"That was risky on her part," he said. "If we can make out who signed it, it could lead us to her. What did her message say?"

"She claims she can tell me where the kids are. She wants me to come to Shute Creek Park, alone, at four."

"Are you sure the guy who brought it to you was on the up and up?" he asked.

"If he wasn't, he's an even better actor than Stewart. He seemed pretty confused by the whole situation, but I got his name and number. I told him it was a prank, and that his information would help me retaliate."

"And he didn't ask for any kind of response?"

"No, although he did try to pick me up."

"*He tried to kidnap you?*"

"What? No! He told me I was hot for a pregnant woman and wanted to get a raincheck for coffee."

"*Oh.*" Perhaps realizing he shouldn't have sounded so surprised, he hastily added, "And you are."

I snorted. "Please. That's the least of my concerns right now."

He was quiet for moment. "So we need to be careful if we contact him," he said. "We don't want to make him suspicious enough to go to the police."

"Agreed." Kind of. I was having second thoughts about keeping this whole thing from Joe. Busy or not, he'd want to know, particularly given he'd just found two bodies. That meant it was more important than ever to find Ashley and Mikey soon, but it also meant the situation was more incredibly dangerous.

"The note said Shute Creek Park. I presume she's talking about the picnic and beach area?"

"My thought too."

"There aren't many places to hide there, and there's one road in and out, which means she'd be trapped if we showed up with a group of men." He pursed his lips. "Does she seem like she'd do something stupid?"

"I don't really know her well enough to guess," I confessed. "But she's been careful when she's tried to see me in the past. I think she'd be extra careful now."

"Then she must have another way to the spot." He paused as though to consider it. "She's probably usin' the creek."

"The creek?" But that made sense. We'd had a lot of rain, so she wouldn't have to worry about it being too shallow to get a small boat or canoe in and out.

"So what do you plan to do?" he asked matter-of-factly.

"I don't know."

He was silent for a moment. "Who else have you told?"

"No one else knows, Dermot. Only you."

Another moment of silence. "And why do you suppose that is?"

His question caught me by surprise. "I called you this morning and told you what was goin' on. Why wouldn't I give you an update?"

"But you haven't told the others about Vera's request." He paused. "I think we both know what you plan to do, and that influenced your decision to call me instead of the others."

He was right. I was going to meet her, of course. Joe would never, ever let that happen if he knew, and Jed would likely be opposed as well, even though he'd been my guardian on most of my past dealings with the criminal world. Neely Kate, I knew, would insist on being at my side. I had to admit that they all had just cause to be worried, but I'd never gotten the impression that Vera was dangerous. I suspected she wanted me to come alone because she was frightened.

Joe had the legal route covered, and it sounded like he would be occupied for the rest of the day. In case the Vera situation was a bust, I needed him to keep at it. And as for Jed and Neely Kate...I couldn't banish my memory of that vision. I'd do best to keep them away from any possible trouble.

Maybe my subconscious was just trying to convince me I was doing the right thing, but if I could only pick one person to help with this task, I was certain that Tim Dermot was the right choice.

When the dust cleared, I only hoped everyone else was just as convinced.

"In regards to Simmons, I think keepin' it from him is a good call," Dermot said. "He'll insist on sending deputies, which will likely spook her."

"Agreed," I said, although it didn't totally sit right with me. I wanted Joe to trust me, and although I wasn't lying to him, this was another instance of me not including him.

"Carlisle is your call, but I think the less people involved in this the better."

I had another flash of Jed's face from that vision I'd had of him and Neely Kate. He'd looked so sad.

"We'll keep this between you and me," I said, feeling nauseated. There was no right call here. Just the one that ticked enough boxes for a possible best outcome.

"Okay, then. I say you drive into the park with your truck, and I'll hide in the backseat to make sure you're covered."

"And if she has other people with her?" I asked.

"I doubt she will, but I'll have some men for backup out on the highway, waitin' for my order."

My stomach twisted. "Surely it won't come to that."

"I guess we'll find out soon enough."

"If she shows. She got spooked at least twice before, so it's probably better to go in alone." But I still couldn't help thinking Joe would have a fit.

"You up to this?"

I bristled. "Of course I am."

"Don't misunderstand me, Rose. I know ordinarily you'd be up for anything, but you've got more to think about right now. You could be putting the baby and yourself at great risk. You can't run. It will be hard for you to react like you normally would. There's no shame in saying this is too much."

I was tempted. I hadn't had any run-ins with criminals in months, and I felt like I was off my game. My edge had softened. Plus, Dermot was right—the fastest I could move was a brisk walk. I hadn't even been able to run after Muffy the night before. There was no way I could run for my life. And yet, Vera had been trying to talk to me for months, and her message had indicated she could bring me to Ashley and Mikey. How could I not go?

"No," I said slowly. "I have to do this. I fully admit that I'm scared, but I need to do this."

"There's no shame in admittin' you're scared. In fact, I'm relieved to hear that you are."

"Then feel plenty relieved." I sucked in a breath. "There's something else I need to tell you."

"I'm listenin'."

"As much as I loathe to get into my personal life, part of the reason I went to see James last night was to find out if he had anything to do with the break-in at Mr. Gilliam's office, but the other was personal." I took a breath, brushing a few strands of hair from my forehead, and told him about the paternity papers I'd drawn up and James's refusal to sign them. "When I asked him about it last night, he refused to address it. But when Neely Kate and I were at Merrilee's this morning, Carter showed up and said *his client* had a change of heart, but there were two conditions. One, I give up on finding whatever was stolen from Violet's attorney's safe, and two…" I paused and steeled my back. "That I spend forty-eight hours with him, with no contact with anyone else. Before the baby is born."

"I see…"

"After I took Neely Kate back to the nursery, I went to see Carter. He gave me a number to a burner phone so I could contact James to arrange our *get-together*."

"And did you contact him?" he asked, his tone not giving anything away.

"Yes, although in typical Skeeter Malcolm fashion, he didn't tell me squat. I told him I'd give him a few hours, not forty-eight, but he told me it was an all-or-nothin' deal, then hung up."

He didn't respond for several seconds.

"Well?" I asked.

"We already know he had something to do with that break-in, so that one's no surprise. And the second…" I heard an edge in his voice. "I know it sounds like a personal matter, and it likely is, but if he's lookin' to start something back up with you, it seems like odd timin'."

"He said that I could have come to see him sooner and was pissed that it was something about kids that made me reach out to him again. He seemed bitter, so I can't imagine that's what he wants."

"And he won't tell you why he won't sign the paternity papers?"

"No."

"How adverse is he to havin' a kid?"

"His attorney tried to give me a twenty-thousand-dollar check to abort and had an appointment already set up in Little Rock. That should tell you."

"And you declined, of course." He paused. "And he didn't take that well."

"No. He said I'd chosen an unplanned baby over him. He mentioned again last night that I'd chosen the baby over him."

"So what if he doesn't want to rekindle your romance? What if he wants to take the baby from you?"

"*What?*"

"Skeeter Malcolm is a ruthless man. He sees your choosing a baby over him as a betrayal. He doesn't tolerate betrayal."

I shook my head before realizing he couldn't see it. "No. He would never do that."

"Didn't he already try? He pushed you hard to get an abortion."

"But he thought the baby was nothing then. Now it's a *baby*, and he told me that he'd never tolerate abuse of children." He'd left J.R. Simmons' good graces when he'd refused to murder a child.

"Who says he's gonna *kill* the baby? You obviously want this baby, so what better punishment than to take it from you?"

I gasped in shock.

"You're two weeks from delivery, so you're safe to deliver at any time. And forty-eight hours is plenty of time for him to bring someone in to induce labor and take the baby."

I stumbled backward and sat on the edge of my desk. "No. He wouldn't do that."

"Maybe the man you knew wouldn't do that, but the man he is now…I think *he* might."

Panic raced through me. "I have to tell Joe."

"You haven't told him yet?"

"No, but to be fair, I just found out and he's busy with the murders south of town." Tears filled my eyes. "Joe would kill him if he did such a thing." My heart was pounding with unfettered alarm. "Literally *kill* him, Dermot. And he wouldn't be careful about it."

"Then maybe you should hold off tellin' him. Let me do some checkin' around. See if anyone's put out feelers for a midwife with access to Pitocin."

I couldn't believe we were having this conversation. Despite everything, I didn't believe James was capable of such a thing.

Dermot's tone softened. "This is all a lot of speculation. For all I know, he's plannin' to use that forty-eight hours to woo you and create a happy little family. Maybe that's the reason he won't sign the papers. He's just been too stubborn to admit it." His tone turned dark. "Or maybe he won't sign them because he doesn't want anything tracin' this baby back to him. Have you had a paternity test?"

"No. I didn't need one. There's no doubt this baby is his."

"Like I said, nothing tyin' it to him but your claim."

"But Carter had legal papers drawn up. His own attorney. Surely *that's* admission."

When he answered, I heard pity in his voice. "Do you really think Carter Hale would turn over something damaging to his most important client?"

We both knew the answer to that one.

He pushed out a sigh. "Let's table this for now and focus on your meeting with Vera. It's nearly two. Let's meet at the Stop-N-Go outside of Sugar Branch at 3:45. It's only about ten minutes from the picnic area."

I was still stuck on Dermot's horrible suggestion about James, but I forced out, "Okay."

"Hey," he said. "We're not gonna let anything happen to your baby, okay?"

Tears flooded my eyes. "Okay."

"You all right to drive? Do you want me to pick you up on the way down?"

"No," I said. "I'm good. Besides, I might have a few places to go before we'd meet. It'll work out better this way."

"Don't be gallivantin' around town," he said. "I suspect you're fine with Malcolm. He's makin' a power play, which means he wants you to come to him. The station wagon stalker is momentarily taken care of. All that's left is Carmichael. You want me to put someone on you for protection?"

"Carmichael still thinks I owe him a favor. He's not gonna hurt me until he thinks I've fulfilled whatever purpose he has planned."

"And what if this is it?"

"No," I said softly, my head starting to pound. "He would have contacted me by now if this was it." Not to mention I'd seen a vision of him last summer. He'd led a band of men, preparing an attack—likely against James—and I'd been there with him. That was his purpose, even if *he* didn't know it yet.

"Okay, I'll see you in a couple of hours. Let me know if anything else comes up."

"Thanks, Dermot."

I hung up the phone, sick to my stomach over Dermot's suggestion. He was right about one thing: Skeeter Malcolm issued punishment for betrayals.

Did James Malcolm?

Chapter
Twenty-Four

I had a little less than two hours before my meeting with Vera, but I couldn't bear to sit and wait. Not when I felt so much uncertainty about everything, including whether James was furious enough with me to do something terrible.

It occurred to me that there might be one person I could ask about his state of mind.

Grabbing my purse, I left the office and headed to the opposite end of the square, walking past the thrift store that had been rebuilt after it had burned a year ago. I kept going several blocks until I came to a tiny diner tucked out of the way and mostly ignored.

I stood outside the Greasy Spoon, wondering if this was such a good idea after all. For one thing, it made me sad. I'd come here with James back when we were friends. Colleagues. Back when he'd respected me.

This was the place where we'd written a list of rules for our cooperation.

But I wasn't here for a trip down memory lane. I was here to talk to the woman who had known him nearly as long as he'd known Jed.

Inhaling a deep breath, I walked inside and let my eyes adjust to the dim interior. Booths lined the exterior wall embedded with windows, and the other wall had a long counter with ten stools pushed up to it. A TV hung on the wall, tuned in to a game show. I started to head toward the booth James and I had sat in, but I'd never fit, so I took a seat at the counter, hoping Sandra was working.

She came out from the back seconds later, offering me a weary-looking smile. "Miss Rose."

I was startled that she remembered me, and then alarm set in, making me reconsider this decision. Why had I risked coming here? Of course she was loyal to him and not to me.

She must have seen my fear, because she gave me a warm, nonthreatening smile. "Rose, you're safe here. You hungry? I can cut you a fresh slice of strawberry pie."

"That's okay," I said, remaining in my seat but ready to bolt. She ignored me, turning toward the small refrigerated display case on the counter. "I've got apple and coconut cream too, but strawberry seems to be everyone's favorite." She cut a slice and served it to me on a small plate. "Mr. Malcolm likes it too." With that comment, she met and held my gaze. "Why, I left one at his place yesterday."

Other than Jed, Sandra was the only other person who knew about James's house in the woods. He had her come to clean and stock him up with food twice a week, but he'd claimed she was in the dark and didn't know it belonged to him.

The air left my lungs, and I started to jump out of my seat, but she covered my hand with hers, squeezing tight.

"It's okay, Rose. You're safe. I saw you outside and sent the fry cook out on an errand. It's only you and me."

"James said you didn't know it was his house."

"I'd always suspected," she said, "but I didn't know for sure until *you* started goin' out there."

"I made him sloppy," I said, my heart sinking.

"You made him happy." Sadness filled her eyes. "When you stopped goin', it broke him, girl."

"He pushed me away, Sandra. And then…"

"The baby?" she asked, glancing down at my belly then back up to my face. "I ain't dumb. I can do the math. That's why he pushed you away. That and this dreadful business he's gotten mixed up in."

"You know about his business?"

Frowning, she nodded. "Enough to know he's on a dangerous path."

"I know. I tried to stop him, but he's mad because I refused to get rid of the baby."

"He's scared he's gonna end up like his own father, and I confess, at this point, he ain't far off. He's drinkin' all the time and meaner than a snake." Tears filled her eyes. "As much as I love that boy, I'm not sure I'd trust him with a baby."

My throat burned as I stared at the untouched pie. "I loved him, Sandra. I loved the man who met me here last year. The man who saw me as an equal." I realized he'd shared more with me back then, when I was the Lady in Black, than when I'd become his girlfriend.

"But do you love him now?"

I slowly shook my head. "Not the man he's become."

She gave me a long look. "He loved you too. Maybe still does, but between the alcohol and the bitterness, he's drowned out everything good in his life. Jed. You. The chance for a family."

I started to cry.

"Now, now, girl. I tried to help him, and I know you did too. The only thing you can do is move on with your life," she said, tears streaming down her face. "You've got to think about that baby. James made his bed. Now he's got to lie in it."

I started to sob in earnest, realizing another part of my connection to him was falling away. Part of me didn't want to let him go, while the rest of me wanted to run far and wide.

"He's mixed up with some *bad, bad* men, and I suspect this is gonna end ugly. You and the baby can't be anywhere near that."

I nodded, and the baby kicked hard. I put my hand on my belly as another contraction grabbed hold, and I started to breathe through it.

Concern filled Sandra's eyes. "You in labor, girl?"

I shook my head. "No." I breathed a couple more times, then said, "False labor." I added, "Don't look so worried. I've been to the hospital twice now, and they just keep kickin' me out."

She gave me a worried look but nodded, waiting.

When it subsided, I said, "Will you still look after him?"

"I'll do the best I can, but he's pushin' me away too," she said. "And honestly, when he brings those men in here, it scares me something fierce."

I sat up straighter, realizing this wasn't all about me. "Do you feel unsafe, Sandra?"

"James is falling into a pit, and some days I feel like I'm the only one he can still see at the top." She gave me a sad smile. "I'm not leaving him until the bitter end."

Did the fact that I was leaving him behind make me smart or disloyal?

She must have seen the look in my eyes, because she shook her head. "No, girl. We all got parts to play in this fiasco, and goin' down with the ship isn't yours." Leaning over the counter, she placed a hand on my belly. "*This* is your part to play, to have this baby and give him the life James never had."

I started to cry again.

"And one day, when your baby's old enough to understand, tell him that there was a man who tried to make a better life, but he got lost in the weeds." Her chin quivered. "Promise me that you won't let your baby get lost in the weeds."

"I won't," I said through my tears.

"Go have a good life, Rose Gardner. Give that baby the life James deserved all along."

She turned and limped to the back then, her shoulders shaking with sobs.

Oh, James. You didn't think you mattered to anyone, but my heart isn't the only one you've broken.

But I didn't just have myself to think about anymore. I'd grown up thinking my momma didn't love me because I was lacking, and there was no way in hell I was going to let my baby feel that way about one of their parents.

I headed back to the office, but instead of going inside, I got into my truck and headed south of town, toward my future... and my past.

Chapter Twenty-Five

I t wasn't hard to find the murder scene. Half a dozen sheriff cars and two state police cars were parked on the side of Highway 83. Crime scene tape had been set up, and from behind it I couldn't make heads or tails of what was going on. It didn't matter. That's not why I was there.

I parked well behind the law enforcement vehicles as well as some lookie-loos who were standing on the shoulder, craning their necks to get a good view.

I walked past them and marched up to the first deputy I could find.

"This is a crime scene, miss," he said with a frown. "You can't be here."

"I'm here to see Chief Deputy Simmons. Can you get him for me?" When he hesitated, I added, "Tell him it's Rose. It's important."

His eyes flew wide as his gaze dipped to my stomach before rising to my face. Holding up a hand, he said, "Wait right here. And don't let that baby go nowhere."

I gave a nod. "We'll wait."

He rushed off and another deputy walked over with a curious expression. "You need to go back with the others." He gestured to the group of bystanders.

"I'm waiting for Chief Deputy Simmons."

He took in my stomach and understanding washed over his face. "You're the mother of his baby. It's your niece and nephew that are missin'." He grimaced. "I'm surprised he called you already. They're not announcing any details yet."

"He didn't tell me anything. That's not why I'm here," I said. And because I couldn't help it, I decided to take a chance. "But I just came from Sonder Tech, and they're really torn up about what happened."

Irritation flickered in his eyes. "It's already been leaked."

I didn't answer. It had, but I hadn't heard it from Sonder Tech. "They said Calista was a good salesperson. And that she really loved her boyfriend. It's a shame they were shot in the chest."

The deputy frowned in disgust. "Fake news. They were shot in the head." Then, realizing what he'd said, he became panicked. "You didn't hear it from me."

Neely Kate would be so proud of me, but I felt dirty knowing I'd tricked an officer of the law to spill information about the crime scene. Still, I was glad I knew, and better him than Joe. Now I could focus on the important part of my visit.

For the tenth or so time since I'd gotten in the truck to drive here, I considered whether I should tell Joe about my meeting with Vera. He'd be upset, justifiably, but Vera seemed harmless, and if it got us to the kids sooner, the benefits far outweighed the risk. But Joe would insist on coming, and he'd likely want to bring more deputies. One look at any of them, Joe included, and she'd take off running.

No, this was something I had to handle by myself. In the unlikely event things went awry, Dermot had it covered.

The baby shifted before another contraction kicked in. I had just finished riding it out when Joe came running toward me with fear in his eyes. With good reason—I had never shown up at a crime scene before, and he had to fear something terrible had happened.

"Rose?" he called out, still six feet away. "What's wrong?"

He stopped in front of me, grabbing hold of my arms as he searched me for injuries.

I slowly shook my head, tears springing to my eyes. "So much is wrong, but it finally became clear to me that one thing is very, very right." Lifting my hands to his cheeks, I stared up at him, wondering why it had taken me so long to figure out something as obvious as the nose on my face.

Confusion washed over his features, then hope.

He slipped an arm around my back, slowly pulling me close like he'd done with our first kiss on Momma's front porch nearly two years ago. Only now, our baby was between us, and I couldn't mold my body to his like I'd done that night. Instead, our bodies cradled the baby we would be raising together. A strange sensation stole over me, as if the past and the future were brushing into the present, filling it out as if with a painter's fine-pointed brush.

I smiled up at Joe, brushing my thumb across his cheek, tears stinging my eyes, and he smiled back.

The first time I'd kissed Joe had been playful and tender. It was my first kiss and he'd known it. He'd laughed at my request to make it a good one.

There was no laughter this time. We'd traveled a weary path to reach this place. We'd shared laughter, to be sure, and I knew there would be plenty more of it, but this moment was one of reverence. When he held back, I realized he was waiting for me to come to him—he'd pulled me to him, but he was giving me one last chance to decide, to change my mind. Which only made me more certain this was right.

Closing my eyes, I lifted onto my tiptoes and spanned the remaining distance between us to press my lips to his. That strange feeling, of the past and future converging in one moment, washed over me again. It was a feeling of forever, I realized. Feeling his mouth on mine again sent a rush of butterflies through my stomach, as if it really was our first kiss, but the sensation was deeper for the fact that we'd walked through fire and found each other on the other side.

Longing filled my soul as Joe lifted his hand to my cheek, deepening the kiss but keeping it just as tender, just as reverent, and I felt cherished, worshipped. Understood. He knew me now, truly knew me, and he loved me more than he had in the beginning, and the same was true of my feelings for him.

Joe released a growl, pulling me closer, and a fire rushed through my body, making me forget everything around us. There was only me and this man and our future, and I took everything he offered and more.

When he pulled back, panting, he searched my eyes.

"I love you, Joe," I said. "I want you to belong to the baby, but I want you to be mine too."

Still cupping my cheek, he stared at me in amazement. Hope poured from him like light. "But... are you sure?"

"I've never been more certain of anything in my life."

He kissed me again, softer this time, and the passion blended with contentment and peace.

"Uh... Chief Deputy Simmons," someone called out.

Joe lifted his head and kept his arm protectively around me as he turned to face Deputy Randy Miller, who was smiling from ear to ear.

"I really hate to interrupt." His grin spread. "Like *really* hate to interrupt..." Then his expression turned serious. "The forensics team has something they want to show you."

Joe looked torn.

251

I gave him a quick kiss on the mouth. "I'm not here to keep you. Only to give you that message."

His gaze searched my face, as though looking for something. He must have found it because he gave me that grin again, the one that rippled across his whole face. "You have no idea how happy I am that you did."

"I love you, Joe," I whispered. "I want to spend the rest of my life with you."

"I love you too, Rose. I never stopped. I've loved you since I kissed you on your mother's porch." He kissed me gently as he held his hand against my belly.

The baby gave another hard kick just as a vision set in.

James was holding a gun on me—on Joe—from six feet way, his face full of contempt. "You thought you could take what was mine, Simmons?"

"You could never deserve them, Malcolm," Joe's voice said in disgust.

"Maybe not, but neither do you." He lifted the gun so it was pointed at me center mass. Then he pulled the trigger and the deafening report made my ears ring. I felt intense pressure on my chest, followed by a rush of white-hot pain.

The vision faded and I mumbled, "James is gonna kill you," into Joe's mouth.

He pulled away, his hand lingering on my face, and there was so much love in his eyes, my heart felt ready to burst. "I love you too. I'll see you at home."

Then he turned around and headed back to the scene.

I watched him in shock and disbelief, unable to process what I'd seen.

A new deputy walked over to me and gave me a sharp rebuke. "You need to leave, miss. You'll find out what happened here right along with everyone else in Henryetta. When we release it to the press."

I considered telling him I'd just been talking to Joe, but I was still in too much shock to process what was happening. I walked back to my truck in a daze. I had to stop this, but how?

Should I spend the forty-eight hours with James? Would that convince him to leave Joe alone?

I was in no condition to sort it out now, not this close to my meeting with Vera. I considered calling Neely Kate, but she'd want to get together immediately to powwow. No, I'd wait until after my meeting with Vera.

Dermot and I weren't supposed to meet for another forty-five minutes, though, and the Stop-N-Go was about twenty minutes away, so I decided to stop at Henryetta Veterinary Clinic to see Muffy. Maybe it wasn't the best idea given what Levi had said to me, but he'd also told me that Muffy needed me—and right now I needed her.

Maria, the new receptionist, smiled when I walked into the waiting room. A man sat in a chair holding a dachshund dressed in a hot dog costume, but the cloth mustard was dropping off the back, looking like it was a string of yellow poop that was still hanging on.

"Your girl's a trooper, Rose," Maria said.

"That she is. Would it be okay if I see her?"

She got up from behind the desk. "Of course. Let me take you back."

I cast another look at the man, but the dog let out a vicious bark, and its owner bared his teeth too.

I jumped back in surprise.

She ushered me through the back door. "Don't mind Mr. Weiner and his dog Schnitzel. They take themselves *way* too seriously."

I followed her into the kennel room and found Muffy lying on her fleece blanket, her eyes closed. Her body rose and fell with her labored breathing, and I fought the urge to cry.

"I know she looks bad," Maria said. "And she *is* pretty sick, but she's a fighter. She's too stubborn to let a station wagon, of all things, take her out."

I released a chuckle as I swiped a tear. "That's true."

"Just tell her that you love her, and you can't wait until you can take her home."

Maria opened the kennel door, and I did just that, telling Muffy that Joe loved and missed her too. And that the three—and then four—of us would be a real family when she came home, just like she deserved.

But then I saw a glimpse of James's face, twisted with hate, and I wondered if I'd just issued Joe a death sentence.

My bitterness and anger toward James shifted to something dangerously close to hate. If James killed Joe, I'd kill him myself.

Pushing the dark emotions away, I stroked Muffy's paw, hoping she could feel my love. She stirred a bit and released a soft whine, looking up at me with the saddest eyes I'd ever seen. I leaned over and kissed her gently on the head, telling her I'd be back later to check on her.

I was a bundle of nerves the entire drive to Sugar Branch—worried about Joe. Worried about meeting Vera. Worried about James's demands and Dermot's suggestion that he might try to steal the baby. Worried about Muffy. Worried about the kids and even worried about Mike.

I sent Joe a text using my voice app.

I just saw Muffy. She's still the same, but I told her how much we both love her.

He texted back right away.

Thanks for the update. I love both of you.

I had to save Joe, and I refused to give him up to do it. Our paths had branched together again, and I wanted to walk down it with him by my side—I wanted that with a ferocity that surprised me. No, I was going to figure this out as soon as we found the kids and this particular mess was over. Because I couldn't accept any alternatives. My heart just couldn't take it.

I didn't have much longer to think on it because I pulled into the Stop-N-Go parking lot, and Dermot walked out of the store.

I parked in front of a gas pump and inserted my debit card as Dermot approached. Fitting the nozzle into the truck, I told Dermot, "You finish up here. I'm gonna go pee."

"Haven't you heard the saying, 'You should have gone before you left'?" he asked with a smirk.

I gave him a sassy look. "I did."

I didn't tell him that I'd left the office nearly two hours ago.

When I came back out, Dermot was already in the backseat of the truck. I climbed inside and started the engine, taking a deep breath.

"It's not too late to change your mind," he said softly.

I'd had that very thought, but I couldn't back down now. Not with everything on the line. I needed to get Ashley and Mikey back, and if Vera knew something, I had to risk going.

I lifted my chin and gripped the steering wheel. "Nope. We're doin' this."

We drove the rest of the way in silence. When I saw the partially hidden sign that said Shute Creek Picnic Area, I turned onto the long dirt road that led to the creek and drove toward the pea gravel parking lot that was mostly gray packed ground. Three concrete picnic tables flanked the left side and a rocky beach was in front of us. There weren't any cars in the lot and no sign of Vera.

"Don't get out yet," Dermot said from the backseat. "Wait and see if she shows herself first, and while we're waitin', get out your cell phone and call me. Then I can hear the conversation."

"I don't have a pocket to hide it," I said, my anxiety rising. "Wait. I have a sweater with pockets in the back." Unbuckling my seat belt, I tried to turn around to get it, but as with everything lately, my stomach got in the way.

Finally, Dermot, who was hunched down in the back, groaned. "Where is it? I'll hand it to you."

"Under your feet."

He shifted and grabbed the gray sweater and handed it to me.

It took some maneuvering to get it on, and then I called Dermot. Once I was sure we were connected, I put the phone in my pocket.

We waited a couple more minutes, and I was beginning to doubt that Vera would show when she emerged from the trees next to the picnic tables. She was wearing a dress and the cardigan Preston had mentioned. Her hair was pulled back into a loose bun at the back of her head, but huge chunks had fallen out and hung around her face and down her neck. She gave me a wary look, then glanced toward the road as she took a few steps closer to a picnic table.

"She's here," I said quietly.

"Alone?" Dermot asked, lying on the backseat.

"Yeah."

"Okay, go out and meet her."

I opened the truck door and headed over, leaving my purse—and gun—in the truck. But it would have looked suspicious to bring my purse, and I hadn't had target practice in months. Not when I worried it could hurt the baby's developing eardrums. I was safer without it. Dermot would protect us.

"Vera?" I asked as I walked toward her.

"How do you know my name?" she demanded, her eyes wide with fright.

Oh, crap. She'd never told me her name. I'd heard it in a vision. "You accidently mentioned it when I saw you in December."

"No, I didn't," she said defensively. "I was careful."

"It doesn't matter how I know it," I said softly as I took a couple of steps closer. "What matters is why you've tried to contact me multiple times."

"I didn't mean to run over your dog."

That sent a spike of pain through me, but I'd assumed as much. "I know. She's gonna be okay."

She looked scared to death, and I worried I was about to send her running. Dermot could likely catch her, but I suspected that wouldn't get us answers. I needed her to volunteer the information. "I'm not upset. I just want to help you."

She started to laugh, but it sounded a bit hysterical.

The hair on the back of my neck stood on end and I considered running back to the truck, but instead I stood in place, waiting for her next move.

"You're not here to help *me*, you stupid twit," she said through her laughter. "I'm here to help *you*."

I wasn't sure I believed that. In December, she'd told me she was in more trouble than I'd know what to do with. Her note had said she could help me find the kids, but what if that had just been a ploy to get me to meet her? I was starting to reevaluate Vera's level of threat.

Trying to quell my expectations, I took a step forward. "Okay. Then help me."

She stopped laughing, staggering over to the picnic table closest to the creek and leaning against it. She was unbalanced and unpredictable. The smart thing to do would be to leave, but I wasn't ready to let this go yet. She'd been the one to reach out to me. She *wanted* to talk to me. I just needed to let her work her way to it.

I sat down on the bench seat, my back to the tabletop, and waited. I didn't want to scare her off, and the more I talked the more I put this whole discussion in jeopardy. She was close enough now that I could see bruises on her face like someone had hit her.

"Why do you care what happens in this county?" she asked.

Her question caught me by surprise, but back in December, she'd said she knew I was the Lady in Black. "Because I live here." I placed my hand on my belly. "I'm gonna raise my baby here. I have

257

friends and two businesses. But I want *everyone* to be safe—not just the people I care about, everyone. I would hope everyone else feels that way."

"Everyone else doesn't go traipsing around in a hat and veil," she sneered.

"I haven't worn a hat and veil in over a year."

She started to say something, then stopped and took a seat at the opposite end of the bench, facing outward like me.

"The boy you had with you in December," I said. "Is that your son?"

She hesitated, then nodded.

"And a daughter?" She'd been hiding in a closet with a little girl in my vision.

Her eyes flew wide. "How'd you know?"

I shrugged. "Lucky guess, but I'm sure you want them both to be safe too. Just like I want my baby to be safe."

"It ain't always that easy, you know?" she asked, her hands shaking in her lap. "You make bad decisions, and suddenly everything is spiraling out of control."

"I know a thing or two about that," I said. "We can't change what we've done, but we can control what we do goin' forward." I paused and lowered my voice. "If you need help, I can give it to you. I've helped others. Just tell me what kind of trouble you're in."

She was quiet for a moment, staring out at the creek.

"How did you find out that I'm Lady?" I asked.

"People talk."

"People in the criminal world. I'd never seen you before last December."

"I know people, and I ain't just talkin' about Mark."

"Mark?" Then it hit me. She was talking about Mark Erickson. Riviera—Vera.

Vera was Mark's girlfriend.

I tried to temper my excitement. She might actually be able to help find Ashley and Mikey. "Do you know anything about my niece and nephew?"

"I can take you to them."

"Then let's go," I said, getting to my feet.

"Not so fast." She got up and came toward me. When she was only a couple of feet away, she reached inside her sweater and pulled out a handgun. Grabbing my arm, she pointed the gun at my belly. "I know one of you's in the truck and the others are in the trees," she shouted.

My breathing turned fast and shallow. My head was faint. "Vera, I only want to help you."

"I asked you to come alone," she said, her eyes wild, "and you brought those men."

Her gun jabbed hard enough into my belly to leave a bruise. "Vera, I'm *beggin'* you. Please don't hurt my baby."

"Then them men better get their asses out in plain sight." Her voice rose as she called out, "You're startin' to piss me off. I'll shoot her. Don't think I won't."

The truck's rear door opened and Dermot slowly got out, lifting his hands up in the air. "It's just me, Vera, so don't do anything hasty."

"You're a liar!" she shouted, her fingers digging deeper into my arm. "I seen a couple of guys in the trees!" She jammed the tip of her gun into my belly, her finger on the trigger.

I told myself to calm down. I could usually reason things out when I was in danger, but I was so consumed with protecting my baby, I couldn't think straight. My instinct was to call out to Dermot, but he wasn't a stupid man. He'd know how to handle this.

Wouldn't he?

"Johnson, Murphy," Dermot called out in a conversational tone. "Come on out so our hostess won't be so jumpy."

Two men emerged from the trees close to the dirt road, both holding shotguns. Dermot had told me his men would wait by the county road, but I wasn't surprised he'd had them hiding in the woods. He'd probably thought it a sensible precaution.

"That's right," Vera said, "come closer and drop your guns on the ground."

The men shuffled closer, about twenty feet away, but they kept their weapons trained on Vera.

"Throw down the guns!" Vera shouted, jabbing my stomach again.

I cried out in pain.

One of the men lifted his gun to eye level, and Vera dropped her hold on my arm and lunged behind me as a gunshot went off.

I resisted the urged to scream. I was fairly sure the bullet had whizzed past only a few feet beside me and lodged into a tree behind us.

Vera was behind me and grabbed my left arm while thrusting the gun under my chin. "I should kill her for that!"

"Drop the guns!" Dermot sounded pissed as he stepped in front of his men. "Drop the damn guns!"

They tossed their guns to the ground.

"Now move up closer to this guy in front," Vera said, the gun barrel jamming into the skin under my chin, but I realized her hand was shaking.

"Do what she says!" Dermot shouted, then leveled his gaze on us. "Vera," he said, softening his tone. "I apologize for my men's hasty actions, but you have to understand that you're pointin' a gun at the Lady in Black and threatenin' her baby. They're a little defensive of her."

"So tell them to back off!"

"No one's armed, Vera," Dermot said in his perfectly reasonable tone. "You're in control, so let Lady go and we'll all go on about our day."

"You're not gonna let me go, and we all know it!" she shouted.

Dermot took a step forward. "I'm a man of my word, Vera. I swear to you, if you leave Lady unharmed, we'll let you walk away. Free and clear."

"They will." Could I safely push her arm away so that she'd shoot in the air if the gun went off? I shifted my weight as though to gauge the possibility.

"What are you doin'?" she asked, pressing the gun to my belly again.

I froze. "I'm due to deliver any day. My back hurts. I'm shiftin' my weight."

"Well, stay still!" she hissed in my ear.

I stopped moving.

"What now, Vera?" Dermot asked. "Tell us what you want to do."

"I'm thinking!" she shouted, sounding like she was close to crying.

"Vera," I said softly. "Dermot's right. He's a man of his word. You tell him what you want, and he'll make sure it happens. I guarantee it."

"You were supposed to come alone," Vera said into my ear. "Why didn't you come alone?"

"Did you really think I would?" I asked.

"No," she said, sounding resigned.

Everything happened in slow motion after that.

One of Dermot's men reached behind his back, pulling out a gun.

Vera pulled the gun away from me, pointing it at him and pulling the trigger.

Then, before I could even think to stop her, the gun went off, again and again, in rapid fire.

The sound was deafening, startling my baby. They jumped in my belly and began to move around in protest.

The men fell and leapt to the ground, Dermot too, and I had no idea if she'd shot them or if they were in defensive positions until one of the men from the trees started to crawl away, and Vera shot him in the back. He fell to the ground and stopped moving.

Horror filled me like poison.

"What did you do?" I cried out, trying to pull out of her grasp, but her fingers dug in deeper.

"I told you," she said, starting to cry. "You should have come alone."

Chapter
Twenty-Six

C learly, I'd underestimated Vera on a massive scale.

"Come on," she said, tugging my arm. I was sure she was going to drag me to my truck, but she started pulling me toward the woods instead.

My mind was racing. How many shots had she taken? Six? Eight? How many rounds did her gun hold? She hadn't changed the clip. Did I take a chance that she'd used them all?

She'd just gunned down three men in cold blood. I had no doubt that she'd shoot me too if she had any bullets left, and I didn't have much hope of running. I let her push me toward the woods, but I cast a glance back at the men, trying to see if Dermot was okay.

"Go!" she said as she jammed the gun into my back.

"Vera," I said, trying to keep my wits about me. "Let's just take a minute to think this through, okay?"

"Do you wanna see those kids or not?" she shouted.

"You have them?"

"I told you I knew where they were in the note!" she shouted, waving the gun around.

"You're right. You did." Holding my hands in the air, I tried to keep my voice steady as I slowly turned around to face her.

Her eyes were wild, and she looked as freaked out as I felt. I wasn't sure if that was a good thing or not.

"I'm a trustworthy person!" She jabbed the gun in my direction as if to prove her point.

"Okay," I said, my hands still in the air. "But everyone says they're honest. How was I to know? I was gonna come by myself, but Dermot, he wouldn't let me."

She narrowed her eyes. "He ain't livin' with you. That sheriff's deputy is. What's he care?"

"That's right," I said. "I'm with Joe, but Dermot… he's got a lot invested in the Lady in Black. He's counting on me to help keep Hardshaw out of the county."

She snorted. "It's too damn late for that. They're already here." Her voice broke, and I saw tears in her eyes.

"I know," I said, relieved she was talking. I was getting through to her. "I know Mike's workin' for them. Was Mark mixed up with them too? Is that why he was killed?"

Her back stiffened. "You think you know it all, but you don't know shit. Now turn around and start walkin'."

"Wouldn't it be easier to take my truck?" I asked.

"Easier for you, but that's not the plan. Now march." She gave me a shove and I fell backward, landing on my butt hard enough to make my teeth clamp together. A wave of pain shot up my back and my stomach hardened into a cramp.

"Get up!" she shouted.

"Contraction," I said through gritted teeth as it took hold.

"Don't you be fakin' goin' into labor." She waved her gun toward me. "You ain't gonna get no sympathy from me. I was choppin' wood right up until I gave birth, squattin' next to my bed."

I couldn't hide my horror. "You didn't go to the hospital?"

"And neither will you if you decide to have that baby now, so I suggest you get up. We've got a trek ahead of us."

When the contraction subsided enough for me to get up, I rolled to my side and pushed up, wobbling as I got to my feet. "Where are we goin'?"

"You sure do ask a lot of questions," she said. "We're goin' to see Mike's kids. *Now hurry.*"

I knew it was a bad idea to leave this area. If she took me somewhere, I might never be found. I doubted she'd just let me go after I'd watched her commit multiple murders, but at least this way I might get to see the kids. It would give me a chance to get us out of this, and that was the best I could hope for now. "Okay, but I'm not dressed for a hike."

"You'll do. Go."

I headed into the trees, realizing we were following an overgrown path. We walked for a good five minutes before I heard running water. The woods opened to a small clearing next to the creek, and Vera motioned for me to walk toward the water.

Both sides of the creek bank were about a foot and a half to two feet above the water. The creek was moving fast, but the six-foot-wide bed looked like it was only a couple of feet deep. There was a larger clearing on the other side, with woods surrounding it.

"Take off your shoes and socks."

"We're crossing the creek?" I asked in surprise.

"Why else would I tell you to take off your shoes and socks?" She shook her head in disgust as she leaned over and unlaced her boot. "You ain't very bright, are you?"

Another contraction hit me, and I breathed through it as she removed both boots, tucking them under her left arm.

"Well, get to takin' them off," she said, pointing her gun at me.

"I'm not crossing that rocky creek bed with bare feet," I said. "I'll fall and possibly hurt my baby."

"You ain't gonna hurt your baby," she said. "You already fell and you're just fine. But suit yourself. I don't want to hear any complainin' about your soggy shoes." Gesturing toward the creek, she said, "Well, get goin'."

If I hadn't been pregnant, I would have stepped over the edge, but I didn't trust my balance, so I sat on the creek bank and scooted my feet into the water and stood.

"For shit's sake," she snapped. "Quit stallin'."

"I'm not stallin'." I took a tentative step. And then another, catching myself as my foot slipped on a slick rock.

Vera came up behind me, maneuvering easily, and climbed onto the other bank. She perched there, smirking at my slow progress as she put on her boots.

When I finally reached the other side, she shot me a look of contempt. "You're not what I expected."

"And what was that?" I asked as I ungracefully climbed over the creek bank and got to my feet.

"Someone badass."

"Sorry, you caught me at one of the least badass moments of my life," I grumbled. "But bein' badass is more than holdin' a gun," I added, getting pissed. "Killin' unarmed men isn't badass."

She started to respond but cut herself off.

"You shot my friend. He wanted to help you, Vera. That's why he came." But a little voice inside me insisted that it was my fault too—that if I hadn't agreed to this cockamamie plan, Dermot and his men would still be alive—and the guilt was almost too much to bear.

"You think I'm stupid?" she spat out. "He came for *you*, but for the life of me, I can't figure out why every criminal in the county is chasin' after you like you're the best thing since sliced bread."

"Because it's not about my looks or the weapons I carry. It's about earnin' their respect."

"By lyin' on your back?" she asked in disgust. "Do you even know whose baby you're carryin' in your belly? Last I heard, you're not even married."

"Joe Simmons is my baby's father." And he was going to kill her if anything happened to either one of us. But it seemed like a bad idea to mention that. I wouldn't put it past her to shoot me and leave my body to rot, hoping I was never found. "I'm not discussin' my personal relationships with you unless you care to share yours."

Delight filled her eyes. "Well, there's some of that backbone I kept hearing about."

If she wanted backbone, I'd give it to her in spades. "Do you know where Mike is?"

"If I knew where that bastard was, I probably wouldn't need you."

"Why didn't you just call the police?"

"I don't trust police."

"And you called me?" I countered. "You don't trust me either."

"Well, I'm havin' plenty of second thoughts about that decision." But she didn't look like she was telling me the truth. Or at least the full truth, not that I was surprised. She gestured toward the trees. "Let's get going."

She steered me toward an opening, and she was right, my feet were squishy and uncomfortable in the wet shoes, but I knew better than to complain. The dirt beneath my feet turned to mud with each step for a while.

We'd been walking for several more minutes before my stomach tightened and now an all-too-familiar wave of pressure squeezed my uterus. I tried to keep walking, reasoning that I'd get to the kids sooner that way, but soon the contraction became too intense for me to keep moving. Grabbing hold of a nearby tree, I leaned my forehead against it as I waited for it to subside.

"Damn, girl," she said, sounding startled. "I think you're really in labor."

"Like hell I am," I snapped. I wasn't having my baby in the woods with a murderer. I was having my baby in the hospital with

Joe supporting me every step of the way. Besides, I had two more weeks.

She shrugged. "Whatever. As long as you make it to where we're goin', that's all I ask."

Make it to where we were going. Not once we had the kids and were safe.

Had Vera laid a trap for me? It wasn't like I had a choice whether to go with her or not, and even if I did, I'd still go with her. I had to get the kids.

We continued walking deeper into the woods, each step bringing us farther away from anyone who could help me. Where was she bringing me? I only had Vera's word for it that we'd find the kids at the end of this, and I certainly didn't trust her. "Who took the kids?"

"You'll find out soon enough."

"Who killed Mark?" I asked. "Hardshaw? Denny Carmichael?"

"You don't know shit," she sneered.

"Then educate me."

Her mouth clamped shut and we continued on in silence for another ten minutes, but I had trouble keeping my balance as we started up an incline. I had to grab tree trunks to stay upright.

"Are you usually this graceful?" she asked in a snarky tone.

"I can't even see my feet. Are we almost there?"

"We're close."

I estimated the trek had taken about forty-five minutes or more. Which meant this plan had taken some thought and coordination. I also estimated that we'd been heading southwest... in the general direction of Denny Carmichael's land as well as the Collards' stronghold. It wouldn't surprise me to find out either Carmichael or the elder Collard had taken the kids. The real question was why.

"We're getting close," Vera said, sounding nervous. "We're gonna need to be quiet from here on out."

As if on cue, another contraction hit me hard.

I stopped and grabbed another tree trunk as I waited it out, this one more intense than any I'd experienced before.

Vera moved next to me, placing her hand on my belly. "Girl, that's a damn contraction if I ever felt one. Your uterus is clamped tighter than a bear trap."

I didn't protest, instead deciding to use the opportunity to force a vision. *Am I gonna find the kids?*

The vision was hazy and almost in slow motion. I saw Ashley's dirty, tear-streaked face, and Mikey clung to Vision Rose's neck, only their faces were fuzzy and the colors were distorted. I was looking up at Vision Rose, my side pressed tightly to her chest, and she was talking, a sound that comforted me even though I couldn't make out what she was saying. She looked exhausted and scared but unharmed.

Then I heard a male voice, only I couldn't make out the words, just the consonants and vowels, and an arm reached for Vision Rose from behind. Everything faded to black.

"We're gonna find Ashley and Mikey," I said.

"I told ya we were, but we gotta hurry before you pop out that kid," Vera said, several feet in front of me now.

I swiveled my head in surprise. When had she moved past me? My visions usually took a second, maybe two, but I could tell several seconds had passed. That was odd.

"Comin'," I said, more subdued as I followed, trying to sort out the significance of the vision. Why had the words sounded so garbled? And why had Vera been pressed to my chest? She certainly wasn't my favorite person, and I had an inkling I wasn't hers either.

I stopped dead in my tracks, horror and shock washing over me.

I hadn't had a vision through Vera's eyes. I'd had a vision through my baby's.

"No. No. No." I shook my head, panic setting in as I realized what it likely meant.

Vera stopped and turned to face me. "What are you babbling about?"

"I need to know where those kids are, Vera," I said, my voice rising. "Who's holding them and how much farther is it?"

She hesitated, staring down at my belly. Her mouth twisted to the side, and she seemed to be mulling something over. Finally, she nodded, determination filling her eyes, and said, "The Collards have them. Gerard and a couple of his sons. They're holdin' 'em in an old icehouse."

The Collards? Did Brox have anything to do with this? I was surprised at the disappointment that thought carried. He'd had my back twice during encounters with his father. I'd thought he had a higher moral code than his father and degenerate brothers.

I covered my forehead with my palm as I thought this through. "Close to the house?"

"No, it's by the old cabin. Deeper in the woods."

I nodded, trying to remember the layout of the property from my trip there last year. "I suppose the only road out is the lane that leads up to the house? The way the house is situated, I suspect they always have a good view of who's comin' and goin'."

"You been there before?" she asked in surprise.

"Yeah." I took another breath, trying to come up with a plan. "The house faces northwest. Where is the icehouse in relation to that?"

"About a quarter mile to the west."

"So not close to the house. What about a guard?"

She shook her head. "They don't keep anyone there from what I can tell. They bring 'em food and water."

"They must be locked in. Do you have anything to break the lock?"

"They ain't locked in. Them boys have a bar across the door so the kids can't open it."

I nodded. "That's good. So we should be able to get in and out. We'll bring them back this way. Did you bring any flashlights? It's gonna be gettin' dark soon."

"I get you to the kids, and you're on your own after that."

Did I believe her? Was she setting me up so the Collards could hold me hostage too? Then again, it seemed like it would be easier for the Collards to just snatch me. Shoot, they'd successfully kidnapped me twice before.

"I only said I'd get you to the kids. I never said I'd help you escape."

And she'd killed or grievously injured the people who could have helped me do just that.

"You brought me here close to sundown," I said in disbelief. "Why didn't you bring me here sooner?"

Her voice broke. "You're lucky I brought you here at all!"

"Why did you come to see me those other times?" I asked. "Why did you come to the nursery?"

"'Cause Mark wasn't in so deep back then," she said, looking a little embarrassed. "I thought maybe I could scratch your back and you could scratch mine."

"What was he involved in, Vera?"

"Hardshaw."

"And Mike too. That's why you said you could help me." I took her silence as confirmation.

"Him and Mike and Pat. They were a trio. That woman at Sonder Tech was their contact."

"What did they do for Hardshaw?"

She turned away from me. "I don't know."

"Bullshit."

Anger flared in her eyes as she turned back to look at me. "Mark wouldn't tell me. He got his orders from Beauregard. I told him not to do it, but Beauregard told him they needed an electrician—one who had access to restricted areas—and he said they'd pay good money for it."

"What restricted areas?"

"The courthouse."

I sucked in a deep breath. The courthouse. Hardshaw could want any number of things there, but I couldn't help thinking they'd be most interested in access to Mason's investigation on them.

"What were they after?"

She shook her head. "I ain't got no idea. He'd just tell me not to worry about it, but Mark started actin' all nervous a few weeks ago, and then Collard took them kids last weekend. Mark told me he was gonna meet with Mike on Tuesday night. He said I should be ready to run when he got back." Then she seemed to think twice and added, "He said if he *didn't* come back, I needed to tell you where the kids were, then run."

"So why didn't you just *tell* me?" I asked. "I could have come on my own! Dermot could have brought an army of men!"

"Or you would have told your sheriff deputy boyfriend. Then you'd track me down and take my kids. This gives me time to get away. I'm running far, far away."

I held my breath, releasing it slowly. It hadn't sounded judgmental, but I was properly chastised. Why hadn't telling Joe been the first thing that popped into my head? Now there was a good chance I was going to get myself, the baby, and Ashley and Mikey killed. But I took comfort at the thought of the four of us together. If I could get to them, I'd figure the rest as we went.

"The whys don't matter anymore," she said with a weariness I hadn't heard from her before. "Denny Carmichael caught wind that Mark was involved and started puttin' pressure on him, wantin' to know what Hardshaw was up to." She gave me a quick look. "He used to deal for Carmichael. Back in the day. Carmichael thought he could get his hooks in him."

"I'm sorry he was killed," I said honestly.

"Sometimes you don't have a choice in what happens." Then she turned around and started walking, leaving me to follow.

I stood in place, half tempted to turn around and run back to my truck. But I couldn't turn my back on Ashley and Mikey, if she was telling the truth about where they were being held, and there was no doubt she'd catch up to me. How would she handle my escape?

Not well. She'd likely shoot me and be done with the matter. Especially since she was telling me out of obligation, not her moral code.

The phone was still in my sweater pocket. Turning to the side, I pulled the phone out of my pocket and checked the screen. No service. I wasn't surprised, but maybe I could use it later. I had a feeling I'd need it.

None of this felt right. I suspected she was drawing me into a trap, even if the kids were being held by the Collards, but I had no notion of how to derail it.

Should I try to overpower Vera and then… what? Head back to my truck? Attempt to steal the kids away from the Collards?

But attacking her wouldn't have been a sure thing if I hadn't been pregnant and likely in labor, and it was unlikely to turn out well in my current condition. The only thing I knew to do was continue forward, and count on my vision coming true.

Even if half of it scared the bejiggers out of me.

Chapter
Twenty-Seven

Two more contractions hit me before we made it to the edge of the clearing surrounding the icehouse. They were stronger than anything that had sent me to the hospital before. I estimated they were now five minutes apart, and I assured myself I had plenty of time to get the kids back to the car, hopefully without alerting their captors, and make it to the hospital in time to have the baby with Joe by my side.

Vera and I stood about six feet deep in the trees, watching. The four-foot-tall dilapidated structure was about as tall as it was wide, and a two-by-four in brackets was keeping the door closed. The building looked like it would fall over in a strong windstorm. I had no doubt a grown man or woman could probably bust their way out of that heap, but two little kids? Not likely.

The hair stood on the back of my neck. Something wasn't right, but I couldn't figure out what was setting me off.

"This is where we part ways," Vera said, her voice shaking.

I grabbed her wrist. "You're not gonna stay and make sure they're still in there?"

Not that I'd counted on her help, but I also didn't want her to run straight to the Collards to bring them down on me.

Her eyes narrowed, but I saw fear in her gaze too. "Nope. I only promised I'd bring you here. Nothin' more, nothing less."

She tried to tug away, but I tightened my grip as another contraction hit.

I forced a vision. *What trap has Vera laid?*

The vision quickly engulfed me. I was outside, surrounded by trees, and bullfrogs croaked so loudly it would likely drown out any cry for help. A dark pickup truck was parked to my right and a man stood in front of me, but I couldn't bring myself to look up at his face. I focused on his feet instead.

"I brought her to those kids just like you said," I whined in Vera's voice as I stared down at a pair of brown boots with a scuffed left toe.

"And did she get them out safely?" a man asked. I could hardly make out his words over the sound of the frogs, but I knew that voice. Terror swamped my head.

"I don't know," I said. I knew that wasn't the answer he was looking for, yet I knew better than to lie. "You told me to make sure she got them. Nothin' else."

"I meant for you to make sure she got them out safely. What was happening when you left her?"

I hesitated, knowing full well he'd want to know it all, but telling him might be a death sentence. I looked up into the face of Skeeter Malcolm. His cold, dark eyes bore into me as he trained a handgun at my head.

"What happened?" he repeated.

"The Collards…," I sputtered, my mouth so dry I could barely speak.

"Did they capture her?" he asked in barely controlled rage.

"I don't know. They were comin' out when I took off, and I heard gunshots—"

Skeeter's face turned dark, and I was sure I was facing the devil himself. "Did they shoot her?"

"I don't kn—"

The sound of a gunshot filled my ears milliseconds before everything faded to dark, tossing me into the abyss of death.

I forced myself out of the vision and found myself staring into Vera's pissed-off face. "Skeeter Malcolm's gonna kill you."

Her eyes flew wide and she gave another hard jerk, pulling herself free, and took off running through the trees in a different direction than we'd come from.

I took a second to digest what I'd seen as my contraction eased. Vera hadn't brought me here at the behest of her boyfriend. James knew the Collards had the kids, and instead of going to save them, he'd had Vera—unstable, murderous Vera—bring me on a mile-long hike while I was thirty-eight weeks pregnant. Why? And what about the end of my vision? He'd killed her in cold blood. He hadn't liked what she had to say, and so he'd killed her.

Jed and Sandra were both right. The man I'd loved was dead, and the part of him left behind was using me in some elaborate scheme. What was his endgame?

But I couldn't think about James right now. I had to focus on freeing the kids, so I could get them back to civilization and have my baby. In my vision, Vera had said she'd heard gunshots, which meant someone was around to shoot at me. But they could only shoot at me if they knew I was there. Staying in the trees, I'd walk around to the back of the icehouse.

If the Collards were watching, they were probably listening too, so I had to be careful picking my way through the undergrowth and dead leaves, a difficult task given I couldn't see where I was going. Still, I managed to make it to the rear of the structure, hidden in the trees, without setting off any obvious alarms. My heart was pounding in my chest, but I forced myself to wait. Given that my contractions were five minutes apart, I needed to time my dash to the icehouse between rounds.

Every nerve in my body was taut with expectation and fear as I waited, so when the next contraction hit, it felt twice as painful as the ones before. I tried hard to hold back the moan building in my throat, and I could hear Joe's voice in my head, coaxing me through it, just like we'd done while practicing.

"That's right darlin', just breathe. You've got this."

I started to cry, stuffing my fist in my mouth as a moan forced its way out anyway. It wasn't supposed to be like this. I was supposed to be in the hospital with Joe holding my hand and feeding me ice chips. A doctor was supposed to deliver my baby and wrap him or her in a clean blanket. Joe and I were supposed to bask in our love for the baby. It was all supposed to be joyful.

Most of all, it was supposed to be safe.

Skeeter Malcolm had taken that from me too.

Holding on to a tree next to me, I bent forward, trying not to give in to my fear and my pain, trying to find relief, but the pressure continued to build.

"Breathe, Rose. Breathe," Joe coaxed in my head.

I'm sorry, Joe. I'm so sorry.

"Just breathe, darlin'."

Finally, the contraction reached its peak and started to ease.

A warm trickle flowed down my leg.

My water had just broken.

Panic filled my head, but I refused to give it power. If the kids were in that building, I was getting them out, and we were leaving together. Nothing else was acceptable.

Once I could walk, I crept toward the back of the structure and bent over, relieved when no one shot at me. Pressing my ear to the wall, I waited, hoping to hear something, anything, to tell me that they were indeed inside.

Nothing.

I probably only had about four minutes left before the next contraction hit, so I took a deep breath and hurried around the side of the building, stopping before I reached the front. Peering around the edge, I squatted, taking comfort in the fact that the entrance to the icehouse was already veiled in shadows. I looked for any signs of the Collards, but I realized they'd likely be hiding—and doing a much better job at it than I ever could. I'd just have to take a chance. With my body pressed to the side of the building, I reached around and slid the two-by-four out of its brackets, tugging it free.

I heard a whimper inside.

"Ashley?" I whispered.

"Aunt Rose?" she cried out. "Aunt Rose!" The relief in her voice was nearly my undoing, but I forced myself to keep it together—for them and for the baby. She started to cry.

"Shh," I told her, my voice tight with tears. "You need to be quiet, okay, honey?"

"Okay," she said through her sniffles.

"Is Mikey with you?"

"Yeah."

My heart sank. "Mikey?" I called out softly. "Can you walk?"

When he didn't answer, Ashley whispered, "He's scared."

"That's okay," I said, trying to sound encouraging. "I'm here to take you home."

"To Daddy?" she asked with a tiny sob.

I wasn't sure what to say, so I lied. "Yes. He's very worried. Now we have to hurry. I unlatched the door, but I want you to push it open the tiniest of cracks and send Mikey out to me, okay?"

"Okay."

It was a huge risk. The Collards might shoot them coming out, but I reasoned that they wanted the kids alive, otherwise they would have killed them already. They might shoot me if I came around the corner, but I doubted they'd shoot at the opening door if they didn't see anyone on the outside. And maybe the shadows would conceal the front of the building enough that they wouldn't notice—so long as the kids didn't open it too far.

Peering around the edge, I saw the door open a sliver and Mikey's face appeared, his eyes wide with fear and his cheeks flushed.

I reached out a hand to him and gave him a big smile. "Take my hand and stay close to the wall, okay?"

He hesitated.

"It's okay, Mikey," Ashley said in a grown-up voice. "It's Aunt Rose. She's gonna help us." But he'd hardly seen me since Violet had died, and six months to a three-year-old is literally one-sixth of his life. He barely remembered me.

Slowly, he reached out a hand and I grabbed it, tugging him out of the building and around the corner. The door banged against its housing, the dull sound of wood against wood as I held him close. Smelling of sweat and urine, he wrapped his arms around my neck and clung for dear life.

I held Mikey tight for several seconds, kissing the top of his head before I pried him loose, then held his face between my hands. "I have to get Ashley out and then I'll hold you, okay? We're all going home together. Now."

He nodded, and I gently pressed him against the building at my back, then peered around the side to make sure we hadn't drawn unwanted attention. I figured I was about two minutes from another contraction, and I didn't want to have one out in the open. Especially not with the kids at my back.

"Ashley, do what your brother did, okay?" I called out softly. "But we need to try not to let the door bang this time."

"So they don't hear us."

A sob built in my throat. Six-year-olds shouldn't have to consider such things. Poor Ashley had seen her mother fade before her eyes, and now she'd been a prisoner to some bad men. Her childhood had been taken from her much too soon. But I couldn't fret about that right now. I needed to get the kids to safety.

"That's right," I forced out. "Now come on out. Slowly."

The door cracked again, and Ashley's dirty, tear-streaked face appeared, her eyes wide.

"Good girl," I said. "Stay as close to the building as you can."

She did as I instructed, taking my hand as she pressed her tummy against the building and slipped out of the icehouse. She didn't release the door until she was safely out, and then she let it close softly behind her.

I tugged her around the corner and hugged her tight, kissing her too. "Such a smart girl."

Mikey threw himself at the both of us, nearly toppling me over.

"I want to go home, Aunt Rose," Mikey whispered, his tiny voice cracking.

"So do I. Let's go. We're gonna play a game of Church Mouse. Do you know how to play?"

Both kids looked up at me wide-eyed, shaking their heads.

"You have to be as quiet as you can," I whispered. "Even when you walk. We can stop playin' when we get farther away, okay?"

They both nodded, and I realized they fully expected me to get them out of this. They felt safe because they were with me.

I'd never felt more lacking in my life.

"Okay," I said, forcing a big smile. "We're gonna run into the woods behind the building. Then we'll walk in a sort of circle until we get to the path. Are you ready?"

They both nodded again.

I got to my feet, bending my knees to remain hidden behind the squatty building. Holding both of the kids by the hand, one on either side, I led them to the corner of the building.

Taking a leap of faith, I tugged their hands. "Run!"

They ran beside me, Mikey struggling to keep up, but we made it into the trees without being shot at. That part of Vera's vision hadn't come true. Yet. But I didn't have time to sit around, resting on my laurels. We had to keep putting distance between ourselves and the Collards.

Dropping Ashley's hand, I leaned over and picked up Mikey, settling him as best as I could on my hip. "Follow me," I whispered.

She nodded with wide eyes.

I started picking a path through the trees, trying to find bare spots for us to place our feet. We'd nearly made it to the path when I felt my stomach tighten.

I slipped Mikey off my hip, setting him down on his feet, then squatted next to him.

"What are you doin', Aunt Rose?" Ashley asked in a whisper, sounding genuinely curious.

"I have a tummy ache," I said, giving her a tight smile as the pressure grew. "I just need to rest for a moment."

"Okay."

I tried to force myself to relax, knowing full well it would hurt less if I wasn't tense, but I was too on edge for any deep breaths to fix this. We were much too close to the icehouse for comfort. If I cried out, one of the Collards might hear me—and it might bring them right to us.

Tears stung my eyes, but I told myself not to cry. I didn't want to scare the kids and I needed to be strong for the baby. Labor took hours and hours. Especially for a first baby. I had plenty of time to get to safety.

The contraction continued to build, and I tried to find a focal point—a dark spot in the tree trunk in front of me—breathing like I'd learned in childbirth class, but the pain intensified, and a moan built low in my throat.

I put my fist in my mouth, concentrating on not crying out.

Ashley watched in terror, and although I would have given anything to comfort her, I had to pour all my focus into keeping quiet.

It finally peaked, and as the last of it faded away, I forced myself to stand, my legs shaky. I held my finger to my lips as I grabbed Mikey's hand and led the kids to the path.

I had about four and a half minutes before I had to do it all over again, which meant we had to be as far from here as possible.

Chapter
Twenty-Eight

Mikey didn't make it very far until he couldn't walk anymore, so I picked him up and tried to carefully navigate the tree roots on the path. The fact that I was going down a small incline didn't help. If I'd been clumsy before, I was twice as bad now.

We'd made it no more than fifty feet before the next contraction hit—which lit a new fear in my heart. It hadn't been four minutes since the last one, more like two. I found a spot with a rock on the side of the path and set Mikey down. The contraction started to ripple through me, and I got on my hands and knees, a position that seemed safer given where we'd stopped.

"What are you doin', Aunt Rose?" Ashley asked with wide eyes.

"My tummy hurts again," I said, trying not to freak out. Going downhill was slower going than climbing up, and I was starting to wonder if we were going to make it to the truck let alone the hospital before the baby came.

The contraction continued to build, even stronger than the one before, and I started to cry, wanting Joe more than I'd ever wanted anything or anyone in my life. I wasn't supposed to do this alone. He was supposed to be here with me.

But seconds later, the only thing I could think about was riding through the pain. I rocked back and forth, breathing in for a count of four and out for seven. This one seemed to last longer, and as it eased, I said, "Ashley, get my phone out of my sweater pocket."

"Do you want me to call Daddy?" she asked.

I gave her a tiny smile. "What does it say at the top?"

"No service."

"Look at you," I said, rocking back on my heels as my stomach continued to relax. "You're such a good reader. But that means we can't make any calls. Now, I'm giving you two jobs, okay? One, you need to keep checking to see if those words go away and bars take their place."

"Okay."

"And second, do you know how to use the timer on a phone?"

She nodded. "I use it when I read. I have to read for twenty minutes every night. Two-zero, two dots, zero-zero."

"Okay, then," I said, trying to sound cheery. "I need you to time two things, okay? I need you to time how long until I have my next tummy ache, and then I need you to time how long it lasts. I know it's a big job—"

"I can do it, Aunt Rose."

I opened the lock screen and pulled up the timer app. "I know it's been a bit since the last one went away, but go ahead and start it."

"Are you havin' your baby, Aunt Rose?" She stared at me with a serious expression, and she looked so much like my sister in that moment it took my breath away.

I reached out and cupped her cheek, missing Violet something fierce. "Not if I can help it. Not here. Which means we need to get goin' again, okay?"

She nodded and started the timer, then took Mikey's hand. "Come on, Mikey. I'll hold your hand through this next part."

He got up and the two of them started down the hill in front of me. I made better time without Mikey on my hip, but we hadn't made it very far when another contraction hit.

"Ashley, how long?" I asked, deciding to keep walking as long as I could.

"One, two dots, three-two."

"One minute and thirty-two seconds." Which meant they really were now two minutes apart. Crap. Crap. Crap. That wasn't good. How much farther until we made it to the creek? At this pace, probably forty or more minutes. "Stop the timer and start again, but keep walking."

She tapped on the phone and gave me a look of surprise. "You don't want to stop?"

"Not yet. Let's see if we can get a few more feet."

A few more feet was all I got before the contraction seemed to possess every part of my being. I grabbed a tree and fell to my knees, crying again.

"Come on, darlin'," I heard Joe say in my head. *"You've got this."*

"I don't have this, Joe," I said through my tears. "I don't have this." But as the contraction began to fade, I got back up on my feet, my entire body shaky.

Both kids stared at me in fear.

"It's okay," I assured them. "I'm okay."

"Do you want me to stop the timer, Aunt Rose?" Ashley said in a small voice.

"Yeah."

We continued like that for nearly thirty minutes, me pushing through as much of the pain and discomfort as I could. The sun wouldn't set for a couple more hours, but the dense growth of the trees and the surrounding hills blocked the sunlight, making some areas of the path dark. We could use the flashlight on my phone, but the phone's battery was at twenty percent. It wouldn't be long before it was dead.

I couldn't help wondering when the Collards would figure out that the kids were gone. I hadn't replaced the bar over the door, which meant they'd probably notice sooner rather than later. Would they know where to look for us? Maybe. They knew how to live off the land, which meant they were probably trackers.

We needed to get to the truck before they found us.

Mikey was scared and weak from lack of food. He got too tired to continue walking, so I put him on my hip and clutched trees to hold us upright. And when the next contraction hit, I focused on a rock about fifteen feet ahead, telling myself that I could only stop if I made it to that spot. Somehow I did. The contraction washed over me as I set Mikey down. I fell onto my hands and knees, unable to hold back my agonized cries. I rocked back and forth, praying God would see fit to let me have help with this baby, because I didn't want to deliver it alone.

"Rose?" Dermot called out while the contraction was peaking. His voice sounded distant.

Now I had to be hallucinating. Sure, I'd been hearing Joe alongside me, but that had only been in my head. It sounded like Dermot's voice was directly in front of us.

"Who's that, Aunt Rose?" Ashley asked, her eyes wide with fear.

"You heard him too?" I asked.

She nodded.

"Dermot!" I shouted, starting to cry again, this time in relief. He wasn't dead. How was he okay?

"Rose? Keep callin' out to me!" He still sounded faint, but he was out there. We weren't alone anymore.

"We're on the path," I said, taking in a deep, cleansing breath. "Restart the timer, Ashley."

I grabbed a tree trunk and pulled myself to my feet, then picked up Mikey again. I had two minutes to get closer to the truck. And to Dermot.

We kept calling out to each other until the next contraction hit. Dermot found me on my hands and knees trying to breathe through the pain.

"Rose?" he asked as he approached. Then he realized what was happening and he blanched. "Jesus. You're in labor."

I didn't answer because it seemed obvious enough, but the next thing I knew he was kneeling next to me, rubbing my lower back.

"You're doin' great," he said in a soothing tone. "Slower breaths. How far are they apart?"

"Two and one and half," Ashley said.

"What?" Dermot asked, rubbing slow circles.

"Two minutes apart," I panted out, the pain increasing. "A minute and a half long."

"When did your water break?" he asked, sounding perfectly calm. I wondered how he knew, then I realized my pants were still damp.

"I don't know." The pain was so intense, I could barely focus on his words. "Half an hour?"

"You've got this," Dermot coaxed. "When this contraction's over, I'll check to see how dilated you are."

That thought should have horrified me, and with most other people it would have, but I trusted Dermot. He was a nurse practitioner. He'd patched me up before, and I'd seen him help plenty of other people too. He'd help me get through this.

The contraction eased and I fell face down, my butt still up in the air.

"Is it done?" Dermot asked, his hand still on the small of my back.

"She tells me when it's done," Ashley said with plenty of attitude, channeling my sister again. "I'm supposed to time them."

"Sorry," Dermot said in a light tone beside me. "I'll wait for you to tell me. You must be Ashley. And *you* must be Mikey. I'm Rose's friend, Dermot."

"Are you gonna help us?" Ashley asked.

"Sure am."

"Why is there blood all over your shirt?"

Panic gripped me as I sat up to face him. Sure enough, his upper right chest was bloody. "You were shot."

"I patched myself up. I'm fine. Let's worry about you." But I could see his face was still pale, he was slow to move, and his right arm was tucked in close to his side. "I'm gonna check you now, okay?"

I nodded and started to pull down my pants, but it struck me that my niece and nephew were both watching, probably horrified. "Ashley, you and Mikey go ahead, okay? We'll catch up. We should be close to the water I was telling you about."

"Okay, Aunt Rose," she said, but she gave me a dubious look before they started down the path.

"That girl's wicked smart," Dermot said, already opening a small bag and placing a glove on his right hand. "She takes after you." He pulled out a tube of lubricant.

"She gets that sass from her mother."

"Then maybe it runs through the Gardner women."

"Do you want me on my back?" I asked, terrified this would hurt. Terrified of what he'd find.

"Whatever you're comfortable with," he said. "Seems like you've been laboring well on your hands and knees, so let's try that."

I tugged my pants down to my knees and faced forward, feeling a little embarrassed now.

"This is gonna be cold," he said, and I braced myself for the invasion. He took longer than I expected, and about ten seconds later, he withdrew his hand and pulled off his glove. "We need to get goin'. Can you still walk?"

"How dilated am I, Dermot?" I asked, pulling my pants back up.

He called out, "Ashley, do you have any service on that phone?"

"I'm supposed to tell Aunt Rose when it has bars."

"Which means there's still no service," I said, getting to my feet. "How far am I, Dermot?"

"I haven't had an L&D rotation in years, Rose, but I'd say you're about a nine. You'll soon be feeling the urge to push, but don't, okay? We need to cross the creek."

He wrapped an arm around my back to usher me along, but I pushed him away. "Cut the bull, Dermot. You've always been straight with me before, and I need you to be straight with me now. What's wrong?"

He looked me square in the eye. "Rose, your baby's breech. I felt the foot when I was checkin'."

I shook my head, fighting my rising hysteria. "No. The doctor said everything was good. Head down. You're wrong," I said, starting to walk, but my legs felt like noodles.

"I'm not wrong. Sometimes it happens," he said, taking my right elbow with his left hand. "Has the baby been active since your last appointment?"

"He or she's been movin' around a lot the last day or so, but I figured they were tired of bein' cramped." Fear made it hard to choke out the next words. "Can you deliver a breech baby?"

"I will if I have to."

"Have you ever done it before?"

"No."

289

"Okay, then," I said with a brisk nod. "So if I feel the urge to push, I just won't. Problem solved."

He gave me a pitying look but didn't say anything.

"I thought you were dead, Dermot. Are the other two guys okay?"

Frowning, he shook his head. "I would have been here sooner, but I passed out after she shot me." He shook his head. "When I came to, I called for backup, patched myself up, and went after you, which wasn't easy. I took a few missteps—I hadn't realized she'd crossed the creek—but I was never so glad to hear your voice."

"You have no idea how relieved I was to hear yours. Thanks for comin' after me."

He glanced down at me. "Rose, I promised I wouldn't let anything happen to your baby."

I bumped my shoulder into his arm. "Thank you."

"What happened to Vera?"

"She led me to the Collards' property. They were keepin' the kids in an icehouse. Once we got there, she told me her job was done and took off. I managed to sneak in and get them out, then we started down the path. I keep expectin' them to find out the kids are missin' and come after us."

"Let's hope we can get out of here before that happens," I said as we continued on the path, Dermot leading the way. The kids hiked about ten feet in front of us.

"When did your labor start?"

"I don't know," I admitted. "It may have been goin' on all day. I just figured it was more false labor. The contractions got a lot stronger before we reached the Collard property. My water broke before I got the kids out."

"You rescued them in active labor." He looked back, grinning a little as he shook his head. "Of course you did."

"Don't glorify it, Dermot. I did what I had to do. No more. No less."

"Did Vera mention why the Collards took them?"

"No. And I haven't had a chance to ask the kids if they overheard anything."

"It would be better to wait until they feel more secure," he said, turning back to grab my arm and make sure I didn't trip over a tree root. "The danger's not over yet, and they're bound to sense that."

I had to agree. "Ashley's been asking for her dad."

"That's a rough one."

"No word on him?"

"None."

"Skeeter sent Vera to me," I said. "I had a vision." I described it to him and then, on impulse, told him about the vision of James and Joe.

"What's Malcolm up to?" Dermot asked.

"I don't know, but I want no part of it."

We caught up with the kids before my next contraction hit. Dermot helped me keep walking until I couldn't take another step, then eased me to my hands and knees. He rubbed my back again, telling me I had this, and that I was doing great. And there was no denying I was doing much better with him here. Only I still wanted Joe.

I had two more contractions before we heard the sound of the creek, and when the next one hit, the urge to push hit me like a freight train.

"I have to push, Dermot!"

He moved in front of me, inches from my face. "No, you don't," he said in a calm voice. "Look at me. We're gonna breathe through this together."

"I can't stop it," I cried. Every part of my body screamed to push.

"Yes, you can," he said. "Now breathe with me." He started chanting, "He. He. Ho. He He. Ho."

My eyes locked with his and I did as he said, concentrating on the pattern, and soon the urge began to ease.

When it subsided, I realized Ashley and Mikey were staring at me in fear.

"It's okay," I said with a reassuring smile. "My baby wants to come before we get to the hospital, and we're tryin' to stop it. I'm okay."

Ashley nodded, but she didn't look totally convinced.

"Okay, kids," Dermot said. "We're almost at the clearing, and once we get there, we're gonna run."

"I don't think I can run," I said. Truth be told, I wasn't so sure I could get to my feet, and Dermot must have sensed it because he grabbed my hand and tugged me up.

"I know," he said. "We're gonna do the best we can."

We'd just reached the clearing when Dermot stopped. "Everybody quiet."

I shot him a questioning look, but he was tense, straining to listen to something, and then I heard it too. The crack of tree branches behind us.

"I think they're up ahead," a man who sounded a lot like Carey Collard, Gerard's son, called out.

"We need to hide," Dermot whispered.

The creek was twenty feet in front of us. "You take the kids across," I said. "I'll wait here."

"What?" he whisper-shouted, his eyes hard. "No. I'm not leaving you."

"*Yes.* Trust me when I tell you I wouldn't suggest this if there were any other way. It took me forever to cross it the first time. It's not gonna happen. And if the kids stay here, they might make a noise and give us away. So take them across, and I'll hide until you get back."

"Rose."

"You *know* this is the best plan. We need to get them out of here, away from danger."

His resolve wavered. "I made you a promise, Rose."

"And you're gonna keep that promise," I said. "You have a gun, right? Do you have two?"

He gave me a long look. "You're due another contraction any minute. What are you gonna do then?"

"I'll figure that out when it happens. You're wastin' time. You know we need those kids out of here. You and I can deal with the Collards together."

He gave me another look, then dug into his bag and pulled out a handgun, offering it to me handle first. "It has a full clip and here's another round." He passed it over with his other hand. "Hide in the trees, off the path." He grinned. "But don't shoot me when I get back."

"I won't," I said, forcing a smile as I dropped the clip into my sweater pocket. "I need you to keep your promise."

I headed deeper into the trees, catching a glimpse of Dermot grabbing Mikey with his left arm and holding him to his chest as he ran toward the creek. Ashley ran behind them. Once Dermot had crossed the stream, he lowered Mikey onto his feet and raced back to pick up Ashley, who had started to climb down the bank. Once he made it to the far side, the kids took off running into the trees. He stood at the edge, likely debating whether he could make it back to me before the Collards reached the clearing.

"I know you're out here somewhere, Rose," Carey Collard called out. "I've been listening to you chatter for a few minutes now. Sounds like you're in labor, but what I'd like to know is who's with you."

I held my breath, praying my next contraction took longer to kick in.

"I *also* know you took those kids, and I'm gonna need them back."

293

I considered telling him he'd get them back when hell froze over, but I didn't want to give my position away. When I turned back to check on Dermot, he was gone.

And even though I was grateful he'd listened to me, a chill shot down my back. My baby and I were in this alone.

Chapter
Twenty-Nine

The footsteps came closer, and Carey called out, "*Ashley…* I'm gonna hurt your Auntie Rose if you don't come out of where you're hiding right now."

I sure hoped Dermot told the kids to follow the path to my truck. In hindsight, I should have checked my phone for cell service. I could have called Joe.

But none of that mattered right now. I needed to focus all the energy I had left on hiding from a man who would take great pleasure trying to find a way to humiliate me and put me in my place before he killed me. Carey was a misogynist who'd always hated the Lady in Black.

I headed through the woods, moving upstream and hoping Dermot had gone the same way. I didn't make it far before the next contraction kicked in, and the urge to push was even stronger this time. I stopped and squatted next to a tree. I couldn't *he-he-ho*, but I wasn't sure I'd be able to get through this contraction without making any noise.

"Ashley," Carey sing-songed. "Come on out."

My stomach cramped up and everything in me wanted to push. I released a small moan.

"I hear you, Rose," he called out. "You can't hide from me."

The pressure increased and my uterus clamped down. I released an involuntary cry, unable to fight the urge.

Carey laughed, sounding closer. "I hear you, Rose."

Not yet, baby. Not yet.

I still held the gun, hoping I could keep my wits about me enough to shoot him, but I wasn't sure I'd manage. If he found me right now, my baby and I would probably both be dead.

Joe, I'm so sorry. I screwed up everything.

Impossibly, the contraction grew stronger, and I couldn't stop myself from pushing, or from crying out again, long and loud this time.

Carey appeared between two trees, grinning from ear to ear, his shotgun slung over his shoulder.

"Well, if that isn't a picture."

I kept my hand with the gun tucked behind the tree, still riding out the contraction, trying not to push and failing.

"Cat got your tongue?"

"Why did you take my niece and nephew?" I asked through gritted teeth.

"Where are they?" he asked, glancing around. "You might as well tell me. We're gonna find them."

Only Carey didn't have anyone with him, and I hadn't heard any other voices besides his.

"You don't have anyone with you," I guessed. "You're the only one lookin' because I bet *you* were supposed to be watchin' the kids, and you can't go back without them or your daddy's gonna whip your butt."

His eyes bulged as his hands fisted. "My daddy doesn't run my life." He looked close to hitting me.

"If you say so," I said as the contraction eased. "I bet you don't even know why you were holdin' those kids in that icehouse."

"I know why they were there," he said.

"Do you know that Skeeter Malcolm knows you had them?" I prodded.

His eyes widened slightly, and he started to say something but stopped. "Malcolm?"

"He's the reason I knew they were on your property."

"Is Malcolm with you?"

There was no way I was going to answer that. "Worried that he knows your daddy's business?"

"You're lyin'."

"Then how did I know where to find my niece and nephew? If you tell me why you had them, I'll tell Skeeter to let you get away."

"Your former brother-in-law's the crooked one. We took them to coerce Beauregard to tell us what he knows about Hardshaw."

But Carey was a bad liar. His shifty eyes gave him away.

"Where's Malcolm?" he asked. "You claim he's here, but there's no sign of him."

I hadn't claimed anything of the sort, just insinuated, but I wasn't about to point that out. "And where do you think the kids are?" I asked. "Someone had to get them to safety."

"Malcolm would never leave you to save some kids. But then again, last I heard, he wants nothing to do with you."

"Well, if you want to see him so badly, you can just stick around and find out for yourself. Or you can run on home."

"I ain't goin' back without those kids," Carey said.

"You should reconsider," Dermot said to my left.

I shifted my focus to see him standing at the edge of the trees, his gun trained on Carey.

"Just toss the gun down and we'll let you go," Dermot said.

Carey snorted. "You think I'm gonna believe that?"

"I'll hold back for Lady," Dermot said. "If it were up to me, I'd just shoot you and be done with it."

"I need those kids," Carey said, sounding more desperate. "When they show up and those kids are gone, they're not gonna be happy."

"So you took them for Hardshaw?" Dermot asked. "Have you Collards joined forces with them?"

"If you can't beat 'em, join 'em," Carey said. "We got a nice arms deal with 'em. You might consider reaching out to them yourself, Dermot."

Which explained why James knew where they were—and also why he wasn't willing to openly interfere, not that I was excusing him for any of it.

"So they had you take the kids to pressure Mike into doin' something he didn't want to do," I said. "But what?"

"This isn't for the womenfolk," Carey said. "You'd best stick to doin' what women were meant to do—deliver babies and cook for their men."

"Why did they want them?" Dermot asked.

"Hell if I know. Rumor has it that Beauregard's about to turn state's evidence. I suspect they're wanting to hold on to those kids to keep him in line."

Mike was turning himself in? Did Mason know?"

"What a bunch of sick bastards," Dermot said in disgust.

Carey shook his head. "Hardshaw's movin' in, so your best move is to join them, Dermot."

"We're never joinin' those assholes," Dermot barked. "And you're a fool to consider it."

Carey laughed. "You believe what you want, but I'm still gonna need those kids. We'll lose the deal if we ain't got 'em."

My stomach tightened, the urge to push growing. My breath came in pants as I fought it.

Worry covered Dermot's face, but Carey's eyes lit up. "You're comin' with me, Lady."

"She's not goin' anywhere," Dermot said.

298

Carey turned and trained his gun on Dermot, and all I could think about was how Vera had shot Dermot earlier because of me. I wasn't going to let him get hurt again.

My contraction continued building, but I lifted my own gun and aimed it at Carey. "Move away from him, Carey. Now."

Carey laughed, and I knew he was going to shoot Dermot, but I still couldn't bring myself to pull the trigger.

But a shot rang out and I screamed, because it hadn't come from me, which meant my own inaction had really gotten Dermot killed this time.

My uterus clamped down, but I fought against it with all my might. I couldn't push for a multitude of reasons, the least of which was Carey was shooting my friend.

But it was Carey who fell, and Dermot rushed over to me, his face intense.

"Don't push, Rose."

I dropped the gun as I started crying. "I'm sorry. I didn't shoot him."

"You were a little busy," he said. "Now don't push."

"I can't help it."

"Yes, you can. Breathe," he coaxed. "He. He. Ho."

I nodded, repeating the chant.

"I'm gonna need to check again," he said, sounding worried.

"Not here," I said, staring at Carey's lifeless body. "I'm not havin' my baby here."

"Okay," he said. "We'll move once the contraction is done, okay?"

"Okay." Once it ended, Dermot helped me to my feet and we started walking toward the creek, but I could feel something between my legs, and I looked up at Dermot in a panic. "The baby's comin' now."

"We just need to try to cross the creek before the next contraction hits. The truck's not too far. The kids are there waitin'."

The kids. How had I forgotten about the kids? But I knew they were safe, and I had more pressing concerns. "No, Dermot," I said, reaching between my legs. "It's comin' *now*."

He pulled me to a halt. "I need to check, Rose."

There was no way I was lying on the ground, not out in the clearing all exposed, so I got down on my knees, tugged my pants down over my hips, then got on all fours.

Dermot reached between my legs, and he cursed. "We're not goin' anywhere, Rose. You're right. They baby's comin'."

"Is the baby still breech?"

"Your baby's foot is hanging out, and I need to help the rest of the baby come out." The tremor in his voice scared me.

I shook my head. "No. Not here. I can't."

"Rose, we have to deliver now. The cord might be compressed."

Fear swamped my head. "What do I need to do?"

He hesitated. "Take off your sweater."

I started to question him, but another contraction was building, so I slid it off and handed it to him. "Now what?"

"Lie on your back. I'm going to need to pull off your pants."

"Okay," I said, not liking either suggestion, but I didn't have a choice.

Dermot helped me onto my back and tugged off my pants, then laid my sweater across my lap and upper legs. He opened his bag and started to put on a pair of gloves. "Let me know when the next one starts."

I nodded, terrified. "Please don't let my baby die, Dermot."

"I promised you that I wouldn't let anything happen to your baby. I don't make promises lightly." His eyes were dark and determined.

"It's starting now."

He knelt between my legs, wearing a serious expression, but his eyes were kind. If anyone could get me through this, it was Dermot. "You can push this time, but stop when I tell you to, okay?"

"Okay."

"Then let's deliver your baby. Now push."

Bracing myself up on my elbows, I pushed, but the pain between my legs made me scream.

"I'm sorry, Rose," he whispered. "I've got to deliver the baby's butt and then the other leg."

I nodded, crying again, but another rush of pain had me screaming.

"Rose?" I heard Joe shout from far away. "Rose!"

"Joe!" I shouted in disbelief, then cried out again as I pushed.

"Rose, I'm comin'!" he shouted, sounding closer now.

"Good, Rose," Dermot said. "The butt's out. Now I'm going to deliver the other leg, then we'll wait for the next contraction to deliver the rest of the baby."

"How did Joe find us?"

Dermot frowned. "I don't know." There was more pain, and then he said, "Both of her legs and her butt are out. Try to rest until the next contraction."

"Her?" I asked.

"Your baby's a girl."

Wonder stole over me. My baby was a girl. She was almost here with me.

Worry filled his eyes as he stared toward the other side of the creek. "I don't like bein' out in the open like this, but I'm not comfortable movin' you to cover either. Not with the baby like this."

"Are you worried more Collards are comin'?"

He didn't answer, but the glare he was casting over my shoulder suggested he thought the threat was coming from the other side.

I had a moment of fear about how I was going to explain this situation to Joe, but it all evaporated when I heard him shout my name in a panic. "Rose?"

I glanced behind me as he emerged from the trees on the other side of the creek.

Dermot looked up, his gaze darting toward the trees. "Who else is with you?"

"No one. I have deputies on the way," Joe said, standing on the bank. "What the hell's goin' on?"

"We're havin' a baby over here. You better hurry if you want to be part of it."

I suspected Joe meant more than the obvious, but he seemed to accept it, cursing as he stumbled across the creek, splashing water everywhere. But then he was by my side, kneeling next to me. "You're havin' the baby *now*?"

"Yep," Dermot said. "The legs and butt are out, and we're waiting for the next contraction to deliver her chest, shoulders, and head."

"Her?" Joe asked, looking shell-shocked.

"Dermot says we're havin' a girl," I said, looking up at him with pleading eyes. "I know you thought it was a boy . . ."

"We have a girl?" he said, sounding thrilled. "I only care about having a healthy baby, but why are her legs out? She was head down at your last appointment."

"These things happen," Dermot said. "But we're halfway there."

My abdomen tightened. "Another contraction's comin'."

Dermot drew in a breath as though preparing himself. "Okay, same thing. Push until I tell you to stop. We're gonna deliver her shoulders now."

"What can I do?" Joe asked, sounding frantic.

"Get behind her," Dermot said. "Help her sit up and brace her back."

Joe maneuvered behind me, resting my back against his chest.

"I'm sorry, Joe," I said. "You were supposed to do this with me."

"It's okay," he said, rubbing my arms. "I'm here now."

I started pushing.

"Good, Rose, good," Dermot said. "Her back and chest are out. I'm workin' on her shoulders now, so I'm gonna be tugging and turning her."

I pushed and soon the pain between my legs was too much to bear and I screamed, leaning my head back on Joe's chest.

"You've got this, Rose," Joe said, then shot a worried look to Dermot. "Should it hurt this much?"

"Ordinarily, no," Dermot said, focusing his attention between my legs. "There's one shoulder and arm." He glanced up at Joe. "The baby's presenting in a way that makes it more difficult for Rose to deliver." Then he twisted the baby and my pain increased.

I screamed as Joe encouraged me. "You've got this, Rose. You're doin' great."

"And there's the other shoulder and arm," Dermot said, sounding relieved. "You need to stop pushing now, Rose. The head is next and we're gonna need a full contraction for that."

The urge to push was still strong.

"I can't," I cried out, overwhelmed by the pain and loss of control of my body.

"Yes, you can," Joe cooed in my ear. "Our baby's almost here. You can do this, Rose."

The contraction began to ease, and I collapsed against Joe, spent.

"That's good, Rose," Dermot said. "Rest and we'll be ready for the next one." Dermot kept his hands between my legs, holding the baby.

I leaned forward and saw the lower half of my baby's body hanging out of my body, then panicked. *"Dermot is she okay?"*

"I'm trying to keep pressure off her cord, but I'd really like to deliver her with the next contraction, okay?"

I nodded. "Okay."

I closed my eyes, wondering how I'd fallen into this nightmare, then realizing full well how. It was my own doing, but the fact I'd found and saved Ashely and Mikey helped ease my guilt. I only hoped Joe saw it that way too.

"I'm sorry, Joe."

"Shh," he said softly. "You focus on delivering our baby."

"Another one's comin'," I said, bracing myself up on my elbows again.

"A nice gentle push," Dermot said. "I'm working with her head now, tryin' to flex it." He sounded distracted as he pulled her body upward. "Big strong push, Rose. A really big one."

I pushed with all my might and I felt her come free.

"You did it, Rose," Joe said in awe. "You did it."

Dermot cradled her and rubbed her chest and thumped her feet.

"Why isn't she cryin'?" Joe asked, starting to panic.

"Dermot?" I called out.

"Give me a second." He pulled a bulb syringe from his bag and suctioned her nose and mouth, then turned her over, her chest on his hand, and smacked her butt. "What's her name?"

"We haven't picked one yet," Joe said.

She let out a weak cry.

"Come on, baby," Dermot said, giving her a gentle shake. "You can do better than that."

She released a loud wail, and a huge smile spread across Dermot's face. "That's better." He grabbed my sweater and wrapped it around her, then gently placed her on my chest. "Rose, meet your daughter. Baby, meet the best mother you could ever hope to find."

I stared down at her face. Her eyes were closed as she wailed, full strength now. Her cheeks were pink, and she had a dainty nose. Her head was sparsely covered in fine dark hair. I couldn't have imagined a more perfect baby. I couldn't believe she was mine.

I glanced up at Joe and smiled. No. Ours.

"She's perfect, Rose," Joe said in awe, still supporting my back.

I nodded, crying, studying her again. I couldn't believe I'd grown this miracle inside me. "She is."

"We still need to pick a name," Joe said.

I glanced up at him. "I like Hope."

Lord knew we needed more of it.

He smiled down at me. "I love it. How about Hope Violet Gardner?"

"No," I said. "Hope Violet Simmons."

His eyes lit up.

"I love you, Joe. You're this baby's father. She needs to have your name."

"It doesn't matter if she has my name or not. She's my daughter no matter what."

"I want to go home, Joe. Take me and your daughter home."

He gave me a soft kiss on the lips, happiness radiating from his eyes. "Gladly."

Chapter Thirty

B ut I couldn't go home, not right away.

Joe called an ambulance to take me and Hope to the hospital to be checked over. He wanted to wait in the clearing for the EMTs to come, but I insisted on going back to check on the kids. After he took off his jacket and wrapped it around my waist, he carried me over the creek, baby Hope cradled in my arms, and Dermot walked beside us to make sure we didn't fall. I insisted on walking part of the way to give Joe's back a break, but the first time I slowed down to catch my breath, he picked me up and carried us the rest of the way.

Ashley and Mikey were inside the truck, and they rushed out to greet us when we emerged from the trees. Mikey threw his arms around Dermot's legs, and Dermot picked him up and held him.

But what I found conspicuously absent were the two dead bodies of Dermot's men. There was no sign of violence at all. Dermot said he'd called for backup. Was it to look for me or just to clean up the mess?

"Aunt Rose," Ashley said. "Did you have your baby?"

"I did."

Joe set us down on top of the concrete picnic table, and Ashley scrambled onto the seat to look at the baby cradled in my arms.

"Ashley," I said, my voice breaking. "Meet your new cousin, Hope Violet Simmons."

She looked up at me with wide eyes. "That's my mommy's name."

"That's right," Joe said, putting a hand on her shoulder.

"I want to see," Mikey said, wiggling from Dermot's grasp, then running over and scrambling onto the table and throwing his arms around my neck, Ashley next to him as Joe wrapped an arm around my back. Baby Hope was looking up at us, and I knew this was the moment from my vision.

Dermot hurried over and tugged Mikey away, asking him if he wanted to throw rocks into the creek. Ashley ran after them and soon both kids were distracted.

I lifted my gaze to Joe's. "How did you know where to find me?" I asked, realizing he'd just shown up out of nowhere.

"You can thank Ashley for that," he said. "I'd been trying to call your number all afternoon, but it went straight to voicemail. Ashley found my number in your phone and called me, telling me there were bad men tryin' to get you. Jed already suspected Denny Carmichael might have had something to do with why you weren't answering your phone, so I was already down in the area, trying to figure out a good reason to get onto Carmichael's property to search for you. But then Ashley called and described where you were, and I remembered it from the investigation last summer. I was less than ten minutes away, but I got here in about five."

"My niece is one smart girl."

"Just like her aunt," he said in a somber tone.

"You don't have any questions about how I got here or why I was with Dermot?"

He studied me for a moment. "I'm gonna trust that you felt you had no choice. I'd like to think you wouldn't knowingly put yourself or the baby in danger." His voice lowered. "Did you do anything illegal?"

I shook my head. "No. Vera sent me a note sayin' she'd take me to the kids, and Dermot said he'd cover me."

He didn't look pleased. "Looks like that plan went awry."

Talk about an understatement. I told him about everything that had happened, from the note Vera had sent to finding Dermot out in the woods on my way back to the truck with the kids.

"He wasn't with you when you got the kids off the Collards' property?"

I cringed. "No."

"You got those kids out of that icehouse while you were in labor?" His voice was sharp.

"I couldn't leave them, Joe. Vera ran off. I was gonna have to walk back anyway. I figured it would be safer to take them with me."

He nodded.

"I'm sorry."

His mouth twisted into a tight smile. "You have a big heart, Rose. And I would have likely made the same call, but *so many* things could have gone wrong. I'm lucky I'm holdin' you now."

"I know."

"But we're also lucky Dermot knew how to deliver Hope. If you'd been out here alone… you both could have died."

I didn't want to think about it.

"Why didn't you tell me about the note?" he asked, sounding hurt. "Or even Jed? Why did you turn to Dermot?"

"We were worried that Vera would get spooked. You know she'd tried to make contact with me several times before and ran. I worried if she saw any hint of a sheriff's deputy, she'd run. After you found the bodies of Calista and her boyfriend, it felt like there was no time to waste. Dermot figured this was our best option to find them."

"Dermot," he said with a frown.

"He's my friend."

He nodded with a grim look. "You found the kids all right," he said, "but at what cost?"

He was right. There were three dead bodies, and soon to be four (unless my vision didn't come to pass), from this escapade. We had Ashley and Mikey, but had there been a better way?

"Promise me you'll be more careful from here on out," he said. "Promise me you'll tell me what's goin' on. While I haven't hid my general dislike of your role in the criminal world, I think I've proven that I'm more tolerable of your Lady in Black tasks. We both want the same thing—we just have a different way of tackling it. If *I* promise to listen as your boyfriend and not the chief deputy sheriff, will *you* promise to come to me?"

"Yes," I said, looking up into his worried face. "I promise."

Sirens blared in the distance and soon lights were bouncing off the trees as the ambulance pulled into the parking lot, along with several sheriff's deputies.

Dermot insisted on keeping the kids busy while the EMTs checked out me and Hope, even though it was clear he needed medical assistance too. But he refused care, and the EMTs said they needed to take me, Hope, and Ashley and Mikey to the hospital, which we'd expected, but I was worried about Ashley and Mikey riding in the ambulance without me. Dermot said he'd ride with them in one ambulance; Hope and I were in another, and Joe took my truck, telling me that Mike's parents would meet us at the hospital and take the kids with them.

"Mike's parents?" I protested. "I'd rather leave them with Neely Kate and Jed."

"They're scared out of their minds, Rose," Joe said. "They know Mike's parents better than they know Neely Kate and Jed, and they really need familiar faces just now."

"But what if Mike shows up and tries to take them?" I asked.

I might never see them again, something I couldn't take.

"I'll assign a deputy to stand guard."

"And what about Dermot? He shot Carey Collard. Will he be in trouble with the prosecuting attorney?"

"No. He was defendin' you from that maniac. I'm more worried about what Gerard Collard's gonna do when he finds out Dermot was the one to pull the trigger. It could mean an all-out war."

"Surely Gerard Collard will be behind bars," I protested in outrage. "He kidnapped my niece and nephew."

He nodded, but I could tell he didn't think this would be the last trouble the Collards would make.

I let the EMTs load me onto a gurney, even though it felt ridiculous, while I cradled Hope close. She had fallen asleep and I studied her sweet round cheeks and her tiny nose, so full of love I felt like I was close to bursting with it.

The hospital pronounced Hope perfectly healthy, but I needed some stitches after what they deemed to be a traumatic birth. My doctor wanted us both to stay in the hospital overnight, but she left the decision up to us because there was no medical need. Hope had already successfully nursed, and I just needed time to heal.

Joe had Neely Kate bring Hope's car seat from the farm so we could take her home. When Neely Kate walked into our hospital room, I was alone with the baby. Joe had left to make some phone calls about the crime scene.

Neely Kate stood in the doorway, holding the car seat and my hospital bag. The longing on her face as she studied the bundle in my arms made my heart hurt, but I told myself that soon she'd have her own baby girl to love.

Unless they lost the baby and that was her deep sadness in my vision. I prayed that wasn't it. Her heart couldn't bear it.

"Hey," I said with a soft smile.

"Hey, yourself," she said, moving closer. "Joe told me everything. You scared me to death, Rose Gardner."

Hope was in my arms—the need to keep her as close to me as possible was overwhelming. I gave her an apologetic smile. "I know. I'm sorry. Come meet your goddaughter."

"You had a girl?" she squealed, rushing forward and setting the car seat and bag in a chair. "Joe refused to tell me that part." Perching on the side of the bed, she grabbed the bottle of hand sanitizer on the nightstand and squirted a generous portion onto her palm before rubbing it in. "Does she have a name yet?"

"Hope Violet." I looked up at her. "Simmons."

Her mouth parted. "You're givin' her Joe's last name."

"He's her daddy. Of course she should have it." I grabbed her arm. "Neely Kate, I told Joe that I love him. That I want to be with him."

She frowned. "Are you sure you weren't emotional from the delivery?"

"I told him earlier this afternoon, after I had a moment of clarity." I gave her a sad smile. "It became very apparent to me that James is no longer the man I fell in love with. He's Skeeter Malcolm through and through." I told her about my chat with Sandra at the diner, my visions of James shooting Joe and Vera, plus Dermot's hypothesis about why James had wanted me for forty-eight hours.

"But you had the baby, so will he try to kidnap her now?"

A cold chill washed down my back. "I don't know."

Would he really go that far? I'd like to think not.

The color left her face. "He shot Joe and Vera in cold blood in your visions."

I could understand what she left unsaid. James viewed Jed's departure as a betrayal. Would he go after Jed too?

Joe walked in soon afterward and took Hope from my arms, cradling her to his chest.

"Hello, Hope. I'm your daddy, and I promise to love and protect you until the day I die," he said in a soft voice.

Her eyes fluttered open and she looked up at him.

My heart filled to the brim, watching the man I loved holding my baby, whom he clearly loved with every fiber of his being even if she wasn't his biological daughter. "She recognizes your voice," I said. "Just like she recognizes mine."

He smiled as he looked down at her. "I know all those baby books say so, but—"

"No," I said softly. "I had a vision of her. She recognized my voice, even if she couldn't understand what I was sayin'. She took comfort from hearin' my voice. I know she takes comfort from hearin' you too."

Joe looked up at me with tears in his eyes. "You had a vision of her?"

I nodded.

Neely Kate slid off the bed. "It's late, and I need to let y'all get home and get some rest. I'll be over tomorrow, okay?"

"Promise me you'll come," I said. "I have no idea what I'm doin' and Violet's not here to help me."

She took my hand in hers. "I promise. I don't know either, so we'll figure it out together."

Hope was in a hospital gown, so Joe laid her gently on the bed and we undressed then redressed her in the onesie I'd packed in the bag, scared we were going to break her as we maneuvered her tiny arms and legs in and out of the sleeves and her leggings.

I laughed once we had the last button snapped. "I think that took us nearly ten minutes. We're in trouble."

He laughed too, so much happiness in his eyes, I was nearly blinded by it. "We'll get faster. It just takes practice."

Back at home, we put her in the travel bassinet in my room, and neither of us slept much because we both insisted on checking on her every half hour or so. She woke up twice to nurse, and Joe sat up with me, offering to get me a glass of water or Tylenol for the pain.

All three of us were sleeping the next morning when the doorbell woke us.

Joe bolted upright and checked his phone. "It's Randy Miller."

I heard him race down the stairs and open the door, and once I checked on Hope, miraculously still asleep, I shuffled down the hall, stiff and sore.

I heard Randy's voice as I made my way down the stairs.

Both men glanced up when a stair creaked, and alarm washed over Joe's face. "Rose, you probably shouldn't be climbing up and down the stairs."

"Dr. Newton said walkin' is the best thing for me. It will help me from gettin' stiff." I offered the deputy a smile. "Good morning, Randy."

"Good mornin', Rose. Congratulations on your daughter."

"Thank you. I'd introduce you, but she's sleepin'."

Joe greeted me at the bottom of the stairs and wrapped an arm around my back.

"Sorry if I woke you," Randy said with a sheepish smile, "but I have news for Chief Deputy Simmons." He gave Joe a questioning look. When Joe nodded, he continued, "We found Vera Pullman's body a few miles south of where we found Calista and Pat."

I gasped, and Joe's hold on me tightened. I wasn't surprised, but I still hated that she was dead. "What about her children?" I asked in a sudden panic. "She had a little boy and girl."

Randy grimaced. "They were at Vera's mother's trailer. We found them when we went to tell her about her daughter."

I nodded.

"There's somethin' else," Randy said, then took a breath. "Mike turned up at the state police headquarters early this mornin'. He said he'd heard the kids had been found. The state police refuse to tell us much more."

"Do you think he's tryin' to work out a deal?" I asked. "Carey Collard suggested Mike was about to turn state's evidence. That

Hardshaw had kidnapped the kids to coerce him into keeping quiet."

"Turning state's evidence seems likely," Randy said. "He showed up with his attorney. Deanna Crawford."

Joe frowned. "The state police might not be forthcomin' with what he tells them."

"But it affects us too," I protested.

Joe shrugged. "It's politics." But he didn't look happy about it.

"How's Dermot?" I asked, scared I'd gotten him in trouble with the law.

"He gave his statement and we released him. He was protectin' you when he shot Carey Collard." Randy turned to Joe. "We got a warrant for the Collard property, but there was no evidence the kids had been there, and the kids couldn't describe who took 'em."

"So you didn't arrest Gerard?" I asked, my stomach sinking.

"Not yet," Randy said.

"That's not a surprise," Joe assured me. "The prosecutor's buildin' a solid case. And since Gerard Collard's not a flight risk, it's better to let him collect his evidence."

The two of them talked for a few more minutes while I started a pot of coffee. The home phone rang, and I answered it with my heart in my throat when I saw Henryetta Animal Clinic on the caller ID.

"Rose," Levi said when I answered the phone. "I wanted to give you an update."

I leaned against a counter. "Okay."

"Muffy's doin' great. She's sitting up and her tail's wagging. I'd like to keep her for the rest of the day, but she'll be ready to go home tonight."

"Thank you, Levi," I said, closing my eyes in relief. "We'll be out to pick her up later."

"I hear congratulations are in order," he said warmly.

"Word sure does travel fast."

"Small towns. Should I be expecting Maeve or Neely Kate?"

"Yeah," I said, "one of them will come get her." I knew either one of them would be eager to pick her up. "Thanks, Levi."

As I disconnected the call, I heard Joe and Randy tell each other goodbye. The sound of a door shutting, softly, confirmed he'd left, and I headed into the foyer to tell Joe about my conversation with Levi.

"That's great news," Joe said, beaming.

The baby started to cry, and Joe headed toward the stairs. "I'll get her."

I laughed. "You're just lookin' for an excuse to hold her."

Pausing on the stairs, he grinned from ear to ear. "Guilty as charged."

He bolted up the stairs and I followed, albeit much slower. The baby's crying soon stopped, and when I reached the hall I found them in the nursery. Joe was holding Hope, showing off her new room to her. "I painted the walls, and your momma and Aunt Neely Kate painted the trees for you. I hope you like it, although you might be a little traumatized by them given where you made your entrance to the world."

Joe must have sensed my presence, because he turned around to face me. "Just givin' her the official tour."

I leaned into the doorframe, smiling so wide my cheeks hurt. "I can see that."

He walked over, holding the baby so tenderly, I thanked the heavens I had this man in my life to help me raise our daughter. But the vision I'd had, of James killing Joe, hung over my head. I knew I had to tell him. He had a right to know, even if it spoiled our happiness.

Was Joe's death the deep sadness Neely Kate felt in her vision?

"Joe, there's something I need to tell you."

His smile faded. "Okay."

"When I came to see you yesterday, I had a vision."

He stopped in front of me with a frown. "What did you see?"

"Skeeter Malcolm. He was pointing a gun at you, and he accused you of stealing everything that was his. Then he shot you."

He took a deep breath, then nodded. "Okay."

"Okay? It's *not* okay," I said. "I can't lose you."

He lifted a hand to my face and gave me a tender kiss. "You won't. I promise."

"You can't promise me that, Joe."

He smiled with so much tenderness it stole my breath. "I'm not goin' anywhere, Rose. I won't leave you. But now that we know, we'll be ready."

We'd both be ready.

I'd fought my whole life to find the happiness I had now. I'd be damned if I would let Skeeter Malcolm steal it from me. James had had his chance, and he'd thrown it away for money and power. But Joe had been there through thick and thin. I could count on him to love and protect us. The only thing I could count on from James was heartache and misery.

I was done accepting heartache and misery. I was choosing joy.

And God help the man who tried to take it from me.

It All Falls Down
January 21, 2021

Printed in Great Britain
by Amazon